I0760856

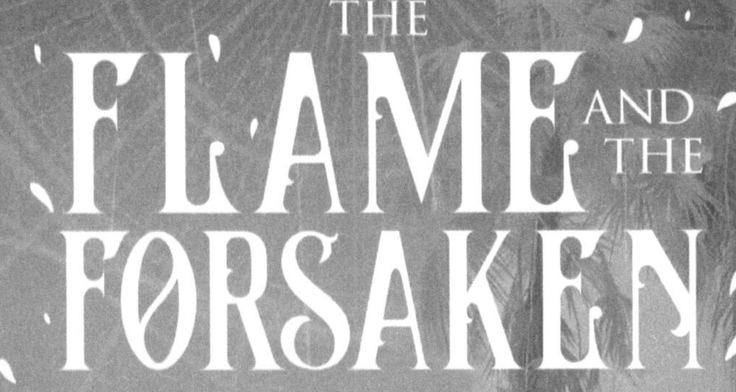

THE BOOK OF ALL THINGS

USA TODAY BESTSELLING AUTHOR
SARAH M. CRADIT

ISBN: 978-1-958744-46-8

Cover and Interior Design by The Illustrated Author Design Services
Map by The Illustrated Author Design Services
Hardcover Art ("Wrecked") by Koti Komori
"Whoever We Want to Be" Art by Salome Totladze
Mariel and Erran Portraits by Ivy Gwendolline
Editing by Novel Nurse Editing

Publisher Contact:
sarah@sarahmcradit.com
www.sarahmcradit.com

For the stubborn, the willful, the passionate, the ones who were told they must change to fit society's demand. Adapt and explore, but never change. You were already perfect.

PRAISE FOR THE FLAME AND THE FORSAKEN

"The Flame and the Forsaken delivered everything I crave in romantasy: simmering tension that burns into love, emotions that resonate deep in my bones, and a plot that won't let me go. And enemies falling in love while shipwrecked? Hell. Yes. I now have a new favorite trope."

~*Tessonja Odette, author of A Rivalry of Hearts*

"Another fantastic read from one of my favorite authors! Sarah M. Cradit is a wordsmith who constantly weaves magic into her stories, and I absolutely loved every single page."

~*Elle Madison, author of Scarlet Princess*

"Trapping a female Robin Hood in an arranged marriage to King John's handsome son results in a wild romance of aching and mending hearts. Add the rigid societal structures and political intrigue of a lush fantasy world and you get the Flame and the Forsaken."

~*Angelina J. Steffort, author of Wings of Ink*

"Absolutely electric! The way Mariel and Erran orbit one another is complete perfection!"

~*Casey L. Bond, author of The Last Lost Girl*

"Erran and Mariel's arranged marriage romance was absolutely breathtaking, and the combination of Erran's quiet strength and quick-wittedness as well as Mariel's fiery and vivacious personality made for an epic and explosive love story that could be written about in the stars."

~Sarah Elyse Rodriguez, bookstagrammer at Spellbinding Reviews By Sarita

"I was hooked from the first page! There is something about Sarah's writing that pulls you right in, and she has a gift of building worlds and weaving incredible stories, and this one was no exception. Readers who adore enemies to lovers fantasy romance are going to eat this UP."

~Ky Venn, author of Justice in Magic

INTRODUCTION

There exists a kingdom set upon an isle, surrounded by a sea no one has ever traveled beyond. The Kingdom of the White Sea it is called, or simply the kingdom, for they have no other name for it.

The individual Reaches—Northerlands, Southerlands, Westerlands, and Easterlands—once ruled themselves. Two centuries past, the Rhiagains washed upon their shores, claiming to be gods. From gods, they became kings.

Erran Rutland, heir apparent to the wealthy Whitecliffe stewards, has no love for royalty. His love, Yesenia, was sold by King Khain in marriage to an enemy house, and there wasn't a thing he could do to stop it. He was equally powerless against her falling for the man. When his grief turned self-destructive, resulting in a public humiliation after he begged her to leave her husband, his father decided it was time he settled down.

One day Erran is nursing a broken heart, and the next he's married to a woman so unsettling, he knows he's being punished. If he doesn't toe the line, he'll lose everything, including the admiralty, the birthright he's been training for his whole life.

Mariel Ashdown has more than her share of reasons for disdaining the man she married. The Ashdowns had once been barons, until the Rutlands first starved them and then stole their land from under them. Mariel and her brother, Destin, are the only survivors from their once-close-knit family, having lost both parents and a sister in the famine.

Her light in the darkness is Obsidian Sky, a band of rebels she has led since the age of twelve. Through masks and diversions, they slowly take from those who have taken from them, and return what they pilfer to the people. They're the greatest thorn in the side of Erran's father, Rylahn, who has offered temptingly high bounties for the arrest of even one of the outlaws.

But small heists only do so much, and they'll never right all the wrongs with simple midnight coach robberies. So when a drunken Destin sees an opportunity to place Mariel right in the belly of the beast, he takes it.

Mariel almost refuses, until she realizes the advantage this will give her: a seat at the supper table of the man she most needs to take down…a chance to hear about a job far bigger than anything Obsidian Sky could ever have hunted down on their own.

And then she does.

What's coming could change *everything.*

Flip the class structure on its head.

Return the wealth to the people.

Figuring out when and where, though, continues to elude the gang, until the steward lets slip the details she needs.

When an unfortunate situation forces their hand, Mariel and her friends have no choice but to push forward with the raid, even though they have no plan and no time to make one.

Meanwhile, Erran has suspected for a while that his wife has been up to something, and has been following her. Weary of her everlasting iciness and fearful of his father's threats to disown him if he can't get control of his marriage, he's determined to find the cause and put an end to it.

What he discovers makes no sense.

The absolute insanity that follows makes even less.

But one thing becomes excruciatingly clear, as they both fight for their very survival.

Their shared loathing only hurts their slim chances of living through this ordeal, but putting aside their hatred will be easier said than done.

WHITECLIFFE

Keep
Goldsea Spires

Reach
Southerlands

Steward and Stewardess
Rylahn Rutland
Hestia Leecaster Rutland

Steward's Children
Erran Rutland, 21
Sessaly Rutland, 18

Other Rutlands
Rehor Rutland (Rylahn's father), deceased
Drummond Rutland, ancestor

OBSIDIAN SKY

Origin

Remnants of the abandoned foothills village on the banks of Loch Ethereal, Mistgrave

Leader

Mariel Ashdown Rutland, 22
a.k.a. Shadowstep
a.k.a. the Flame

Other Members

Destin Ashdown, a.k.a. the Whisperer, 27
Remy Perevil, a.k.a. the Tactician, 25
Augustine Perevil, a.k.a. the Needle, 20
Alessia Terrowin, a.k.a. the Sword, 23
Magnur Koss, a.k.a. the Stone, 32

Past Residents of Mistgrave (Deceased)

Astin Ashdown, father of Destin and Mariel
Ofaelia Braeloch, mother of Destin and Mariel
Angelika Ashdown, sister of Destin and Mariel

OTHER SOUTHERLANDERS

Warwicks
Lord Khallum Warwick
Lady Gwyn Dereham Warwick
Lady Korah Warwick
Ransom Warwick

Laws
Damian Law
Artesia Law
Samuel Law
Aliksander Law

Strongs
Argus Strong
Hamish Strong
Yanna Strong
Jesse Strong
Ryan Strong

Garricks
Lem Garrick
Foss Garrick
Esta Garrick

HOWLING SEA
N
W
E
S
MIDNIGHT CREST
ICEBOLT MOUNTAIN
MIDWINTER REST
WITCHWOOD CROSS
WHITECAP
NORTHERLAND RANGE
FOREST OF LYCANA
WULFSHEAD HAVEN
9
TORRIN'S PASS
6
WESTPORT
EASTPORT
DUNWOODE
1
DARKWOOD RUN
SALTHILL
WULF'S NECK
7
MAYKE
SALEEN
ASGILL
2
DRUMAIN
BYTHESEA
TERMONGLEN
RUSHWOOD
12
WHISPERING WOOD
VALLEYBROOK
STREAMSTOWNE
EVERLEIGH PIKE
EVERHART THICKET
WILDWOOD FALLS
PARTH
RESPLENDENT RELIQUARY
THE SEPULCHRE IN THE SKIES
10
5
BRIARHAVEN
THE SEVEN SISTERS
GAP OF EVER
GREENFEN
FIONN'S PASS
RIVER RUSH
WINDWATCH GROVE
PINE BLUFF
WHITEWOOD
OLDCASTLE
OAK HILL
WHITE SEA
3
EAST DERRY
IRON HILL
BLACKPOOL
STONE MAWR
NEWCARROW
4
SANDYMOUNT
GREENCASTLE
GOLDTHORPE
SANDYCOVE
LEECASTER BAY
11
HORNSEA
PORT WORTHING
CAMP ATONEMENT
GREYSTONE ABBEY
WHITECLIFFE
8
CAMP RESTITUTION
1.) NORTHERLANDS
2.) HINTERLANDS
3.) WESTERLANDS
4.) SOUTHERLANDS
5.) EASTERLANDS
6.) ISLE OF BELCARROW
7.) DUNCARROW
8.) WASTELANDS
9.) WULFSGATE
10.) LONGWOOD RUSH
11.) WARWICKTOWN
12.) WHITECHURCH
KINGDOM OF THE WHITE SEA

LIKE WALKING INTO
A STORM
WITHOUT A CLOAK

ONE
LOCH ETHEREAL

Suffering through a belated marital idyllmoon with an unbearable princeling, on the lake that had once belonged to her family until it had been stolen by his, was a perverse sort of torment, even for Mariel Ashdown.

She leaned onto the balcony overlooking the dawn mist wrapping Loch Ethereal below. The fog made it impossible to see from her vantage point, but one of hers was almost certainly waiting below, just as they'd promised when she had told them where she'd be forced to spend the week after her husband's "triumphant return" from months away at sea.

The mossy, thatched banks had disappeared, trailing into and blending with the dense morning air. The once-tranquil lake embodied the sinister authority of its subjugators, a warning and a reminder of the thin veil between past and present. It was far too cool for a swim, but she was already imagining herself stripping away her layers, recalling the icy jolt of first contact that would remind her she was still—unlike almost everyone she had ever loved—painfully alive.

Erran would still be peaceably sleeping, like all men with no conscience with which to burden themselves. He was no doubt exhausted from his most recent naval conquest, which had kept him away for the entire three months of their arranged marriage. He'd already been planning the campaign when their fly-by-night union had come about, and it had been too late to send another in his place. At least, that was what his mother kept saying, as though Mariel was nursing a broken heart in his absence. It had been all she could do to nod solemnly and play the doting, mooning wife.

She hadn't seen her husband at all since the wedding, actually, until four days ago when he'd shown up with his too-pretty, hangdog face and, a scandal following him that made her disgust for him an easy part of the act.

There was still time to make her rendezvous and be back before the attendants—every one of them a spy for his father—sounded the morning meal bell, upon which she and her princeling husband would sit in rigid silence and pretend they weren't secretly dreaming of killing one another.

Mariel tore her eyes away from the lake and started down the hall. To her surprise, there were no attendants there, nor any following her down the stairs. She stepped into the balmy morning without encountering a single soul, which seemed as suspicious as it was fortuitous, though she lived perpetually on edge, always anticipating danger. It was the life she'd chosen, one of secrecy and shadows and peril. But her only witnesses at the early hour were the crickets and songbirds slowly waking the world up.

Still, sneaking off, right under the nose of her "naval hero" husband, was reckless even for her. No one could know who she was when the sun disappeared in the evenings, but if *Erran* found out…

He couldn't. Hers wasn't the only neck that would swing.

The dew in the air coated her skin from the moment she stepped into the lush forest. It painted the leaves so shiny and green, they seemed spun from silk. The Southerlands were known for endless tropic coastlines and salt-hardened traders, but the Lake District was a hidden gem, stretching between the Rutlands' seaside territory in Whitecliffe all the way to the foothills of the Easterlands range in the north. Many wealthy barons owned cabins along the twelve lakes, but not because they'd purchased the land legitimately. Any records claiming otherwise had been signed by the same people who plundered through life like the conquerors of old.

The hardest lesson Mariel had learned, and early, was that while the wealthy could buy anything they desired, their real thrill came from stealing it.

Mariel paused at the end of the worn path to look back at the garish monstrosity that had been built in place of her modest childhood home. The juxtaposition of memory and reality fueled her vengeance and gave her the last bit of resolve needed to continue on.

She followed the tall reeds lining the banks. Frogs croaked from thatches of pads, which broke up the soft mossy algae of the otherwise-still surface. How she and Destin and sweet Angelika had played and played as children, skipping rocks through the thick stew of colors...even then, they'd known their time was stolen. They'd read it in the increasingly haunted stares of their mother and father as they'd slowly starved to death.

Soft light painted an orange band across the grass. She closed her eyes and looked up, breathing deep. Home. Not the way it had been, but still hers. Land didn't recognize gold. It recognized like. Love.

A fluttery whistle snapped her attention back. She ducked low and listened. When it came again, she cupped her hands over her mouth and sounded her own in return. Once. Twice.

Reeds cracked underfoot. She stood slowly, trying to guess which one of her friends had come for her.

Her heart skipped when she saw it was Remy.

Or, as the barons they frequently robbed knew him as, the infamous Tactician.

The corner of his mouth pulled into a slow grin. She matched it as she moved closer, knowing, even before he held out his arms for her, where she would land. When he locked around her, she allowed herself the briefest interlude of vulnerability, releasing a breath into his warm chest. He pulled back, still smiling, and brushed the gesture along her forehead with a sharp inhale.

"The Flame lives," he jested.

"Aye." Mariel snorted and broke the embrace. She scouted the area once more, but they were alone. "Barely. Was touch-and-go for a while."

"How much time do you have left on your sentence?"

"Four days." She crossed her arms. "Though *days* with that one are measured in far longer terms than the ones we know."

"He was bound to come home eventually. Unless you were hoping he would drown?"

"Even I'm not so cruel," she retorted, though she'd be lying if she claimed she'd never thought about the prospect.

But if the princeling *had* died at sea, she'd never get what she needed. Months alone with his family had produced no valuable intelligence. He was the key. She knew he was. If not, it would mean she'd married him for nothing, and she couldn't live with that.

Remy scratched a hand through his shoulder-length blond hair. "Has it been so bad?"

"He's been avoiding me ever since his idiocy in Warwicktown. He thinks...that I care about his foolishness with Yesenia, which is absurd. Better he believes it though. Makes it easier to stay in character." She tilted her head back in the frustration she couldn't show to anyone else. "I ken the attendants have reported to the steward we haven't been sharing a room though. Feckin' spies, the lot of them."

"Aye, but at least you're home, for a spell," Remy said, glancing around with a poignant grin. "I try not to think about how much I miss Mistgrave...this lake..." He shook his head, then tipped a nod behind her. "Whose idea was this atrocity, anyway?"

"The palatial cabin?" She rolled her eyes. "You've seen Goldsea Spires. You know how high the Rutlands aim."

"And always fall short. They don't ken the soul of a place. The blood running just under the soil, the heart pumping life to the fish, the elk-kind, the crickets and frogs..." He seemed to have more to say, but his lips pursed in disgust. Unlike the rest of her friends, Remy and his sister, Augustine, were technically from the Easterlands, from a town just north of the Southerlands border on the other side of the line from Mistgrave. But they'd spent enough time with Mariel and the others to adopt a softer affectation of the rough salt-and-sand accent associated with the Southerlands. Like hers, it was a composite of both worlds and, for the work they did, useful for blending in.

"Three months of him away has given me plenty of time to think, but I confess I wasn't ready for him to come back. He'll be expecting a wife when he settles, and I know what I signed up for when I agreed to this, but so far..." Mariel groaned. "Ah, I didn't sneak out here to talk about the useless princeling, so please tell me you have something new about the private auction we can use."

Remy rolled his neck, revealing the ink she'd given him right at the edge of his collarbone: a black sword piercing a cloud, their group's insignia. Beneath it was a map and quill, his personal signature. She'd been hesitant when he'd asked her to do it. If he were captured, it was as good as a signed confession he was a member of Obsidian Sky—and a proud one. But Remy feared a cage more than a scaffold. "Augustine learned there's a dealer organizing the thing, but no name. No location yet either. Alessia is making her tavern run over the next few nights, to see if she can get any drunkards to spill more, but I ken those organizing the event are deliberately keeping the details close to their vests."

"Hmm." Too close. Mariel's own father-in-law was the architect of the whole thing, and he'd mentioned the auction exactly once in her presence. She drummed her fingers against her biceps. "And still no date?"

"Could be next week. Next year. Whoever knows, they're keeping the details close."

"Nay, not next year. They won't wait that long. It'd be like offering infinite spirits to a man lost to the drink and expecting him to pace himself." As nice as it felt to be close to someone she loved, she challenged fate with every minute she lingered. If anyone saw them, they'd assume she was having an affair, which, while safer than the truth, would only hurt her objective. "If we don't find out when and where—"

Remy's hands shot out and gripped her cheeks. "We won't let what happened to us happen to others. Now that the heir apparent has returned, you'll get what we need, and those robber barons will tuck tail and slink back to their keeps and castles, humiliated and penniless. It will *change* the way they do business, forever, and they'll finally know we're more than just a nuisance to swat away." He was quiet for a moment. "And then you can be done with all of this and come home to us."

Preventing more commoners and gentry from having their land stolen in an illegal, private auction for the nobility was Obsidian Sky's principal goal, and the plan was to intercept the gold and dump it into the sea, where it would belong to no one. The outlaws had agreed it was the only way to ensure it never fell back into the hands of the powerful. But Mariel couldn't stop thinking about how that much wealth could *change everything*. It could feed entire villages. They could do so much more for the people than they'd ever done with their midnight heists. The others were afraid to dream big, but they'd lost sight of the very reason they'd formed Obsidian Sky, to quash such powerlessness and keep it from ever returning.

Even Remy wasn't ready for that conversation. She didn't have long to get him there, but it was more time than she had available that morning.

Mariel lowered her eyes and nodded. "I should go. The silk stocking will be wanting his breakfast soon."

He swept in and kissed her—brief, chaste, but near enough to genuine intimacy to remind her how cold her existence had been since the light had gone out in her life...since her mother and father and sister had died, leaving her and Destin to choose whether they'd suffer as their loved ones had or risk everything by fighting back.

Perhaps she could have made a love match, or at least a tolerable marriage, had she opted to sit back and let others continue to run roughshod over them, generation after cursed generation.

But Mariel Ashdown, known as the Flame to her enemies and Shadowstep to her admirers, would spend whatever minutes, hours, days, or years the Guardians had planned for her in fearless rebellion.

No indecisions.

No regrets.

She joined her forehead to Remy's, exhaled, and nodded.

Erran knew Mariel was hiding something from him, and while he shouldn't care, he damn well did.

As he watched her slip through the hall and down the steps like a vengeful sprite, clearly pleased with her duplicity, he wanted nothing more than to call out to her and watch her expression dissolve when she realized she'd been caught. But then he'd never know where she was headed.

There was no love lost between them. How could there be when *love* had nothing to do with their cobbled-together, last-minute handfast? The past few months at sea had been...a reprieve from his new reality. From the marriage he had been given no choice in. But he *was* her husband, like it or not, and he had a right to know what she was up to—and a responsibility to protect her from herself.

Not that she wanted or needed his help. Behind her painted-on smiles, her loathing was palpable.

Erran supposed that was his curse. He'd loved one fiercely independent woman and had become shackled to another, the second an unhappy consequence of the first.

He cleared the porch and stepped between the tall reeds. Fog coated the tops, obscuring the two paths she could have taken. But he'd learned to track from his grandfather Rehor, and Mariel hadn't bothered to cover her footprints. If nothing else summed up their farce of a marriage, it was her thinking him too pretty and stupid to be a problem.

He trudged east, dodging dewy stalks. He'd never liked Mistgrave, or any of the lake district, unlike the rest of his family who treated it like a secret stash of splendor. Being so far from the sea unmoored him, made him feel as though the earth was closing in on all sides, his death knell in the form of shrilling crickets and croaking frogs. He already missed his crew and ship, Perseverancia, and yearned for the day when he'd assume command of his father's fleet and spend his days at sea, beneath the swelter of hot days, falling asleep to the gulls' cries.

As he rounded the east bank, he heard the voice of a man. Mariel's drifted on the end of whatever he'd said, followed by her long, drawn sigh. Erran slid his boots to cover the squish and inched closer, until he spotted Mariel's long, dark waves through the reeds. Her head was tilted up at the man holding her, someone Erran didn't recognize. Whoever he bloody was, he was looking at Mariel the way Erran had always looked at Yesenia.

A dark clench formed in his belly. It wasn't jealousy. His father couldn't have picked a more incompatible pairing for him than the stony-eyed, mercurial Mariel Ashdown. But the trip to Loch Ethereal was a not-so-gentle nudge to push Erran and Mariel to finally consummate their union and bring an heir. His father had eyes everywhere. Her dipping out to meet a lover was more than foolish. It was dangerous.

After brushing Mariel's hair away from her brow, the man tweaked her ear and dashed off, disappearing between a thicket of bowing trees.

With a distraught look at the sky, Mariel raked her fingers down her cheeks.

Erran eased a hard breath through his nose and marched over. She whipped her head up in alarm, but he wasn't giving her a chance to speak first. "Have ye lost your mind then, Mariel?"

Irritation flashed across her flushed expression, but humor was quick to supplant any evidence of it. She smirked with her entire face in a startlingly swift recovery that she must have assumed was convincing. "It's fine when you want to go chasing skirts, Errandil, but if I have a congenial meeting with an old friend, I've lost my mind?"

No one, not even his blessed mother, called him by that atrocious name, not until Mariel had learned it at their wedding and decided it was an enjoyable way to get under his skin. "Willnae even dignify that with a response."

Mariel scoffed and tried to brush past him, but he side-stepped into her path, flipping her annoyance to disgust. "I realize this is a challenging concept for a Rutland to embrace, but I'm nay your property. I'm allowed friends."

"Friends." Erran flung his arms out with a dry laugh. "Oh, aye? Friends? Kiss all your friends then?"

"I donnae *answer* to you either. And, eh, you can drop the phony salt-and-sand brogue around me. Your grubby mates aren't around to judge you for being soft, and it won't impress me."

"Impress you?" Erran was speechless. Humidity clung to his skin, but her accusation hung heavier. He'd always switched between accents without even thinking about it, because he was sensitive about his privileged Whitecliffe upbringing, which was far more refined than what most of his mates had experienced to the north and west. The Rutlands were one of the few families who neither looked nor sounded like they were part of the Southerlands at all. If one really wanted to insult them, they made the inevitable comparisons to the gold-laden tree-dwellers in the Easterlands who lived better than kings. "And why in the bloody Guardians would I ever want to do that?"

"Aye, well, that's better. You're more tolerable when you speak with the gold pacifier in your mouth, tucked right where it belongs." She tried again to get past, but he held his ground. "Think I won't stab you just because your family bought me?"

Erran had no doubt Mariel would stab him, but a conversation needed to happen, away from the ears and eyes of his father's staff. "Listen to me, Mariel—"

Mariel's hands shot to her hips in a snapping gesture that cut him off. Her eyes flashed with a dozen competing reactions, so fast he could read none of them. She was both cornered doe and raging bull, engaged in a silent battle with herself.

"We didn't *buy* you, all right? Our marriage was brokered like any other. And I'm no more keen on it than you are, but do you not remember why we were sent to this lake to begin with?"

Mariel burst out laughing. "Because you were, what, *two* days back from sea, and you couldn't keep your spindle away from a married woman?"

"I did not…" Erran grimaced, bracing. He'd already learned that there was no such thing as a simple conversation with her. "Nothing happened between Yesenia and me. You know that."

"Because she can't stand the sight of you anymore. Chose a *tree-dweller* over one of her own, which…" Mariel whistled. "Even I can feel the sting of *that*."

He bristled, drawing rigid. "I don't have to explain myself to anyone. Not even you."

"Who's asking you to?" Mariel threw up her hands, incredulous. "Why did you follow me?"

"Had a sense." Erran chewed the inside of his mouth, once more preparing for her inevitable fire. "Seems I was right to be suspicious."

Her eyes rolled. "Mark it in your diary."

Erran dragged his hands down his damp face with a groan. "We both want the same thing, you know."

Her grin was murky, but she kept her response to herself.

"To be left alone? To do as we please? To not hear another of my father's loaded lectures about duty?"

She laughed and gestured around. "Aye, well."

"You know how we get that, don't you? By playing *nice,* for feck's sake. By…at least *pretending* we wouldn't like to chuck each other into the White Sea and be done with it all. And by not sneaking about at dawn and meeting strange men, which will surely be news to my father by, oh, noontide today."

Mariel's unctuous grin faded. "No one followed me."

He gaped at her. "I'm standing *right here.*"

"No one whose tongue I'll have to cut out for informing on me."

She was right; he was the last person who'd tell Rylahn Rutland she was up to nothing good. In that, he might actually be her ally, not that she'd see it that way. "Who was he, anyway?"

"None of your concern," she retorted.

"If he accidentally gets you with child—"

"Unlike you, I'd never even entertain dodging my vows, no matter how I…feel." Her eyes pinched, narrowing. "And there wouldn't be such pressure, would there, if your chin-wagging sister hadn't spread false rumors about us expecting."

Sessaly was as much a thorn in his side as Mariel's, but her false declaration that Erran and Mariel had a bundle on the way was more than an irritation. When Erran had to confess to his parents it was not true—and how the only thing they'd consummated was their aggravation for each other—the disappointment had come down like a landslide on the dunes. *For Guardians' sake, it's not that hard to bed a woman, Erran. You've done it before!* Rylahn had roared, in front of everyone, before storming away.

If only you knew you'd found me the most disagreeable bride in all the Southerlands, Father.

"Sessaly is a pain. I'll give you that," Erran said after a wary pause. Sunrise cast a pale orange hue over the lake. Others would be looking for them soon. "But do you not…Do you not realize we can't avoid this forever?"

"Managing your family is your job, not mine."

"They're your family now too."

Mariel tossed back a cackle. "Oh, aye, is that why my brother is always invited for supper?"

"Perhaps if he could hold his *drink*—"

Mariel lifted a silencing hand, but her ear was turned toward the lodge. "Someone's out there."

Erran turned at the sound of shuffling and muted voices. It was Calvan and Eleanor, the married caretakers. All staff in the house reported to them, and they reported everything of note straight back to Steward Rutland.

There was no good reason for Erran and Mariel to be whispering angrily in the reeds at dawn, and he could already imagine how it would be relayed to his father, right after they'd explained the "blissful couple's" failure to share a bed.

Mariel glanced at him. Her eyes moved in time with her thoughts, no doubt calculating the perfect rationalization, just as he was. But there was only one that would appease his father.

As soon as he spotted Calvan's bright-red hair rounding the bend, Erran snaked a hand around Mariel's back and yanked her against him. Her eyes glared first, the rest of her catching up in a body-wide clench. He locked his mouth to hers, hushing her indignant groans with louder moans of his own, counting the seconds until he could release her and put the unfortunate moment behind them.

"Ah, pardon us, sir. Ma'am. We didnae intend to intrude on such a *private* interlude, but we've had a surprise visit from the stewardess, and she's waiting for you both in the dining room."

Erran nearly swallowed his tongue. *Mother. Great.*

"Thank you, Calvan," Mariel said sweetly, murder flashing in her irises when she turned them on Erran.

"Very well. You'll come straight to the dining room?"

"Aye, right behind you," Erran called, still rooted by Mariel's death stare and the inevitability of a lecture from his mother. "I'm *sorry,* all right? It was the only thing I could think of to cut off suspicion—"

Mariel cut him off with a stinging slap. "Don't you ever, *ever* do anything like that again, for any reason." Her nose flared with a slow breath. She seemed to be forcing calm upon herself. "Nay... unless...*until*...I say you can."

"Forgive me." Erran laid one hand on his cheek, raising the other in penitent surrender. "Won't happen again."

"And why would they have been suspicious to begin with? Did you even think..." She trailed off, casting her gaze toward the lake. "I ken it'll keep your mother and father pleased for a spell though."

"For a spell," Erran agreed, still recovering from her reprisal. "But we need to talk about this. About having bairns. We can't avoid it forever, no matter how much we might want to."

"You wanna talk about it? Here you are then." Mariel's tongue lashed over her lips. "I don't give a Guardian's fig what your mother and father want. I need time." Her shoulders lifted in a defeated sigh. "Now, what are we gonna do about your mother? She's here to spy, aye? You didn't ken she was coming?"

"Nay, I didn't." Erran glanced up at the mist-covered lodge, shaking his head. "Maybe the staff told them about the separate beds."

"Don't recall us piling on top of each other being part of the marriage contract."

"Well, officially..." Erran might have smiled, if his belly hadn't already soured from the strained exchange.

"Your parents don't even sleep in the same bed. Not even the same apartments."

He shook his head. Even discussing simple things with her took great patience. "They did when they were making bairns, and as far as they know, that's what we're doing." He flexed his hands at his sides. "I didn't ask for this marriage either, but there's no getting out of it. We have to find a way—"

"Did you not hear me when I said I wasn't ready?" she replied, thunderous. "Or are you in the business of taking *everything* you decide is yours?"

"Can I finish my sentence?"

She turned her nose up and waved, scoffing to the side.

"We have to find a way..." He continued slowly, as though dealing with an errant child. "To show them we're making an effort. If we walk in there with you looking like...like..."

"Like what?"

"Like you're going to stab me."

She grinned.

"Right, so if you can't control *that*, then they're going to make our lives very difficult. I heard Father talking to Steward Law about having attendants stay in our bedchamber with us to make sure we..." Erran twisted his mouth.

"That's an archaic, revolting tradition no one follows anymore." Her brows furrowed. "He wouldn't dare."

"He might. The man's already bloody arsed with me over the Yesenia thing. Thinks I've shamed him before all the Southerlands. The forsaken son."

"Only shame in what you did is not fighting harder for her," Mariel said, surprising him. "Is it any wonder she ran off with a tree-dweller? At least the Quinlanden lad was willing to go where he wasn't wanted for the love of her."

"Is there..." Erran squinted, tilting his head and shaking off the wound she'd intentionally inflicted. "Is there something that me...that *I*, personally, have done to you that causes you to treat me like a feckin' dog?"

"You disparage dogs with such a comparison." Mariel sized him up with a look so full of vitriol, he felt compelled to take a step back. "Time to put on a fair show for your mummy."

If Hestia Rutland had married into any other family, Mariel might have had a fondness for her.

She had an oddly cheering presence, with her bright-orange shawls, elaborately plaited hairstyles, and thick gold boots under leather gowns that were equally dressy as utilitarian. Rumor had it that under those billowy skirts, she always had two daggers, one strapped to each thigh, and that when she was still a Leecaster, she had welcomed occasions to use them. She had an unexpectedly gregarious laugh that made Mariel wonder what she must have been like before she'd joined the wealthiest family in the Southerlands.

But the woman sitting across from her in the dining hall had been a Rutland for longer than she'd ever been a Leecaster, and the way she held the narrowing in her eyes, as she watched Mariel and Erran in agonizing silence, was something she'd clearly perfected in her married years.

"Are you not going to eat, Mother?" A note of anxiousness emphasized Erran's careful words.

"Trying to decide if I have an appetite," Hestia replied smoothly. Her eyes shifted toward Mariel. "I'm sure you're aware it has come to my notice you requested a separate bed from your husband."

We'll be getting right down to it then.

Mariel glanced at Erran, then admonished herself for even considering they were allies. "Aye, well—"

"It was me, Mother," Erran said, cutting in. He swallowed a sip of his drink. "I've been feeling poorly since I returned from Warwicktown and didn't want it to pass to Mariel as well."

"Poorly how?" She stared at him, clearly unconvinced.

Mariel held her breath, waiting to see how the exchange played out.

He nodded at his belly. "Nothing you'd want to hear about at mealtime."

"Or any time," Hestia said with a sour grimace. "Are you feeling better now?"

"On the mend."

"Then I'll inform the staff that you and your wife are ready to cohabitate." Hestia traced one finger along the edge of the tablecloth before leaning in. "Unless it's not what you want?"

It was Erran's turn to look at Mariel. She offered a light, reluctant nod, still chiding herself for her inability to control her temper outside with him. She'd lost her cool, and even considering her role as the "wronged wife," she'd gone too far.

Sharing a bed was the last thing she *wanted*, but keeping the Rutlands happy with her was the only way to keep them from looking more closely at her interest in their business dealings.

"Of course it is," he said with a grin that deepened his dimples. Mariel buried her face in her bowl of fruit and silently cursed every Guardian, including the sixth one.

"Then I'll see it done." Looking far more pleased than she had when they'd started their meal, Hestia turned again toward Mariel. "And how is your aunt, pet?"

There was no aunt. "Sick Aunt Anna," Mariel and Destin's father's supposed aunt, was just her excuse to disappear in the evenings.

The best way to lie was to tell the truth, so Mariel answered just as she would have if Hestia had asked her how her midnight heists were going. "As well as can be. Every visit I ken she gets stronger, though it'll be some time before she no longer needs me at all."

"You have a kind heart, Mariel. I do hope she'll understand that when you have bairns, though, she won't see you near as much."

Mariel forced a smile. "I ken she will."

"Perhaps your brother could take over helping her?" There was no malice in Hestia's expression, but just because she didn't say what she was thinking didn't mean Mariel didn't hear it just the same. *We both know he can hardly take care of himself, and we both know why.*

"One day, perhaps," Mariel said tightly.

"If not, I'm sure we can find someone suitable for her. We certainly won't let her suffer." Hestia divided her attention equally between them. "I'm afraid I'll be leaving just after morning meal. Your father needs to travel to Port Worthing this afternoon to sign some documents relating to the auction. I'd forgotten my promise to the stewardess that I'd share some of my lace patterns with her, so I'm joining him."

Mariel perked, pretending her thrall was for the fruit on her plate. An overheard conversation between Erran and his father on their handfast night had been her first awareness the auction even existed, but with Erran gone for months, she'd been relegated to the background of important matters.

"Port Worthing?" Erran asked, after chewing a mouthful of meat—tidily, with his mouth closed and a napkin against his lips.

Mariel almost laughed imagining him try to fit in with her friends as they passed a sloppy mug around the campfire and tossed picked-clean bones of rabbits and foxes at each other across the flames.

"I thought they were holding it in Sandymount?"

"Port Worthing is where they're performing inventory and storing the gold until it's time."

Port Worthing and Sandymount, Mariel thought, her heart racing. It was far more than she had any right knowing, so it was important her disinterest was convincing. But when she tried to take a bite, she was so focused on the conversation, she missed her mouth.

Erran waved his fork. "I still don't understand why we're having this auction. Or why we're entitled to sell the land at all when we don't rightly own it. Are we starved for gold?"

Hestia sent a cautious glance Mariel's way. She folded her hands atop the table. "If you have questions, Erran, your father is the one they belong to." With a sigh, she turned her eyes toward the window. "You know, I can see why he wanted this place. Have you ever known such true quiet?"

Mariel watched, amid a glimmer of hope, as Erran processed his mother's words. He'd come so close to seeing the problem when he'd reminded his mother the auction was nothing but stolen goods. But he only nodded and returned to his food, leaving Mariel deflated and foolish for thinking there might be more to him.

"Mariel, will you join me briefly in the gardens before I leave?" Hestia asked, though it was not a question at all.

"Of course, Stewardess," Mariel said, nodding low in the appropriate reverence for her mother-in-law. Acting was not a skill Mariel had expected to collect on her journey, but it had proved as useful as any other she'd honed, especially now that she was no longer looking in on the enemy's lair but was right in the center of it.

"I've told you, pet. Mother will do." Hestia smiled. "Shall we then?"

Mariel followed the woman down a small staircase and out a narrow door leading to one of the few things that remained intact from when Mariel had run and played there: her grandmother's garden. But though it hadn't been plowed over, neither had it been tended, and as a result, it had become overgrown and unruly. Only time kept it from being the next victim of the Rutlands' plundering.

"The adjustment hasn't been easy on you, has it?" Hestia asked as she dodged a thatch of thorny weeds. "Marriage is often so hard in the early days, especially for women."

Mariel wasn't sure what answer the stewardess was looking for, what words would satisfy her. "I've endured harder times."

"You have, haven't you?" Hestia's sidelong smile was genuine, warm. "You've lost so much, Mariel. Indeed, more than most your age ever should. Now, you may have been conscripted into this family on account of my son's unseemly behavior in Warwicktown, but I *do* want you to feel like you're one of us. To feel at home in all our homes. Is there anything I can do toward this effort?"

Hestia had been nothing but kind to her, but the woman's smooth manner served as a reminder she could withdraw her warm cordiality with a flick of her wrist. She might have started her marriage in similar circumstances to Mariel, but she was all Rutland now. "Nay. But thank you."

"I realize you were brought up in a very different world than I was. Women had to work *and* rear their bairns. But you'll have a dozen governesses at your disposal, should you desire them. You needn't give anything up, as long as you've done your duty. And while we as women have many tasks and errands and responsibilities, we have but *one* duty, no?"

Mariel hadn't yet addressed, even to herself, the pressure from all sides to bear Erran's children. It had always been her hope that she'd get what she needed and she could simply...disappear. But if her mission failed...if something went amiss and they were forced back to the start...

No. She couldn't even consider it.

"And my son is a most comely man, with many achievements already behind him and far more ahead. Marriage into our family has afforded you a level of comfort and access you'd never have known otherwise." Hestia stopped and looked directly at her. "You're fortunate is what I'm saying, Mariel. More than you seem to realize."

Tears of anger sprang into her eyes. *Fortunate?* And whose fortune were they standing upon at that very moment? Whose fortunes had built every brick...weaved every tapestry in their gilded life? And how could Hestia Rutland even say such words when she *knew* she was standing on stolen Ashdown land? Was she so blind to her husband's own faults that she'd lost any semblance of perspective? "Have I done something to compel you to say these things?" Mariel couldn't help asking.

Hestia balked slightly. "It's rather what you have not done, dear."

"We've been married three months, and he's been away for all of it," Mariel replied, her defensiveness mounting. *Careful.*

"But now he's home. And a child will never happen at all if you refuse his bed," Hestia answered smoothly. "There are no whispers that do not return to my ears. Oh, love." She sighed. "You could do so much worse, but you'd never do better."

Mariel recoiled, stung. "Stewardess—"

"You think me cold and unfeeling, but how I wish I'd had a woman in my life to counsel me when I married Rylahn. Might have saved myself years of heartache." She smiled sadly. "He's a good man. They both are. If you had to give up a love of your own in this venture, remember that Erran did too."

"There was no other love." Her mind spun with how quick-footed Hestia was, and how unprepared Mariel had been for it. Erran's foolishness about Yesenia in Warwicktown had actually been a blessing, for it had given Mariel the opportunity to play the wronged wife, which was a fair cover for her disgust of him. But Hestia was telling her she saw past the act, for what it was. Guardians help them all if she ever learned why. "It's more complicated than that."

"You think I don't know we stand on ground that once belonged to your family? Or how it came to belong to ours?"

Mariel held her breath. She hadn't expected any of them to address it so boldly.

"Expecting equity in this life is a path to great unhappiness, Mariel. This system was here for thousands of years before us, and it will outlive every last one of our descendants. Lamenting the unfairness of life is like spitting into the air to assuage a drought. You are not entitled to the disappointment that follows." Hestia swept a hand along Mariel's brow, brushing stray hair back. "You're prettier than her, you know. Yesenia. There's a warmth in you that was always lacking in her. When his heart settles, he'll see it. He'll see he's lost nothing really, nothing that couldn't be gained another way." She drew herself straight. "But we cannot wait for a man to come to his senses. Erran has always understood duty and will do his, if you show him you are willing."

Not for one second did Mariel believe Hestia would ever be someone she could show her heart to, but it was harder that the woman was, in her way, being kind. She was trying to help Mariel see the future didn't have to be filled with despair. But Hestia was a product of the system she spoke of, shaped and molded over the years to accept the unacceptable. Mariel could never, ever let that happen to herself. "I understand what's expected of me."

"And perhaps, should the bedchamber whispers grow warmer, I may be able to persuade my husband to return this property to the Ashdowns. To your brother, who is now the head of your family line. The last Ashdown male."

Mariel missed a step, her boot catching in a tangle of morning glories. She glanced over and found the stewardess watching her like a hawk. In all her dreams and goals as the Flame of the Obsidian Sky, Mariel hadn't considered her ancestral lands could ever be theirs again. She'd given up on that fantasy, focusing instead on how to keep such a loss from happening to others. If she were to put her own needs first, hers and Destin's, there was nothing more important than the Ashdown land coming home. It was all they had left of themselves.

But this isn't about me, or Destin. If I ever forget that, I will have regained my heart at the expense of my soul.

"Consider my words," Hestia said with a patient smile. "But not for too long, pet. The future of this house rests upon your shoulders, and you'll find others will not be as understanding as I am should this ice not thaw."

Hestia's retinue was parked at the entrance to the lake road that would take her southwest to Port Worthing. Erran waited for her there, watching for signs of her vibrant attire through gaps in the forest.

"Darling." Hestia appeared suddenly from the side and swept the air by his cheeks with phantom kisses. "Thank you for seeing me off." She looked past him, through the forest that covered any view of the quiet lake. It was so unlike the ambers and ochers of the Golden Coast that he could believe it was another world altogether. "It *is* lovely out here."

Erran recalled what Mariel had said that morning, about the land being stolen, but his mother had made it clear questions should be directed to his father. "How long will you be in Port Worthing?"

"A night. Two at most." Hestia brushed her hands down his arms with a fussy sigh. "You must win her over, Erran. The way things are now are not sustainable. Your father is worried, and I'd say he has good reason to be."

Erran shifted his gaze to the ground, shaking his head. "I *am* trying. Mariel is…She's challenging. But I'd never force myself upon her."

Hestia looked almost stricken. "Of course not. No one would suggest that."

"All I'm asking for is some patience and understanding."

Her smile was placating. "Love, actions have consequences. Throwing yourself at Yesenia like an undomesticated lapdog was unwise, and her rejecting you, while prudent on her part, turned a mild scandal into a public humiliation. Rutland men do not grovel. At least not outside the privacy of their bedchamber." Her arms lowered back to her sides. "You have the Rutland charm and more than your share of the good looks. I advise you to use them."

He pressed his lips tight to keep himself from saying that Mariel was immune to any so-called charm he might possess, because it would only make matters worse. His mother had no interest in excuses or explanations. Her sage advice had once been a central part of his life, but as he'd aged into adulthood, she'd started turning his questions around on him. Asking *What do you think I should do?* only garnered a *What do* you *think you should do*?

"You should know," she said carefully, "your father will announce his retirement soon. His leg has gotten so much worse while you were away, and he worries it's starting to erode his esteem amongst the men in his fleet. I'm going to tell you what he will not, because he wants you to figure all of this out yourself and not be pressured by the prospect of avoiding punishment. The admiralty should be yours, Erran. It's your birthright. But he worries the men won't respect your leadership after all that's happened. You know what they've been calling you, the forsaken heir. He's been quietly preparing Aliksander Law as a potential replacement for you, should you not…sort the matters of your house." She leaned in close. "We cannot let that happen, love. Aliksander will be a part of this family soon, but he is a *Law*, not a Rutland, and his and Sessaly's son will be a Law. I say again, it is your *birthright.* Your future son's birthright. If your private matters are not soon resolved, you will lose everything and gain nothing for it."

Erran's blood rushed away from his face. His father had made plenty of insinuations but had never come out and said the admiralty could ever go to someone else. It was a Rutland operation—a Rutland legacy, built over the past two centuries. Not only had he been waiting his whole life for the honor but he'd been actively training for it since he had been six years of age. He'd spent years at sea. There was nowhere else he felt more like himself. More whole. Without the admiralty, he had nothing else to drive him. Nothing else to sustain him.

Not even Yesenia had meant as much to him.

"How do I fix it? She's…She's still sore about what happened with Yesenia, which was nothing except humiliation on my part. I've been naught but kind, no matter how cross she is." His voice cracked, a weakness his father would have criticized and his mother would likely reprove. Asking at all was missing her point, that he needed to resolve his own trouble, for if he could not, how could he ever lead a fleet of forty-seven ships? Eight thousand men?

But she surprised him when she brought a hand to his cheek with a tender cupping. "My darling, Mariel is hurting. She has lost so much, and her grief prevents her from seeing what she's gained. It's not enough to be kind…I sense she is isolated and feeling as though nothing at all is familiar to her. And then you disgrace her reputation and yours? Of course she's sore. If her own husband does not see this, does not care, then one cannot really blame her for being cross, can they?"

Erran lowered his gaze back to the ground. He thought again of Mariel's bizarre claim the loch had once been her family's. Of all he didn't know about her. "You're wrong if you think she could love me." *Or that I could love her.*

"And what, my dear, does love have to do with marriage?" Her mouth pulled into an impudent grin.

He couldn't help rolling his eyes. "You and Father aren't the best example, if you want to make that point."

"Love came after the children, after our duty was behind us and we were free to consider our own needs." Hestia reached for her carriage door. "I must go now, or we'll have to stop somewhere else for the night. You'll find your way, Erran, because you must. But your first obstacle is accepting that marriage is a business transaction, not an arrangement for chivalrous romantics like yourself. Consider what Mariel most *wants*, what *gain* would be worth the sacrifice of her pride, and you may find the answer is closer than you realize. You don't need her to love you, or to love her in return. If that is your aim, you will fall woefully short."

TWO
THAWING THE ICE

Erran watched Mariel pace the darkly lit bedchamber like a restless fox. She was fully dressed, still wearing her weapons. She always wore them, even to breakfast, like she was expecting a violent melee to descend at any moment.

The woman was a complete enigma to him.

But he didn't have to solve her. He just had to tolerate her. "What did my mother say to you?"

"I ken you could guess," she replied without losing momentum.

"And your response?"

"Told her what she needed to hear."

"So…a lie?"

"Aye, I suppose."

"What's going on here?"

"What?"

He waved a hand at her and made a walking motion with his fingers.

"We don't know each other, Errandil. Don't fuss yourself trying to make conversation. We can do our duty without…that."

Was she actually suggesting she was fine with intercourse but talking to each other was a step too far? "Maybe I just don't see the merit in being miserable all the time, Mariel."

She shook her head with a bracing look at the ceiling. "You'd never know if I was miserable. First you'd have to know what my joy looks like."

"Miserable with *each other*," he said, his belly tight in readiness for whatever her next retort would be.

"Aye, well, you seem miserable enough on your own without my help."

Erran didn't expect anyone to understand his predicament. *Love,* particularly the romantic kind, was a happy accident for a noble, not an expectation. As his mother had so poignantly said just that morning, only after duty came personal fulfillment.

He'd always assumed that when the time was right, he and Yesenia would tell their families how they'd felt and a marriage contract would follow—not even because they were in love but because the Rutlands were one of the few houses in the Southerlands with the pedigree to wed a lord's daughter.

But then the king had sold Yesenia off in a political marriage to their enemy in the north. That much they might have overcome, as Erran had been more than ready to fight to bring her home. Except, she *had* come home, and she'd been *in love* with the tree-dweller.

Erran had pulled Khallum aside later to find out what hypnosis the Quinlandens had used on her to change her into an entirely different person, but his best mate had cut the matter off with a harsh, almost pitying *confounds the feck outta me too, mate, but my little sister loves the bootlicker.* Loves *him, loves him, ye ken? Let it go.*

Loves him, loves him. Never had a phrase left him so defenseless.

Still, he'd thrown himself at Yesenia's feet, practically begged her to remember what they'd shared. He'd promised to fight for her, to do anything necessary to free her, and she'd looked him dead in the eyes and told him she'd chosen the Easterlander.

Word got back to his father of how he'd behaved, and Rylahn had already been cross with Erran after having to arrange a last-minute union to keep him from running off to the Easterlands like a lovesick fool. But for Erran to debase himself further, when both Yesenia and he had spouses of their own? It was simply not how Rutland men behaved.

But that was how Erran had ended up on an involuntary idyllmoon at Loch Ethereal with one of the most unsettling women he'd ever been around. "If that's how you wish for this to go."

Mariel turned, looking at him for the first time since they'd been banished to the bedchamber by his mother, right before she'd swept off into the afternoon like a gentle storm. Her sigh was expectedly contemptuous but just barely, like she'd lost the heart for full-blown animosity. "You have your life. I have mine. So in here? Let's give each other peace."

"I just don't understand how you expect this to go. What happens in six months, a year, when there's no sign of a bairn coming?"

"Who said there won't be one? I know what's expected of me." Mariel shrugged. "But then, what if I'm barren? Seems the annulment that would follow such failure would make you happy."

"Guardians, what a blessing that would be," he whispered under his breath. His brows furrowed in a thought he didn't share. He'd heard of women who secretly sabotaged their fertility behind their husbands' backs, but suggesting such a thing would be like throwing oil on a fire. "Mother knows what is—isn't happening in our bedchamber…on our wedding night or since I've come home. The only way to fix that is to fix the problem."

"Would you like me to make some unsavory noises for the guards in the hall?" Her eyes fluttered in petulance. "Like a barn animal?"

Erran's brows creased further. "Is that what you sound like when you…" He left the rest unsaid. He didn't actually know what a woman sounded like when she came undone. Yesenia had always pushed him away when he tried to pleasure her.

Ever briefly, she looked affronted. "Aye, well you'll never know, will you?" Her eyes softened, like she regretted the words but didn't know how to say so.

It took him a few more moments to work up to what he wanted to say. "I have to say something, Mariel." Erran pulled a chair from the writing desk and sat backward, eyeing her. His mother's ominous words had played on perpetual repeat in his thoughts. Mariel might have been the last woman he'd ever choose, but if he couldn't bring her around to his side, he'd lose everything that mattered. His birthright. His honor. For *that* he could close his eyes and his heart and do what was required. "You keep saying you were sold into this marriage, but there was no… no *forcing* you. Your brother signed the pre-contract. You signed the contract. So I don't ken why you're now acting like a prisoner of my family."

She appeared taken aback by his question, her mouth opening in the start of an answer that never came.

"Am I wrong?"

Mariel shook her head. "Submission and permission have different definitions."

"Submission?" He scoffed. "When have you ever known any Southerland woman to be submissive?"

"You ken what I mean."

"Do I?"

She said nothing.

"So the man in the reeds this morning, is he the one you really wanted?"

Mariel gave up on her pacing and dropped onto the edge of the bed, her languid gaze pointed toward the row of windows overlooking the loch. "He's not my lover."

"Then what?" He leaned closer. "What is he to you that he would sneak onto our property to come visit you before dawn?"

She ruminated before answering. He couldn't help wondering at all the responses she'd abandoned. "Khallum. Samuel. Hamish."

"What about them?"

"Your mates, not quite kin but the closest to it."

Erran nodded. "All right."

"That's what he is to me," she said, looking just past him. "Like kin."

"You've never mentioned him before."

"You've never asked me about my life before I came to Goldsea Spires."

"Haven't I? Perhaps because we've had so little time together." He knew he hadn't. Even his mother knew how shameful little interest he'd taken in his wife's past.

"Right."

"Mariel, be fair. You're not exactly a *reasonable*—" The cutting look she gave him made him reconsider finishing.

"Your mother knows we're standing on stolen Ashdown land. She doesn't hide it or smooth it over with pretty illusions. Why do you pretend?" She finally looked at him, her mossy eyes piercing his with cool indictment.

Erran sputtered. "Can you explain what you mean by that?"

"You don't know?"

"If I knew, I wouldn't be asking, would I?"

Mariel shifted a weary, withering glance toward the ceiling. "You're either a feloniously terrible liar or you really do know nothing, and I can't decide which is worse. Truly I can't." Her hands lifted and then fell with her gaze. "I don't ken why I'm even explaining this to you. You're just a…" Her words collapsed with an open-mouthed sigh.

"I *want* to know." Erran reached without thinking, his palm skating across the bony part of her knee. His own horror reflected back at him through her stunned glare as she shot to her feet in defiance. He tucked the offending hand under his leg. "Tell me. Please."

Mariel looked down at herself like she'd gladly be rid of her own skin. "You want to know? Then ask your father, Errandil. I'm calling for a bath."

Mariel didn't have time or energy to waste in bickering with the princeling, but he wasn't wrong. He hadn't outright called her a hypocrite, but he would have been well within his right to.

She *had* signed the contract, and she *did* need this marriage, but it wasn't so simple.

It had started with Destin…her beautiful, broken older brother. He had good days, and he had bad days, but the bad days were far more memorable, filled with drunken blunders and far too many messes for her and the other Obsidian Sky outlaws to tidy up. She couldn't remember the full set of circumstances that had led to him accepting a significant coffer from the Rutlands and Warwicks in exchange for Mariel's hand—because *he* couldn't even recount it reliably—but she'd never forget the moment he'd told her.

I just need to know why, Desi. Why you would do such a thing? With them. *To* me.

It seemed…I don't know, Mare. I thought if you could get close to them…It seemed like the right thing…Oh, Guardians…Guardians, I'm so sorry. I'm so cursed, feckin' sorry…

All right, all right. It's going to be all right. We'll figure it out. Shh, get some rest now.

His tears were the most devastating thing, and she could never hold onto her anger for long when he cried. Every single time, it was like he was shedding the full weight of his lifelong grief, only for it to build itself back up again, readying for the next violent spill. And she, the younger of the two by five years, had assumed the imperfect role of protector of his light.

Once he'd passed out from exhaustion, Mariel had worked her mind around what he'd done and how to move forward. A pre-contract wasn't a contract, and she *did* have rights as an independent adult, no longer under the care of parents. She could refuse to sign, and had fully intended to, until she considered the rare opportunity it provided. *I thought if you could get close to them.* To be *in* the nest of vipers itself. Obsidian Sky had Augustine on the inside, as one of the stewardess's seamstresses, but it wasn't enough. A seamstress could only get so close, hear so much. If Mariel agreed to marry the princeling, she would be seated at the same table as *the* man they needed to take down. If she worked the son just right, she could mold him into her perfect, unwitting informant.

She'd had three months to work herself up to the task. But as soon as Erran returned, she'd led with anger, not with the cunning that had kept her and her friends safe for so many years. It was baffling, inconvenient, and counterproductive, but she somehow couldn't stop herself.

If Augustine were there, she'd tell Mariel yesterday didn't decide tomorrow. It wasn't too late to reset, begin anew.

Mariel had stolen more gold and jewels than she could ever account for. She'd bested men at swordcraft and was quicker with her bow than others were with words. She'd lied and schemed and evaded capture for over a decade and protected her brother and friends from the same. But somehow, sleeping with the enemy seemed a step too close to cliff's edge?

There was another... slight complication, if she could even call it that. The rumors about Erran Rutland's handsomeness had been understated, if anything. He was exasperatingly gorgeous, words he'd never hear her say aloud and she preferred not to think either, but fortunately, when she looked at him, she saw only the dust and ashes of the land the Rutlands had stolen and sold to their friends. His charming dimples became the disrupted earth of landmines used to drive people from their own homes, his curved smile reminiscent of a surreptitious path of an unexpected blade entering through the back.

She had never lain with any man, or woman. All those nights curled up in the arms of Augustine—the other woman's hand draped over her waist, fingers spread across the cave of her belly—Mariel had certainly *thought* about it. Any desire she'd felt had come hand in hand with safety and respect. Both of the Perevil siblings, Remy and Augustine, had lighted something electrifying in her, but the unpredictable nature of their work kept her from ultimately surrendering to what felt right. Love was merely another weapon for the enemy to wield against her.

Mariel's hand shifted to her abdomen as her thoughts returned to such nights. She traced it down her wet skin, half wondering if even momentary pleasure was too great a distraction. But she was drained, body and soul. She craved the safe return of her tranquil evenings in Augustine's arms, when she could almost forget that her life wouldn't allow for anything more.

She bit down on her lip when her hand breached the water and traveled between her legs. Her eyes closed as she slipped lower in the bath, getting comfortable.

Mariel shot up in the water when violent, booming thunder shook the keep. The brass mirror crashed to the stone floor, shattering.

Erran had the door open so fast, she was almost impressed. His wide eyes met hers, then slid downward, to where she still had one arm under the water. The hand on his sword hilt slowly fell away, while hers splashed to the side in the bath like a fish caught on a hook.

It seemed he was on the verge of speaking but backed out, closing the door gently without a word.

Breathless, she darted her eyes around the room, as if there were anything to ease her absolute mortification. But he couldn't know *what* he'd seen. She hadn't even had the chance to do anything interesting. Erran discovering she knew her way around her own body was inconsequential and not the worst thing that could happen. He could have overheard the conversation with Remy.

She pushed to her feet, sending water splashing onto the stones, and climbed out, stepping gingerly around the shattered glass. After wrapping herself in a robe, she stormed from the bathing room back into the bedchamber.

"You always walk in uninvited on a woman having a bath?" Her whole body was hot, head to toe, from the discomfiture, from the water, from...

Erran faced away, looking out one of the windows at the rain with both hands wrapped around the back of his neck. His shirt was rolled to the elbows, revealing his tense, muscled forearms. "I heard the crash after the thunder hit. I came to see if you were all right, and..." He turned his head over his shoulder, his stare on the wall. "You aren't just any woman, you know. You're my wife."

Mariel tightened the belt on her robe and stepped closer. She *could* do this. She had to. Continuing to be contrary only further compromised her goals. "You're right," she said quietly.

He spun all the way around. "What's that?"

"I said you're right, but I'll take it back if you don't...wipe that..." She waved a hand. "That look off your face."

"What look?"

"That self-satisfied smug—" She fisted her hands, then released them. "I cannot refute the points you made earlier. I *did* sign the contract, aye. It wasn't...not because I wanted to, but because... It was the prudent choice."

Erran crossed his arms and leaned against the frame, listening.

"But I signed it," she said, moving close enough that she could safely reduce her voice to a whisper, mindful of how others were always listening. Her calm gradually returned, and she remembered she didn't have to surrender her control to anything. To anyone. "I'm not ready for what your mother expects of me, but we've got to earn ourselves a reprieve from everyone's meddling ears. We both need that reprieve. You ken?"

He offered a light frown. "Would help if you laid it out."

"You're still in love with Yesenia." She posed it as a statement, but he nodded weakly in answer. "I was not in love before we married, never have been. Never wish to be. But my old life still matters to me. And I will not give it up. I couldn't care less who you love. If she'd take you back, I'd turn the other cheek—mind my own business—as long as it doesn't get back to your meddling parents." Her breath was shaky and uneven, her hands traveling to the belt of her robe. She drew from every bit of resolve within her as she opened it and let the silk fabric slip to the stones in a soft whoosh.

Never had she so openly bared her physical self to anyone.

The light inward gasp from Erran had her toes curling to keep from reaching for the robe again. "Do you see these scars?" She pointed at two faint white gashes, one near her breastbone, the other, a longer one, across her torso. "Childhood injuries," she lied—not fully a lie though. She'd still been a child when she'd earned them.

"Aye," Erran croaked. His hand pulled at the stubble on his chin. His eyes danced between his cautious assessment and the nearest corner.

"I want you to brag to your mates about us, and when you do, mention the scars. Make sure everyone can hear when you do. There's no way you could know about either of them unless you'd seen me in the flesh."

Erran nodded slowly. "Seen and noted." He coughed to clear his throat. "Should I do the same…"

Mariel brushed a hand across the air, indicating he should.

He removed his empty sword belt first, unclipping it and laying it across the arms of a nearby chair. His suspenders came next, then his shirt, revealing the other half of the view she'd gotten earlier. Hard lines cut across his tanned flesh, tightening with his movements as he unlatched his trousers and tugged them down. Her mouth watered in defiance of the power she still—barely—wielded over the moment.

It was the bewildering twinge of weakness that made her say, "That's enough. I can…There are freckles on your chest. Have them elsewhere?"

Erran glanced down at himself. "Aye, my inner thighs. Knees. Back of the calves, at least in the warmer months. Feet. Toes, anyway."

"Cock?"

He blurted an unflattering laugh. "Nay, not there."

"You can get dressed."

He seemed almost comically relieved as he yanked his trousers back into place.

Mariel snatched the robe from the floor and disappeared behind the armoire. She took a moment to gather herself. "Aye, so you understand then?"

He appeared just on the other side, close enough for her to hear his raspy breathing. "Thing is…I never bragged to my mates about Yesenia. I always felt what we did was just for us."

"You'd be lying, not bragging." She shrugged her nightgown on, tugging it over her still-damp skin. "Think of it as playacting, and you'll find it comes easier."

"You sound like you know a thing or two about it."

"I might."

"Do you lie often?"

"When I need to."

"Have you lied to me?"

"Aye."

Erran snorted. "At least you were honest about that."

She nearly laughed, but shared jokes were for friends, and they were not friends, even if she didn't find him near as galling as she'd expected to. He could be an ally, and she needed him to be, but for only as far as it served her. Forgetting who he was would undo everything she'd worked for. His kindness and beauty were curses, blights of ignorance. And ignorance, in her experience, could be as dangerous as malice, if not more.

Mariel emerged from behind the armoire. "Everyone lies, Errandil. Either from necessity or greed or just boredom."

"Not me," he said, defiantly shaking his head. "What else do I have, if not my honor?"

"Honesty and honor may start with the same letters, but they are not the same," Mariel replied, looking up at him. "You said outside we share the same wants. Would I be right in saying you don't want me any more than I want you?"

He hesitated before nodding. "Not because there's anything *wrong* with you, Mariel. You're..." A frown preceded his next word. "Interesting."

"Wasn't fishing for compliments. Only way to get out of doing the thing is lying about doing the thing. We go on long enough like that, act convincingly enough when eyes and ears are turned our way, they'll assume we gave it our best. Enough time passes, we either start actually sharing a bed or...or they'll grant us an annulment, because you need an heir." *And by then, I'll have what I need and can walk away.* She tossed a glance at the door, beyond which the servants were undoubtedly scrambling to make sense of the whispers they couldn't hear. "If we don't do this, they'll never give us peace."

He followed her gaze, his expression thoughtful. "So this is to be our marriage then? Lies and evasion?"

"Wouldn't you prefer an annulment to being stuck with me the rest of your life?"

Erran looked down at her. "Honestly? I don't know."

"How?" Her frown deepened. "It's a simple question."

"Aye, but I don't know if the answer is. My responsibilities as heir are what they are, but I never considered I'd have a loveless, cold marriage such as this one."

She nearly felt bad for him, how he'd lost Yesenia. There'd have been no better husband for the only Warwick daughter. But losing a childhood love held no mirror to all Mariel had lost. All that her people, and many other peoples, had lost, on account of his father.

"You can take as many lovers as you please. There'll be no jealousy from me. In front of others, we play the happiest of families. We convince them we're doing our duty whenever we step beyond these doors. When alone, we don't have to pretend. We respect our separate lives." She paused and then said, "That means turning the other way when I want to see my friends. Maybe even covering for me from time to time. In return, I'll do the same." The next part was a lie, but it needed to be said. He needed to believe she would one day be the dutiful wife he required. Only after she had what she'd come for and was gone like a wraith would he realize he'd been had. "And when I'm ready, we'll do what we must."

Erran seemed completely lost for words. He pursed his lips in a stilted breath, one hand knotted in his dark, wavy hair. "If that's what you want."

"And my brother."

"What of him?"

"I want him at supper here once a week."

"That's not up to me, Mariel. He'd have to—"

"I know," she said softly, her eyes flashing wide at the door to remind him they had to keep their voices down. "I *know* he has troubles. No one knows it better than me. But he's my *family*, and he's all alone, and if I cannot bring him here, then I'll have to spend more time away from the Spires, which means…"

"More interference from my mother and father," he said, his eyes slowly shuttering in understanding. Not a complete idiot then.

"Aye. And more problems we don't need. Either of us."

"I'll talk to Mother." He didn't explain why he'd chosen to start with her, but Mariel knew. Hestia Rutland was a smooth negotiator and would cede ground to get what she wanted. Rylahn expected fealty to fall into his lap without giving up anything.

Mariel glanced at the bed. "It's big enough we never have to touch each other…"

"You want the left or the right?"

"Right."

A flash of disappointment crossed his face as he nodded. The right had probably been his side.

"I can take left if you prefer," she said, feeling unexpectedly generous. For the first time since they'd said those cursed vows, they were in *something* resembling accord. Their plan would offer her the freedom she needed, and she wouldn't have to explain herself because Erran would do it for her. As long as she kept the peace—and her animosity at bay—he'd have no reason to betray her, even as she was betraying him.

"If it's no trouble," he said, looking back at her.

"None at all." Mariel waited for him to climb in before slipping onto her side. She'd been sleeping in the guest quarters while he'd been gone, as Erran's apartments were being renovated in his absence. The guest bed was nice, but nothing like what she'd just crawled into. His sheets were luxuriously soft, slightly thicker than silk, and made of a material her family would never have used even when they could have afforded it. She slid her legs along the smooth fabric, torn by how lovely it felt and how wonderful the sleep ahead would be, all the while reminding herself she could never *ever* allow herself to succumb to the lure of the comforts offered by the Rutlands and their world.

If she could commit to what she'd proposed, it would be over soon.

Destin's tortured cries entered her thoughts. Remy's resourcefulness born of horrors. Augustine's warmth amid the cold. Alessia's fierceness against the lions of the world. Magnur's quiet strength that held them all aloft.

For them, she wouldn't rest until she'd set the world to rights.

For herself, she wouldn't forget who she was and how she'd been made.

And as for the Rutlands, by the time her work was done, they'd forget none of their names ever again.

THREE

THE TOAST AND THE DANCE

Mariel hid upon one of the twelve columned balconies of Goldsea Spires overlooking the milky coastal cliffs. Beyond, the cresting waves of the White Sea ebbed as the tide washed out. Tall palms bowed and shimmered along the balmy breeze. She breathed in the briny nocturnal air and held it until her peace superseded her nerves.

The distant ocean roar defeated all other sounds. Though it wasn't the perfect stillness of a lake, the crashing surf made her chest soften, easing its feverish cadence of the past hours of drink and dance and music. It was the party they were supposed to have had three months ago, after their hasty handfast, but Erran's campaign at sea had forestalled something she'd preferred to have gotten out of the way months before.

The Golden Coast had never been home to her, but she'd just returned from the one place that *had* been, and the foreignness had been nearly unbearable.

She'd been twelve when her parents had died of scurvy, after feeding what meager fruit and greens they'd had left to their two surviving children. Afterward, she and Destin had been taken in by Remy and Augustine's father, but then Sir Perevil, too, had died after drowning his desperation too deep in a bottle. Many of the adults in their small world had been taken by either the malnutrition or the despair, leaving a surplus of children to fend for themselves. Remy, who had been away at Oldcastle on apprenticeship at the universities, returned and attempted to assume domicile of his father's estate, until that, also, had been stolen from underneath them. *Too young* was the official reason, which was merely an excuse, like all the other justifications the Rutland supremacy had concocted for tyranny.

It was on one of their late nights, starving and cold, when the four orphans had conceived of the first and barest of bones of Obsidian Sky, starting with the question: *What if it didn't have to be this way*?

A few nights later, Remy overheard two drunkards talking about the gold they were hauling for their wealthy patron in Sandymount. The inept guards had stumbled to their room that night without even bothering to secure their wagon. When Remy came home, laughing about the idiots in the inn, Mariel had told him they needed to go back, that they could do so much good for others with that gold. He hadn't argued—had even confessed he'd been thinking it himself but didn't want to scare her with such a reckless suggestion. But the only thing Mariel dreaded was a lifetime of the same suffering they and their people continued to endure.

A year later, they'd rescued Alessia from a sex trader they'd robbed outside Warwicktown. Magnus had come a couple of years after that. He'd been a hired muscle, hauling a cart they'd targeted, and had unexpectedly turned his coat and joined them instead.

Obsidian Sky was the only family Mariel and Destin had left.

No one inside the lavish pillared keep could ever be.

Fingertips brushed her back. She spun almost fully around before she saw Augustine's wild braids whipping through the air. The redhead winked at her and puckered her mouth in a brief air kiss before moving to the far end of the balcony, becoming a silhouette as she blended with the curtain.

"What are you doing here?" Mariel whispered. Augustine, as one of Hestia's seamstresses, had more access than most of the staff, but she'd never be in their inner circle. They certainly weren't inviting her to their parties.

"I live here," Augustine said, grinning.

"You know what I mean."

Augustine tilted her head back with a deep breath. "I'm relieved you survived your week in purgatory."

"Could have been worse," Mariel said, her stare on the wispy curtains dividing them from the elaborately festooned terrace, where far too many people were drinking and dancing and carousing. She was close enough to the party to hear the trailing bits of conversation, raucous and grating. "He and I have come to an arrangement."

"Oh." Augustine tucked her chin in amusement. "Is it *that* big, then, that you'd throw it all away for pleasure?"

"What?" Mariel gaped at her. "You're surely not implying what I *think*—"

"Ah, you're too serious sometimes." She watched Mariel closely, like she was testing her. "Some of the other girls here talk is all, especially now that he's come home from securing even *more* ships and trade agreements for his father. Yesenia Warwick wasn't his first or his only."

"Course not." Mariel shook her head. "When have men like him ever had to practice discretion or moderation?"

Augustine crossed her arms. "Your arrangement then?"

"As long as others believe we're doing our duty, we live our separate lives and cover for each other. It only has to last as long as it takes me to get what I need about the auction, which should be any day now. If everything goes to plan, I'll never even have to sleep with him."

"And you trust him?"

Mariel scoffed. "Nay, but he believes he has even more to lose than I do. Cannot bear to disappoint his daddy." She laughed. "Or his mommy."

Augustine made a *hmm* sound. "And so you're out here alone and not celebrating with all the other somebodies?"

"I've been doing my part all night." Mariel leaned over the balcony with a stretch. "Smiled at his dodgy mates, laughed at their bawdy humor. I let his mother introduce me to dozens of people whose names I only bothered to learn so we can add them to our list of enemies. Even kissed the princeling again to help sell the facade, which was no small thing, Auggie, let me assure you."

With a soft, trailing laugh, Augustine said, "I'd have let him dodder me by now, lacking any better ideas to placate him and the other nonces."

Mariel's eyes narrowed. "You're just as clever as your brother." Augustine—otherwise known as the Needle—had skill with sewing and weaving that was only a cover for her innate ability to thread herself through the most unlikely spaces and situations. Whatever Augustine couldn't glean from slipping indiscernibly through the spaces of the influential, Alessia gained through taking powerful men to bed—with the occasional brute force from Magnur.

The rest was up to Mariel.

"Remy misses you," Augustine said distantly. Her eyes were turned on the sea.

"And you?"

The redhead grinned. "I can just watch you while you sleep. Being the Needle and all."

"Not now that I have to share a bed with him." Mariel's own grin faded into the gentle silence that followed. "I've been thinking about how I'll leave this place. If I can't get what we need, that is. Obviously I won't stay here forever."

"You'll get it," Augustine assured her.

"It's happening soon. Any day now, but I...No one's talking. Rylahn hasn't even been joining us for meals. You know we have to time this *just right* if it's to work. Too soon and the gold won't be there yet. Too late and the equivalent of an army will await us, alongside every damned baron in the Rutlands' territory."

Her friend grinned. "Maybe you *should* sleep with the princeling. I hear he gets loose lips when he's consumed by his, eh, carnal desires."

"I would never debase..." But she would. If she had to, she would. "Does he now?"

Augustine nodded from the shadows. "So they say."

"Not loose enough that you've gotten wind of what we need though," Mariel said, shaking her head. "I'm afraid time isn't on our side anymore."

"And you still think this..." She peered behind the curtain, into the hall dividing the balcony from the rest of the terrace, before continuing. "This auction will be enough? And then we can retire from all this?"

Mariel had never come out and said it like that. Not because she didn't believe it *could* be enough. The sheer quantity of gold that would be stored there would change the face of the Southerlands forever. Whether the money was thrown into the ocean, flattening the class structure, or redistributed to its rightful owners, the entire system would turn on its head. Upheaval would follow, but they'd be on the proper end of it this time.

But she'd never said it that way because the thought of Obsidian Sky disbanding—of their work no longer being necessary, of having to figure out what the hell to *do* with her days and nights—was gutting.

Mariel's gaze followed the dark coastline. Dozens of ships lined the horizon, all part of the Rutland fleet. To the west, all the way in Devon, the modest ship she'd won in a billiards game, the *Mistwitch*, was anchored at sea, waiting for her. She'd sailed her only a few times before her marriage, and none since. She'd had no formal training and wasn't especially skilled with any of it, but she could manage well enough in the shallows of coastal waters. Often she dreamed of rowing out, climbing aboard, and navigating alone into the dark unknown. If not for Destin, she might have. "You should go before someone sees us talking."

"I only came to ask if you'll be able to slip out tonight. After the toast and dance, of course."

"Tonight?"

"You didn't forget. The golden egg?"

Mariel hadn't forgotten, but the small, insecure side of her had wondered if they'd forgotten *her.* If they would just go ahead without her. She smiled to cover it. "Never."

"And he won't be a problem? The princeling?"

Mariel shook her head. "We have an understanding, as I said."

"What does he get out of it, Mar?"

"Same as me. Freedom. Whatever he wants, really."

"The one thing he truly wants is out of his reach, shacked up with a tree-dweller in the Easterlands."

Mariel laughed. "She cannot be *all* he wants. He's weak, but he's still a man. Still has needs."

"You're right. He also wants the Rutland admiralty, but whispers tell me his inability to domesticate his bride is forcing his father to consider alternatives."

Mariel cocked her head to the side. "That cannot be true. The steward would be a fool to hand over their legacy to someone other than his only son."

"Truth to a wraith extends as far as belief. I can only tell you what I've heard...what he tells the maidens he beds as he's complaining to them about his impossible wife."

Mariel considered the weight of that. It could work for or against her work. If Erran fell out of his father's favor, an annulment, when the time came, would be a simple request. But if his father was so cross with him, then it was possible Erran would be left out of important matters, like the auction. And that couldn't happen.

Each path ahead had been closing one by one, until only one was left for Mariel. She had to keep Erran in his father's good graces and pray she wouldn't need to keep up the act for long.

The thought filled her with a sudden fury, directed at *him.* If he'd only just *lied* to his father, like a normal son, there would be no disfavor. Now they were both crushed into a corner.

But *she* was the impossible one? What was he doing talking to his conquests about her anyway?

"You always know what you're doing, of course." Augustine's fingertips brushed Mariel's bare arm as she slid by. "I've heard naught but fair things about the princeling from the rest of the staff, but does that nay raise your suspicions even more? Is anyone so free of danger and darkness, Mariel? Or are some better at hiding it than others?"

Mariel left without answering.

"Ye finally snog her and all ye wannae speak about is her *scars*?" The ale in Hamish's thick hand sloshed in time with his vivacious laughter. He snorted, his head shaking at Erran. "Mate, yer doing it wrong. Khal, tell him he's doing it wrong."

"It's 'cos he's lying," Khallum muttered, grinning into his own mug before taking a swig. "When have ye ever known our Erran to be good at it?"

"Ask your mothers what I'm good at." Erran's face heated, despite the sea breeze sweeping through the fluted columns into the sumptuously trussed terrace, where everyone they knew was gathered to celebrate a union they'd already celebrated once before. The heady aroma of the extensive florals from Mistgrave mixed with the tang of seawater in a nauseating combination of a world he hated and a world he loved.

Although he'd thought Mariel's idea a prudent one when she'd suggested it, as he stood in a huddle of his closest friends, he wondered how he could have ever thought they'd buy any of it.

"Good at feckin' or lyin'?" Hamish nudged Erran, his good-natured smile turning somber. "Donnae need to put it on for us, mate, aye? We know ye ain't happy. Cannae judge ye for the heart wantin' what it wants. I married for love, after all."

"Lying," Khallum said, answering Hamish. "We'll not be discussing the feckin', lads, seeing as he learned it on my sister."

"Oh, aye." Hamish's eyes widened at his error. "Aye indeed."

Erran breathed in through his nose, fighting a frustrating sway. He hadn't seen Mariel in some time, not since their saccharine-smiled greeting line to kick off the party—and the impromptu kiss she'd landed on him for show, after warning him against the same behavior—and then handed her off to his mother. "Just…donnae run your mouths where my father or mother can hear, aye? They're already displeased with me."

"After ye just added all that to yer family's legacy?" Hamish scrunched his nose in disbelief.

"Who are ye talking to? Telling tales? Come on now." Khallum belched and banged a fist on his chest. Hardly a year had passed since the untimely death of his father, Khoulter, and his ascension as lord of the Southerlands. He'd tried distancing himself from his long-standing reputation as the vulgar libertine of the group, but there were still flashes of the old Khallum, reminders of the before times. "But if she's giving the same story to Gwyn and Yanna, or any of the other women…Well, the wives are even more keen than us. They could look at the shore and tell ye if even a grain of sand was missing."

"Isnae a lie, that," Hamish agreed with a tilted nod.

"Donnae even know where she is." Erran shrugged, but he was growing concerned. He'd agreed she could dip out near the end if they could play nice until the toast and dance, but he was starting to fear she'd actually left hours ago. His anxiety had been making the slow climb for a while, but he could hardly feign smiles anymore.

Samuel nestled into the group with a full pitcher. He whistled at their half-full mugs with a scolding head shake. "Falling behind, lads. I've been gone long enough that you should have been empty by now. Would you put such disrespect on the names of your fathers?"

Hamish downed his, made a sputtering sound, and thrust his mug out. "Properly shamed, Sam."

Samuel chuckled and topped him off. "Erran, Sessaly stopped me on the way back. I'm supposed to tell you they're calling for the toast and dance now. She seemed rather...excited at the notion."

Erran smiled without joy. He'd barely touched his own ale. Every drop that hit his lips sent a curl of uneasiness through him. He wondered again where Mariel was. Who she'd been talking to. Whether she'd said something he'd be working to unwind over the next few days. If she was even still there...or had deceived him, sabotaging her own damn scheme.

Erran caught his father watching from the other side of the terrace. Between them, over two hundred Southerlanders drank, cursed, and whirled to the lively music, a mix of piped and wooded instruments. Rylahn wore his admiralty regalia, donning the red and gold of Warwicktown, the Southerlands capital, as well as the symbol of the Rutland standard, the jagged alabaster crags of Whitecliffe. Their eyes stayed locked, his father's expression as smooth as stone. Erran nodded at him, unsure if he'd just been silently scolded or praised.

"Are any of Mariel's people here?" Samuel asked. He'd taken no mug for himself. He was the teetotaler of the group, their voice of reason and confidence. His father, Steward Damian Law, was the treasurer for the Southerlands, and a top adviser to the Warwicks. Sessaly would be marrying into the family soon, betrothed to Samuel's younger brother, Aliksander. The Laws hailed from a region of the Southerlands as wealthy as Whitecliffe, but unlike Erran, Samuel didn't put on pretense by affecting an accent that wasn't natural to him.

"What people?" Khallum scoffed. "It's only the brother, and he's nay fit."

"So there's no one here for her?" Samuel frowned.

"I tried," Erran said. "Father thinks Destin would make a scene and..." He almost added *he's not wrong,* but guilt stayed him. Samuel's observation emphasized the fact that Mariel had no allies at Goldsea Spires. If anyone should have been willing to advocate for her, it was her husband, and he'd folded at the slightest disapproval from his father.

Khallum clapped him on the shoulder. "For the best, mate. You're already up to yer neck in it."

The music halted. Conversations dwindled before dying to whispers as everyone turned toward the west end of the room, where Rylahn and Hestia stood waiting to speak. Sessaly dashed in beside them, a blur of dark curls and pink frills.

Khallum broke away from Erran and the others and headed to the front of the room, where he was expected to make a brief speech as lord of the Southerlands.

Erran's heart did a somersault. *Just stay through the toast and dance, then you can leave, and I'll make whatever excuse you like,* he'd told Mariel, and she'd agreed. So where was she?

"Aye, it's true what they say about a Rutland party. *Much* more civilized than many of us are used to," Khallum joked, breaking the patient silence of the celebrants. His voice carried all the way to the back of the terrace, where Erran was still rooted in place with Hamish and Samuel. "It's tradition for the lord of the Southerlands to bless the unions of stewards. Should be my father here, but..." He cleared his throat with a cursory glance upward. "You're stuck with me instead. Deepest apologies, and may the Guardians see fit to bless the couple anyway."

A ripple of subdued laughter moved across the room. Erran couldn't even make himself smile. His mouth was a bed of cotton. Samuel gave his shoulder a brief squeeze.

"I've known Erran since we were bairns, crawling around on the sand, giving our mothers heart palpitations."

More laughter.

"He's a good man. Mariel, ye couldnae find a truer heart than his. But I ken you already know that, or he'd be a dead man by now, since I have it on good authority you're even fairer with a bow than he is with a sword."

Erran craned his neck, rising onto his toes, but he still couldn't see her.

"You're telling half-truths, Lord Warwick!" Mariel cried, emerging breathless from one of the vestibule arches as she pushed through the crowd. "For I'm better with a sword too. Or should a lady keep such particulars to herself?"

The guests laughed even harder, roaring and clapping as she made her way to the front.

Erran's whole body sighed in relief, only to draw tight again.

"I detect a pattern with you and capable women," Samuel teased.

"Didnae choose *this* one," Erran said before finishing his ale and setting it on a table.

"Sometimes choice follows decision."

Erran scrunched his nose at Samuel's unwelcome wisdom on the matter.

Hamish nudged him. "Better get on wit' it then. Willnae end if ye cannae begin."

"Remember, you're supposed to say something nice!" Samuel called after him, chuckling.

Erran made his way through the crowd in a daze, trying to smile as hands from all over clapped him on the shoulders and squeezed his arms. It was meant to be a joyous occasion, and he should feel what they all felt for him. But all he could think about, surrounded by the people who had shaped his twenty-one years, was that it should be Yesenia Warwick standing behind his parents, not the feral tomcat who would just as soon watch him get mauled by wulves as share his bed.

Sessaly winked at him in an especially theatrical fashion, her lips pursed as though she was privy to some great secret they all shared. He wished someone would clue him in on it.

"Behave," he warned his younger sister as he passed her. She made a little indignant chirp. Their father had indulged her ill-mannered behavior for far too long, and she was irrecoverably incorrigible.

Khallum and Rylahn both clapped, while his mother smiled tolerantly. Erran nodded at all three, forgetting everything he'd planned to say by the time he stepped in beside Mariel. He flung a quick glance her direction, noticing that while she was beaming at everyone, her eyes glowed with cool wrath, amplified by the soft brushes of candlelight.

"It is tradition," Hestia said, "that our couple, who were denied a proper party after their handfast, share something they've come to adore about their spouse. It can be anything." She grinned impishly, to more laughter. "Now remember, before you speak, Erran and Mariel, you have to dance with one another when you're done. Choose your words prudently, for you *also* have to sleep beside each other when night falls."

"Lassies go first," Rylahn said with a light nod at Mariel.

Khallum bit back a grin and looped his hands behind his back, his eyes directed at the stones.

"Aye?" Mariel nodded, whistling through her teeth. Her cheeks were two splotched balls of blooming anger. He couldn't fathom where it had come from, when she'd seemed perfectly fine earlier—fine for an untamed banshee anyway. "Well, all right. How hard can this be? Just one thing is all I have to come up with?"

Erran braced through the subsequent chuckles her gibe had earned. But though everyone else was laughing, Mariel was obviously not.

She glanced his way before stepping forward. "One thing I adore..." She tapped her hands on her crossed arms, sighing. Her face pulled into an exaggerated wince, her eyes squinting upward. "Ah! I *do* have one. Before I met Errandil, I was blissfully unaware that men, or anyone for that matter, could have freckles on their feet. But he has the most *adorable* ones, would you not say, Stewardess? And so many more on his knees, his calves, his shoulders...elsewhere..."

"Adore his *feet*, do ye?" Khallum asked, just loud enough for those at the front of the room to hear over the laughter.

Erran's face was on fire. He couldn't say anything, couldn't even react without making it worse. Was that the real reason she'd been so eager to see the marks on his body? To make him think they were allies so she could weaken and humiliate him? And implying he had freckles on a cock she had utterly no interest in toying with was untenable. He'd have preferred she just slap him on the face and be done with it.

"Mariel, dear, you've surely not seen many Southerland feet then," Hestia said, gentle warning in her tone.

Rylahn cut in. "Is there nothing else you'd prefer to say?"

Mariel's eyes skirted the crowd. She *appeared* in perfect command of herself, of the moment, except Erran could see the light twitch in her pinky, resting against her leg...the tension turning her jaw into a razor's edge. "I ken I could speak of how much he loves his mates."

Everyone nodded in approval.

"*So* much so that he puts on a poor salt-and-sand affectation when they're around, and speaks like a proper tree-dweller when they're not. And we all know our Errandil has a *special* relationship with tree-dwellers, don't we?"

Erran's belly seized in fury. She *was* trying to humiliate him, and from the few looks he dared catch from his friends, family, and peers, it was working. They were amused, perhaps confused, but it was the pity...Ahh, he could almost read the precision of their thoughts. A man who couldn't even keep his own wife from emasculating him was no man at all. He'd rather be known as a cuckold.

Mariel stepped back, having done more than enough damage. She still hadn't bothered to look at him.

"Erran, it seems your wife has chosen to go to war with her words," Rylahn called. He sounded playful, but Erran knew better. "Will you do the same with yours?"

I could tell them all about your lush of a brother. How I caught you fondling yourself in the bath. How you snuck off to be with another man on our own feckin' idyllmoon.

Sessaly prodded. "Erran?"

"Well, I..." He couldn't decide whether to speak with an accent or without. Either way, he'd be ridiculed, thanks to her. "I willnae..."

"Ye what? Will...nay?" Khallum asked, chortling. He was genuinely amused, more than Erran had seen from him since his father had been murdered by the king.

"Quit taking the piss," Erran retorted through a clenched jaw.

"Mixed audience here, mate. Could be either version of yourself."

Erran rarely wasted time on such a useless emotion as hate, but in that moment, he hated Mariel.

But if he retaliated, it would only magnify her insults, validate how they'd disturbed him. The only answer was to do the opposite.

So he laughed. He laughed with everyone laughing at him, all the while stabbing her with his eyes as he matched her fury, glare for glare. "My wife has my measure, I see, just as my mates do," Erran stated with a terse shrug. "I ken I could tell ye all some things. Mariel is a capable woman, as are all Southerland lasses, and you wouldnae be surprised to hear me numerate the ways." *And thank feck I don't have to, for I prefer not to make a liar of myself.* "But one value we share is our love of family. And while I know she misses hers, I hope the Rutlands can, in at least some small way, provide what she's been without."

Instead of the laughter and taunts that had followed Mariel's revelations, Erran's left the room quiet. A few *awws* cut the silence as many smiled warmly at whoever was beside them, or slipped a hand into their spouse's.

There, wife. Now don't you look the fool.

Erran tucked his head low and started away, catching the warm breeze flowing freely through the open veranda. What he needed was to stand with his toes in the sand and his eyes facing the sea, remembering that no matter what Mariel said, he was salt and sand, through and through. A man's accent, the amount of leather in his skin… Neither of those things defined what was in his blood, and always would be.

"Son. The dance," Rylahn said, assertive.

Erran froze. His shoulders pinched back as he turned. He flashed a smile. "Oh. Right."

He couldn't even look at Mariel as he stretched a grudging hand to lead her to the center of the room, where the revelers had parted to make way. But instead of taking it, she marched past and went ahead of him. It was another cruel and unnecessary slight after he'd extended a sign of amity with his own "adoration."

Most dances in the Southerlands were lively feet-stompers, but not the nuptial dance. It was a slow, intimate affair called the sand and sway. He'd expected Mariel to revolt when he reluctantly took one of her hands in his, resentfully placing his other at the small of her back, but she was surprisingly pliant, falling into formation.

The melody, a heady composition of string instruments, carried their pace. Other couples began to salt and sway as well.

"What the bloody hell are you playing at?" Erran brushed the words close to her ear, through his teeth, smiling joylessly at those watching. "We agreed to be allies. To play *nice.*"

"Aye, that *was* nice," she said defensively. The antagonism in her voice was cut with something else, something he hadn't heard before but was clear enough now. Hurt. "As nice as they'd believe, given all the whispers about us. Some, as I understand it, from you directly."

He had no idea what she was talking about, but he didn't care. She was well out of order, and he was already sick of it. "You want me to believe you didn't enjoy that?"

"I was only performing my part." Mariel straightened, and his hand slipped lower. "They expected another Yesenia. I tried to give them one. I thought you would approve."

His arm at her back tightened. "Yesenia would never have humiliated me like that."

"Did I say anything untrue?"

"You willnae—" Erran grunted, grinding his teeth. He could almost feel her smirk form against his shoulder. It was an equal defeat, whether he kept up the accent or dropped it. "Will not make me the fool here. I know what you were doing. Getting your stabs in where you could. Is it because I couldn't get Destin an invitation?"

"I never actually expected you to stand up to your father," Mariel said, a touch of unsteadiness in her defiance. "You never do."

"So it *is* about that." Erran scoffed, shaking his head. Her hand felt like quicksand on his, and he couldn't wait to be rid of the cloying sensation. "Instead of blaming me, perhaps you could look at your brother's deviant behavior for what it is."

"My brother is a wounded man. Did you ever ask your father about Mistgrave? About the loch?"

He'd squandered several opportunities to ask, though in every case, there'd been something more pressing. "All men are wounded, Mariel. It's the way of life."

"And why is that, Errandil? Do you ever ask yourself, or have you been on the side of the oppressor so long, it doesn't even occur to you there may be those not as able to defend themselves from tyranny?"

"What is this really about?" He missed a step, throwing off their rhythm. "Everything was…fine at Mistgrave. Was fine the past two days since we've come home. And now you're acting like I've shat in your porridge when you should be acting like you cannot wait until everyone leaves so you can be alone with me."

Her shoulders released their pinch, softening her posture. Her neck rolled in a stretch. "I know I said I wanted you to brag to your mates about us, but talking shite about me to your conquests?"

"What *conquests*?" he shot back, growing hot again. "When would I have time for those, when I'm so busy trying to placate my wife and father?"

Mariel scoffed, readying with a hard breath in. "I don't care who you fuck. I care who you spill your secrets to."

"So when I say I've done no such thing, you're still going to trust the words of fishwife gossip instead of me?"

"Why would they lie about such a thing?"

"Why would *I*?" Erran exclaimed. He groaned quietly when others turned their attention on them. "My mother welcomed you with open arms, Mariel. My father has been kind. Sessaly is…Sessaly, but she's like that with everyone. She was worse with Yesenia. They never got on."

"Can't help working her into a conversation, can you?" Mariel's hand constricted atop his, her head tilting back and up to look at him. "You're lucky it was me who ended up sharing your life and not someone capable of actually loving you. Because there's no room for three in a marriage, is there? Especially not when one is as 'insufferable' as you tell others I am." She broke away as the song came to a close, her chest rising and caving. Her smile seemed real enough, but nothing in her eyes implied an ounce of joy. "I did my part tonight, even if you didn't like the way I did it. Now do yours."

Astonished, Erran watched her slip into the crowd and disappear.

Khallum drew up beside him moments later. "And we thought my sister was a challenge. You've got your hands full with that one, aye?" He clamped a hand over his shoulder. "And we already knew about the accent *and* the freckles, mate, so liven up. There's ale to be drunk and lassies to dance with."

FOUR
THE GOLDEN EGG

Mariel crouched low, her eyes in a squint and her ears listening for sounds, friendly or hostile. She and Alessia were hidden in a thatch of thorny bushes at the edge of a small clearing, Magnur not far off. The others were in their regular positions, passing signals that would make their way back to where Mariel and the two warriors of the group waited to be deployed. Remy and Augustine guarded each end of the road, while Destin patrolled the forest in between.

"You hear that, or did I imagine it?" Alessia whispered. She wrapped her arms around her slim jacket, warming herself. She was called the Sword because of her training as a blacksmith's daughter and her role as the group's armorer, but also due to her adeptness in wielding the steel she forged. Magnur, Alessia's sometimes partner—the largest man Mariel had ever laid eyes on—had begun his days in Obsidian Sky as the Sea, an ode to his force and unchangeableness, but their targets had dubbed him the Stone for his implausible size, and that was the name that had stuck.

"I heard it," Mariel replied and waited until Destin's trill echoed a second time. She shifted to free her quiver from of a thatch of thorns. "Get ready. Remy's should come anytime now."

"He went north, right?"

Mariel nodded toward the north end of the road. "I saw him pass by ten minutes ago. Augustine was already south."

"And Destin?"

"You heard his signal."

"Isnae my meaning, and you know it."

Destin had been reading the forest in preparation. The Whisperer, he was known as, but only by the others in the group, for Mariel had pushed from the very start to keep his role inconspicuous. Ever since their parents and sister had died, he'd been reading the dangers of the world like he was tuned just for them. It wasn't magic, even if it sometimes seemed like it was, but an almost empathic connection to the world, similar to how advanced trackers could discern all manner of detail from things that were inconspicuous to others. He was not the tactical genius Remy was nor the warrior Alessia and Magnur were. He had no tangible skill, like Augustine, with which to make a name for himself. And he was not fiercely resilient, like Mariel. He had to be invisible because he would never survive capture. Mariel only kept him in the group because it was better to have him near and know what he was up to than worry about the trouble he'd find if he was not.

"He's dry tonight," Mariel answered tersely, followed by a warning look. *For now,* she added in her head.

"He doesnae need ale to self-destruct, Mar."

"Nor do any of us. Shall I take your place then?"

"If you say he's fine..." Alessia was clearly unconvinced but held up a hand in surrender and ducked lower before slinking off to take her position on the west side of the road.

For the first time in over an hour, Mariel was alone.

She used to enjoy her rare moments of quiet reflection, but in her weeks as the "pining wife," she'd been forced into more than her share. She was still reeling from her antics on the terrace, and in desperate need of some inward wisdom, but she had none to give. *Months* she'd plotted and planned and sat in her impatience, knowing once he returned she would have to be ready to move on their agenda. It was an enigma even to herself why she'd behaved so poorly, going against her own plan to convince others they were warming to each other...why her tension had flamed into fury when Augustine had told her the way Erran had talked about her to the women he took to his bed.

She didn't *care* about any of that. His idiocy with Yesenia worked in Mariel's favor. Really, so did his wandering penis. If he spent his energies on a constant stream of housemaids, he'd leave her alone, and they could, maybe, make it through their short marriage without doing anything that would haunt her nightmares forevermore.

Just playing my part, she'd said, as if it explained any of her behavior. He was rightfully confused, and if she couldn't extract her head from her ass, she'd sabotage everything she'd worked for over the past ten years. She'd let down the only family she had left, when they'd given up everything for a vision she'd convinced them was the path to their salvation.

But those were troubles for later, when they weren't moments away from the wagon arriving.

Mariel snaked a meandering path through the bushes until the road was visible again. A canopy of leaves fanned the sides of the narrow passage, rustling against the peaceful breeze that had followed a quick, hard rain that had glistened against the moonlight. She peeked up long enough to find both Alessia and Magnur, each posted on opposite sides of the road and holding the ends of a stretched wire. Remy would be too far to spot, and Destin would be hiding by now, but where was...

Mariel drew to a stop when she saw the nightgown-clad Augustine "stumbling" down a rut in the road. Hers was the first trap, which rarely worked as well as it used to, since Obsidian Sky was a known hazard to high-value wagons. But even vigilant men could not always resist a beautiful, helpless woman.

The second, the wire, was in case they did.

Mariel listened for the familiar creak of wheels carving through rutted dirt. She timed reaching for her arrow with a thud of the caravan hitting a pothole and used the next loud diversion to pull the folded vellum from her pocket and tack it onto the tip of the arrowhead.

Augustine shrieked. The carriage came to a stuttering halt.

"Sirs! Sirs, help me! Please help me!" Augustine cried. Her white nightgown flapped in the moonlight as she approached the wagon.

"Whoa!" The driver held a hand out. He nodded at his copilot to move again. "Lass, you need to clear this road right now—"

"There's a man, and he…he…" Augustine ran backward as the wagon drew nearer to her act. When they'd first adopted the ruse, she'd look over her shoulder by instinct, sometimes giving away the trap just behind her, but years of the act had made her execution near flawless. "Would you abandon your daughter in need? Your sister?"

"Miss, we are under strict orders to stop for no one. Donnae ye ken there're bandits on these roads? Best I can do is throw you some bread."

Mariel nocked the arrow, careful not to tear the message at the end of it. *Almost there.*

"Will bread heal these wounds?" Augustine gestured wildly to the red splotches on her white nightgown, courtesy of three overripe tomatoes.

"Steward Rutland has advised no coaches should stop in these woods—"

"Do I look like a bandit, sir?" Augustine's agony was so convincing, Mariel almost wanted to comfort her.

"Well, nay, but they're known for employing such trickeries. Go on now. Off the road, miss. It will be all right. We'll send help back when we reach town."

Mariel held tight to her test and waited. Waited. She narrowed her eyes, searching for any sign of Magnur and Alessia, but they were too good to be spotted once they'd settled into place. Unlike rope, the wire could not be seen by the men in the caravans until it was too late, but the horses would spot it and break free, leaving the cart to fend for itself.

It was true what the man had said, that they were known for the distressed honeypot ploy, but it was one of over a dozen they used, and the variety should have kept their adversaries on their toes.

They were so close to the wire, so why wasn't Augustine signaling?

And then it came. A single glance in Mariel's direction, so quick no one else would have been suspicious enough to follow it, but it was all Mariel needed. She loosed the arrow and waited for the gasp, then stifled a snort when the man's hat came detached from his head and pierced the tree several feet to his left, pinned by her arrow.

"Haven't lost my aim yet," she whispered, pleased with herself.

The driver gaped at the hat and note, leaning over the side of his wagon to read the message.

Obsidian Sky wishes you a pleasant evening, sirs!

"Feck the Guardians and all..." The man groaned, his eyes following the note even as his carriage continued, headed straight into the second trap.

Mariel couldn't see them, but she knew Magnur and Alessia were backing in opposite directions, stretching their wire high and taut. It was too late for the driver or his cohort to do anything but yell, "Trap!"

The carriage skidded to avoid the collision, but the horses were already rearing, snapping their reins and darting off in opposite directions as the wagon slammed to the ground. Alessia and Magnur rushed forward to surround the men and their broken caravan, while Augustine to stand guard in the road.

"Why you're just bairns!" declared the copilot, holding his hands out. Even from her vantage point in the woods, Mariel could see he wasn't armed, which was stupidly shortsighted of anyone traveling the roads with expensive cargo. He was worried about bandits but not ready for them? "Take off your masks and show us who you are."

"Our qualms are not with you!" Mariel shouted the words from the forest. She nocked another arrow and released it, enjoying the sharp whistle as it sailed through the leaves and landed an inch from her first one.

The hatless man stared at the tree, dumbfounded.

"But they shall find their way to you just the same should you resist us."

"Where's the Flame?" The driver limped forward, blood staining his trousers from the fall. "Where's your leader?"

No one, of course, knew Mariel was the Flame, but it suited their purpose for others to continue believing it was a man authorities had been searching years for. It was a blow to her pride that she could never reveal to the craven barons they'd been bested by a *woman*.

"Here's all ye need to know, grunt," Alessia said, sauntering closer with a grin. Her dark-blonde hair was stuck under her hat, part of her disguise, but her smoky voice was unmistakably feminine. "We're taking what we've come for, but it's up to you whether ye end up in the gulch."

Magnur stood quiet and rigid, like a boulder.

While Alessia educated the men about their unfortunate predicament, Mariel drew smoothly toward the road, and the wagon. She clipped her bow into her back strap and drew one of her daggers instead, stepping sideways until she was so close, she could hear the men's labored breaths.

She caught Magnur's eye. His face moved not an inch, but the single blink told her he'd seen her and was ready if the men turned.

Mariel held her breath and climbed carefully aboard the wagon. It was a mess of bags and ropes and trash, which would take longer to sort through than they safely had time for. At any point, Remy or Augustine could sound the whistle, and—

And then it happened. Mariel strained, listening for which direction the sound had come from.

Remy.

They had two, maybe three minutes, to find the jewel and flee before whoever was on the road arrived on the scene.

Mariel calculated her options. The back of the wagon was a quagmire of scattered items and trash, a shot into the wind. *If I were escorting a rare golden egg valued the same as the annual taxes on a small village, would I store it in such a sty?*

Or would I keep it close?

She landed in the dirt and stepped quietly onto the road to shake her head at Magnur, who was tying both men to the tree she'd shot. His nose flared in aggravation, but he returned to his task.

"Is it you, big man? Are you the Flame?" one of the men asked. Terror edged his flippant tone.

"You're wasting your breath and our time," Alessia snapped. "Where is it?"

Mariel withdrew her bow and nocked another arrow, aiming at the men as she came around the side of the wagon. "Hand it over. Now."

"We're just poor merchants—"

She smacked his temple with the arrowhead. "Give me the egg or you die here."

"I wouldnae choose such a dishonorable death for myself," Alessia spat. "Ye donnae ken that what they take from others, they take from you? Would you die for men like them?"

Magnus tightened the last bit of rope with a tug and a grunt. "There. Going nowhere."

"Last chance, merchant," Mariel warned. Her heart was itching to address the panic that they were mere moments from disaster, but she'd learned to tease it, to trick it into waiting for the moment to pass. "Hand it over or don't. We'll have our egg either way."

Magnur caught Mariel's stare over the men. He had a hunting knife pressed to one of their throats, and it would take even the most subtle nod to get him to use it. He wouldn't hesitate… wouldn't break her gaze either. But though they'd injured some in their dealings, and had certainly threatened worse, execution was not part of their agenda. The irony of killing men over a golden egg—men who were just as much victims as Mariel and her friends were—was not lost on her.

She'd abandon the heist altogether before she'd let that happen.

Mariel lowered into a crouch. "We have a tracker in the forest. He can smell you. Sense you. Follow your stench all the way to whatever family awaits you. Now, I'm sure he'd rather enjoy a hearty meal than burn a family home to cinders, so let's agree it's not worth destroying lives over a golden egg you'll never benefit from either way."

"Will ye at least feck us about? So we look like we put up a fight?" the driver asked. He tried to dig in his pocket, but his bindings prevented it.

Alessia snaked a hand down and did it herself, then withdrew a weighted golden egg the size of an aubergine. She winked at Mariel and then darted into the forest. Her sharp cries, signals to Remy and Augustine to withdraw, echoed after her. Mariel prayed Destin, wherever he was, was doing the same.

Mariel grinned at Magnur. "Seems like the least we can do. Aye?"

Magnur's face brightened in amusement. "Aye. Won't take but a moment."

Erran watched Khallum drop coins into the mugs of the four women he was recruiting to join him later, wondering where his friend would even find the stamina for such an ambitious endeavor.

Even though their entire crew had become either married or betrothed, Khallum still roped them into ending a party in a brothel.

Hamish, before meeting and falling ass over head for his wife, Yanna, used to join in the entertainment, but Erran never had, nor Samuel for that matter. Erran always had too much on his mind to let go long enough to forsake consequence—particularly the variety that had healers visiting Khallum every month or so to clean up his messes—and Samuel just didn't believe in indulging in illicit distractions.

They'd always been an odd bunch, the four of them, but despite his discomfort in a hall of midnight repute—the shrill music and drunken laughter so loud, his ears hadn't stopped ringing—Erran never felt more at home than he did with his three oldest friends.

"Look how they watch him. Every single one, dying for a coin in their cup." Samuel shook his head and sipped his milk like a dainty madam.

"Aye, even the ones who know better," Erran quipped, and they both laughed. "Ken he'd notice if we left?"

"Doesnae miss a whit, our Khal," Hamish said, slopping ale all over the place as he wedged between them. "Remembers every one of their names too. Stunning commitment, innit?"

"I prefer fealty to home and hearth, but it suits him," Samuel said, conceding as far as he ever would. "And Gwyn doesn't seem to mind."

"She minds," Erran said. "But what can she do about it? She didnae choose the marriage any more than he did. She's a Northerland lass. Might not be their way."

"It's the way of all men," Hamish retorted. "Until they find themselves, course."

"Not all of us can just stumble upon a beautiful, helpless woman in a port and marry her." Erran laughed. Hamish hadn't told them the full story of Yanna, only the parts they'd seen themselves: she'd been homeless, abused, desperate...and pregnant. But Hamish had seen something in her eyes that had turned his entire world on its head. He'd taken her back with them that very day, and they'd been wed within a fortnight. Their oldest son, Jesse, as far as anyone else knew, was Hamish's. Erran and his friends were quick to shut down anyone positing otherwise.

"Mariel is lovely, Erran. I'm sorry we didn't get to meet her sooner," Samuel said. "Reminds me of Yesenia, but with fewer, ah...spines."

"Aye, but the lass was prickly tonight," Hamish replied. "Erran likes 'em tha' way, I ken. Flogs himself for sport."

"*Is* she lovely?" Erran swallowed a mouthful of ale to drown his distaste. "Cannae see past her displeasing attitude."

"And you have accentuated our point." Samuel shook his head at Khallum, who was still winning over the lasses he'd bed later. "I'd think you two would get on swimmingly. Remind me, Hamish, who his first infatuation was, before Yesenia?"

Erran shook his head tightly at them both in sharp warning.

"Oy, Esta Garrick!" Hamish boomed, slapping his knee. "Course, she wasnae half as hairy then..."

"Feck off." Erran grunted at him. "I was a bairn, you tosser."

"Still plowed her," Hamish muttered, cackling into his ale. "Bairn or nay."

"Fourteen is plenty old to know better," Samuel replied, grinning with mischief. "Is that why you didn't attend her handfast? Were the feelings too...raw?"

"I didnae attend her handfast because the Garricks are uncivilized." Erran groaned through his teeth, remembering how Yesenia had taken a dagger to Esta's brother, Lem, for bullying her brother. Maybe Mariel was right and he did always find a way to work Yesenia into a thought. He only knew he missed her still. "I expect this nonsense from Khallum but not you two."

"We're just trying to cheer you up, mate." Samuel leaned over the table and slapped his shoulder. "Did you at least talk to her? Was it an attempt at humor?"

"She's like walking into a storm without a cloak. All I can think about is how I can get to safety without losing too much in the doing." He eyed Khallum, still smoothly charming his chosen ladies, wishing, for a moment, that his own needs were so simple. "She says it's about Yesenia and some maids I allegedly consorted with at the Spires, but I donnae ken I believe her."

"What maids?" Hamish asked, his eyes growing wide. "Donnae recall anything about pretty maids."

"There *were* none."

"Why don't you believe her?" Samuel asked.

"Because to care about who I spend my hours with would require some sort of harmony or attraction, and she has neither. And aye, feeling's mutual. So feckin' mutual." Erran sputtered into bitter laughter. "She doesnae even *know* me, and you'd think I'd murdered her family, down to the last."

"Did ye?" Hamish waggled his brows. Ale foam stuck to his beard.

"Be serious," Erran gruffed. "Never even met her until Father came home one day and told me he'd picked me a wife. I had no choice in the matter."

"Where did your father find her?" Samuel crossed his arms and leaned back. "I don't remember you saying."

Erran pursed his mouth. "All he'd say was that she was 'unproblematic.' What he really meant was 'lowborn' and 'easy to control.' Suppose he was right on one point."

"Must've been right cross wit' ye to pair his only son wit' a lake rat," Hamish said. When Samuel shot him a look, he asked, "What? Donnae mean nothin' by it. It's what they call lake dwellers, innit? Leastways the ones with no family name?"

"Ashdown is a name, Hamish."

"Aye, never said otherwise."

"You know they used to be barons, the Ashdowns?"

Hamish frowned. "Oh, aye?"

Samuel shook his head and turned back toward Erran. "Where does she think you are tonight? If she's sore about the chambermaids, she won't much like you in a brothel until dawn."

His friend's questions were right. Valid. The ones he *should* be asking. But it assumed Erran had valid answers. Nothing about Mariel's behavior made sense. By all accounts from his mother, she'd been perfectly congenial in his absence. Polite. Pliant. Nothing at all like the spitfire who'd slapped him in Mistgrave and humiliated him in his own home in front of everyone. "Couldnae say, Samuel. She went off to be with her brother before the party ended."

"She always carry a mask when she goes to visit her brother?" Hamish asked.

"Sorry?"

"She had a mask in her hand is all. Saw her from the balcony. Do they play mummers together?"

"Guardians, Hamish, mummers is for children," Samuel scolded.

Erran sat up straight. That *was* curious. "You sure that's what you saw, Ham?"

"Aye, sure as anything."

"And she was headed north, aye? Toward her brother's place?"

Hamish squinted one eye, his face pulling up on the same side. "Oy...nay. Nay, she went east actually. Aye, was east, toward the village."

Mariel wasn't done keeping secrets then.

Well, *he* was done with her keeping them.

"Excuse me, mates." Erran pushed back from the table. His blood boiled with unknowns. He'd been back hardly a week, and already he'd tarnished his own reputation, with Mariel all too happy to make it even worse. He might not be able to fix the first, but he'd be damned if he let her errant behavior push him out of the admiralty. "It seems I need to go find my *wife*."

Mariel nursed the heavy golden egg between her hands. At her feet, beside the log she was sitting on, was a mug of the old cider Remy had procured from a taverner who was going to throw it out because it was past its expiry. She hadn't touched hers, but the others were on their second or third rounds. Their glossy eyes and swelling laughter were a sign it hadn't lost its potency at least.

Even if she'd wanted some, she was too distracted to command her body to lean or her hand to reach for it. What she should have been doing was loosening up and joining them, as she'd always had before she'd signed her marriage contract. Even in Erran's months away, she'd still felt free, like herself. Old Mariel would not have tensed at the potential snag in their plan, the way she had when Remy had sounded the bird call. She would have relished the small bit of challenge it posed in an otherwise now-rote routine they could all perform in their sleep.

It was always the same. Isolate, subdue, steal, flee. Retreat to camp, eat, drink, enjoy the merriment, distribute the spoils to the people in need. Do it all again when the next opportunity landed in their laps.

Mariel couldn't make sense of where her own head was at. She'd had far longer than she'd imagined to learn the ways of the Rutlands, without having to share a bed or life with one. At first, she'd been annoyed he was leaving her for so long, forcing her to endure life in his family sphere longer than she'd ever intended. While she hadn't known about the auction before the marriage, she'd assumed there would be *something* like it, some big win she could lead the Sky to and then declare her short marriage a victory for the cause. When he'd gone away to sea, a test run of the eastern coast to prove he was ready for more, she'd taken the slight loss on the chin and made the best of it, biding her time and learning the keep and their ways. She'd reminded herself it wasn't the worst thing for her to have more time to ready herself for what, even then, she'd known would be her toughest act yet.

She hadn't seen him at all until after he'd returned from Warwicktown, shame shrouding him and his family after he'd begged Yesenia to leave her husband. It might have been better for everyone if she *had*, because then Mariel's nearly histrionic performances would have been more reasonable.

"You're not drinking. Or singing. Or doing much of anything other than staring at that ridiculous wad of gold," Augustine whispered, craning sideways with an inebriated grin. She batted her lashes at Mariel, which made her laugh. "Would you prefer we retire to our tent? Just you and me?"

Mariel lowered her eyes toward the forest floor and shook her head. "Nay, sorry. It's not about the heist. I wasn't myself at the party tonight, and I need to do better."

Augustine's smile faded. Her expression clouded. "He deserved everything you said."

"You heard, aye?" Mariel shook her head. "I humiliated him."

"He deserved it, Mar."

"But I'm not there to humiliate him, Auggie. I *need* him. *We* need him." She watched Destin accidentally slosh whiskey into the crackling fire, sending it roaring briefly higher. Magnur shot him an irritated glare as Destin stumbled away with his bottle without saying a word.

Augustine pulled herself erect. "Be careful about needing him too much, Mar. He's a volatile man, who would let you starve if it meant filling his own plate."

"Were you not just telling me you've heard naught but good about him?" Mariel laughed. She'd clocked Augustine's strange fascination with Erran, but she didn't know what to make of it yet. "Which is it? Is he a diabolical lion or a tender little lamb?"

Remy's brawny arms hooked around Mariel's neck as he pulled her head back for a teasing kiss. "What are you two she-demons whispering about over here? Hmm?" He squished between them on the log. Augustine groaned. "And why are you not drunk, lass?"

Her malaise aside, Mariel's fondness for spirits had waned as Destin's problem had increased. The others loved him too, but their world was one of high stakes. The reward was helping others, but they bore all the risk. Every heist was a new opportunity to meet the noose. Drinking themselves into oblivion was a small vice in comparison.

"Long night for me," she replied, trying to smile. "You had no problems with the buyer?"

"I meet him at dawn with the egg. He'll give us exactly what we ask. Alessia's coming with me, and she'll deliver the gold to the Whitecliffe miners straightaway, minus our small cut."

"Good." Obsidian Sky retained less than five percent of their bounties, just enough to fund the jobs and ensure they didn't starve. "How close was the other caravan?"

"You had time." Remy patted her knee. He turned a tight smile toward Alessia and Magnur, who were wrestling for the keg spout. Destin had drifted farther from the group and was drinking alone near the edge of the clearing. "We've had closer calls."

It hadn't felt like that to Mariel. Her anxiety as they'd worked the men over, waiting for danger to arrive, had reminded her of the early days, when they were still testing the waters to see what they could get away with. Gone was the confidence of the Flame at her peak, when she'd ignored the bird calls and the peril and charged forward with intrepid bravado.

Nothing had felt the same since she'd joined the Rutlands.

"Excuse me," she muttered and pushed to her feet, rushing off before their confusion could reach her ears. On the way to Destin, she caught Alessia's eye. She'd stopped playing with Magnur long enough for concern to pinch her face, but Mariel shook her head to indicate she was all right, despite that she was not. Heist nights were for revelry, not for whatever was going on in her head.

"Hi," she said, sidling up next to her brother with a warm squeeze.

"Hi." Destin's smile didn't make it to his eyes; it never did anymore. "How was your party?"

Mariel snorted. "Be glad you weren't there. It was *monstrously* boring and then I made a proper arse of myself."

Destin laughed. "That's not like you."

"I don't know what's gotten into me. Maybe I'm…I don't know, losing my touch."

"I wish I could be there to help you, Mar. I feel neutered out here." Destin took a swig from his mostly empty bottle and wiped his mouth on his sleeve. He pointed his glossy gaze at the moon. "Remy and Auggie act like they're my mother and father, and I ken it's because they feel they need to be."

Mariel nudged him. "They love you, same as I do. That's all."

"Hm." Destin emptied the bottle and chucked it into the forest, where it disappeared. "I'm older than all of you, except Magnur." It never should have been the Flame leading the Sky at all, at least in his mind. He was supposed to protect Mariel, not the other way around. But for all he couldn't forgive himself, nor could he seem to change.

"We all have our role to play, Desi," Mariel said, plopping a soft kiss on his cheek. "And I could not play mine in there if you weren't playing yours out here."

"You mean if they weren't looking after your indigent older brother?"

"I said what I meant," she stated firmly, giving him a gentle shake. "If anything, *I'm* the one neutered, having to watch everything I say, do…having to pretend I don't dream of wringing every one of their necks. It's harder than I thought it would be."

Destin considered her words for a moment. "What's he like?"

"Who? Erran?"

He nodded.

Mariel balked. "I barely know him."

"You're his wife."

She blurted a laugh. "Do you know how strange that sounds when you say it so casually?"

"Will you ever forgive me for it?"

"Aw, Desi," Mariel said, her heart heavy as she pulled him in for a squeeze. There were nights she didn't sleep at all, wondering if she'd wake to learn he'd been dredged from the river or thrown into jail. Her fear for him had no end. "You saw a clever opportunity and you took it. You acted like a leader. I'm the one who needs to screw her head on straight and finish this."

Destin hugged her tighter, sniffling. "You're a good liar anyway. How long can you stay?"

Mariel kissed him again, sighing her regret. "I should go. Now that he's back from sea, they'll be less likely to turn their cheek at me visiting our 'sick aunt.'"

"Poor dear Anna."

They both laughed, and for a moment, she remembered what it had once been like, when they were children and unencumbered by so much trauma. When Angelika's crystalline laugh still rang through their halls and their mother's oyster stew could cure any ill.

"Be safe," she whispered and slipped off through the trees without saying good-bye to the others.

Erran lost Mariel's trail on an old service road, but he soon realized why when he stumbled upon an abandoned caravan half in the ditch. He followed the path all the way to the caravan itself, where her footprints ended, but not only hers. There were at least three others he could discern.

The entire scene was confounding. Whoever had been driving the wagon had left it seemingly in a rush after being clipped by a…wire lying across the road? The tree nearby had some severed rope at the base and one of those anachronistically friendly notes from Obsidian Sky tacked to the bark, a group of bandits of which he was all too familiar. They were the bane of his father's business, and for as steep as the bounty was on any one of their heads, it was a wonder none had ever been caught.

There were only small signs of a scuffle, nothing serious.

He was almost certain she'd been there when the wagon had lost its battle, because of the way her footprints traced the edges of the wreckage, like she was intentionally stepping around it. From there, they disappeared into the forest.

Obsidian Sky wasn't known for violence, but what if they'd kidnapped her?

Erran knelt to get a closer look at the boot prints at the front of the wagon when he heard someone coming. He swiftly squatted and angled quietly around the side until he again had a view of the road, one hand on his hilt.

With a surge of relief, he immediately recognized the long, dark hair, but gone was Mariel's smug swagger. She moved quickly, her hands crossed over her chest and her head down, and although it was hard to tell by squinting in the darkness, he was almost sure he saw tears cutting lines down her face.

A strange flutter filled his chest, followed by a stab of guilt, like he'd been spying on her—and though he *had*, until that moment, he'd felt wholly justified, expecting to catch her in the act of something heinous or untoward that would explain her hostile attitude.

She stopped abruptly and turned. "Who's there?"

Erran slowly rose, unsure whether to smile or hold up his hands in some sort of apology. Instead he announced himself with a throat clearing. "I came upon this mess and feared the worst. What happened here?"

"*Errandil?*" Her posture went rigid, and he again recognized the firebrand who had humiliated him in front of everyone he had ever known. "You following me?"

He stepped out with a flippant shrug. "What if I am?"

"I told you where I was going." Her arms locked over her chest.

"You said you were going to see Destin. He lives the complete opposite direction of this road."

"I never said I was going to see him at his place."

"So you're fine then? You weren't caught up in this Obsidian Sky mess?"

"Do I not look fine?" She swept her hands over herself.

Erran's concern shifted when he pieced it together. "You went to see *him*, didn't you? The cad you met in Mistgrave? After I asked you to be more careful?"

"What kind of man slinks about at night trying to catch his wife up to no good?" Her laughter split the night. "I really don't think you want me to answer that."

Erran gritted. Whatever pity he'd felt for her fled with her barbed words. "The kind who knows when he's being *lied* to, Mariel. It was your idea for us to play nice and..." He gestured around. "You were clearly *here* at some point. Did you see it happen? Why *are* you here?"

"You're so good at mysteries, can you not solve this one? Obviously I robbed the men and chased them off, all by my little old self," she said with an insinuative grin.

Erran buried an exasperated groan. "Be serious."

"But I am." She blinked petulantly. "They put up such little fuss. It wasn't a very taxing challenge." She lifted one shoulder.

He marched toward her and she flinched when he neared, lighting a new anger in him. "You think I would *hit* you?"

Mariel's throat contracted in a hard swallow. "I know better than to trust any man who hasn't earned it."

"I don't need you to trust me, but I will ask you to stop insulting me." *I need to calm myself or we'll just keep going in circles. She could go like this all night.* "Mariel, secrets never belong to just one person for long. If whatever you're up to is big enough to hide from me, my mother and father *will* find out. They may already know."

"There's nothing to know. I went to see Destin at a friend's homestead. That's all." She turned but didn't leave right away. Her entire demeanor shifted, became heavier somehow. "Erran, look, I..."

He waited for her to finish, but moments passed and all she offered was silence. "What? You what?"

"I miscalculated tonight at our party. I was upset about Destin not being there and wasn't my best self. I'm...still not." Her stare traveled to her boots. She dug the toes of one into a root bisecting the road. "I'm sorry. I'll try to do better."

His anger softened. In what little he knew of Mariel, apologies didn't come easy. "I perhaps could have prepared you better."

"Aye, but…I'm not asking you to lessen what I did. I can admit my own faults." Her mouth puckered in what was nearly a grin. "For what few I possess."

There was something almost charming about her when she wasn't trying to take his head off. "This will get easier if we're on the same side."

Mariel nodded at the ground. "But then you'll have to stop telling tales to your conquests."

Erran shook his head wildly. "I truly don't ken what you're—"

"I don't *care* who you dodder, I told you." She looked up. "But if they're people I have to see day in and day out, women who serve me food and prepare my clothing, then I'll thank you not to make it harder for me."

He had no idea where she'd gotten the idea he'd been snogging the entire kitchen staff and then some, but she wasn't going to believe him no matter what he said or how he said it. "And I'll thank you not to hide things from me."

"For the second time in our marriage, it seems we agree on something." Her smile was so forced this time, he laughed. "You aren't going to try to be chivalrous and offer to escort me back, are you?"

"Well, we are going the same way, and it *is* rather dark…"

She scoffed, mouth twisting. "I draw the line at taking your arm."

He snorted. "Wouldn't dare offer it."

Mariel grinned.

Erran shook his head and held his arm out, gesturing for her to go ahead. "After you."

FIVE
AMATEUR OUTLAWS

Erran noted it right away. It wasn't merely the energy at the brightly accoutred breakfast table on the lower veranda, subdued and solemn, because that wasn't unusual. The mood of all who lived the Spires followed the mood of the steward, and Rylahn Rutland was often a quiet and intense man when not at sea, favoring his own company to that of others.

It was more the furtive glances passed between Erran's parents, who often conducted their most important conversations in the subtext of charged silences, but rarely in a way that left Erran feeling squarely on the outside of whatever was happening.

It was just the four of them that morning—he, Mariel, and his parents—as Sessaly was engaged in one of her many pre-wedding appointments. It was just as well. She wouldn't have resisted the urge to call out how strange their parents were acting, and that never went well.

Erran waved a hand over his plate to indicate to the maid passing by that he needed no more pork. Whether he could eat any of it at all would depend on the first words spoken, and as he watched his mother and father pull sips from their morning tea or stab the contents of their plates, he wagered who would go first.

It turned out to be the last person he expected.

"I wanted to…ah…thank you both for such a lovely evening," Mariel said.

From the startled looks they shared, his parents were just as surprised, like they'd been stirred from a long sleep.

"It's so good to have Erran back home, where we can focus on…" A stretch pulled her jaw taut, but it was so quick, he could have just as easily missed it. "Starting a family of our own."

"Aye." Rylahn wiped his face on his napkin and tossed it beside his plate. His coiffed hair shimmered on the balmy, plummy breeze passing through the portico. "You have a full season before he returns to sea, and I'm encouraged to hear you intend to make use of it."

Hestia casually watched the conversation, despite her obvious interest.

Erran went from concerned to suspicious.

"We do. We very much do." Mariel reached for her tea, her hand briefly forming a soft fist before wrapping around the goblet. "In fact, we've already started."

Erran choked on his tea, waving a hand when his mother shifted her attention to him.

"I trust if you require anything, you'll let my wife know," Rylahn said, without looking up from his plate. His gaze swung briefly aside, fork paused midair, but his thoughts seemed to be anywhere but the bedroom activities of his son and Mariel.

"The stewardess has been generous with her kindness and advice, and I will not hesitate to speak up should there be needs I cannot meet."

Erran wrinkled his brows until they ached, but neither of his parents seemed overly suspicious at Mariel's turn of mood. Her acting was damned near convincing. If either of them had seen how she spoke to him in private though, they wouldn't have bought a word of it.

Rylahn's cutlery clattered to his plate. Everyone startled. "Mariel, I regret I have unfortunate news, but I'll ask that you receive this information as gracefully as you can manage."

Mariel's plastered smile froze. "And what news would that be, sir?"

His broad shoulders rolled back in a gesture Erran recognized well. His father was clearly annoyed, but it wasn't the general kind, easily resolved. Whatever troubled him had created an unnecessary and unforgiveable distraction. "It seems your brother has been taken in by the law in the wee hours of the morning. He's presently locked away in a regional jail north of Whitecliffe."

Mariel shoved her hands under the table, her chest swelling. "For…" She cleared her throat. "For what was he arrested?"

"Ludicrous, really," Hestia said with a tight, jittery laugh. "He wouldn't be the first to falsely claim to be the Flame, but certainly the most preposterous."

A blank stare was all Mariel could muster, but it gave Erran the push to say something. "When are we riding to free him?" he asked.

Mariel whipped her gaze his way. Confusion flared in her irises.

"Not today or anytime soon." Rylahn snapped his fingers, and his plate was swiftly cleared. He offered a curt nod in gratitude. "I'm expected in Sandymount by midafternoon."

"We're not going to *leave* him there?" Erran asked, stunned. He couldn't blame his father for not wanting to parade the drunken imbecile in front of their friends and acquaintances at a party, but abandoning a family member to rot in jail was not the Rutland way. It wasn't the way of any gentleman. "If you have business in Sandymount, then I'll go to the jail."

Mariel remained silent, staring through the columns and into the sea. There was almost no color left in her face.

"You will not." When Rylahn stood, so did Hestia and Erran, but Mariel didn't move. No one reproached her, which was good, because Erran might have lost his mind. No matter how he felt about her, there was wrong and there was right, and his father was wrong. "We cannot be seen to be relying on nepotism when there is so much attention on this Obsidian Sky gang these days. He'll be questioned and no doubt released when they determine him incompetent of what he claims."

"But that could take days!" Erran was astonished. "Can this business in Sandymount not wait until this crisis has passed?"

"I am afraid not." Rylahn refastened his waistcoat with a gentle cough. "The unfortunate theft of Baroness Alden's golden egg last night has ignited a sense of irrational fear in some of the other barons, and they've demanded we move the auction up. Tomorrow, it seems. I'm going to meet with Banner, the broker, to inspect the gold, which should arrive this afternoon if the weather holds." He garbled a sigh. "I'll be glad when this unfortunate auction business is behind us, for it's been far more trouble than any of it is worth. If you'll excuse me."

A flurry of attendants followed him, his limping bootfalls echoing across the marble and then fading into the background din of the bustling keep.

Erran looked at his mother. "We're really doing nothing?"

"You heard your father." Hestia's mouth puckered. He saw the truth in her eyes, that she was not aligned with her husband, but she always fell in line no matter her feelings. "This will blow over."

Mariel seemed to be completely focused on breathing. Her mouth moved, but she didn't speak.

"Mariel?" Erran whispered.

She looked up in a flash, forging a smile. "I'm fine."

"You're not," he said quietly. "I wouldn't be either."

"You are only feeding her anxiety, Erran," Hestia chided. "Her brother is clearly no thief or criminal, and the officials will suss that out quick enough. Now finish your meal before it grows cold."

Mariel pushed back from the table. "If you'll pardon me, I need to...tell my poor aunt before she hears it from someone else," she said, fleeing before anyone could respond.

Erran dithered between following her and heeding his mother's command for unity. "If he's not free tomorrow," he said, searching for the right words, "then I will free him myself, Mother."

"I do not recommend crossing your father right now, Errandil. You know what's at stake. Her brother placed *himself* in this situation, quite unnecessarily. Is a man like that worth causing further divide between yourself and the admiralty?"

"The two should have no intersection. Destin is *family*."

"Alas," she muttered.

"Mother!"

"Perhaps you're right. If anyone must be on Mariel's side in this, it's her husband." She wiped her face with a fluttery look upward. Her eyes lingered on the vibrant mural of the Golden Coast, commissioned by Erran's ancestor, Drummond Rutland. "I've lost my appetite. Do *nothing* unless I say to, Erran. I mean it. No one has a better read on your father than I, and you must trust I have the interests of this *entire* family in mind when I advise you to calm the storm in your heart and let time and reason do what it must."

Erran nodded to defuse the tension, but he had no intention of listening to his mother.

Mariel's claim of visiting her aunt might have sounded reasonable, but he knew precisely where she was actually going, because it was exactly where he'd go if Sessaly was in Destin's predicament.

For all of their sakes, he needed to be at the jail *before* it happened.

Mariel was almost to the central hall when an exuberant Sessaly came bounding toward her.

"Oh, Mariel! Do forgive my absence at morning meal. I was with my charms tutor—" Her smile froze. "Is something wrong?"

Patience on reserve and nerves frayed beyond repair, Mariel nonetheless tried to seem pleased to see her sister-in-law, who was nothing like any of the young women she'd been raised around.

Sessaly's only concerns in life were being the first to secure new gossip and not missing the monthly textile bazaar, where she'd pick out her dress patterns for the next season.

And what the bloody hell was a charms tutor?

"I've been called to see my aunt."

"Oh, dear." When Sessaly frowned, it was a perfect inversion of her smile. "Is she…"

"I'll know the situation better when I can see her." Mariel's focus was still pointed ahead, where she needed to be, not proffering reassurances to someone who could not care half as much as she pretended to. Mariel had to speak with Remy and Augustine immediately. There was a way to fix this, but they had to act fast.

"Can I do anything to help?"

Mariel's attention briefly returned to her. The girl's expression was earnest, which could have been a result of practice, though it didn't seem inauthentic. But she had no time to tease out her true intentions. As with Hestia, there seemed to be two sides to Sessaly's motivations, and neither woman was to be entirely trusted. "I think a visit will lift her spirits. Will you excuse me?"

"Oh, of course!" Sessaly called after her. "But I am here if you need me, sister!"

She waited until she was clear of the outer gates of Goldsea Spires and then shifted to a jog, lifting her pace every few yards until she was running so fast, the years melted away and she was again the little girl who had raced her siblings around the lake until they were all delirious. She was usually the victor, enough to take the wind out of Destin's sails, so she started letting him win to lift his spirits, which were so easily defeated, even then.

Mariel stopped at the town stables to rent a horse. Even though Hestia knew she was going to see her "aunt," the Spires stable boy would no doubt report her comings and goings, and she had no idea when she might return.

Remy lived above a forge in town, his rent paid by doing odd jobs for the blacksmith. It was a small, cramped apartment, one she'd spent many days and nights in herself before her marriage, and it was the closest thing she had to having a place she still thought of as home.

Augustine was already there, as was Alessia. Magnur was working his shift as a guard for a local marine merchant.

Mariel bent over her knees to catch her breath. Remy passed her a cider in silence when she stood, which she shook her head at and blurted, "I know how we can get him out."

Alessia laughed from where she sat atop a crossbeam that cut through the center of the pitched room, her feet dangling. "We're many things, Mar, but jail breakers aren't one of them."

Remy guided Mariel to the table, where Augustine sat in silence, watching them approach. "We won't just abandon him. Of course we won't." He rubbed her back while she got settled. "What's your idea then?"

Mariel expected resistance. They'd be right to offer it. There would be no time to plan, to account for contingencies. It was all risk with only a hopeful reward, and if they failed, Destin could rot away in a cell forever, which would be convenient for her in-laws. But while she did not exactly believe in fate, she did believe in providence. The Guardians were fickle, but it didn't mean they wouldn't provide to those willing to receive. "First, tell me what happened last night after I left."

"None of us knows," Augustine said softly. Her red braids were wound in a messy knot atop her head, like she'd slept crudely in them and hadn't yet met a mirror. "He left not long after you, and then the rest of us dispersed. Alessia and I came here with Remy because I had the night off, and we were both too sozzled to do much else. A few hours later, Magnur showed up in his guard's uniform and told us Destin had been jailed for declaring loudly in a tavern that he was the Flame."

"No one believed him, of course," Alessia said. "But the lawmen are under order to take all claims of banditry seriously, so unless someone presents evidence on his behalf, he'll wait to stand trial, where they'll either see clearly he couldnae possibly be the Flame, or..."

"Or he'll crumble under the pressure is what you mean to say," Mariel snapped. "Which is why…why we cannot let him spend even another night there. You all know that, right? Even if you don't care about my brother—"

"Mariel." Remy folded a hand onto her forearm. "We love Destin, same as you. You're speaking from fear."

She bowed her head, wringing her hands. An unsteady drip from Remy's broken sink thrummed between her ears. An idea was forming in her mind, and even to her it sounded hazardous. Preposterous. But if it *worked…*"They moved the auction up because they're getting nervous. Last night spooked them. It's tomorrow, in Sandymount. The steward is headed there now to speak with a broker, Banner, who is the one in charge of the whole thing."

"Really?" Augustine's mouth dropped open. "Tomorrow?"

"The auction is tomorrow, aye." Mariel clenched for the next words. "Our best chance is today."

"Well, that's just too soon, innit?" Alessia crossed her arms. "We'd need weeks to plan. Even in the best circumstances, five, six days at a minimum? It was a nice dream, Mariel, but it was always a longshot."

"Would we though?" They were all staring at her, waiting to make their oppositions. Even Remy. She had always found the right words before, but they had become harder, because as she was the Flame, her passion burned brighter than her own personal aims. She could separate Mariel from the equation and truly *become* her other persona, the arbiter of justice for those who most deserved it. Never had her heart been so exposed and raw. "If we can just get to Banner—"

"How will this help Destin?" Alessia asked, pressing. "Everyone knows Obsidian Sky isnae just one person. They'll assume his friends went ahead without him."

"Nay," Mariel replied. "They won't. Because how could Destin possibly know the auction had been moved up if he was in jail when the decision was made?"

"And the rest of us?" Augustine asked. "We're nay locked away. Nothing stopping us from learning about the change."

"Mariel is right," Remy said. He dragged his knuckles along the knotted wood of his rickety table, the uneven legs knocking against the ground. "The Flame is the leader of Obsidian Sky. Everyone knows it. They'd never assume we would move forward on such a big heist without our leader."

"That doesnae make it a good idea," Alessia said. "We donnae even ken who this man, Banner, is. Where in Sandymount the gold is being held. We know *nothing* except a name and a date, and..." She groaned, pulling her hands down her tired face. "I want to help him too, Mar. I do. And I want to stick my dagger straight through the eyeballs of every last feckin' man participating in this bloody farce. But I have to think of my ailing mother, who would die without my aid. I cannae get sent away. I'm out." She leaped down and gave Mariel's shoulder a squeeze, dipping low to kiss the top of her head. "I'm sorry."

Mariel flinched when the door closed. She wanted badly to cry, mostly from frustration, but tears had a way of manipulating those around her. If Remy and Augustine agreed, they would do it because they believed it was right, not because she'd struck at their hearts. "I don't expect the two of you to risk your necks for Destin or for me. But I'm going. And you can come or you can stay, but if something happens to me..." She choked down another surge of emotion. Only in decisive action was there purpose or absolution waiting. "Please don't give up on him. Promise me?"

Remy sighed, shaking his head at the table. "And what are you going to do when you meet this Banner, Mar? Say? He'll be well guarded."

"Not if he's at his own home, he won't. I just need to catch him at the right time."

"And when you do? You still have to convince him to take you to the gold. You still have to *get* the gold, which *will* be under guard."

Mariel appreciated their routines and traditions, but she'd always been keener on improvisation. If she was too reliant on the effectiveness of a plan, she wasn't thinking about the dozens of other outcomes, which meant she'd be ready for none. "I'll know what to say when I get there. *He* is the one who will have to get creative, for I'll make sure he knows what will happen if he doesn't."

"You don't even have your mask. Give Auggie an hour to stitch one—"

"I can't wait an hour, Remy. I'll borrow one of yours."

"Not mine. I'm nay letting you walk into this mess alone." Augustine tightened the wad of braids on her head and stood. "Give me a moment to change into some of Remy's shabby clothes, and we'll leave straightaway."

She disappeared into the back room, leaving Mariel and Remy alone.

"I know the plan is weak," she said, sighing. "I'll shore it up on the ride. There's no other way."

"We'll stop and see Magnur on our way out of town. He doesn't have to come, but he needs to know where we've gone, in case things go sideways," he said. "So he has time to run, same as Alessia."

Mariel brightened in surprise. "You're coming?"

"Am I coming? Really?" He smiled wryly. "It was you and I who conceived of this whole thing, Mar. Auggie, Des, they went along with it for us, but you and me... This is *our* show. The Flame and the Tactician. So it was then, so it is now." He pushed back. "If this is to be the end, then it should be us. To the bitter or not-so-bitter finale."

Erran watched Mariel enter a blacksmith shop along the main stretch of Whitecliffe proper, just west of the grand fountain. She'd been in there nearly a half tick of the sun while he waited in an alleyway, trying to keep the horse he'd borrowed from the workers' stables, Vesper, from reacting to every person who passed. If he'd taken his own mare, others might suspect he'd gone to free Destin. That she rented a horse herself was further evidence of her intention.

He hadn't. Not yet at least. First he wanted to see if *she* would try.

But the North Farthing jail was…north, and Mariel had gone into the village. Stopping at the banker's first would make sense, for bonds on incarcerated brigands had become exorbitant, but he couldn't guess what urgent business she might have with a blacksmith.

Certainly she didn't intend to *storm* the jail, sword swinging.

Did she?

The idea was preposterous. But then, so was following her. She'd made it clear she had a right to her own life, and he had no quarrel with that in theory, but his gut was telling him—no, *screaming* at him—that she was headed toward danger. Erran had learned when he was a boy to listen to his instincts. He couldn't recall a time when they'd ever been wrong. While no one had outright called his special "knack" magic, he suspected he had some in him. But as he had no intention of being shipped off to the Sepulchre for years of formal instruction under the magi, he kept his suspicion to himself.

As much as he trusted his intuition, he needed someone else's to either give credence or discourage him from something that might make their tenuous marriage even worse.

The inn where Samuel and his father were staying for their visit was just around the corner. They were still in town for another week, but Samuel's father would likely already be on his way to Sandymount for the auction.

His friend's wisdom was exactly what Erran needed, but he didn't want to take his eyes off the blacksmith shop, so he flagged down a young boy selling apples.

"There's fifty coins in it for you if watch this shop and come get me at Farthingale Inn if anyone steps out of those doors, particularly a young woman with long, dark hair." Thinking further about it, he also said, "Another fifty if you can *subtly* find out what she's doing in there without her the wiser."

"Aye, and will it get me in trouble?" the boy asked, and Erran could see it was going to cost him more than a hundred coin, that the boy had taken one look at his silver-threaded jacket and bespoke boots and clocked him for someone who could do much better than that.

"Two hundred, but if you tell a single soul, I'll find you and gut you like a fish." Erran would do no such thing, but he hoped his menacing scowl was enough to settle the matter.

The boy's eyes lit up. He abandoned his apple crate and held out his hand.

"Half now, half when I get back," Erran said, depositing the coin. "And keep an eye on my horse, will you? Tether her to a post before you head inside."

He cast one last glance at the blacksmith shop and headed for the inn. Fortunately, Samuel was alone, and after listening to the situation, he simply grabbed his waistcoat and followed Erran.

"I don't wish to alert her or frighten her, aye? I just want to keep her out of trouble," he said as they rounded the corner. He spotted the boy dipping out of the shop and jogging across the road to where Vesper was tethered. They headed toward him.

"You really think she'll try to bond him?" Samuel asked.

"There's no bond for him until someone speaks on his behalf or he goes to trial, so all she'll do is cause a stir." He dug the remaining coin from his pocket and regarded the boy. "What did you find for me?"

"Donnae ken anything they were talking about, truth be told." The boy scratched his head with a frown.

"They?"

"Saw 'em through the crack in the door of the apartment upstairs. Man and two women. One was the woman you asked about, I ken." He held out his hand. "Dark hair and the lot."

"And?" Erran pressed, sharing a glance with Samuel. He closed the coin in his fist, the boy's eyes following the movement.

"Told ye, I donnae ken. Something about Sandymount and a man they need to see. Makes flags or some such. Was all nonsense to me. One of 'em said it was too dangerous." He flashed his hand again. "That's all I heard. Swear."

Erran reluctantly paid the boy and watched him retrieve his apple crate and scamper off.

"What business does she have in Sandymount?" Samuel asked.

"Couldn't say," Erran muttered, but a startling thought crept into the back of his mind, followed by a recollection of what he'd seen the night before, when he'd intercepted Mariel on the road at what had clearly been the crime scene for the stolen golden egg. "But I intend to find—"

He froze when three individuals emerged from the blacksmith shop: Mariel, followed by the same man who had visited her in Mistgrave, and...his mother's seamstress?

"I've seen that woman before." Samuel squinted.

"Go get your horse." Erran tucked back into the alley, following the movements of Mariel and her cohorts.

Samuel shook his head. "We're going to Sandymount, aren't we?"

Erran swung onto his saddle. "Aye, and you might just need to catch up to me because I'm not letting them out of my sight."

Mariel knew the way to Sandymount because the nearest village, Devon, was where her ship was anchored. It was close enough to Whitecliffe that she could reach it if she needed to but far enough away that the Rutlands never had to know their daughter-in-law even *had* a ship, let alone that she'd won it off a grizzled buccaneer one sweltering night in a game of billiards.

Even had she needed direction, the line of decorated caravans, transport for the wealthy, would have been easy enough to discern. Her belly turned at the thought of them all lining up to bid on land they had no right to. Mariel wasn't naïve enough to believe stopping the auction would stanch the gluttony, but Obsidian Sky had always been about slowing the bleed. Even if they were successful in stealing and redistributing all that wealth, the men in those positions would never relinquish their power.

"How will we even find this man, Banner?" Augustine asked as they passed under the village gates, riding between two caravans.

"Leave it to me," Remy said. They'd ridden the two hours mostly in silence. "He's a broker, so he'll have banking connections."

Mariel snorted, annoyed but not with him. A banker wouldn't even speak to a woman unless she had her own private account, and there was a sub-zero chance a banker would ever reveal information about the whereabouts of a colleague to one. "Auggie and I can ask around in the taverns. Sandymount is mostly a dry village, but there are two pubs here, so that makes it simple enough."

"Do that, and we'll meet up in an hour just there," he said, pointing at a giant tree in the middle of a square that served as the intersection of the four main roads. "I don't have to tell you both to choose your words carefully. The stewards are already spooked, and the last thing we need is word getting to any of them that people are asking around."

"Well, I don't even have to lie when I say I have a husband in need of a property broker," Mariel said, rolling her eyes. "I'm sure Auggie and I can smile and look pretty long enough to quell suspicion."

"You're both beautiful," Remy said, his tone earnest. "I'd be properly cross if the next time I saw either of you was in a jail cell I had no power or authority to spring you from."

"Who are you talking to?" Mariel laughed and leaned across her horse to nudge him. Her mirth faded. "It wasn't personal before, Remy, but it is now, aye? I don't trust the steward to do a damn thing to help my brother, so it's on us. This is for Destin."

"For Destin," the Perevil siblings replied in concert.

"They've split up," Samuel said.

"Aye." Erran squinted as Mariel took the seamstress's hand in hers and stepped into a tavern near the crossroads. What Mariel was even doing with the girl was confounding, but it was only one piece in the convoluted puzzle his wife had crafted behind his back.

They'd given the group enough of a lead to blend in with the other travelers coming to Sandymount for the auction, which should have had two more weeks of planning. Playing into fear was not a good strategy. Unlike his father, Erran didn't think the event was at risk. Obsidian Sky was a thorn in the side of all Rutlands—and all barons who answered to them—but it was full of amateur outlaws. Petty theft was one thing; pirating a hoard of gold that had to be more protected than the king himself was another.

But there were still those trifling thoughts stewing in the back of his mind, about Mariel, Sandymount...all of it.

"Erran, I have to ask. What do *you* think she's up to?"

It was obvious she was no longer headed to the jail, but it was far too premature to voice his new suspicion, which was ostensibly ridiculous. "I prefer not to speculate."

"Should we then?" Samuel asked. "I take the man. You take the women?"

"Nay," Erran said distantly, his stare locked on the tavern. "We wait, together. Whatever they're up to, it starts and ends with my wife."

Remy was already waiting for them near the tree when Mariel and Augustine arrived.

He wiped a band of sweat from his brow. The sun was blistering; a midseason gift, some called it. "His office is south of here, near the fork that splits you between Leecaster Bay or Devon. Three Points."

"I know it," Mariel said. She remembered seeing a business at Three Points, but it wasn't a broker's office.

"He shares the building with his wife, a dressmaker. The sign outside is for her business, so that's what we'll watch for. They warned me he has important business today and might not be in." Remy laughed and scratched his cheek. "Took all my reserve not to tell them *aye, I'm familiar with it.*"

"All right, so what next then, Tactician?" Augustine asked, quiet enough only for the three of them.

"This is Mariel's show," he said.

"I've been thinking about it the whole ride," Mariel answered carefully. She did have a plan, but it was nowhere near as solid as the others were used to. It was haphazard at best, and its success depended very much on certain particulars falling conveniently into place—another reason she preferred taking each moment as it came. "It's good for us if Banner *is* at his own office. He won't be foolish enough to have stored the gold there, so his place shouldn't be teeming with guards. We just have to find the right pressure point to sway him. If it's the gold itself, so be it. We'll give him a share, and it won't even scratch the surface." She frowned. "But if it was gold, he'd never be trusted with an event like this. It must be something else. I'll know what it is when we get there."

"What are you thinking, Mar?" Remy asked.

"Does he have children…Is he in love with his wife…We'll know when we see where he spends his time, won't we? And we use that, to get him to call off the dogs wherever the gold is stored and get us in. Out. He'll most likely have a wagon we can use, but we'll have to be quick because wherever we go, the law will not be far behind."

"You want to kidnap his wife and child?" Augustine leveled a dubious look at her.

Mariel clawed at her neck, itching from sweat. It wasn't the heat though. She'd never felt so unsteady about a heist, but those were the last words they needed from her. "He only needs to believe we would." She grimaced. "We only have two masks. I may need to reveal myself, but it will be all right. These men are scared of Obsidian Sky, even if they'd never admit it. This is our best chance, and we won't get another."

"Reveal yourself?" Remy scoffed, his lip curling. "You don't mean that."

"They don't know any of us. Our faces mean nothing, not really."

"Auggie and I maybe, but you're married to a Rutland!"

"And I'm a *nobody* in their eyes," Mariel retorted. "It's the whole reason they chose me for their precious son. Even if Banner or his cronies were at our party last night, a hundred coin says not one of them could pick me out of a crowd, because they don't care about *me*. They were there to preen before his father and Lord Warwick." She shook her head. "Even if someone *did* recognize me, would it be so bad? We'd have the gold. I wouldn't need to stay in this sham marriage and pretend to like the princeling and his vapid family. We could..." The next part was hard to say, but it was what they wanted to hear—what they'd been waiting for. "Retire. Keep just enough gold to exist on. Distribute the rest." She pointed south, in the direction of the sea. "The *Mistwitch* is anchored just off Devon. We could go anywhere, after we collect Destin and Alessia and Magnur."

"You'll take my mask," Remy stated, reaching into his pocket.

Mariel laid a steadying hand on his arm. "I won't argue this point. The two of you get the masks. I'll figure something out. It will be fine. If anything goes awry, you ride hard. You run."

"No one would believe him," Augustine said, her eyes clouding in thought. "Banner. If he told people he was assaulted by two *women* and a man, they'd think he was telling tales to excuse his negligence. Wouldn't they?"

"Maybe," Remy said, but he didn't sound convinced. His hand was still fixed to his mask pocket, his eyes studying Mariel. "But this isn't just our lives we're risking. Everyone we help...the miners, the grocers, the dock workers..."

Mariel nodded, tilting her head toward the sky and the scorching sun. "I'll go in alone. If something happens to me, it won't stop you from continuing the work."

"Not a fucking chance am I letting you walk in there without me," Remy said gruffly. "This is really the best way? You believe that? And not just because you're desperate to help Destin but because you *truly* believe it?"

"I've believed since I first heard of the auction. I knew...I knew it was what we'd been waiting for, working toward. Aye, it's a longshot now, without more time to plan, with mere hours to sort things, but what...Remy, Auggie, what if we *win*? What if we actually succeed? Is it not at least worth trying? We may never get another chance like this."

"You are truly insane, Mariel," Augustine said, shaking her head. "But that's the girl I love, and it's the one I've followed for ten years. I go where you go."

"Aye," Remy agreed, sighing. "It's not much of a plan, but we've learned to improvise over the years. We'll think of something when we get there."

Mariel exhaled her heavy relief, wondering if they would still follow her if they knew that, should it come down to it, she planned to sacrifice herself to save them.

Erran and Samuel followed the group for nearly an hour before arriving at the crossroads that split travelers between the small port of Devon and the larger Leecaster Bay.

Mariel and her cohorts dismounted and tethered their horses to a post outside of a two-story building, which appeared to be both residence and business. The flagging sign, hanging from an archway that served as the entrance to the path leading to the door, read *Banner Threads and Weaves.*

His blood chilled.

Banner.

I'm going to meet with Banner, the broker, to inspect the gold, which will arrive just ahead of me, if the weather holds.

He builds flags or some such.

"I'm beginning to understand your suspicions, mate," Samuel said. "If she's traveling with a seamstress, why would she need to come all the way out here for one? Perhaps the woman is purchasing materials? Though it's a long way to come when you have plenty of your own shops in Whitecliffe."

But Erran couldn't speak with the clog so thoroughly occupying his throat.

He prayed his father was meeting the man anywhere but there.

The short, portly woman who answered the door to *Banner Threads and Weaves* wore a beaming smile as she invited her guests in, a gesture that flagged slightly when they explained they were actually there to see Mr. Banner about managing the sale of their family estate, not to commission gowns.

When they'd seen her approaching through the window, Remy and Augustine had quickly pocketed their masks. She'd never let them in looking like bandits, and they needed to at least get a location on her husband.

"Ah. He so rarely receives visitors outside of his village office," Mrs. Banner said with a distant, thoughtful look.

"We asked in the village, and they sent us this way," Mariel explained. "But if we've been misinformed, we're happy to ride back."

"Nonsense. Nonsense. We'll...Come, come." She ushered them in. "Who made your cloak, dear?" she asked Augustine with a favorable appraisal.

"I did." Augustine cleared her throat with a glance at Mariel. "That is...I picked out the, ah, fabric and showed it to my seamstress."

"Compliments to whoever she is, for she should be sewing for royalty."

Augustine beamed until Remy flicked his eyes her way.

"Thread and yarn work is an art, no matter what anyone says about it," the woman said, continuing as she led them down a short hall, toward a light-filled room at the back of the house. "Men, of course, just think their vests and trousers magically appear in their bureaus, like little elves delivered them."

Augustine laughed along with her. She stumbled a bit when her mask slipped from her pocket, and she had to bend in a rush to grab it.

Mariel felt like throwing up. For the first time in a long time, a tingle of regret made itself known in her thoughts.

"I could not agree more, Madam Banner," Augustine said. "A quite underappreciated art, even by the women."

"My mother was a madam. I prefer Nora," the woman said, leading them into a broad solarium. "And how right you are, Miss…"

"Evelyn," Augustine replied without missing a beat. "And these are my siblings, Delia and Marcus."

"Hmm. My own sister and I haven't spoken in years." She dusted her hands against her apron with another broad grin. "Right. You'll be wanting tea."

"That's not necessary. We can just wait for Mr. Banner," Mariel said quickly.

"Nonsense. You're here for my husband, and he'll nay be chiding me for not affording proper care to his guests." Her lips peeled back, revealing teeth that were half gold, half rotted. "Willnae be but a moment."

"Is he here?" Mariel prodded.

"Oh, aye, donnae you fuss yourselves. Sit tight."

"I don't like this," Remy murmured through a tight gap in his pressed lips. "Something is off."

Mariel sensed it too, but they were so close…one conversation away from what they'd waited months and months—*years*—for, and she refused to let fear be what stood in their way. "Patience," she whispered. "We've come this far."

"There's a word for this…this idea that after investing so much time in something, you believe you can't walk away," Remy answered. He stared intently at the door Nora had exited through. "But it's folly. It leads to folly. And this…"

"Mar, I agree. I have a bad feeling." Augustine leaned in until her breath swept Mariel's neck. "If Des were here, he'd feel it."

"But he's not, is he? And he won't be until we come through for him." Mariel rolled her neck, cracking it. She squeezed out a pursed breath. Sweat beaded between her breasts and along her collarbones. "She said her husband was here—"

"Did she?" Augustine replied. "I don't ken she answered your question directly at all, and why is that?"

"You're being ridiculous, Auggie. This woman has no reason to distrust us or our intentions. We have, as far as she knows, legitimate business with her husband."

"Maybe because they're on high alert after last night," Remy said. His head kept shaking. "I just think—"

They whipped their heads toward the door at the sound of boots clanging on stone. Not one pair, but several. Heavy, full of intent. A storm of swords slapping buckles.

Mariel's mouth parted, but all she could do was nod at them both and then the door they'd come in through.

The three of them slowly stood. Remy drew a dagger, but she shook her head at him and mouthed, *Run!*

Augustine was first, launching into a dead sprint toward the entrance. No sooner than she started did the guards rush in.

"Go, go!" Mariel cried, shoving Remy from behind as they reached the door. "Masks on! Split up!"

"No!" Augustine yelled back. "We stick together!"

"As your leader, I am *commanding* you to go the opposite way I go!"

"Just do as she says," Remy barked, practically throwing his sister up onto her horse. He rushed to mount his as Mariel pulled herself astride her own. "Our meeting spot, as soon as it's safe. You *better* be there."

"Stop them!" a man screeched. "Head them off!"

"I'll see you soon," Mariel promised, but as she charged south, she knew better. She waited just long enough to see her friends ride east before turning her horse toward the encroaching guards and crying out, "You want the Flame so badly, lads? Here's your chance!"

Charged with adrenaline, Mariel urged her horse toward Devon and the port that would take her to the *Mistwitch*.

"*Fuck*," Samuel whispered, the first time Erran had ever heard him use a proper curse. "What do you suppose...doesn't matter. Doesn't matter. I'll go after—"

"Follow the others. I've got Mariel," Erran commanded and raced down the hill and through the dust of the three guards pursuing her.

Devon had never felt so far away, but the time passed in a deafening blur of fear and hooves, and before long, Mariel was barreling down the long hill that led into the small fishing village, where she would either steal a rowboat and race for the *Mistwitch* or die trying.

The plan seemed less and less viable as the guards tailing her closed in. Their horses were built for speed and distance, and her rented one was not. They were purposely wearing her out so they could gain on her when she exhausted her mare.

Mariel pushed the poor beast harder and harder, promising they were almost there.

She prayed in bleak desperation that Remy and Augustine had outrun their own pursuers. If something befell them, it would be entirely her fault. They'd never used the word, but if they had, she'd have deserved it. Reckless. That was how she'd been acting all day, no more than when she'd realized what she planned to do. What she should have done was leave Banner's home after the first moment she'd felt something terrible was coming, but instead, she'd let a dozen more moments like that one pass in her single-minded stubbornness to be right.

She shouldn't have gone to Sandymount at all. Her mind, split between the chase and a cataloging of her remorse, pulled no punches assessing her motive. For the first time in Obsidian Sky's history, she'd ignored her instincts and trudged forward in spite of them. It was the one thing she hadn't compromised on, their safety.

Mariel approached her last chance to turn south into the village, toward the docks, but she knew she wouldn't make it. She'd already decided what to do instead, she only needed to dig deep for the courage.

Her horse reared as she slid to a near stop and forced a hard turn to the east, heading down a path parallel to the sea. She gritted down and leaned in for the final push, praying her landmark, the tall, half-leaning stone pine, was still there.

"What's the bitch doing?" one of the men said amid their flutter of course correction.

Her borrowed horse struggled up a small embankment. "Come on, just a little farther. We're almost there," she urged, her forehead tickling his mane. Her heart threatened to pound right out of her chest, and she wondered if that was something that could actually happen to a person.

To find out, she'd need to die, and she refused to go down without one hell of a fight.

Erran had held a safe distance for most of the ride, but when he saw the Devon coastline appear under the midday sun, he knew they were nearing the end of the chase.

He spurred Vesper, knowing full well doing so would reveal his presence to the men chasing Mariel. *Why* they were chasing her and why she was visiting Banner, those were questions for another time, though he wondered if he'd ever get the answers.

There'd been no time to strategize with Samuel about what should happen if he caught up to the other two, but he had to trust his friend would know what to do.

Erran's mind and heart were a labyrinth of confusion, but he was certain of one thing.

He couldn't let those men catch up to Mariel, no matter what she'd done.

Just ahead, Mariel kicked up a whirl of dust as she made a sharp turn onto a path, which led up into the milky sea cliffs that stretched to a peak above the sea.

Other than a couple of mines scattered along the coastline, there was nothing up there but land, for miles.

"What are you doing, Mariel?" he murmured. Warm wind battered his face as he closed the gap with the guards. Her horse wasn't built for such a hard ride and was struggling up the hill. The men *would* catch up, and soon. He had to stop them—or slow them. But how?

A diversion would do nothing. They'd followed her for almost a full half hour from Sandycove at breakneck speed to catch her. He didn't think he could outrun them either, even though he got closer, the best he could do was match their pace. He couldn't push Vesper much harder without harming her.

Erran nearly laughed as a preposterous idea leaped into his thoughts. He hadn't traveled to Sandymount with much in his tack bag, but he *had* brought apples, for the horse. When they were boys, Khallum used to challenge them all to feats of strength, and one had been to see who could hurl something the farthest into the sea. Erran won almost every time, at throwing and nearly everything else they did. He might be known as the "prettiest" of the bunch, and his accent might not be as leathered as Khallum's or Hamish's, but he'd always been the most adept at any sport they engaged in.

He'd never thrown anything while riding a horse to the brink of her limits, but it was the only idea he had.

Erran wrapped his left hand tight in the reins to stabilize himself as he fumbled the other, searching for the clasp on his bag. He couldn't get it unbuckled with all the jostling, so he tugged hard, grunting through his teeth as he ripped the buckle clear off. A couple of apples spilled out and disappeared on the road behind him.

He made a fist over an apple. Killing either of the men was the last thing he intended, so he couldn't aim for their heads. But no matter where he aimed, it would land where it landed. The ride was too unsteady to guarantee accuracy.

It's them or her.

Erran had no damn reason to show her any loyalty when she'd offered him only misery, but still he cocked his arm back and held it in place a moment to count the space between Vesper's hooves striking earth, as he'd heard the great Riders of the Rush did when battling on horseback. If he timed it right…No, there *wasn't* time. That was the problem.

He whispered a silent prayer to the Guardian of the Unpromised Future and launched the apple. It struck one of the men right between the shoulders, and the shock of it sent him toppling off his horse, which rode on without him.

The other guard pulled to a stop, clearly confused about what had just happened, but it was enough hesitation for Erran to break away and surpass them. He rode by, pushing the horse one last time as they climbed another embankment.

When he crested the hill, he spotted Mariel ahead, but she was no longer mounted. She kissed the horse's snout and gave her a pat, releasing her. When she turned back toward the sea, her eyes locked on Erran, widening. Her expression froze that way as she butted up to the cliff's edge.

"No!" Erran cried, dismounting before he'd commanded Vesper to stop. He landed in a painful roll before springing back to his feet and running the rest of the way. "Mariel, no!"

"What are…" Her face, pale from the shock, whipped between him and the sea. "Why are you here? How did you—" She held out her arms. "Doesn't matter. I..." Breathless, she bounded away from the precipice, then launched into a sprint that sent her hurtling over the cliff's edge, her legs scissoring the air as she disappeared into the abyss of sea and sky.

Erran's heart stopped beating altogether for a moment. He raced to the cliff to confirm his fear, that she'd thrown herself to her death on the rocks below, but she popped up from the water and swam against the tide, headed out to sea. In the distance he spotted a ship, anchored in place, and a fresh fear emerged as he wondered if she was planning to go for it, if she was even a strong enough swimmer to make it that far. Lake rats weren't used to the rough and capricious sea like coastal dwellers were.

The guard he hadn't pegged with the apple came up and over the hill, red-faced and screaming unintelligible curses and warnings.

All it would take was to explain to them who he was. The son of the most revered steward in the Southerlands. The best mate of the lord of the Northerlands. The heir to the largest admiralty in the realm.

But revealing himself would ensure the events of the day made it straight to his father's ears. There was no story that would justify him chasing Mariel across the Reach, of her visiting Banner, of him knocking a guard senseless to protect whatever she'd done. The admiralty, everything he'd ever worked for or cared about, would be taken away, and he'd be left with nothing but his shame.

Erran looked once more at the approaching guard, swallowing an enormous lump of dread.

There wasn't time to think of an alternative.

He had two choices, both terrible.

For the admiralty.

Erran held his breath, reared back to gain speed, and dived in after her.

WRECKED

SIX

A SEDUCTION OF ROPES AND RIGGING

The water sent a stinging pain from her toes to her head when her boots pierced through, but Mariel had no time to think, because the force of her entry had sent her plunging deep under the waves. She flailed in alarm but quickly remembered what her father had taught her about the dangers of panicking, so she shifted her conscious effort toward relaxing her limbs, flipping her feet, and angling her arms down to return to the surface.

She gulped in a screeching breath of air, the desperate sound engulfed by the great roaring sea. Her chest was full to bursting. A cool wave swiped her, dragging her under again, but she let her buoyancy lift her back to safety.

The lifting and pulling continued until she got the hang of the pattern. Her bearings slowly returned.

From the sea, the rise of land looked considerably higher than it had before she'd dementedly jumped to what could have just as easily been her death if the water had been any shallower. If she'd hesitated at all, though, she would be in custody.

Or dead.

Of all the things she had ever done as an outlaw, nothing had ever felt so dangerous.

Or so wickedly invigorating.

The sharp rays of the sun blinded her, but with a squint, she could just make out the form of a man, waving his arms from the top of the cliff. He was too broad to be Erran, but she saw no sign of her meddling husband. There wasn't time to wonder why. Whatever else happened, she'd never be able to return to her marriage.

The guard was unlikely reckless enough to jump in after her, but if she didn't hurry, he'd make it to town and procure a vessel that would reach the *Mistwitch* long before her tired body would. Even if she did get there, there was still so much work to do to ready her for sail, and it would take far too long with just one person doing it all.

That was a problem for the future. She had but one job in the now.

Mariel was a lake swimmer, not a sea swimmer, but analyzing the differences was a luxury unavailable to her as she bobbed in the sea, one foul wind from drowning. The White Sea was infamous for its treacherous waves in open water and untenable sailing conditions, but the coastal currents were calm and easily navigable. She could make it.

She would make it.

Mariel turned until she'd fixed the *Mistwitch* in her sights. She closed her eyes and pumped her arms and legs, looking up every few strokes to gauge her ship's distance. Gentle waves carried her backward, slowing her momentum, but she pushed on, counting her strokes and turning her thoughts off.

A hard ache settled into her legs. Her lungs seized in response. She thought she heard someone calling her name, but the sea was so loud, consuming and blending her senses into a morass of disorder. It would consume her, too, if she gave into it.

Water is water. I can do this.

Mariel pushed on, each stroke in direct defiance to her fright, her demand for hesitation and reflection. *One, two, three, four, five, six,* she counted, starting over when she'd lost her place. *One, two, three, four.* She allowed herself another glance up and saw the *Mistwitch* was only a few yards ahead, glittering in the midday sun—anchored and waiting for her mistress.

She dipped under the water and didn't emerge until her hand struck wood.

Sputtering, she crested, swallowing as much air as her lungs allowed. She used the divots in the hull's wooden cage to guide herself to the stern of the ship, where a ladder was fastened. Her heart hammered as she made her way to the back, but it lodged in her throat when she saw someone was already halfway up, stretching a hand down to her.

Erran.

She lifted her elbow onto a thin ledge to steady herself and took his hand. With a grunt, he hoisted her effortlessly up and out of the water, locking her fingers over a rung, but it left her spread between the outer hull and the ladder.

"I have you," he said breathlessly. His soaked hair was matted against his flushed face, seawater dripping down his eyes to his chin. His aquamarine eyes glistened, like how the sea looked when the sun reflected off its surface. "You can let go. Trust me."

I don't trust you a whit, she wanted to say. A wave thrashed her feet and her hold slipped, causing a few of her nails to bend back. She grimaced through the sharp pain. "What are you…doing… here, Erran?"

"Is now the time you want to have this conversation?" His jawline tensed and constricted as he worked to keep hold of her and the ladder. "They're coming, aye? So we can argue about it, or you can accept my help and we can get the bloody feck out here."

"I can…" Mariel couldn't get enough breath to speak. She took a pause. Her bleeding fingertips strained on the wet wood. "Do it myself."

"I could barely reach it from the water, Mariel, and I have half a foot on you. It's meant for going down, not up." His muscles on the arm gripping the ladder strained under his translucent white shirt. "Let go, and swing my way."

It wasn't the time to argue, and she shouldn't have needed the princeling to tell her so. She inched her hand closer, more nails bending along the damp wood as she struggled to stay gripped.

"Mariel, let go already!"

Mariel yelped through her teeth as she released the hull and threw as much momentum as she could toward him and the ladder. His arm scooped her waist, catching her right as her grip on the rung slipped. He snapped her against him with a low grunt, but instead of pushing her up and ahead of him, he climbed up with her tacked to his waist like an adornment and pulled them both up until the gunwale was in reaching distance. She grabbed for it and wormed her way over the side, then crashed onto the deck with a rolling thud.

Erran landed on his feet behind her. This time when he offered a hand, she didn't take it. She needed her wits about her, because the only trouble as bad as the guards pursuing her—after she'd boldly, stupidly outed herself as the Flame to save her friends—was a Rutland discovering her criminal activity.

"Where did you *get* this thing?" Disgust wove through his words as he continued his inspection. "It's not even yours, is it?"

"It's mine," she said tersely, straining for breath. "And I've got only a few minutes to get her readied for open sea. So while I thank you for the rescue, you can go now."

"Go?" His expression widened in bemusement. "You think you can captain this dory yourself?"

Mariel's hands shot to her hips in hot offense. "*Dory*? She's a proper trading craft! And aye, I've captained her myself, Princeling of the Seas. Do ye see a crew?"

"I see a woman who jumped from a feckin' cliff because she couldn't think straight."

"Wh…" she sputtered, unsure what his angle was. It was clear he wasn't leaving, and she didn't have time to argue. "Fine. But once we're off, you'll be explaining yourself, or I'll punt you into the sea myself."

Erran scoffed, squinting as he took in the details of the ship. She knew what he was going to say before he said it. "Aye, it's no dory. I'll give you that. But it *is* a balinger, lass. The draft is shallow. Only good for trading. Transport. It's built for coastal waters."

As if she didn't know. "Aye, and those same waters are going to make it easy to catch up with us, because we don't have thirty men to run the oars, do we?" She shoved past him and raced for the sails, nearly losing her poise on the slimy deck.

He hissed in through his teeth. "We take it to open sea, we might not come back."

"Feel free to return to where you came from then," she replied, baring her teeth as she started tugging on the starboard halyard, twisting her fingers into the knot to loosen it.

Erran appeared on the other side to help. "On three. One, two—"

Mariel bore down and started tugging before he finished his countdown. He emoted a brief chuckle full of reproach, like she was a petulant child, and joined her. Together, they raised the first and then the second sail. It would have taken her thrice as long by herself, but her gratitude never made it past her tongue.

"Tie them off," he commanded.

"I'm not one of your crew. I don't take bloody orders from you," she muttered, wrenching her halyard over the joint.

"Protests the one running from the law," he snapped.

When she whipped her head up to tell him where he could stick his words, he was already done with his side and had gone to the starboard beam, where he was pitched over the side. His back clenched with every tug as he wrested the anchor from the water, something she'd only been able to do with the winch.

He carefully lowered it to the deck and into the cradle, but on his rise, he went notably still. "Mariel," he said calmly.

She closed her eyes and sighed. "They're coming, aren't they?"

"Are you more comfortable trimming the sails or manning the tiller?" His hands fisted at his sides as he watched the sea. "There's hardly a wind this afternoon. It's going to take some doing to catch air, if we can even do it at all."

What he really meant was that managing the ropes and rigging would take strength and stamina, and she was at a disadvantage. It burned her to admit any weakness to a Rutland, but it wasn't the place for pride. "Tiller."

"Go."

She raced to the tiller, sliding again when the ship rolled on the tide. Erran had two ropes in his hands, his hips wide and knees bent. He craned his head back and yelled, "Northeast!"

"Are you sure?" She tried to read the waters, the air, but she was forced to concede he knew far more than she ever would. "It almost seems—"

"Northeast, Mariel!" His feet started to slide. "Come on!"

Mariel put all her weight into cranking the tiller and heaved a relieved breath when it responded. She kept turning until the compass read northeast and then locked it in place before rushing to join Erran.

"Secure the deck and the hatches," he ordered.

For a moment, she was too awed from watching him work the ropes to do anything but gape. His work was fluid and effortless, like a seasoned artist painting the perfect landscape on their first attempt.

"Mariel!"

There wasn't much *on* the deck, beyond some frayed netting and a few empty crates. A handful of rusted tool parts, scattered. The buccaneer she'd won it from had had his men loot the vessel before handing over the deed, and the meager supplies she'd brought herself were on the lower deck, stuffed in cupboards. She hadn't foreseen she might need to be stocked for a harrowing escape. When Erran figured out how ill-fitted they were for where she wanted to go, he'd have plenty more to say about her lack of experience.

She scrambled to grab everything as he teased the sails, working against their lack of wind in a way she never could have managed on her own. Why he'd followed her...why he'd jumped into the *feckin' sea* when he must have known that aiding a criminal would be the final straw for his father, who was already so close to pulling his birthright for his antics...It didn't add up. She'd be more inclined to believe it was one big fever dream, but the nightmare surrounding her was unfortunately very much real. The men chasing them, no less so.

The most depressing realization washed over her: Obsidian Sky was done. Their best work was behind them now, not ahead. Whatever her fate, the others were on borrowed time. The stewards now knew their favorite brigands were willing to take bigger risks, and would stop at nothing to hunt them down, one by one.

Better they chase her forever, than the others, for even a minute.

"They're gaining!" Erran bellowed.

Mariel shoved everything in her arms down the hatch, slammed it, and threw the bolt. The ship listed as they approached the currents most traders avoided. Everyone knew the White Sea took indiscriminately, and anyone who had ever gone too far out to sea had never returned.

She skated again, this time hitting the deck with her hands. Erran's full focus was channeled into his handiwork, a maestro conducting his masterpiece, a seduction of ropes and rigging.

Mariel returned to the tiller and unlatched the lock, planting her feet as they reached the first onset of choppier waters. She craned her neck back to search for the skiff, but it seemed to hold the same distance.

"Tide's going out, and it's taking us along," Erran called, but he didn't sound happy, which perplexed her. The keel was at no risk from seabed collision in the low tidal pull, because as Erran had pointed out, her ship had a shallow draft. And without the wind, they'd need some assistance from nature, or he'd end up snapping his arms trying to manipulate the air.

"Aye, good!" The tiller rumbled under her hands from the force of their direction, turned to a northeast angle against the building current. Her gut burned with shame at how easily he'd assumed a captain's role aboard her own ship, clearly assuming she'd never learned how to pilot the *Mistwitch* at all. It singed deeper when she was forced to accept he was partly right. She'd piloted her a few times, sure, but in shallow waters, where she belonged. They were already farther from the shore than she'd ever been, skipper or passenger.

"Good? How far do you ken we're going, Mariel?"

"Far enough to shake those thugs!"

"You gonna tell me who they are?"

"They're guards." Mariel's boot slipped. She'd keep slipping as long as the leather was sodden. When it was safe to drop anchor, she'd dry her gear and dig out something new.

"No shite. Why are they after *you*?" His shoulders rippled under his still-soaked shirt as he pulled and leaned and gave and listed. She was mesmerized, watching him work. It was almost beautiful, if they weren't sailing for their literal lives.

"You wouldn't believe me if I told you." Her muscles locked as the current tried to force the rudder farther north. She gritted down and locked it back in place. Seawater rose to the east and crashed against the side of the *Mistwitch*, peppering them with spray. A little higher and they'd have been swamped.

"How close?"

"What?"

"How close are they now?"

Mariel turned again and nearly whooped from joy. "They're receding. Erran, they've stopped!"

"Because they know better." He eased off the trimming and tied the halyards. "If we go any farther east, to open sea, we'll capsize. No doubt of it. You have a map in this mess?"

"Of course I have a feckin' map," she replied, flicking a nod over her shoulder. "In the galley, one of the top cupboards."

"You keep your map in the kitchen?" Erran was dubious, his expression edged with judgment. "Ken that means you've never found much use for it?"

"Oh, you can lose the smug look. Some skippers don't need maps." She tapped her chest. "Got 'em in here."

"*All* skippers need a map, and the best ones aren't afraid to admit it," Erran replied with a quick, condescending smile that was far more galling than his assumption of command. He approached, his arms crossed. "How fortunate you are to have me."

Mariel snorted and averted her eyes.

"Aye, you could pout." His lip hitched. "Or you could thank me."

"*Thank* you?" Mariel screeched.

"For saving your arse, for one."

"I don't even know why you're here!"

He stared at her, open-mouthed, his head slowly passing back and forth. "I cannae even fathom how yer mind must work, baring down on me when yer the one who rode hours to meet a man conveniently wrapped up in the most significant business transaction my father has ever made, right after he mentioned it at breakfast, only to be chased into the *fecking sea*, and then you turn your suspicion on me? The one throwing his future away for a woman who cannae even stand him?"

Mariel was taken aback, though she shouldn't have been. What else was he to assume, following her to Banner's and watching the guards hunt her down like the criminal she was? He might be a spoiled brat, but he wasn't stupid. "Well…Well, I see your salt and sand has come back, but where are your mates?"

Erran curled his nose and pursed his mouth. "I'm told it comes out with my anger."

"So does your shite attitude, which I'll thank you to lose." She charged forward a step. "You did *not* have to come."

"Aye, I *did*."

"Why?" she asked.

His nostrils flared with his eyes, burning with intensifying ire. "Because you're my wife—"

"And your property?"

"Will you feckin' stop with such vile accusations!" Erran was thunderous. His arms flew to the top of his head and rested there as he paced short paths before her. "I donnae own ye, Mariel, nor would I wish to, for how...How could any..." His eyes swept her in disgust. "All ye are is lies and rage."

He stormed to the hatch and climbed down. The lid crashed behind him.

Mariel stood in admonished silence, riding the gentle undulations carrying them to sea. It didn't matter what he thought. It never had. She couldn't let any of it get under her skin. Her father used to say, *Never take criticism from anyone you wouldn't solicit advice from.*

She climbed atop the raised stern deck, hand on the storm mast, and waited to see what the guards would do.

Erran realized he'd only been allowing himself the shallowest of breaths when he finally took in a deep one and let it roll from his lungs in a lingering, gentle escape.

The guards had turned around, but that only meant they were returning to shore for a more suitable vessel. It bought him some time to chart a better course.

He found a decent place to drop the six weighted anchors, meant for creating drag in deeper waters, around the edges of the deck. It was a little farther to sea than he was comfortable with, and the occasional waves cresting and swamping the deck set his nerves on edge, but Mariel was right about one thing: they couldn't go back, and they needed to be far enough out for other ships to think better of following.

Whether they would follow anyway depended on what Mariel had done.

While below deck, he'd done a quick assessment of their supplies. She couldn't have had the ship for long, because there wasn't much. Blankets and pillows. A few changes of clothes. A box of torn rope and busted rigging, probably left by whomever she'd pilfered the vessel from. A crate of whiskey. Candles, tossed into a crate with some knives. A couple of rusted axes. A satchel of dried meat, and a filled waterskin, seemed to be the only food and drink she'd bothered with, so either she hadn't anticipated being out at sea for long or she was even worse at skippering than he'd first thought.

He tossed it all back where he found it and returned to the upper deck.

Mariel was seated on a bench on the port side, her arm draped over the side and eyes on the distant outline of the shore. She didn't look up when he approached or sat beside her.

"Don't say it," she said hoarsely. "Please."

Erran held out his hands to show he had no intention of interrogating her—yet. They had nowhere to go. *She* had nowhere to go. And aye, he'd followed her when he hadn't needed to, but he was in it now. Whatever *it* was.

"Will you at least tell me if there's a plan?"

Mariel dropped her hands between her knees and folded down over them. "Will you yell at me again if I say no?"

Erran's irritation flared, but he pushed it down. "I'm sorry. I shouldn't have."

She sighed through her nose. "I shouldn't have said what I said, when you helped as much as you did. I ken if it were only me, I wouldn't have fared as well."

"Guardians, no," he agreed.

Mariel glanced his way in surprise, and something in her expression made him laugh. She laughed too. "I suppose it doesn't hurt to tell you where I got this beauty."

"I assumed you stole her."

The offense he'd been aiming for never crossed her expression. A hint of pride was there, but it drifted into wistfulness. "I acquired her in Goldthorpe."

Erran flinched in genuine shock. "The gambling town?"

She nodded. "Game of billiards. Won her fair and square."

"I didn't realize they let women in there, except..."

"Except the midnight women, there for man's endless pleasure?"

He cleared his throat, embarrassed both because they were discussing midnight women and by Mariel's bluntness. "Aye, I ken that was what I was trying to say."

"You don't speculate? Not at all?"

Erran shook his head. "It's not the business of a gentleman. Or so says my father."

Mariel nodded and turned back toward the sea. "Neither is confiscating lands from men by fabricating crimes and charges."

"Mariel, you can't say something like that if you're not willing to tell me why we're here."

Her brows raised with a sharp inhalation. She waved her hand toward the mast. "You, uh, handled yourself well today. Thank you."

"'Thank you?'" Erran grinned and turned his head toward the sky, in which a distant storm was materializing. "Will you have to kill me now that you've paid me such a kindness?"

"Would do it for less," she replied, but even with her head turned, she couldn't hide her tight grin.

Erran squinted at the darkening skies, the thick clouds pulling together. "We're going to have to make a move soon. This storm doesn't look to be heading toward land, but it is coming our way. If we navigate into smoother waters—"

"Nay." She spun on the bench, her expression hard. "Nay, we cannot. We cannot go back."

"And you're not going to tell me why..." He enunciated each word.

"Not…I don't know. Nay. Not now." Her hands rolled along the edge of the bench, and that was when he noticed some of her fingers were bloodied. "There's no plan. I *had* one, but…I wasn't expecting what, eh, happened, aye?"

"Being chased by guards into the sea?"

She lifted her fingertips with a curt nod.

"Whatever it is you've done, my father can—"

"Your *father*?" Her laugh terrified him. "You go on back, Errandil. I never asked you to follow me…to help me. There's a rowboat attached to the starboard hull, and it's all yours."

Mariel wanted him to react, to fight with her so she could justify her own anger, wherever it had come from. "I'm not going back, Mariel."

She bore into him with a stare that seemed to challenge his words. "Then you're a bigger fool than I thought you were, because your father won't forgive *this* misstep. I promise you."

Foreboding crossed her words, the closest he'd get to an understanding of the circumstances that had her fleeing in a paltry vessel for an unforgiving sea. "Maybe I am a fool," he said, conceding. "But I'm not leaving you to navigate these waters alone."

"He'll take the admiralty from you when he finds out you've helped me. Is that what you want?"

Was there concern in her eyes? "That's my risk to take."

Mariel glanced away with a sigh, shaking her head in defeat and disbelief. "I ken we'll have a better chance of surviving this mess with your skill."

"Skill is part of it." Erran whistled through his teeth. "But… There's not enough food to last us more than two, maybe three days, and that's if we ration. You didn't exactly provision this ship for a long voyage."

"Where's the map?"

Erran handed it over.

She stood and spread it on the bench. "There aren't many islands here. There's Duncarrow and Belcarrow, the king's territories. The others are small, rather inconsequential. Useless for much of anything."

"I know of them." He gritted to temper the annoyance in his voice, because he truly didn't have the heart for another row with her. But he'd been born on the sea. Trained on the sea. Had been groomed to helm the largest, most distinguished fleet in the entire realm. And she wanted to educate *him*? "They're not useless if you're a bird or a boar. Few see fit to travel so far when there's easier hunting on the mainland."

"Aye." She nodded distantly. "But do you really see us making it back to the mainland in this ship anytime soon?"

He wasn't ready to acknowledge his suspicions, or the inciting words she'd howled at the guards before leading them on a wild chase, but it was enough to believe there could be guards at every port soon, if there weren't already. And if any of them launched their own ships in pursuit, Erran and Mariel would be boxed in, with nowhere to go.

He'll take the admiralty from you when he finds out you've helped me.

Well, Erran thought, with a wry twist of humor. *That ship seems to have already sailed.*

"It's going to be rough," he said. "If we can even get there in this thing."

"I can't guess how long we'll be out here. You can still go back."

He scratched down his chin and neck. "If we can make it to even one island in that archipelago, there'll be vegetation we can eat, food we can hunt. A water source. And then we can…" He breathed deep. "Form some kind of a plan."

"Did you hear me?"

"Aye." He stood with a stretch. "Tide is about to go out again. Still no wind, but we'll make do. You want the tiller again or the sails?"

Mariel's face peeled back. "I'll stick to the tiller, thank you."

Erran closed his eyes and felt for the wind's direction. Still weak, but north. They needed to go northeast, but he could work with it. "Let's pull anchors. We've already wasted enough time."

Mariel made slight adjustments in the tiller's direction while Erran played the sails. At times, she caught herself watching him, his shoulders all neat, flexing lines under his shirt, which hadn't yet fully dried. It stirred something in her, which she knew better than to mistake for attraction, but it reminded her she *was* alive... was a real, whole person who could feel something other than vengeance.

She had to grudgingly admit they made a good team. Maybe not in marriage, or in anything else that mattered, but she knew no one else who could have taken over the *Mistwitch* and navigated her with such effortless ease.

As he worked, she saw the man who could one day lead a fleet but never would.

Why he was there—why he'd *stayed* after she'd skirted just around the truth but close enough for him to know her crime was nothing petty—was a secret he held close, just as she was holding her own. She would never have risked so much for him, a bruising realization that stoked her guilty conscience. When the reckoning inevitably came, the power to exonerate them would not be hers to give, but the least she could do was explain he'd followed her from nothing more than some misguided sense of marital chivalry.

"Coming into the Eastern Shelf," Erran called over his shoulder.

Mariel swallowed her pride to ask, "What...What does that mean?"

"The eastern side of the White Sea is actually two distinct bodies of water, and where they meet, there's a...The best way to think of it is a collision of opposing tidal systems. The force can pull even the most hardy ship under."

Her skin prickled with a fear she'd not considered. "Can we go around?"

"Nay. To go around, we'd encounter worse problems." He shifted his stance, and the top sail snapped against the wind. "It's just the first obstacle in sailing beyond the White Kingdom. By far not the hardest, but the islands we want are just on the other side."

"Then how…" She hadn't actually asked, or even wondered, why mariners could never leave the kingdom seas. "What do we need to do?"

"Grip that tiller for your life," he said. "And pray we haven't angered the Guardians too deeply today."

Mariel squinted into the misty afternoon for any signs of the Eastern Shelf he was speaking of, but the sea was the same on all sides: choppy, endless, and misty from the scattered rain. She was still searching when something large and swelling caught in her peripheral vision. Turning, she saw a wall of water coming toward them and screamed.

"Crank it to the east, Mariel!" Erran hollered. His boots slid along the deck as he grunted and tugged at the halyards. "Harder!"

"I'm trying!" Mariel bared down, but it wasn't enough. She was losing her footing, her hold, and the giant wave was coming right at their starboard hull. It was tall enough to swallow them whole. It was all happening too fast for her to adjust. "Erran, what do we *do?*"

"Stay calm and quarter us—ah, steer us at an angle against the wave."

Her heart leaped into her throat and lodged there, thumping and pounding. "I'm *trying*, but it's not *budging*! It's going to swamp us!"

"Trust me and keep turning!"

Ocean spray from the coming onslaught temporarily blinded her. She looked up, wondering how Erran could sound so calm, and was stunned to see him reefing the sails. The bottom one was rolled halfway up, and he tied it there.

"Mariel…We need…the sea anchors…not all of them, just two on each side…"

She wiped her face on her sleeve and peered behind her. "I can't get to them unless I lock the tiller!"

"The tiller will be fine. We just need some drag to pull our rear—"

Horrified, she watched him lose his grip on the ropes and go rolling down the deck and slam into the side wall. "Erran?"

He didn't respond…or move.

"Oh, no, no, no. No, no. Feck. Feck. *Erran*!" She tried to lock the tiller to go to him, but the next wave struck the ship, swallowing her and everything around her in a flood of bedlam. Her throat burst with seawater and she sputtered, gripping the tiller with all she had.

When she finally opened her eyes, the wave had passed, but the deck was engulfed. Water seeped down the drains, but it would overwhelm the bilge, which would need draining soon or they'd capsize.

This is why I need a crew.

But she'd hardly finished that thought when another wave slammed the ship from behind and carried her away. She flailed, scrambling to grab onto *anything*, but she may as well have been sailing through air.

Mariel slammed into something hard, and it knocked the breath out of her. She heard a horrific cracking sound and saw the mast splitting in the center, the top careening right for her. She shielded her head, but a rush of current carried her away just in time for her to watch the wooden pole slam into the sea.

In breathless horror, she saw the ship's bow list toward the water, and she realized she was watching the *Mistwitch* losing her battle *from* the sea.

"Erran," she yelped, but there was no sign of him. He was probably dead, like she would soon be. If she'd been better prepared, if she'd understood this Eastern Shelf, if she'd—

Her world was muffled by another swell that pulled her under. She stopped fighting. It was only making it worse. She was losing the battle either way, but if she conserved her energy—

An explosion of light engulfed her eyes when a dazzling pain struck her dead in the chest. Her arms wrapped around a thick plank from the ship and she held tight to it, wheezing fractured, gulping breaths that were half air and half water, praying to Guardians she didn't quite believe in, as the sea issued its eternal reminder that it answered to no one.

SEVEN
YOU AND VIOLENCE

Brilliant, dazzling beams of light danced off the world, reflecting a thousand tiny rays of magic. Mariel was in another realm, a place where fear and starvation and inequity weren't even words another would recognize, where there was only joy and plenty in endless array.

Mariel laughed, because it was what her heart told her to do. But after, the most unsettling sensation followed, a cloying mouthful of foamy, salty nightmares.

She turned her head and the beauty disappeared. The light turned blinding, obscuring her sense of bearing. An ebbing roar brought her back toward her new, shifting reality, a hint of truth. Warm, wet sand gritted against her cheek…her thigh. Her feet slid through it as she tried to sit and make sense of how fast and completely everything around her had changed.

Her doubling vision made her to swoon into the suction of the sand. Water tugged at her toes and ankles, and she slid in the direction it beckoned. A great pain in her chest made itself known and then other, smaller pains followed as both body and mind awoke to what was real.

Mariel propped herself up with one hand. Her eyes scanned the horizon. To her right was a lush, hilly area, entirely foreign and strangely enticing. She wanted to go there, to climb up into the many shades of emerald and lose herself to the purity of nature.

To her left was a stretch of endless coastline and—

A ship.

Her ship.

The *Mistwitch*.

Mariel went to stand, but her knees buckled, sending her skittering sideways until she recovered her equilibrium. Her stare was fixed on the *Mistwitch*, on a slowly forming story she wished desperately she could erase and write again.

The ship appeared mostly intact, but the bow was almost entirely submerged in the sea, lifting the stern like a whale's tail. The mast was cracked down the center, the top sail drooping alongside the bottom one.

Like a punch to the gut, she remembered everything. The dramatic cliff diving escape. The sudden wave. The capsize. Losing Eran somewhere in the melee.

She whipped her head around in search of him, but all it did was send her head into a swimming mess. She hobbled down the beach in the direction of the ship, her heart plummeting with every step. He'd been unconscious when the wave had swallowed them, and even in her state of disarray, she knew what that meant.

"Erran!" she screamed, but only a raspy squeal emerged. She cleared her throat, thrust her arms at her sides to project her voice above the sea, and called for him again. The defeat in her voice eclipsed any hope she'd clung to. If he was dead, it was her fault. "*Erran*!"

The effort was exhausting. She closed her eyes and worked her breaths into something manageable, and tried once more. "ERRANDIL, IF YOU DON'T FECKIN' ANSWER ME, I'LL KILL YOU MYSELF!"

All around her, pieces of wreckage drifted in and then out with the ebb tide: planks, pieces of rope, and an axe. A sob formed in her throat, and her hands flew to her neck to trap it there, because she couldn't afford any lapse, however transitory, when she was in the greatest danger of her life.

No one was coming. No one knew where she was. *She* didn't even know where she was.

Her knees went soft again. *No. No, I will not fall here. I will not die here.* She lifted one leg, then another and resumed her sweeping, cheerless assessment of the remnants of their doomed voyage.

I never wanted him dead. I never wanted that. Mariel wiped a tear, but it blended with the briny, reedy mess coating her cheek. She started collecting everything she could, chasing planks with the waves, but kept losing her footing in the powerful pull of the receding tide.

She realized it was raining. Pouring, actually, but she was so soaked from the shipwreck, it was hard to discern what was storm and what was sea. Ahead, the darkening sky held ripe clouds, promising more of the same, but it was the encroaching evening that made her skin prickle with anxious dread. She needed to find shelter *before* she lost daylight, and the ship would be too risky.

A shrill screech tore out from somewhere behind her. She turned inland, but it was just more endless forest, far more vibrant and verdant even than the ones that colored the lake district. It reminded her of the paintings in Goldsea Spires of the Hinterlands, the land of the Medvedev, where outsiders were not allowed. But she was a long way from the Hinterlands or the realm proper, and anything so foreign must be evaluated as a danger.

Whatever made that sound was in *there*.

Mariel continued her cursory scan of the horizon and spotted, astoundingly, a small, utilitarian building resembling a shed. It was a neat, modest wooden rectangle with no windows, one door, two steps leading up to it, and no sign of anyone nearby.

She blinked in case she was imagining it, but it *was* real, and it looked to be serviceable. What it was for, what was inside…It didn't matter. It was shelter. The ship wasn't safe. Whatever had screamed from inside the forest, there would be more, and other creatures besides. She'd washed up onto an island mostly unbothered by man, a kingdom unto itself. The shack was the only sign someone had been there before her, but she wondered if she'd discover more evidence if she became brave enough to venture into the forest. What else she might find…

Focus!

Mariel wiped her face and continued through the haze of dusk and rain, in the opposite direction of the *Mistwitch*. She needed to go back, to collect as many supplies as she could salvage and what little food she'd stored, but if there was even a chance Erran was out there, she had only a narrow window to find him.

She wandered in a haze of mist and exhaustion until she'd outpaced the wreckage. With her hands linked over her head, she stared down the expanse of beach and fought another sob. The last of the sun tickled the edge of the sea's horizon. If she didn't turn back now, she'd be salvaging in the dark.

At least I know which way is west.

Reluctantly, she spun around and hobbled toward the ship. As she drew close, she saw that the angle of the wreck had wedged the bow into the shore itself, and the starboard side was pinned against a rock. The unused oars served as dikes, wedged into the sand. Water was seeping inside, but the stern had shifted high enough to be almost entirely out of the water. For now.

Mariel gripped the highest rung on the ladder she could reach, but when she tugged, the sodden wood snapped in her hands. She tried again with a lower one and climbed, pulling herself over the broken one with an aching burst of strength she'd pay for later. Grunting, she squirmed over the gunwale and dropped onto the stern deck, but the pitched angle sent her rolling down the planks and stairs until she slammed onto the main deck with enough force to knock the breath out of her and bring some of that magical light back.

She staggered to her feet, leaning forward to fight the slant, playing a careful game of balance and physics as she inched sideways toward the hatch. She wrestled with the bolt before throwing back the door, then used it as leverage as she angled sideways down the steps.

Mariel looked around the lower deck. The portside hull had a massive opening, through which she could see the increasingly darkening skies. Her mind assembled all the repairs needed to make the *Mistwitch* seaworthy again, but even if she could make them, she didn't have the tools. The manpower. The strength.

She pushed deeper until she reached the galley, where she'd stored what few supplies she'd brought onto the ship, and laughed in traumatized relief when she saw they were all where she'd left them, and mostly dry. She grabbed an empty crate and filled it with blankets, pillows, food, netting, and candles, stuffing them down so they didn't spill out, and then pulled herself along the wall to fight the slant.

When she reached the beach, she peered down the coastline once more, praying Erran would have washed up in the minutes she had been below deck, but the result was exactly what her sinking heart had expected.

Sighing, she started toward the miracle shack when something large caught her eye, propped against a rock.

Mariel dropped the crate and raced down the shore, laughing and sobbing all at once. She fell to her knees, her hands floating above Erran's pale face, and brushed the torn shirt exposing his chest. She leaned in to listen for breathing and moaned in delirious delight when she both heard and felt it. A palm to his chest revealed a strong heartbeat. *Alive, alive, alive.*

You're one tough little princeling, aren't you? she thought, turning his face back and forth, hoping it was enough to stir him. When it didn't, she slapped him. He agitated with a shrill mumble but didn't wake.

"Erran, you listen to me. You feckin' *listen* to me. You're too heavy for me to carry, and if we don't get off this beach soon, there's no telling what might come for us. I heard...Well I don't ken what I heard, and I don't want to, especially not when darkness falls." She winced in silent apology and slapped him again. His face scrunched in pain, one swollen eye cracking open. "There you are!"

"Mar..." Erran's face crumpled, his head falling back to the side.

"Oh, no. No. Don't you feckin' dare." She moved to slap him again, but one of his hands shot up and gripped her wrist.

"You and violence," he muttered. His head lolled back, and she reached to right it. "Where..."

"Can you stand?"

"I don't..." He pressed a hand to the sand, sagging into the effort. "I don't know."

"I can support you, but I can't carry you. I *need* you to get your head on straight, to help me. Can you do that? Erran, please, can you do that?"

His tongue lashed at his bloody mouth. He closed his eyes and nodded.

Mariel slipped one of his arms over her shoulder, bracing herself against a rock. She waited for him to grip before heaving them both to their feet. He reeled, but she held tight, and he nodded to show he was fine, though he didn't look it. She didn't want to even think about his injuries—or her own—until they were safely inside the mysterious shack.

They hobbled up the beach, struggling through the sand and the uneven weight. Twice he seemed to drift off again, so she pinched him, almost smiling at the curses he muttered at her in defiance. He was alive, *alive,* and together they'd find a way out of their impossible predicament.

"Hold onto this wall," she ordered when they reached the shack. She opened the door, then considered there might come a need to deal with the screech from the forest. Her bow was with the horse she'd borrowed. Her daggers had survived the chaos, still strapped inside her sopping boots, and Erran's sword had somehow stayed with him through all the tumult, but whatever had made that awful sound would require something much bigger.

Mariel pulled one of her daggers anyway and held it aloft as she reached for the handle. The door swung open and slapped the outer wall, then bounced back. She waited, counting to twenty before stepping inside.

It was a single room, two tables in the center. Both tables and floor were stained with blood, though it looked old and worn. Hooks hung from the perimeter of the ceiling, some still holding remnants of animal carcasses. They were so timeworn, they'd turned to leather, and the smell of the place was more old and musty than rotting.

"Let's get you inside," she said and helped Erran up the two steps. She settled him on the floor, against a wall. "Stay put. I have blankets and a waterskin and...I'll be right back."

Mariel raced back to the beach for the crate and reached it just as the last sliver of sunlight inched below the horizon. She carried their meager supplies back like they held the answer to all their problems, and she dropped them just inside the door with a heavy gasp of relief.

"All right, I'm just going to—" She glanced at Erran and saw him slumped over. "No. No, come on." His skin was cool and clammy, his lips bluish. He was shivering hard enough to make his boot buckles tinkle. He was going into shock. She needed to get him out of his wet clothes.

Mariel leaped to her feet to rip the blankets and pillows from the crate and quickly spread them out on the cleanest patch of floor. She crawled back to him and unlaced one boot, then another, gritting as she grappled with the leather suctioned to his feet. They came off with a *thwack*, sending her flailing backward.

She started on his trousers next, cursing at him with every grueling tug. It would be quicker to cut them off, but she had nothing else for him to wear, and they had to preserve everything they had, for it was *all* they had.

His sword belt clattered when she shoved his pants aside and worked on his vest and shirt. The blouse had sustained the worst damage, but it was still functional. It would protect him from the unforgiving sun and save him from burns, if he survived the night.

Panting, she surveyed her work, trying to keep her eyes from lingering in any one place for long. He was nearly naked, except for his skivvies. She had *no* desire to see what was underneath, something she hoped he'd believe when he finally came to his senses and realized what she'd done to save him, but she was terrified it would be this one little oversight that killed him, and he was all she had left.

With a sigh, she pulled those off too, averting her eyes. She lifted his arms and wriggled him until he was on top of the pile of blankets, then patted him dry him with another.

Mariel recalled what her mother had done after Angelika's near drowning. Her little sister had looked an awful lot like Erran: color lost, body wracked with shivers, and unresponsive. Mother had stripped them both to their flesh and twined their bodies together to transfer her warmth. Slowly, Angelika had returned to life, while Mariel and Destin had watched on, through stunned tears.

She stared at a trembling Erran and started peeling off her own wet clothing. When she was done, she climbed in beside him, tugging a blanket tight over them, and curled around him from behind. Her eyes closed, her hand reluctantly sliding over him until it was locked against his muscled belly.

Never in her life had she ever been so close to a man. It might have been the last time she'd be close to anyone.

As the rain hammered the roof, Mariel pressed her face to the space between his shoulders, drew a jittery breath, and finally allowed herself a good, long cry.

Erran had no explanation for why he and Mariel were wrapped, naked, in each other's arms, though there was only one that came to mind.

The night returned in sparks. The wreck. Mariel slapping him—repeatedly. The grueling trek up the beach that had seemed to never end.

His entire body ached with its own remembrances.

Fragmented light highlighted the strange cabin, illuminating dust and blood and other peculiarities he decided to save for later.

Mariel was still asleep. He lifted the blanket to see her hand cupped against his torso. Her breasts were pressed against his back, her knees tucked into his. *We're cuddling?* he wondered but could only guess what that was like. Yesenia had never been the cuddling type, something he'd always found disappointing, though he'd never told her so.

Though he couldn't be entirely sure, he didn't *think* they'd had sex. He could imagine no scenario in which she'd even allow it—or that he'd want it.

Erran carefully peeled her away and crawled out of the makeshift bedroll. His muscles screamed in protest, but he needed more clarity than his awkward wake-up had provided.

The shelter wasn't much, but it would keep them shielded from the elements, and that was all it really needed to do. *Make shelter* was the first lesson he'd learned in training for emergencies. *Find water* was the second.

Loosely, he remembered his boots being removed with excessive force. His clothes. Sometime in the night, she'd hung them all, hers included, but even the thought of trying to dress himself was overwhelming. He was too tired just yet to do more than wander.

He rifled through the half-spilled crate of necessities she'd pilfered from the ship, relieved to see she'd grabbed the dried meat, what little there was. Three waterskins too, mostly full. It would buy them time to find a place to fill them.

Reminded of his complete nakedness, he reached for one of the two blankets lying over Mariel and wrapped one around himself. She slept on, and he let her. If not for her, he wouldn't even be alive, and though he hadn't yet put together every piece of the prior evening, he understood she'd borne the brunt of it.

Erran opened the door and stepped into the glow of the morning sun. He closed his eyes, leaning against the frame for support, and took in the warmth before the full weight of reality set in.

The sun was behind him, opposite the sea. Earth's compass.

The high tide lapped nearly to the edge of the forest floor. Boards and other detritus floated in and out on the current. Still wedged against a cluster of rocks was Mariel's ship, its mast split, hull exposed. There'd be no fixing her, not without a lot of help.

And there'd be no help, because no one knew they were there. Samuel only knew he'd gone after Mariel, but neither one of them had known about the ship when they'd parted. Word would soon spread though, about the runaway woman and the steward's son. It was only a matter of time before everyone assumed them dead.

"It's irreparable," Mariel said, wrapped in the other blanket as she pulled up beside him. Her hair was plastered to one side of her head, a mess of briny tangles. "Though I ken that's stating the obvious."

Erran nodded, too tired for the laugh building in his tender belly. "Aye, I ken it is."

"Are you all right?" She sounded like she couldn't land on whether she was concerned for him or ready to let the sea finish its job.

"My head." He winced when his hand touched the knot forming along the back of his skull. "I'll live."

"Despite all my efforts to kill you," she whispered.

Erran was too bone-tired to laugh. He assessed the needs ahead of them. Shelter was secured. Water was next and then fire, but it wouldn't be long before they ran out of food. They couldn't waste a minute. "I want…I *need* to say thank you, Mariel. You could have solved what to me feels like a big problem in your life by letting me die. Not only did you not, but you cared for me, and I know it couldn't have been easy for you."

She sighed deeply. "Erran—"

"Nay," he said, turning toward her. "Let me finish. I owe you a debt I'll never be able to repay, but I intend to try, by keeping us alive until someone comes along and finds us. I've been trained for this, though I never thought I'd need the lesson." He breathed deep. "But one thing that has naught to do with this debt is the explanation you owe me. We'll get our water, fire, and hopefully find some food to last us, but after that, you're going to tell me *exactly* what you were doing at Banner's. And then you're going to explain to me why you told those guards you were the Flame, and why they believed you."

EIGHT
FECK-ALL ISLAND

On their first full day on Feck-All Island—as Erran had grumpily named it, after stepping into a nest of spiders and nearly breaking his ankle trying to dance away—they found the river and the well.

Mariel noted the sun's position, in the center of the sky, which meant they'd been hiking for close to an hour through dense brush and a scarcely marked path. Erran had had the forethought to mark their route by carving small arrows into trees every few meters. The arrows pointed in the direction of their return, so they wouldn't get lost.

They might have reached the river faster, but Erran was quick with the reminders that longevity and sustainability were their goals, not speed. Until they had their food and water sources, they had to assume their resources were finite, as was their stamina.

The river was at least thirty feet wide, and from the surface, it appeared to be about half as deep. Upriver was a series of waterfalls, carved through the rocky cliffs.

"A longer walk than I'd like for filling our skins, but at least we have water." Erran stood on the banks, hands on his hips as he surveyed the river. He knelt and scooped a handful, giving it a tentative slurp. "No heavy taste of minerals. We have no pot to boil with, but I ken it's safe enough."

But Mariel was more curious about the well. "Wells don't build themselves."

He turned, one brow slanted. "Aye? They don't?"

"Shut it," she hissed, shaking her head. "This is now the second piece of considerable evidence we've seen that men come here, often enough to build a curing shed and a well."

Erran turned back toward the river. "Not that often, judging from the condition of our shed. Those carcasses are a year old. More. The dust hasn't been disturbed in at least that long."

"Aye, but it's no minor effort to build a well. You have to excavate, dam—"

"I know how to build a well, Mariel."

She scoffed. "Have you built many wells, Erran?"

He said nothing, which was all the answer she needed.

"Well, I have. It's nay a wee amount of labor. And I wouldn't waste the time building one if I wasn't going to use it."

"When?"

"Excuse me?"

"When did you build wells?"

Mariel took great offense from the skepticism she heard in his mocking tone. "Every time I built a well, it was for a family in need. That's what community really is, Erran. Jumping in to help others, putting them above yourself."

Her words punched a small crack in his peevish demeanor. "What's your point then?"

She approached, lingering a few feet behind him. "The curing shed might be neglected, but this well tells me there could be other discoveries ahead. Better ones."

"Such as?"

"Well, I don't know, but don't you want to find out?" Mariel countered, exasperated with how absurdly thickheaded he was acting.

He reached into the makeshift satchel he'd fashioned from some sack cloth they'd found behind the shed, and he handed her one of the skins. "Let's get these filled, find some food, and head back. We can do more tomorrow."

Mariel snatched the skin from him and stepped in beside him. "Why are you dismissing what I'm saying?"

Erran rolled his lips in with a quick raise of his eyes. "Suppositions are interesting thought experiments, but in an *actual* survival situation, you need sureties. You're playing a game of odds against a foe you cannot beat but might learn to cohabitate with, if you're smart. Even if you're right, we'd spend more energy chasing your ghosts than we can afford, when all we've collected is..." He cast a melodramatic and unnecessary glance into his bag. They both knew what was in there. "A bit of fennel. Oh, and look. *More* fennel."

"And what do you know about survival situations, Errandil, except what Daddy taught you in your Everything Gets Handed to Me Because I Was Born First and Have a Cock training?"

His eyes rolled all the way toward the sky. "The mouth on you is something else. Anyone ever tell you that?"

"I thought foul women were to your taste?"

Erran tilted his head. "As much as lies and deception are to yours, I ken."

Mariel closed her eyes to cool her blood. They had no choice but to coexist, and it would be smoother if they could do so peacefully. "I *have* been in survival situations. I don't refute your point about conserving energy, but hear me out. If men took the time to build a sturdy water source, instead of just filling skins in a river like we planned to, there *will* be more conveniences. Maybe even a food supply. Someone either lived here or came here frequently. There'll be signs of it, if we keep going."

He threaded an exhausted breath through his nose. "I want to be back before the sun reads three in the afternoon. There's another storm brewing, and I don't want to be stranded in this forest when it hits."

Mariel brightened. "Aye, we'll just go a bit farther and then we'll turn back."

"I mean it. I feel like…like we're being watched, and not by people." A clench on the end of his words revealed his error. He undoubtedly thought she'd ascribe weakness to them, and after his little animated speech about survival training, it was clear he wanted her to revel in his masculinity. "Never mind. Forget I said that."

"Nay, I feel it too. Whatever they are, they're dangerous," she said. It had started the moment they'd pushed beyond the boundaries of their known world, the sensation of hidden eyes stalking their movements. Beasts sizing them up for later. She remembered the crazed squeal she'd heard from the beach, and she knew she never, ever wanted to come face-to-face with whatever foul creature had made it.

They filled their skins in silence and continued on in the same fashion. She picked scattered handfuls of dandelions, adding them to Erran's bag, and also chicory root. None of it was what they really needed, but it would help make the dried meat stretch until they had a fresh source.

She wondered what everyone back in Whitecliffe was thinking about their disappearance. Both Erran and Mariel would have been declared missing already, but unless Banner or his men had identified her personally, it was unlikely anyone would tie her to the chase. Erran was easier to recognize, but he must have done a fair job hiding because she'd never sensed, even once, that she and the Perevil siblings had been followed. Unless the guards had gotten a solid look at him before he'd leaped into the sea after her, it was unlikely anyone had tied him to the scene either.

Remy and Augustine *might* guess she'd gone for the *Mistwitch*, but who would they tell? Who *could* they tell without revealing more than they should?

That was if they'd even made it to safety. She prayed with all her heart that they had.

And Destin...What would become of him, if she never made it home? Jails were incongruously lawless places. They could hold a man as long as they wanted, unless strong evidence compelled them to release him or a powerful man came to speak for him. There was no one or way to produce this evidence, now that she'd botched the auction heist. And there was certainly no one to speak for him. Steward Rutland had made his position on the matter quite clear.

She had no choice but to accept she was powerless about any of it.

"Mariel."

She shifted from her haze and followed where Erran was pointing. A fig tree, just off the path.

Mariel broke into a giddy smile and bounded toward it. Erran was slower, still aching from his injuries, but together they filled his makeshift bag with as many figs as it could hold.

"You were right to push us farther," he said when the sack was nearly overflowing. He adjusted it higher on his shoulder. "Can we turn back now?"

She knew in her heart there was more to be discovered, but they had all the time in the world to explore. Nodding, she leaned against the tree, stretching her back, when a sharp glint caught her notice. "What's...What is *that*?"

He turned toward where she was looking. His eyes narrowed. "I...Stay here."

"Don't ken I will," she muttered and followed him through the brush toward where she could have *sworn* she'd seen a window.

Erran thrashed at the stalks and stems to forge a path. Some smacked her in the face on the recoil, but she stayed close at his back until the dense flora made way for an open area. At the center stood a cabin, larger and more impressive than the shed near the shore. A large fire pit, surrounded by logs for seating, had been dug into the ground about twenty paces from the door. There was no sign of recent use, and even the ash was mostly blown away, but it was well-built.

She hadn't imagined the windows. On the front alone there were three, one on the left side of the door and two to the right of it. Vines grew up and around them, and even through a small hole in the pane of one.

It had the same air of abandonment as their first shelter, but that didn't mean it was.

"Well, look at that," he said, whistling. "Should we knock?"

Mariel laughed. "And if someone answers?"

"We pray they're friendly." He patted his sword. "And if not, there's two of us. Aye, I know you can fight too. No need to play demure."

"I would never denigrate my own Guardians-given abilities," she said, scoffing. Nodding at her boots, at the daggers strapped just under the leather, she asked, "Should I?"

Erran shook his head. "We draw nothing unless we must." He approached the door slowly, one hand cautioning Mariel to keep some distance. The first knock sent birds scattering deeper into the forest. The second pushed the door open with a creaky swing.

He glanced back and held her gaze a moment before stepping inside. "There's no one here. You can come in."

If the shed had been a blessing, the cabin was a damned miracle. It was a single room as well but twice as large, and it had been given far better care. There was a table with three chairs, a stove with a hanging pot, and some frying pans resting on the ashes underneath. Along the windowsills was a handful of lanterns, coated in dust. In the corner was a raised cot, though there were no blankets, and next to it, evidence of two others that had broken and were no longer serviceable, their canvas and rods propped in the corner. A cloudy mirror hung cockeyed on the far wall, a metal basin beneath it.

Mariel approached the table and found a map pinned down by rocks. She traced her fingers over the names, faded but readable. Rushwood. Everleigh Pike. Whitechurch. All towns in the Easterlands.

Erran drew up beside her and leaned over the table. "The Easterlands. Interesting," he said.

"Aye." Mariel nodded. "But useless. Why couldn't it be a map of Feck-All Island?"

He chuckled. "The Guardians want us to work for our supper, I suppose. Hey, what's that over there?"

They spent the next few minutes going through crates and bags left by the prior occupant. Bandages, antiseptic, and a needle and thread were among their findings. Every discovery they'd show each other, like gleeful children uncovering some new wonder.

"You ken if we push farther into this forest, we might find a whole keep?" Erran jested as their exploration ended.

"There is such a thing as turning back while you're still ahead," she teased back. "I wonder when the owner might return."

"A problem for another day. We solved most of ours in just a few hours. An unexpectedly fortuitous trek."

He was right. It was a problem for another day. They could have just as easily slept under the rain, at the mercy of whatever beasts prowled the night, but fortune had smiled their way. Only a fool would forsake the gifts the day had brought.

"Oh, and I broke off some flint from the riverbed." He dug into his pocket to show her. "For fire."

She frowned. "I usually rub sticks together."

"If that's how you want to start your fires, go ahead. I'll take the easier way." He sighed. "I suppose we should go back and grab our things? Move camp here?"

Mariel nodded, unsure where the creeping dread had come from. They had food, better shelter, an endless water source…a way to prepare meals and a pit perfect for a large, warming fire. The circumstances could not be better, after what they'd endured.

So why could she not shake the sense something very wrong was happening?

It's the shock, she decided. *You wrecked your ship and washed up on an island. Your nerves are shot. Of course you're anxious.*

"This firepit may be our greatest discovery yet. Did you see how it was reinforced on the sides, for containment? We can safely build a fire big enough to send smoke signals to anyone passing nearby."

"Aye," she said distantly, following him down the steps and into the warm afternoon. "Let's be quick about getting back, Erran."

His hand brushed the middle of her back. "You were right," he said for the second time. "And in concession to my wrongness, rare as it is, I'll cook us up the most delicious fennel stew tonight. Might even throw some dandelions in there, if I'm feeling saucy."

Mariel's expression cracked, though the smile she offered wasn't compatible with the burning in her chest, urging her to get to the shed and back as quickly as possible. She'd never had the magic touch like Destin had, but her instincts had kept her alive through some truly heinous situations, and she wasn't going to start ignoring them now. "How could I refuse such a tantalizing offer from a man who has probably never prepared a single meal in his life?"

The walk back to the shed was quicker. It wasn't just the markings making for a straightforward route, or their confidence in the destination. There was a lightness between them that hadn't been possible before. Erran had actually seen Mariel's smile—her *real* smile, not the practiced one she believed she'd perfected for him and his family—and it made him want to see it more often.

While she collected their few belongings from the shed, Erran wandered down to the *Mistwitch*. She looked no worse than she had before, though clearly no better either. But if any of their fires worked, the vessel would be the first thing a rescuer would see, and they would need to know where to find them.

Erran withdrew the dagger he'd borrowed from Mariel and approached the part of the hull facing the coast. The hole was almost bigger than what remained, but there was plenty of room to carve *WENT INLAND E+ M* on the side, in the largest letters he could manage before his sore arm gave out.

He hadn't reviewed all the ways he'd been battered in the wreck, but there were plenty of wounds to assess. No breaks, mercifully, which meant he'd be back to form within a day or two. It was mostly bruises, one bleeding right into another, no clear beginning or end. But there were a couple of gashes that would need a cleaning if he wanted to avoid infection. The antiseptic had been one of their more fortunate finds in the cabin.

Mariel was waiting for him outside the shed, her arms stretched around the broad crate. He grinned to himself and went to relieve her, but the sharply offended look she shot back had him thinking better of it.

"I could at least take the blankets so it's not so overflowing," he said, but she rolled her eyes.

"You could," she agreed and sauntered ahead of him. Her ass had a light sway to it, full of attitude, and the urge to charge up behind her and toss her over his shoulder like a savage had him questioning whether he'd perhaps sustained a concussion without realizing so.

"Tomorrow I'll try my hand at fishing," Erran said as they passed their first marked tree. "Not much work to fashion a spear, and I saw a few fish pooling in the low tide."

"Might even be able to rig a pole together. There's netting, and I'll bet we could break up some metal, make a lure. The broken cot pieces looked promising."

"You sound like you know this from experience." He glanced her way to see her reaction, which was often less guarded than her words.

"I've made a few in my time," she said with a noncommittal shrug. "There were years Destin and I didn't have a consistent home. Even when we did, there was no food."

"Where were your parents?"

"Dead. Been on our own since I was twelve."

Erran struggled to understand the implication of her words. "You had no adults looking after you after the age of twelve?"

"Not really. Destin was seventeen and still two years from maturity, so the law wouldn't let him take on our father's property," she answered, her tone and step still as casual as before. "My friend Remy, the one you saw in Mistgrave, his father stepped up for a spell, but then he was gone too. It was just the four of us. That's why...he's so important to me. He's family."

"Who was the fourth?"

Mariel's easiness withdrew some. "Remy's sister."

Erran remembered how close the man, Remy, had seemed to his mother's seamstress. He couldn't quite remember her name, but she'd been embedded in their household for several years, and his mother was fond of her. If it was a coincidence, it was a substantial one.

He decided their unspoken truce wasn't the time to ask. Mariel would return to loathing him soon enough. He still had to ask her about Banner anyway, so he might as well store his questions for when the peace had subsided.

"I'm sorry," he said unhelpfully, wishing there *were* something better to offer her.

"Wasn't your fault. You were just a bairn then too."

It was a strange thing to say. Of course it hadn't been his fault, but her words didn't seem accidentally chosen. "Mariel, when I...followed you..." *Careful.* "What I really intended to do was ride to the jail and take care of matters with your brother."

Mariel bucked forward. Her expression waffled somewhere between distrust and disbelief. "And betray your father?"

"I don't see it as a betrayal. If Sessaly had been locked up in error, he wouldn't have let her stay a moment longer than she had to."

She snorted. "The only thing Sessaly is guilty of is chin-wagging, and she's fortunate it's not a crime."

He chuckled. "Aye, or we'd never see her again, least not as a free woman."

"Why *is* she like that? Does no one ever think to restrain her?"

"The few times I tried to intervene didn't go so well for me." He shook his head. "It's my father's doing. He spoils her too much. Thinks she's harmless and won't let any of us disavow him of this grievous falsehood. Say even a word about it and he'll turn on you faster than a hurricane."

Mariel got quiet. "You were really going to the jail? You're not making it up?"

"I thought you might head there, so I followed you, but then you…" He trailed off, worried about veering too close to the conversation that had to happen, but not just then. "Anyway, I—" He froze…tugged on Mariel to do the same. She stared at him in confusion, but he cocked his head and pointed at his ear, to listen.

It was distant at first, but then it seemed as if the ground had erupted in a muted tremble.

"Is…" Mariel's eyes slowly widened. Her chest rose and fell in sharp waves. She turned her head slowly behind them and screamed, "RUN!"

A shrill whine rang through the air, set to more thundering hooves. Erran bolted after Mariel, ignoring every scream and ache his body sang in protest.

The sound came up in a rush and Erran pushed Mariel to go faster, but she was practically waddle-running from the position of the crate.

"Drop it! We can come back for it!" he shouted.

"*No*, it has our *meat*!" Mariel dodged a root, leaping through the air and landing smoothly. "Our *only* meat!"

"I'll get more!"

"Until you get more, it's all we have!"

"Mariel, it's right up on us!"

"Erran, I swear on everything—" Mariel went sprawling over a different root, the crate miraculously landing perfectly upright, aside from some blanket spillage. She, on the other hand, immediately gripped her ankle as she failed to stand.

"Fecking hell," Erran muttered, scooping her off the ground and flinging her over his back. He almost left the crate, but something compelled him to grab it. The pause gave the beast hunting them a chance to narrow the distance, and he could almost feel the hot, stinking breaths on his ass, the spittle of hunger soon to be sated.

Erran pushed his pace, wheezing from the enduring pain. It seemed every tree and bush was moving, swaying in response to the beast's authority. He'd gotten the briefest glance of it when he'd lifted Mariel, its curved tusks and elongated snout more than enough for him to know they'd be speared before he could even draw his sword.

Mariel didn't fight him at all, more evidence of her survival skills. Upside down, she wrapped her arms around his waist from behind, pushing short, tight breaths in and out.

Limbs battered his face, and thorns he didn't have the time or energy to avoid sliced his ankles. He grunted, shifting Mariel higher on his back, and called on his reserves to give him the last bit of strength he needed to get them to the cabin.

"Erran…Erran, let me down. We'll go faster," Mariel said through her panting, but he heard in her voice she didn't mean it, that she was just as terrified of the fate awaiting them if he missed another step.

"It is tempting to offer you as a sacrifice," he muttered through his teeth, gasping when they left the forest and entered the clearing. He bolted the rest of the way and slammed through the open door with enough force to send him and her both sprawling across the floor. The crate tumbled, losing its contents on its way to slamming into the table leg.

Mariel yelped and hissed through her teeth. Erran climbed to his feet and raced to the door, but the beast had stopped at the forest line. Its red eyes peered from between the brush, its nostrils flaring in a sinister taunt. *Come play.*

"What are you...Erran..." Thumping sounded behind him as Mariel hobbled his way. "Close the damn door!"

"He'll come no closer," Erran said distantly. The boar—or whatever it was, as the thing was bigger than any boar he'd ever seen, by far—knew better somehow. It'd seen men there before. "He's watched men hunt. Thinks we have the same tools."

"Or he's playing with us," she replied, gripping the other side of the doorframe for balance. She had one leg coiled up. "If he was afraid, he'd run."

"He's not afraid. He's just waiting to see what we'll do."

"Well, give me your feckin' sword, and I'll show him!"

Erran scoffed at her, only realizing she was looking for a fight after her response, when she made a disgusted sound she'd been clearly waiting to use.

"Don't think I have it in me?" Mariel asked in challenge. Pain etched the corners of her eyes, half-squinted as she balanced one foot.

"Do I think you're foolish enough to charge out there like a loon and swing metal around, praying it lands somewhere useful?" He shook his head. "Aye, I ken you have *that* in you."

Mariel reached for his sword belt and worked to wrench it free from its scabbard. Erran clamped a hand over hers and waited for her futile struggle to end. Giving up, she swung around to face him with a caustic glare that was so full of hatred, it startled him.

"Are you too scared of the thing to realize he could feed us for weeks?" Her tone practically screeched. "If you can't summon the courage, Errandil, at least let me."

"Enticing as it might be at this moment to watch him flatten you with his hooves and feast upon your foul mouth until it can spew its acid no longer, I might regret letting him slaughter you in the morning." He dragged her back inside and slammed the door.

Erran released her near the table, so she had something to balance herself, and stormed to the basket where they'd found the bandages and antiseptic.

"Sit," he ordered, his hands shaking as he dug for what he needed. He found it, turned back, and saw her swaying on one foot, her arms crossed and a petulant scowl on her face. "Mariel, sit the feck down and let me wrap this before you make it worse."

With her eyes locked on his as if she could sear him alive, she hobbled dramatically toward the chair before flopping onto it. She regarded him with fluttery blinks, her nose flaring, holding fast to her acerbic smile.

Erran had never in his life been so exasperated by anyone.

He closed his eyes and breathed deep before dropping to his knees in front of her.

"Not afraid of the boar coming in to join us for some of your fennel stew?" she said, sounding almost flirtatious. Her spittle sprayed his forehead.

"More afraid he'd respectfully decline, seeing how full he'd be after ripping you apart." He tore off a length of cloth in his teeth and lifted her leg by the calf. Her ankle had turned a purplish hue and was already swelling. "If you'd have just dropped the damn basket—"

"You don't want me to hunt him, aye, but you're perfectly fine with him eating our dried meat?"

Erran balanced her leg with one hand and wrapped with the other, annoyed with himself for how gingerly he was being with her even as she was once again using insults to make him feel like less of a man. "Do you really think boars eat dried meat?"

"And why not?"

"For the same reason they wouldn't eat a rotted carcass, Mariel. Their instincts would tell them it's not fresh and therefore not safe! And from the scent of it, the dried meat is probably boar, aye? So you ken *this* boar is just magically the only cannibal boar alive?" He cinched the first wrap, tighter than was necessary.

Her eyes closed briefly, but she voiced no complaint.

"Things I'd expect you to have learned, from all your outlawing."

"Outlawing? Is that even a word? Or are highborns so used to everyone following what they say that you're just inventing them now?" Mariel's expression was curled in disgust, but her hands gripped the chair so tightly, her knuckles had gone bone white. "A desperate enough beast will eat *anything*. That's what I learned all those years in the forests of Mistgrave, wondering where my next meal would come from."

"Your parents," he said through gritted teeth, tightening another length of cloth, "should have had a plan for you if something happened to them. That's naught to do with me."

"What *privilege* drips from the tongue of a boy who thinks everyone has access to the same advantages. A plan, you say? And what would such a plan entail, when most of the adults we knew were dead or dying from scurvy, and our land was being stolen faster than we could build upon it?"

"You say stolen, but the *law* forbids felons from owning land in the Southerlands."

"The law? You mean your father?"

"I mean the law, Mariel." He tied another strip.

"They're the same, and even you're not stupid enough to be blind to it. Who benefits from the land being taken? Men like your father. Who determines what's a crime and what is not? The men who work for him. Ah, what a pretty picture this paints, don't you think, Errandil?"

Heat engulfed his face, burning the backs of his eyes, which watered from anger. His mouth puckered in rage he could barely suppress, but he had to. He had to. No matter how she goaded him, he could not let her see him like that. She was still his wife, at least until they returned home and he secured the annulment he should have demanded months ago. "You take the cot tonight. I'll take the floor."

"I'll nay argue with that," Mariel muttered. "And we may even keep warm, since we held onto the crate with the blankets."

Erran restrained himself, giving her ankle a light tap instead of the squeeze he felt like offering. "Stay off of it." He cast a sigh and a glance at the door, which was drumming open and closed in the building wind. "We'll have to keep watch."

"Watch?" She lowered her ankle to the floor, delicately resting her heel there.

"The door doesn't latch. I could slide the table over, but there's not much weight to it. Nothing else in here would do." He gathered up the spillage from the crate and dug out the bag of meat, then tossed it to Mariel. "I'll take the first."

She looked almost sad as she eyed the bag in her hands. It faded abruptly. "Why? Because you're a man?"

He snorted. "Nay, Mariel. Because I'm neither hungry nor tired anymore, and if I have to spend one more minute in here with you, I'll go feral myself."

"What about the storm?"

"I'm not afraid of a little rain." Erran snatched one of the blankets from the crate and left before she could sling another cutting insult. He draped it over a log and checked to ensure the flint was still in his pocket after their near catastrophe.

Everything she'd said was taking up far too much space in his thoughts, making him angry all over again, so instead he searched for the sticks he'd need to kindle a fire, his eyes always toward the spot where the beast had watched them. There were still a few logs stacked against the side of the cabin from whoever had occupied it last. If they were there much longer, they'd need to chop more.

As he carried his bundle back, an idea came to him. It pissed him off that he was still thinking of *her*, but he still lifted the branch from the gloaming and holding it against his leg in measurement.

Erran arranged the logs and kindling, then used the flint to spark a flame on the edge of the cloth he'd brought out as a fire starter. It flickered and caught on fast, and he quickly dropped it on top of the arranged twigs. Within minutes, it had enough life that he could settle onto the log and relax.

Relax. He wanted to laugh. Even if he wasn't stranded on an island no one knew he was on, there'd be no relaxing when Mariel Ashdown was there to remind him of how fast she could go from warm and fun to a glacier.

He still hadn't worked up the courage to push for the conversation he'd warned her was coming. But demanding answers at this point would only fill in holes, confirming the suspicions her visit to Banner had earthed. He just needed to hear *her* say it. And he needed to know why.

With a sigh, he laid his sword on the log next to him for ease of draw. He extracted her dagger and whittled the branch he'd brought back with him, clearing his mind and heart of a day that had first lifted him but then buried him in the earth.

It was nearly dawn before Mariel finally succumbed to exhaustion. Her thoughts had nagged her into restlessness, sending her conscience into a confused tailspin.

Erran was a figurehead of everything she'd fought against for ten years. He was also a man who had been nothing but kind to her, no matter what profanities or bitterness she'd lobbed at him—a man who had saved her when leaving her behind would have been a guarantee of his own safety and then, as she'd accosted him, had calmly wrapped her ankle because even in his own anger, he could still do what needed to be done.

She used to be capable of such a thing. Before she'd become a Rutland.

When she awoke, not much later, exhausted and swollen, Erran still hadn't come in to rest.

But beside her on the cot was a long branch, carved into a crutch.

NINE
AYE OR NAY

Two days later, the dried meat was spent.

They'd tried to make it stretch. Erran had even offered to halve his own portions, to give Mariel some of her vigor back, but she'd refused. With her injury, he was spending so much more energy than she was. Other than some light gathering by the cabin and throwing together bitter stews from what little they'd collected, she mostly slept. She said nothing beyond what was necessary, and neither did he.

He tidied the cabin and reached for the spear he'd whittled the day before. It might not have been enough against the monstrous boars, but it would hold its own for what he intended.

Erran cleared his throat before approaching the cot, to give her a small warning he was about to speak. Mariel lay facing the wall, but she wasn't asleep. He could always tell because at rest, she seemed actually at peace instead of a tangle of tension. "I'm going to try my hand at fishing. I may be gone awhile."

"Aye," she said evenly. It was the same tone from her all the time anymore. She'd either lost her fight or was storing it up, but he feared more that she was succumbing to the hopelessness his father had warned him about; all men were susceptible to it, when the odds of survival were less than favorable. He'd take her screaming over her malaise any day.

"I've fished this way before. If those snook or seatrout are still hanging about in the tidal pools, I should fare well."

She shifted under the blanket but didn't turn. "All right."

"I'll take the crate."

Mariel nodded.

"You know where to find me, but I recommend staying off the ankle a little longer. I'll be back while there's still light."

"Aye."

Erran pressed his mouth tight. She didn't want to talk. Nor did he, but he would try again later, just the same. They had only each other.

"I'll be back then. There's still a bit of stew left, if you're hungry. Plenty of figs too."

Erran paused, knowing she'd only answer with silence, and when she did, he took the spear and headed for the beach.

Mariel waited until Erran left. She swung her swollen leg over the side of the cot and sat there for a long time before reaching for his conciliatory crutch.

She hobbled to the table and dropped onto a chair. It was another moment before she reached for her boot and slipped it over her good foot. It would be a while before her sprained ankle would fit into anything but Erran's wraps.

The past two nights, she'd offered to take boar watch and tend the signal fire that had so far produced nothing, but Erran wouldn't hear of it. She tried to tell him she wasn't sleeping anyway, but those words, like so many others, refused to come. All the things she wanted to say remained unspoken, apologies and explanations unformed.

He was an easy outlet for her anger, but he wasn't the source. Even her utter contempt for his father couldn't hold a candle to the disgust she felt for her own self—her own failures, which she numerated again and again on her sleepless nights.

In her darkest moments, she accepted they would die there.

But sometimes…Sometimes she recalled the small but important moments when they'd worked together. They made a good team. His strengths balanced her weaknesses, and the reverse was also true.

Apologizing might be more than she could muster, but if he was going to spend the day trying to provide for them, she could do the same.

She locked the crutch he'd made her under her left arm. It wasn't the most elegant solution, but without it, she'd be even more useless.

Never in her life had she used such a word to describe herself.

Mariel grabbed Erran's makeshift satchel, from where it hung on a loose nail by the door, and ambled out into the bright, blinding morning. She maneuvered sideways down the steps. The smoky remnants of the night's fire burned her nose, but it also made her wonder how Erran's nights had been. He couldn't be sleeping either. Sometimes he'd catch small naps on the floor, but it could not have been enough to make up for what he'd been losing.

They'd explored south of the cabin, in the stretch between their encampment and the shore, and west, but not east or north. She randomly chose east and limped carefully into the forest in search of anything she recognized as edible.

Mariel picked more fennel and dandelions, gagging with every tug; if she survived the ordeal, she'd never eat either ever again. She found a lone lagerberry bush she robbed of its entire contents, stuffing a handful in her mouth before continuing.

The world shook, and she stumbled into a tree. The red eyes of a boar pinned her there. She was too injured to outrun it, and by the time she drew her dagger, those long, curving horns would have her impaled. But this creature, unlike the ones she'd heard shrieking in the forest, seemed more curious than dangerous.

Mariel closed her eyes and whispered a brief prayer. When she opened them, the boar was gone.

She waited for the panic to subside and kept straight on, marking arrows on trees as she went. When the brush grew denser, weaving together to prevent smooth ingress, she turned back. That was when she spotted the mushrooms.

When she and her siblings were children, their mother had taught them all about how to spot poisonous toadstools. The ones in the kingdom had one of three defining characteristics; they either had pale spots lining the cap, uneven truffling, or the tiniest spikes along the stem, like the stinging barbs of nettles.

A close examination revealed the cluster had none of these. They were all a boring, dull brown, with no other features to note. She considered the possibility the island might have different species than the realm proper, but one of the core learnings her mother had impressed upon her was that a poisonous plant always had *some* trait meant to deter predators from consuming it.

Mariel broke one off and nibbled the tiniest spot off the edge. She waited a few minutes, and when no ill effects kicked in, she took another bite and then another, eventually finishing the entire mushroom.

Still alive. And slightly less hungry.

She balanced on her crutch and her good leg. Her knee wobbled, weak and exhausted like the rest of her, but it held long enough for her to clear the entire patch and load it into her slinged bag.

By the time she finished, sweat was pouring off her. Her vision wavered with the heat as well, so she continued heading back, allowing herself another mushroom along the way. The surrounding leaves shimmered, some taking on more hues of blue than she was aware even existed. Some reached out to grab her, and she reached back, gasping in delight when one seemed to actually hold her hand. A mushroom, holding her hand!

Mariel was full-on grinning and giggling by the time she returned, delirious with joy from imagining Erran's face when he returned to find she'd roasted up a delicious—and surprisingly congenial!—lunch for them.

Erran's optimism had only earned him two seatrout, despite the hours he'd toiled in the sun.

He'd waited through three changes of the tide before calling it. Though he'd been wishing for a more plentiful run, confirming there *was* fish and he *could* spear them gave him hope for the future. The smoke signal might or might not call a passing ship, as few traveled too close to the islands intentionally, and while there was a chance the men who had built the structures would come back, there was no telling when. They needed the ability to sustain themselves indefinitely, and he was beginning to see it was possible.

On the way back, he refilled his waterskin. He lingered long enough to rehydrate and wonder if Mariel had moved from the cot at all.

She would when she saw the delectable dinner ahead of them. The fennel would be a nice seasoning for the fish.

When he reached the clearing, the sight of Mariel sitting cross-legged on the ground stopped him dead. She was playing with a pile of mushrooms. Counting them…tossing and catching them.

Talking to them.

Erran couldn't make sense of what he was seeing.

"Erran!" she cried, failing a clumsy leap forward and falling sideways. "I…I was going to…Wow, did you see that? Did you see the way it…the *colors*?"

He was speechless. Everything he attempted to say never formed. But he knew right away what was happening. Mariel had foraged hallucinogenic mushrooms, and Guardians knew how many she'd consumed.

Erran set the crate by the door and sank onto a log near her. "Mariel, how many of those did you eat?"

"Eat?" Mariel craned her neck toward him, horrified. "They're my friends. You don't eat your friends. It's true, some of them found their way to my belly, but they *wanted* to go there. They told me. They…"

"All right." He leaned down to scoop the mushrooms, and she practically clobbered him. "Mariel, I'm just bringing them inside."

"But they want to be out *here*! Do you not feel the leaves? The way the forest speaks and holds everything dear and…Even the boars know not to upset them. The boars are afraid of them, and they're afraid of us, my friends told me."

"Right." Erran steadied himself, imagining the long hours ahead. He sighed. "Well, tell your *friends* there's another storm coming. Wouldn't they…" He braced for the inanity of what he was about to say. "Be happier and warmer inside when it comes?"

Mariel lit up, her eyes and mouth widening in tandem. She glanced between the fungi and him. He was glad he couldn't read whatever strange little thoughts were brewing in her mind. "Aye. Aye, they *would* prefer that. You are so wickedly smart and kind, and they would very much like to be your friend too."

"Aye," he muttered and finished picking up the mushrooms. He dropped them in with the fish and then went to gather her as well. He'd have to wait until she was sleeping to throw her "friends" out. "Nay," he said when she tried to stand without her crutch, her tongue between her teeth and her hands straight out like she was about to walk a tightrope. "*Nay*, Mariel."

"I want to show my friends—"

"I've spoken to your friends, and they would like you to listen to me." *For once.*

"Oh." Mariel's mouth puckered, her brows knitting. "Oh, I see. I wouldn't want to disappoint them after all the fun we've had today."

"That would be a travesty," he mumbled as he scooped her up and into his arms. He bent to grab the crutch and saw she'd used it to draw some nonsensical loops and lines in the sandy dirt. "They also suggested you all take a nice nap before supper."

"Will they nap with me?"

Erran nudged the door open. He laid her atop the cot. "They said they would."

She flashed her fingers, curling them into her palms. "Bring them."

It's like dealing with a child, he thought, shaking his head in bewilderment as he entertained her delusions. But there was no way he was letting her consume more. "They said they would like to sleep on the floor. They, ah, prefer the ground."

"Of course they do. Of course, that makes perfect sense. They like the dark." Mariel wiped her smile onto the pillow as she settled in. "How thoughtful of you to listen to them."

A few hours. Just a few hours and she'll be back to ignoring me or cursing me.

Erran pulled a chair across the floor and placed it next to her cot. He'd been excited for a nap, but waking to find her climbing a tree or challenging boars to fistfights was not on his list of things he was prepared to deal with.

"Just rest," he said, suppressing a yawn.

A delectable scent roused Mariel from a series of the most bizarre dreams she'd ever had. In them, she was dancing on top of the ocean with her brother, Destin, climbing the waves like steps. Then it was Augustine, who faded to Remy. Erran was last, sweeping her across the waves with the same effortless finesse he'd used on the sails. Observing them was an endless sea of boars, all wearing beautiful lace dresses and bonnets.

Rain battered the roof and windows. She sat up, worried about everything still outside, but Erran would have taken care of it already.

A familiar sizzle made her heart skip. Meat cooking on a pan. Fish. He'd fished today and brought some back, and oh, how she couldn't wait to shove it all down her gullet.

"Still having conversations with your new friends?" Erran asked, turning just his head as he flipped the fish on the iron pan with a stick.

"Friends?" Mariel rubbed her head, heavy with the remnants of a headache. "What…" The afternoon filtered in. She'd gathered a ton of mushrooms, even eaten a few, and she'd…

Hallucinated. That was what she'd done.

"Oh, Guardians." She moaned, flopping back, her arms crossed over her face. "Whatever I said or did when…I'm sorry. I don't know…"

"Never seen you so happy," he said. "Maybe you should eat them more often."

"Ha ha," she quipped, wondering what else she'd said or done. If she even wanted to know. "The fish smells amazing."

"Got two today. I'll try again tomorrow."

"Were there so few in the pools?"

"Not as many as I thought, and they're fast. I'll need to work on my reflexes." Erran wrapped his vest around the handle of the pan and brought it to the table. The mouthwatering scent pulled Mariel from her mortified stupor, and she went to join him.

"Don't see any spoons or forks, so we'll have to eat with our…" He grinned when she started picking at the flesh and eating. "Hands."

They ate in silence, Erran finishing first. When he was done, he moved to the door, watching the storm.

"I've been thinking about the boars," she said after licking all remaining evidence of the delicious fish from her fingers. "How we could take one down."

"Before or after you devoured mind-altering mushrooms?"

Mariel hung her head in fake contrition. "We have a spear now. Between it and your sword, we'd have the advantage. Spear it to slow it, then stab it when its energy has dwindled. Weeks it would last us."

Erran shook his head firmly. "Not worth the risk. We get too close and miss? He'll be having *us* for supper."

"Do boars eat people or just murder them?"

"Don't know, but is this how you'd like to find out?"

Mariel laughed. The sound compelled Erran to turn.

"Still intoxicated?" he teased.

"Nay, but I am feeling relaxed for the first time in..." She nearly said *days*, but the truth was years. Years and years. Her work was fulfilling, but peace never followed, only the satisfaction of knowing they'd helped another family. Another village. Another mining crew.

"I hate to even bring this up when you're in such a good mood, but I've been trying to work up the courage for days. And then I think to myself, why should I need courage to ask for the truth?" He rejoined her at the table. "Mariel, there's a good chance we're never leaving this island. And if by some miracle we do, neither of us will be the same person we were when we leaped from that cliff. So...tell me." He paused before adding "please."

Mariel's eyes lowered to her lap. She'd been waiting for him to ask again, but she still had no idea what to say. She no longer cared if he knew about her, but she could never implicate the others. He wouldn't believe she'd done it all by herself, and would push for names. Maybe they would die there...Maybe it didn't matter. But *maybe* wasn't good enough.

"I can see you devising another lie in there." He tapped his head and pointed at hers.

"Not a lie, just...Telling you isn't so simple."

"The truth shouldn't be complicated."

"Aye, but it is. This truth is."

"Why?"

She shrugged. "It just is."

Erran twisted his mouth, cast his eyes in thought. "What if I asked you aye or nay questions?"

Mariel considered that. "I ken we could try. But if you ask something I'm not ready to answer, we stop."

"How about this," he said. "I ask you one, you ask me one. And we go until one of us refuses to answer."

She nodded. It seemed fair enough of a compromise. "Aye. I suppose you should go first, since this is your game."

"The whole point of this is to be done with games."

Mariel scoffed and waved a hand. "Don't be pedantic. I said we could try."

"All right." He linked his hands and flexed them. His knuckles popped. "Let's start with an easy one. You grew up in Mistgrave, aye or nay?"

"Aye." Her heart had already begun to race, and they hadn't even gotten to a tough question.

"Your turn."

"Ah…" What did she want to know about him? She'd never cared before, but the past days had her feeling like another woman altogether, and he, almost a stranger, as though she'd just met him. *This* man, the one who could play the sails, spear fish, and scout and track, she liked him, which was a startling thing to realize. "You learned all this survival stuff from your father?"

"Aye." He cleared his throat. "My mother mentioned you had another sibling. A sister. Is she alive?"

Mariel swallowed and tilted her head toward the warmth of the hearth. "Nay."

Erran breathed deep. "I'm sorry."

"It was a long time ago," she said softly. "I know you want to ask how she died, so I'll just tell you. She died of malnutrition. Like my mother and my father."

It was a moment before he said, "I'm so sorry, Mariel."

She licked her lips. "Ah, I guess it's my turn then? Were you telling me the truth in Mistgrave when you claimed not to know the property we spent our idyllmoon on used to be Ashdown land?"

"Aye," he stated firmly, leaning in. "Aye, I *was* telling you the truth. And maybe sometime you'll tell me—"

"Your turn," she blurted.

"Is..." Erran paused. "Is there really an aunt named Anna?"

Mariel's jaw peeled back in a wince. "Nay."

He watched her closely for another second or two before sighing. "Is Destin the Flame?"

"Nay." Her stomach clenched. "Are you still in love with Yesenia?"

Erran balked a bit, leaning back in his chair. "I don't know."

"It's an aye or nay question," she replied.

"Aye, and I don't have an answer for you."

"Why?"

"You can't ask me that. Is Remy the Flame?"

"Nay. Would you rather it was Yesenia here with you on Feck-All Island?"

His neck twitched. "Nay." He spread his hands over the table and looked directly at her. "Are *you* the Flame?"

Blood flooded her face, then rushed away. Her heart thumped wildly, her skin a graveyard of raised flesh. Her breath in was more of a shudder. "Aye."

Erran closed his eyes. He pulled his hands down his face with a protracted groan. "So it is true. Guardians deliver us." He shook his head. "*Now* I understand why you married me. *Finally*."

Mariel asked her next question without thinking. "Do you hate me for it?"

Concern filled his expression. He shook his head slowly. "Nay."

"Nay?"

"Nay, I don't hate you. I never did." His eyes swam with what seemed like pain. "You're the only one who brought hatred into our marriage."

"That's...veering too far from the rules," she said shakily. "Your turn."

He held out his hands, his mouth parted. "I ken I'm done."

"So that's it? You have no more questions for me?"

"I have tons of fucking questions for you, Mariel!" His hands fell to the table with a thud. "But you won't answer them. And I won't make you."

Mariel held her tongue. There wasn't anything else to say, because there was nothing she was comfortable telling. He already knew her darkest secret. The rest belonged to others as much as her.

The room lit up. Thunder split the sky. She started to stand when he spoke up.

"Nay, I have one more for you. I do have one more." He rapped his knuckles on the table. His cheeks were flushed. "Were you trying to stop the auction?"

"Uh…" Mariel was caught off guard by the question, but he'd already put it together, and he was after confirmation, not revelation. "Aye."

Erran cast his gaze away, nodding. "I ken we don't need a watch tonight. The boars will be sheltering from the storm, not conspiring to eat us."

"Erran—"

"Nay. Nay, Mariel. I don't have any talk left in me tonight unless you're willing to tell me the whole story. And you're not, are you?"

Tears pooled in her eyes as she shook her head. She didn't know where they'd come from.

"Thought not." He reached into the first aid basket and handed her a strip of cloth.

Mariel stared at it in wonder until she realized he'd given it to her to dry her eyes. She looked up at him, for once seeing a man not tied to her greatest heartaches. He was just the beautiful, raven-haired, mossy-eyed man who had followed the woman who had treated him with nothing but contempt into the doom of the unknown, knowing full well it would spell the end of his aspirations. "I'm sorry. I really am."

He made a line with his mouth and nodded once.

She watched him exit the cabin, into the storm.

TEN
THE WHISPERER

Destin had been told he was free but not who had spoken for him.

It couldn't have been Mariel. She would have come for him days ago if she had that kind of sway and power, and her absence meant the Rutlands had forbidden it. He couldn't blame them really. To an esteemed house like theirs, he was an embarrassment of liquor and mistakes.

The jailer handed him his dagger and the few coins he'd had in his pocket when they'd arrested him. Well, there'd been a half-drunk bottle of whiskey too, but they'd probably confiscated it for their own enjoyment. After a few—painful—dry days, he didn't much want it back either.

"That's all you had," the jailer said, sounding almost sorry, like most men came in with more. But most men had a name, a proper home…something of worth or value to offer themselves and the world.

"Thank you," he murmured as he accepted his meager possessions.

He stepped out into the sunlight, spreading his arms to absorb the warmth. His joy was short-lived. Two men he recognized but could not name were standing in his path.

"Samuel Law," said the tall, thin one with the face of an accountant. "This here's Hamish Strong," he said of the beefy fellow with a jovial expression.

A Law and a Strong, two of the major houses of the Southerlands—and quite close to the Rutlands. There was no way this could be good.

"Is it the two of you I have to thank?" Destin asked, unwilling to take another step until he understood the situation better.

"Don't thank us just yet," Samuel said, exchanging a wary look with Hamish. "Mariel and Erran are both missing, and we think you might be the only one who can help us find them."

Destin was stunned. "Missing? What do you mean? How?" Erran too? It made no sense. Mariel would never run off with the princeling.

"Come wit' us," Hamish said, swinging an arm toward the hitching post, where three horses were tethered.

"Where?" Destin hadn't moved.

"We'll tell ye when we see fit, lad," Hamish retorted, but Samuel lifted a hand, staying him.

"Whitecliffe. Beyond that, you'll have to trust us."

Destin snorted. "I don't even know you. Trust you?"

"I'm certain you can at least acknowledge we have the same aims. We want our friend back. You want your sister back. Aye?"

Destin wobbled his head a bit before nodding. What the hell kind of mess had Mariel gotten herself into? He was supposed to be the troublemaker of the family. "But what makes you think I know where they are?" Mariel could have been with the Perevils, or even Alessia or Magnur, but Erran being missing as well made it highly unlikely.

One thing was sure: the two men pretending to be his new-found friends knew a lot more than they were saying.

"We already questioned her friend Remy Perevil. He wouldn't tell us much, but he looked concerned enough for us to discern he had nothing useful to contribute," Samuel said. "Augustine, however, has gone missing from her post at Goldsea Spires, which leads us to believe she is either with Erran and Mariel or had reason to flee."

They know about Remy? And Auggie? "Why...Who is Remy—"

"Oy, donnae start with th' games, son. Sam here saw yer sister visit him, aye? We *know* ye know him." Hamish crossed his arms. "I can go back in there, tell the jailer I was wrong about ye."

Destin glanced back at the jail he'd spent the past four days in. He had no reason to trust these highborns, but he could do nothing for Mariel in a cell. "How long has she been missing?"

"We'll answer yer questions when ye answer ours," Hamish said. He clapped Destin's back in a gesture that seemed affable but sent him skittering forward a few steps with a gulp. "Sorry. Donnae ken me own strength sometimes."

"Hamish." Samuel sighed, shaking his head like a disappointed father. "Shall we?"

Their destination was a pub right across the road from Remy's flat. An intimidation tactic, Destin was sure, but they'd already played their hand where Remy was concerned. Knowing they'd already questioned him took the edge off.

After the barmaid brought their ales around, Samuel said, "Let me assure you Steward Rutland is sparing no expense in the search efforts."

"For the princeling, I'm sure," Destin said with a snort. "No one would go to such lengths just for Mariel."

"The wife of a future steward? You'd be wrong, Destin. But they're both missing, and my instincts tell me whatever Steward Rutland has going, it won't be what finds them, because there's something else going on here, something rotten. Do you agree?"

Destin didn't know whether to agree. If Mariel was missing, and she wasn't at Remy's, and even *Remy* was concerned, then it was already a bigger problem than he knew how to solve. He pushed his ale away. "One of you can have this. I'm off the drink for a while."

"A wise decision," Hamish muttered, both of his furry brows raising.

"I don't partake myself. Hamish will have no problem managing three mugs, I'm sure." Samuel folded his hands neatly over the table. "Tell us about Banner."

Destin screwed his face in confusion. "About what?"

"Not what. Who. Edwin Banner, the broker in Sandycove."

"I genuinely don't know who you're talking about." Destin sat back. "Never heard the name before."

Hamish muttered something about lies, but Samuel's patient gaze was still trained on Destin. "I believe you. I know when a man is a liar, and you're not a particularly good one, so I've heard. Edwin Banner was in charge of an important auction for Steward Rutland, an auction that was supposed to take place the day Erran and Mariel went missing, but was put on hold after Mariel rode to the man's place of business. He sent his guards after her. Erran followed, and it was the last I saw either of them."

Destin's mouth widened into a stunned O. He'd only been locked away for a few hours when she'd ridden to Sandycove. In that time, she'd somehow managed to not only get the name of the man managing the affair but had gone to see him.

And then gone missing.

Samuel glanced at Hamish in a shared look. "So you do know what we're talking about, just not all of it."

Destin looked down and nodded. "I may have heard something about the auction."

"Would it surprise you to hear your sister, as she was giving chase to two of Banner's guards, declared to everyone present *she* was the Flame of the Obsidian Sky gang?"

He tried, oh how he tried, to hide his shock. He knew he'd failed because of the looks the men were giving him. "Why… would she do that?"

Hamish rolled his eyes. "I ken ye know good and well why. I ken ye know a whole lot."

"I managed to return and convince Mr. Banner it would not be in his best interest to go claiming a woman was our Reach's most famous brigand, the ire of all stewards, but the longer this goes on, the more I fear his restraint will wane." Samuel sighed. "Remy and Augustine were with her. They rode for Whitecliffe. She rode for the coast. I followed the siblings. Erran followed his wife."

Mariel, Mariel, Mariel. What have you done? "I don't know what to say."

Hamish shook his head. "A cornered man cannae find his tongue for the life o' him. But we ain't going to th' law, lad. Whatever yer sis was up to, Erran is in it now too."

"We just want to find them. That's all," Samuel said. "I realize you have no good reason to trust us, but whatever you tell us, we promise not to repeat."

"Aye. Swear on our mothers," Hamish said.

"We've already deduced Mariel was going to do *something* to impede the auction. Halt it, confiscate the gold, sabotage the men attending…We can only guess. We're already halfway to the truth, Destin. We just need you to provide the rest."

Destin was in a no-win situation. He could say nothing—*should* say nothing. If the Rutlands, who had no limit to their resources, hadn't found them yet, then it grew increasingly unlikely they would. But if he told the truth…He could already imagine the lack of surprise in the knowing glances of his mates, who always said he'd be the one who inadvertently outed them.

But Mariel had boldly outed *herself*. She had to have her reasons, but she wasn't there to share them.

"I…" Destin cleared the dry thatch in his throat. "I don't know where she is. But aye, she's the Flame. And I'm the Whisperer."

Hamish scoffed. "Never heard of no Whisperer." He counted on his fingers. "There's th' Tactician, the—"

Samuel shushed him with an icy look. He gently nodded at Destin to continue.

"Remy and Augustine..." There was no point in finishing. They didn't care about the others.

Hamish whistled through his teeth. "We jus' tossed a rock into a wasp's nest."

"It is quite the revelation," Samuel replied, not looking nearly as bowled over as his friend. "And one I'm very curious about, but at present, I am only in need of information that will lead to their whereabouts. So tell us, where would Mariel go if she was in trouble?"

"Ahh..." Destin eyed the row of ales. He'd never wanted a drink more. "Remy's, but you said she wasn't there."

"Where else?"

"My place, but I ken you've already checked there."

"Where else?"

"There isn't...There's a spot in the woods where we sometimes meet, but there's no shelter there. It's not a place one stays for long."

"What 'bout th' other members of Obsidian Sky?" Hamish asked.

Hearing the men speak their name aloud so casually was like a slap to the face. He couldn't help that Remy and Augustine had been revealed as outlaws, but he wouldn't add Alessia's and Magnur's names to their bank of knowledge. "I don't know. There is nowhere else. Our family home..." He didn't finish.

Samuel nodded, processing. "*Think,* Destin. Erran followed her *somewhere.*"

"I don't—"

"Think!" Hamish boomed, rattling the mugs and drawing curious eyes from onlookers.

Destin knit his brows at the man who certainly *looked* like a brute, but it was clearly all bluster. He was soft on the inside, like

Magnur. Didn't mean Destin wanted to test it though. "You can't imagine how badly I want to find her, but you both know more than I do."

"You know more than you realize. You know her better than anyone," Samuel said.

"But I wasn't there. I didn't see her ride…" A wild thought struck him. "Which coast was she riding toward?"

"Devon, if she stayed on the same road."

Destin blurted a laugh. He looped his hands over his head and looked up at the candelabra hanging above him. *Mariel, Mariel, Mariel.*

"Nothin' funny about any of this," Hamish grumbled.

"Tell us," Samuel said, unruffled.

"It's insane," Destin said. And it was insane. She hardly knew how to captain the damn ship, let alone flee in it. And with Erran? "And a longshot at that. But I ken I might…I might know where she was headed."

ELEVEN
BOAR

Mariel was up before Erran, though she hadn't really slept much at all with their last conversation repeating over and over in her head.

His patience. His resignation. There was no anger but certainly disappointment, and that she could understand because she was disappointed in herself too. He'd put aside their differences and recognized the necessity of working together, the great equalizer of circumstance that had made them peers. Friends, even. But she'd met his attempts with erratic mood swings and maddening half-truths.

She didn't know how to apologize, at least not yet, but there was something she could do. He couldn't know about it until she was done—another lie, but for a good purpose.

Mariel tiptoed around the cabin as best she could with a twisted ankle, collecting the spear, her daggers, and the satchel, in case she found anything new to forage. Her crutch she tucked under her arm but didn't use yet, wary the thumps would rouse him. She checked once more to be sure he was asleep, and snuck out.

They'd identified a few trouble spots during their exploring and had avoided them.

That morning, she was headed directly into one.

Erran might not think they could take down one of those monstrous boars, but the shed, cabin, and well told her differently. Men *did* come to the island, often enough to build an infrastructure capable of supporting their hunting. She'd seen the old carcasses hanging in the shed by the coast. They weren't small.

Her bow would have made the task far easier, but people had been hunting boars with spears forever.

She had not, but if she let inexperience hold her back, Obsidian Sky never would have become what it had been.

Past tense. No matter what happened, their days as outlaws were behind them, at least as a collective group. Maybe the end had been imminent for longer than she'd realized. Alessia had been losing interest for a while. She enjoyed her honest work as a blacksmith and dipped out of their group celebrations earlier and earlier. Remy had grown more reticent, perhaps a side effect of getting older, but he'd also expressed repeatedly that he wanted Augustine out. He was afraid she'd be hung by the Rutlands if discovered, and Mariel wasn't sure he was wrong. Magnur...Well, Magnur was down for anything. He never questioned the work or what it required. He would follow Mariel until she told him not to.

And Destin. Sweet Destin. He should never have been a part of any of it. Everything they'd done was a reminder of what they'd lost, a perpetual loop of pain and sorrow tempered only by the brief rushes of successful conquests. But every one sent him descending further into melancholy. Maybe putting their heists in the past was exactly the thing he needed to finally move forward.

Mariel hobbled along, drawing closer to where they'd seen the densest concentration of the boar-like creatures. Someone had told her once that boars were communal when younger, choosing to live in packs and only becoming solitary when they reached their old age. She guessed that meant the trouble spot was probably a young pack.

Her belly rumbled at the promise of the feast awaiting them. She grinned, imagining Erran's face when she presented her peace offering. The shock, followed by admiration and, hopefully, reconciliation.

As she neared the spot, she heard the snuffling, snorting sounds they'd come to fear. Deception was a lot harder with a crutch, but there was enough natural forest noise to muffle her search for a spot that would give her both a clear shot and a safe vantage point.

It took her a while before she accepted there wasn't one, at least not on the ground.

Mariel scanned the trees, and her eyes landed on one that had a good system of branches. She used to love climbing as a lass, hearing her father's proud voice encouraging her as she went higher and higher. She'd scaled a couple in their heists too, but never with a sprained ankle.

She peered upward, sucking her teeth. All she had to do was climb high enough to keep the boars from being able to reach up and gore or bite her.

Mariel set the spear in a valley of branches, found a good solid place to pull, and, with her good leg, pushed to hoist herself up.

Panting, she gave herself a quick break before inching herself farther in. She strained, nestling the spear on a higher branch, and climbed higher.

The ground seemed farther than she'd expected when standing beneath the tree, but it was certainly high enough to protect her. Only problem was she couldn't see much from the center of the tree, where she had the most protection and stability. She'd need to slide outward on a supportive branch to get a clearer view.

The one she was on seemed like it would do the trick. She gave it a couple of hard bounces to test but stopped when the leaves rustled.

Mariel tucked the spear tight to her armpit and carefully, quietly, pulled herself along the branch until she had a clear view of the ground. Two boars were grazing on the same bush. They hadn't noticed her yet. She saw no others, but they could have been nearby.

The tricky part would be finding a way to sit, balance, *and* throw the spear, but she only had to wound a boar. Once it no longer posed a threat, she would give it a clean death, a dagger across the throat.

Once the first one was hit, the second would realize the danger and run. But if she missed...If she missed, they'd all come for her. There'd be nowhere to run and no safe way to descend.

She inched slowly down the branch, the spear pressed between her palm and the branch itself. The morning was already hot. Sweat peppered her face...the back of her neck. Wiping it wasn't an option, or she'd lose her tenuous balance.

Almost there, she thought with a triumphant inner cheer. She'd always been an excellent shot. Bow, spear, crossbow. Erran had done a good job carving the weapon, using a heavier wood that would catch good air and wouldn't easily splinter. *I can do this.*

The branch bowed, sending leaves shimmering to the ground. One boar stopped eating for a moment, snorted twice, and resumed.

Now that she could get a good look at them, she was stunned at their size. And these were the younger ones?

Mariel arched her back as she pushed upward, attempting to swing her legs down so she was straddling the branch, but as she did, the spear slipped from her hand and went crashing to the forest floor. Both boars abandoned their grazing and started toward the fallen spear.

"Cursed hell," she hissed, wincing from her terrible, terrible error. There'd be no easy way to return for it, because of where it had fallen, without being spotted by the very beasts she was trying to both avoid and kill.

Erran could make another spear, but that wasn't the point. She couldn't return empty-handed. Her gesture had to say all she could not.

Think. Think! There were thinner branches, some longer than others. One seemed long enough to reach the ground, but even if she could graze the spear, she had nothing to hook it. *Unless* she also used the leaves to make a sling of sorts, but even then, the boars had been spooked and—

A loud crack broke the silence. She'd only just registered what it was before she went crashing to the ground.

The force of landing knocked the air out of her. She'd landed on her bad ankle, and the pain was absolutely blinding. Her crutch was still propped at the base of the tree, and she wasn't even sure she could *crawl* far enough.

Low snorts drew closer. She looked up, still gripping the fallen branch, and found both boars staring right at her. One bared his lower tusks, revealing sharp orange teeth. A viscous wad of drool plopped onto the fallen leaves. Its breath smelled like years-rotted cabbage.

Mariel stopped breathing and went as still as she could. There was no chance of outrunning them, even if her ankle wasn't useless. With certain bears, one could sometimes play dead, but she had no idea if it worked on boars. She guessed not, by the way they were sizing her up.

A sharp whistle pierced the air. One of the boars squealed, whinnying in pain as it started galloping away. It made it as far as the bush it had been munching on before buckling to the ground.

The other boar darted into the brush, its hooves shaking the earth in its hasty departure.

Mariel, stunned and delirious with pain, watched Erran stand over the dying boar with his sword. He knelt and dragged it across the beast's neck, just as Mariel had planned to do, and waited for it to bleed out before coming to her.

"Where...the spear..." She couldn't get any more words out.

"I made three. You didn't notice?" He knelt and gently peeled her away from the branch. "Are you hurt? Where?"

"Just…my ankle. What are you doing here?"

Instead of answering, he scooped her into his arms. He knelt to grab the spear she'd dropped, and then her crutch.

"We have to get out of here. There'll be more," he said and took off.

"No, the boar. Erran—"

Mariel bolted awake. She'd passed out from the pain. "Erran…"

"Just hold on."

"The boar. The meat."

"I know, Mariel." He raced through the forest like she weighed nothing.

"I wanted to…wanted to surprise you." Her head lolled toward his chest. She was losing her battle with consciousness again.

"You surprised me all right," he quipped, but she heard a softening in his tone.

He kicked the cabin door open and carried her to the cot. She was hardly settled before he'd dragged over a chair and the first aid basket. "You're bleeding."

"No, it's my ankle." Mariel swooned in her delirium. "Just my…"

Erran tore a cloth with his teeth. He poured antiseptic on her arm, and she screamed. "Arm's fine, is it?" he asked, working to dress the wound she hadn't noticed before.

"I'm sorry," she murmured. "I'm sorry."

His eyes swept her body. "I need your trousers off."

"Huh?"

"There's blood on them. It means you're wounded…just…" He unbuckled her pants and tugged before she could protest.

But one look down confirmed what he'd said. "Oh Guardians. That's a deep…"

She awoke again, this time to Erran stitching her thigh.

"What are you sorry for?" he asked as he tied the bandage.

"Last night." She licked her cracked lips. "And today."

"I'm going to re-wrap your ankle. Some of the bandage must have caught on the branch, because half of it's missing." He rooted around in the basket for the thicker roll. When he hunched over, she saw the sweat blooming across the back of his shirt…the harsh breaths lifting his shoulders, strained from tension.

"It was going to be a peace offering," she said. Her eyes closed in longer intervals, but she resisted the call to pass out again.

"I told you it was a bad idea. That we were outmatched."

"And I didn't listen. I know. But *you* killed one, Erran. We'll… We'll eat for weeks on that meat."

"I only killed it because…" He sat up and wiped his forearm across his brow. His jaw tensed, flexing with his breaths. "Because I was too terrified to stop to think about whether it was a good idea."

The full weight of the morning hit Mariel like a wave. She'd nearly died. He'd saved her for a second time, but not before deciding that endangering his own life was an acceptable risk. "Thank you," she whispered.

Erran flicked his hand and returned to wrapping, but he kept messing up and starting over. Finally, he flopped back in his chair, brimming with annoyance. "Be serious. You wanted to surprise me? To apologize?" He pushed to his feet, sending the chair toppling. "Next time just say the words, Mariel."

"I didn't…" *Didn't know how. Didn't want to. Didn't have the words. Didn't, didn't, didn't.*

"Think? No. You didn't think. You didn't think about what might happen to you out there, what might go wrong. What it would do to *me* if…if you'd *died* out there." He grunted in frustration, his hands laced over his head as he paced to the other end of the cabin.

Mariel's heart missed a beat. "No," she admitted, swallowing. "And I'm sorry for that too."

"Are you?" he asked, still facing away.

"Yes, Erran. I *am* sorry. For…everything. For lying to you. For marrying you when I could hardly stand to look at you. For putting you through far more than you deserved out here when all you've done is try to make peace." She tried to push up onto her elbows, but stars danced in her eyes, and she went sprawling back onto the cot. "I've always been better at *doing*. And I thought providing for us would show you what I couldn't find the words to say."

He didn't speak for a full minute. "You just said them well enough."

Mariel's visceral response was to demand to know why he'd even followed her to begin with, but her instincts had gotten her into enough trouble, creating a rift that wasn't necessary and had only hurt them both, in a time when they needed to be united. "I don't want to fight with you anymore."

He turned around. "I never wanted to fight with you, Mariel."

A flash of her old self came out. "Nay, but you didn't want to marry me either."

"You think me a lovesick fool who can't see past his heartache? That I miss her so much, I could never..." He pressed his mouth tight, shaking his head. "I *didn't* want to marry you. The first day I met you, you had this...this obstinate look about you, and I *knew* we'd butt heads. I knew." His head kept shaking with his unsaid thoughts.

"I married you..." Was she really going to say it? Could she? She swallowed her pride and tried. "Because I needed to get close to your father."

"Aye, I gathered that." His chin dimpled. "So you could steal from him."

"Nay. So I could take back what was never his."

Fire flashed in his eyes, but he didn't put voice to it. He sank onto another chair and hung his head between his legs. "I want to...rage at you. Call you all sorts of awful...but I'm just relieved you're finally speaking truth in your words. These past months finally make sense."

"I don't know if you care or if it even matters now, but the most maddening thing for me was discovering you weren't a bad person after all." Tears trickled down her cheeks. "I thought you were spoiled and entitled, but you absolutely stunned me with what a good man you are. I couldn't understand how you could be a Rutland and also be so honorable, and I decided not to see those things. To see only what I needed to see to keep going. I think I've been doing it with everything in my life for so long that I no longer know right from wrong, good from bad." She wiped her face. "I can't apologize for Obsidian Sky. I won't. But I'm sorry you were put in the middle of something that has nothing to do with you."

"I don't know why," he said quietly. "But I believe you."

She laughed through her tears. "I'd assure you of my honesty, but it would mean little, wouldn't it?"

"You asked me last night if I hated you..." When he glanced up, she was shocked to see he was crying too. "I'll ask you the same thing now."

Mariel bit her inner lip and shook her head. The tears were spilling so much, her vision blurred. "Nay. I don't hate you, Erran."

He stood and made a slow path toward her, then dropped onto the edge of the cot. "Let's start over, Mariel. Let's forget...forget who we were *out there* and be who we wish to be *here*. Forget my father. Forget your extracurricular activities." His mouth twitched. "Forget all of it. I just want..."

"What?" Her voice creaked.

Erran pulled one of her hands into his and held it there. "To know you. To *really* know you."

She wanted to ask why, but that was her defenses kicking in, protecting her. The truth was she wanted to know him too, and she could think of no better place than the little world they'd stumbled upon and made their own. "Aye. I'd like that."

He blinked hard and sniffled once. "Right. You're fading. And I have a boar to dress."

"Can you haul him back yourself?"

Erran shot her a look as if to say, *really*?

Mariel mimed sewing her lips shut.

He laughed.

She laughed with him.

"I'm sorry as well." He released her hand and stood. She felt a pang of grief at him leaving her side. "I shouldn't have dismissed your idea about the boar. I was being stubborn. And if you hadn't...gone out there and made yourself bait—"

Mariel gave himself a playful smack. "My idea wasn't a bad one, all right? The branch did me wrong."

"The branch. Right."

"I had a clear shot!"

"Were you planning on making a cannonball of leaves, or..."

"If I wasn't laid up on this cot..."

"You'd what?"

"Come closer and find out."

"Save your threats for when I return." He grinned down at her. "Rest up, outlaw. Tonight, we feast."

TWELVE

PLEASURE UNDER THE SHAME OF SECRECY

Mariel wrapped herself in a blanket and hobbled down the steps of their cabin at dusk. Pinkish hues wove patterns through the violet, and for a moment, watching with her eyes and heart wide, she understood what people meant when they talked about their souls being at peace.

Erran looked up from his log and smiled. "There you are. Did you rest?"

She nodded and joined him, lured as much by the smoky call of the boar's meat roasting on the spit he'd fashioned as she was the perplexing realization that in the hours she'd been asleep, she'd missed him.

"Almost done." He badly repressed another grin. "Close your eyes."

"What?"

"I have a surprise."

Mariel laughed nervously. "I don't like surprises."

"Even if they're good?" He waggled his brows, his eyes lit up like a pleased puppy's.

She huffed a playful groan and obliged, wondering what had come over her that she'd so easily give in. "Do your worst."

A couple of seconds later, she felt him unwrap one of her hands from the blanket. He peeled her fingers open and pushed something wooden into them. "Drink," he said.

"Drink what?" Mariel peered at him through one eye until he scowled at her, and she shut it again.

"Drink," he urged.

"If this is poison, I *will* come back and haunt you," she warned, bringing the mug to her lips. Before she could draw a sip, the oaky, sharp notes of whiskey hit her nose. "*Nay*. Erran! This is what I think it is?"

She could hear the glee in his voice when he said, "Aye."

"Don't tell me you learned distilling in survival training?" She opened her eyes and tilted the mug toward her mouth, then relished the burn on her tongue, her throat.

"You flatter me," he said, laughing. "I wandered back down to the shore to check my traps and happened by the shed. There were some trunks stacked along the back side, and I hacked them open—"

"*Hacked* them open?"

"Aye, I also found an ax on the beach." He nodded over his shoulder. The half-rusted tool was propped against the side of the cabin, near the woodpile. "Good thing too, as we're almost out of wood."

She'd forgotten all about the ax. It could have made their lives easier if she'd remembered to go back for it. "So you *hacked* these trunks open like a madman. Go on."

"What, should I have used my teeth?" Erran shook his head. "One of them was full of bottles, so I brought a few back." He uncorked the cap and filled her mug higher.

"Could have used this when you were stitching my leg," Mariel said. She raised her mug. "To…new beginnings."

Erran grinned and lifted his mug to hers. "And getting to know one another."

Her eyes locked with his as they both went to take sips and seal the toast. Something compelled her to hold the gaze, and neither did he look away. To ease the flutter in her chest, she smiled and turned back toward the fire. "It smells amazing. Thank you."

"Amazing? If I made this back in Whitecliffe, the kitchen staff would draw and quarter me." He chuckled. "No salt. No spices. Just.. fennel. But it will fill our bellies, aye?"

Mariel nudged her shoulder against his. "It will taste amazing because we worked for it. It wasn't handed to us."

Erran stared into the flames with a drowsy expression. "Aye. We did." He pushed forward off the log, withdrew the stick that had eight dripping pieces of meat, and brought it back to them.

She reached for one and he made a *tsk* sound.

"You want to add burns to your growing list of injuries?"

She pouted, withdrawing.

"Thought not." He blew on a piece dangerously close to falling off the end of the stick, tapped it with his finger, and pulled it off. He lifted it to Mariel's mouth, his own amusement at the act a reflection of hers.

"I haven't had anyone feed me since I was a bairn." She laughed but still found her mouth opening for him, her tongue making space for the meat. His finger scraped her teeth as he withdrew, still watching her...waiting. The explosion of juices in her mouth had her eyes rolling back, a moan escaping.

"That good, aye? Would you like a moment to yourself?" He laughed and blew on a second piece, taking it for himself.

"Aye, I would. Just, ah, give me the rest of the stick and—"

Erran swatted her side, making her giggle. She finished her whiskey, belched, and thrust the mug out toward him. It had been ages since she'd enjoyed spirits, but if there was ever a time to let go, it was a night like this.

"Demanding woman," he muttered and refilled her.

"Aye, but you like it."

"Uh, *nay*."

"Esta Garrick and Yesenia Warwick would beg to differ." She regretted the words immediately, because they hadn't been spoken in good faith. Bringing the past and other women into an otherwise pleasant evening felt like breaking an unspoken rule. "I'm sorry. I was out of order."

"Nay…nay. You're right." Erran returned his gaze to the fire with a deep inhale. "Mariel, you remember how you accused me of working my way through the lasses at the Spires?"

Mariel sputtered in embarrassment. That, too, belonged to another life, another time. "I shouldn't have. Wasn't my business."

"It was untrue anyway." He rolled his tongue along the inside of his lips. "Esta and Yesenia are the only women…I ken I just don't have carousing in me the way Khallum does. The way Hamish did, before he met Yanna. It seems like it could be fun, and I ken it *should* be, and then I look at a woman and think, that's nay how I want this to be. Pleasure under the shame of secrecy is no pleasure at all. Not for me."

"You don't have to explain yourself to me," she said slowly, though she was hanging on every word. She *wanted* him to share more of himself.

"Esta, we were both so young, and it was…Aye, it was a blunder, let's just leave it there." He chuckled to himself, lost in a memory he didn't share. "Yesenia was no blunder, but you never see things as they are until they're done, do you?"

Mariel swallowed. Something about hearing Yesenia's name on his tongue made her uncomfortable. "Aye, there's truth in that."

"Mariel." He handed her another piece of meat and propped the stick against the spit. "Will you tell me more about what you and your brother and the others were doing? Not the…the parts you *can't* tell me, but there must be parts you can."

She clenched in defense, drawing the blanket tighter. Her throat was scratchy and dry when she responded with a suspicious "why?"

He turned sideways on the log to face her. "I'm not trying to trick you. Out here, who would listen? But even if they find us and bring us home, I would never…I just want to understand you better."

"I see." Mariel eyed the meat in her hands. "What do you want to know?"

"You said you were on your own after your parents…after they died of malnutrition. Was it money?"

Mariel scoffed. With highborns, it was always about money, always so simple. "Gold was scarce, but even more scarce were greens and fruits. The lake district had always been so fertile, and I ken…More powerful men wanted it for themselves. It was your father and his thug barons who imposed a steep tax on the food. *Our* food. We grew it, cultivated it, toiled over it, and then suddenly found ourselves unable to afford to eat it." She stared into her mug, watching the amber liquid ripple as she swished it. "And without proper nutrients, a person can only survive so long before their body turns on itself."

Erran went quiet. His mouth parted slightly, a gentle breath the only sound. "I had no…I had no idea."

"My parents. My sister." Mariel hadn't spoken the words in years. Everyone close to her already knew the story. "The mothers and fathers of so many of my friends. Villages, once so vibrant and full of life, slowly went barren. And then…" She wrapped herself tighter. "Then came the land theft. And we lost that too. Families were accused of crimes that had never happened, or in our case, the Ashdown land was confiscated after my parents died. The lawmen who came to claim it said children could not own land, not even held in a trust until their maturity, and that was that."

"My father…" Erran composed himself. "My father did this?"

"It's happening all over. Your father was just the one whose actions hurt me and my loved ones the most."

"And what…What did you hope to gain with this marriage? Access to his ear, to sway him?"

"Guardians, no. Powerful men only listen when other powerful men are speaking. What did I hope to gain? Information." She smiled sadly. "Anything I could use to even slightly balance the wrongs that had been done upon the common people. When he spoke of the auction, I dreamed too big. I should have known it was too much for our little group."

"What were you going to do?"

"The others wanted to dump all the gold in the sea, so no one could have it. So it could never be taken back." She shook her head. "I believed it was worth the risk to redistribute it to where it belonged. Remy said the stewards would just steal it again if we did, and maybe he was right. But it shouldn't be so fecking easy for anyone to do what those men have done."

"You're right." Erran's voice croaked. "It shouldn't. It's *wrong*, and I don't even know what to say, Mariel. I really don't. Except that I should have known and not been so…so willfully blind. *I could* have known, but I didn't care."

Her heart softened toward him. It had been softening inch by inch, even before he'd leaped off a cliff after her. He wasn't his father, but he should have known. He should have cared.

Considering that, her urge to comfort him was bewildering. "You know now," she whispered.

Erran's hand slid from his knee to hers. His expression contorted, traveling a range of emotions. "I understand now why you've always been so angry toward me. You had every right to be."

Mariel tentatively inched her hand closer. Her pinky tickled his. "I'm not angry with you anymore, Erran. You're no more responsible for your father's atrocities than I am for not knowing how to save my parents and sister."

"You should be." He angled his face away and wiped it on his sleeve. "If we ever…If the Guardians see fit to bring us home, I *will* fix this. Somehow, I will fix it." A hard, shuddery breath pulled him erect. "I can't bring them back, but I can make it right." He sniffled and lifted the amber bottle. "More whiskey?"

Mariel shook her head, taking him in. The glisten in his thoughtful eyes, as green and deep as the forest surrounding them. The flush coloring his entire face. His mouth, arched with penitence, with the expectation of words he didn't know how to speak, something she understood, because she didn't either.

"Rain is starting." Erran held his palms up. "We should go in."

She nodded and helped him tidy the area. Her gaze followed him, watching how he bent, how he cradled the whiskey, and how he kicked sand over the fire. They were perfectly routine actions, but she wondered how she'd never noticed the way he bent at the knees…the short, measured kicks that were just enough. The strangest, most obvious thing occurred to her as she realized he was a real, whole person, not the caricature of a steward's son she'd made him out to be. It had been a choice not to see it. To see him. A choice that suddenly fell short of her expectations of herself.

Erran stood at the base of the steps, waiting for her to go first. "What?" he asked when she didn't go.

"Nothing, I…" Mariel hobbled up the steps, her heart a racing mess. It wasn't the spirits; she'd hardly had enough to do much more than relax her. It wasn't a feeling she'd ever experienced at all, but some part of herself recognized it, and it was that part that turned, flung her arms around his neck, lifted her up onto her toes, and touched her lips to his.

Erran's surprise echoed against her mouth. Mortification flattened her impulsiveness as she started to apologize, to explain herself, but the words caught when his hands reached down to grip her face and cradled it. His eyes skimmed her, his mouth parting, and then he crushed his warm, soft mouth to hers, dissolving her words. The unexpectedly gentle caress sent her aflame.

He pulled back, reading her again. "It's not the whiskey, is it?"

Mariel bit her lip and shook her head when she couldn't find words.

"Thing is, I want you, Mariel. I want you more than…" Erran's artless candor, his confidence in saying what he meant, had once annoyed her, but now…"But only if it's what you want."

Her flesh tingled from her fear of doing the wrong thing—saying the wrong thing. She'd never felt so exposed, but what scared her more than the vulnerability was the comfort in it. The understanding she was safe, if she wanted to be. "It is what I want."

His thumb caressed her cheek. He hoisted her into his arms, kissing her again and again and again, his lips skating her chin, jaw, and neck before returning to her mouth.

Erran's boots joined the cacophony of fresh rain and her erratic heart as he slowly carried her to the cot.

She was practically trembling as he tenderly undressed her from the waist down. He was extra careful when the fabric of her undergarments brushed her stitches, and he leaned in to kiss the edges of her angry flesh. Her head fell back from the strange intimacy of the act. To hear the others in Obsidian Sky speak of sex was to envision a sweaty tangle of desperation and regret.

His mouth brushed between her legs, his hot breath waking a part of herself she'd only indulged in her most private moments, when she needed the release that nothing, not even the heists, could provide. When the tip of his tongue parted her, she cried out, bearing down in modesty that was unnecessary. There was no one to see. To judge. The island—this life, this world—was theirs.

"You can let go, Mar," he whispered, his breath hot on her nethers, and she did, releasing the world to allow it to fall away. Even the rain was part of another life…the boar, the whiskey. As she climbed higher, safer, she thought of nothing except how beautiful it was to be wholly present and open with another.

Mariel's thighs instinctively clamped when she climaxed, but Erran was unfazed, his arms still wrapped around her legs, his tongue taking her further than she'd ever been on her own. Oh, Guardians how she wanted him. She couldn't remember ever wanting anything more.

Erran peeled back and waited for her to recover, wearing a boyish smile she wanted to kiss and keep forever.

She nodded to show him she was fine, more than fine. The throbbing between her legs was all-consuming, pounding in time with her heart and irregular breaths as she considered what would come next.

He lifted her legs and eased her onto the cot, climbing up and over her, still so careful with her wounds. One hand scooped under her back to hold her aloft as he used the other to peel away her shirt.

His came off next. She ran her fingers along the hard lines of years at sea. Privileged or not, he'd worked hard to prove himself, to earn his place. He'd shied away from nothing their adventure demanded, and though she wasn't used to anyone else being in charge, she realized she *liked* his assumption of control. She never knew how badly she wanted someone to look after her until Erran had decided himself her protector.

Erran deftly wriggled out of his pants. When his torso came down over her, his erection dragged along the length of her, sending her eyes rolling back with longing. He nestled into place, one hand reaching down between them to guide himself into place. "What a mess we are, Mariel," he whispered, breathless.

"Nothing wrong with that, as long as we're together," she answered and boldly lifted, provoking a surprised reaction from him. Then something changed in his eyes, the lightness of the moment passed, and he drove into her, knocking her entire world off its course.

"Ahh," she moaned, the stinging, burning pain unexpected but not more than she could handle. He slowed to check on her, but she wrapped her arms around his neck and pulled him in for a deep kiss, gliding her tongue over his, showing him what she wanted, that she could handle all of him.

Erran's rhythm was smooth and lyrical, like his skill with the sails. Every inch of her, including the parts she hadn't explored, illuminated under his touch like lightning coursing through a desert. His gentle but frenzied thrusts seemed to manifest their fears that the moment couldn't last, couldn't be real. That they were still the Erran and Mariel of Goldsea Spires, products of worlds that would forever be at odds.

Erran caressed her face, his hands traveling her neck. He whispered her name there, and the syllables had never sounded so beautifully handled. Arcing back to look at her again, his head shook in slow passes, his voice cracking. "I never realized how gorgeous you are until now. I must have been blind, because..." He trailed off.

Mariel ran her hands up and down his muscled back. "We see what we think we need to see." Her eyes closed, losing herself in his movements.

"Everything I need is right here." Erran solemnly pressed his mouth to hers. "And here," he said, brushing his lips along the hollow of her neck. Tears sprang to her eyes, and he swiftly dipped in to kiss the corners. "It's all right, Mariel. The past can't reach us here."

Mariel tightened her grip around him and buried her face in his neck. "Don't stop. Please."

Erran wrapped his arms around her and hoisted her onto his lap, the two of them entwined in a perfect knot of desire and need and desperation. Mariel had no sense of how long they stayed there, him plunging upward into her and her riding the rhythm, but when he pressed his mouth to her temple and shuddered, she knew it wasn't nearly long enough.

She waited for him to get up and leave, the way Destin and Remy had always said men did after sex, but he didn't. He nestled down and pulled her against his chest.

"Mariel, was this your first time?"

Mariel launched into a panic, recounting everything she must have done wrong for him to know. "I...Aye, it was. Was I terrible?"

Erran squeezed her tight, planting a long kiss atop her head. "Nay...*Nay,* you were amazing. But you were bleeding, and had I known, I could have been gentler."

"You didn't hurt me." She angled her head upward to look at him. "Do you know how you can tell?"

He shook his head.

"Because you're still *breathing.*"

Erran burst out laughing and gave her a gentle shake. "Fair play."

"Why did you think...You assumed I'd been with other men?"

"Well, aye..." He tripped over his words. "I assumed you were lying to me about the man who came to visit you. Remy."

"Remy is family. I wasn't lying about that," she said, though it wasn't so long ago she'd wondered if he could have been more. Imagining it now was like trying to fit a square oar into a round bolt. "Like a brother."

Erran got quiet. "And me? What am I?"

"You're..." The words didn't come because she had no answer. So easily she could have said *nothing* even a week ago. "I don't know. All I know is we can be anything we want here."

"What if I said I wanted to be your family?" he whispered into her matted hair. "But *not* like a brother?"

"We can be anything we want here," she said once more, snuggling closer. "And lucky for you, I want the same thing."

THIRTEEN
MY LITTLE MYSTERY

Mariel finished wringing Erran's clothes after a wash in the river, draping them over a line they'd fashioned from the old netting. He grinned at her from the side as he mimicked her actions, having just cleaned *her* clothing. *If you're going to wash mine, it's only fair,* he'd said, and not only could she not argue, she found it incredibly sexy.

It didn't hurt that he was naked. And obnoxiously stunning.

Over the past week, the barricade between them had been dismantling. They'd fallen into a smooth rhythm, dividing some chores and doing others together, adhering to a schedule that helped establish needed structure. With her ankle on the mend, she could do more every day. She taught him how to craft a bow from branches and boar guts, and he taught her how to repair his fish traps. Her skill with tanning hides into leather proved useful, and he showed her exactly how he'd carved the spears. Even when they'd parceled their tasks between them, they followed each other, never apart for long.

They truly could be anyone they wanted there, and she knew who she wanted to be…who she wanted him to be.

"Your first time washing clothes, I ken?" Mariel teased, jumping sideways just in time to avoid him swatting her bare ass.

He gingerly draped her blouse over the line and turned toward her. Mariel conjured what little remained of her self-control not to look down. "At home, of course not. At sea, we had a sailor whose secondary job was to take care of the washing for all the men."

Mariel made a gagging face. "You all must have hated him, sending him to manhandle all your filthy skivvies."

Erran chuckled. "Believe me, there are worse jobs on a ship." His tongue parted his lips, and he swept his gaze over her. "Ready to test my soap?"

Mariel was certainly looking forward to cavorting with him in the river after an afternoon of chores, but she had serious doubts about the semi-hard goop he had in his satchel. She'd made soap herself when gold was scarce, but they'd had the tools to do so. Erran had fashioned his from the boar's fat, boiling down half-burned wood ashes from the fire pit to make lye and adding the cursed dandelions in a hopeful but ultimately failed attempt to mask the crude scent of the tallow.

A twinkle in his eyes gave him away. He kissed her and bolted for the river, calling back, "Last one in gets to try it first!"

"I don't feckin' think so, you cheater!" she shrieked and raced after him, overtaking him just as they reached the bank. Her feet collected the first splash, and she was so occupied with whooping and hollering her victory, she didn't notice him come up from behind, lacing his arms under her into a sweeping scoop. She squealed as her feet kicked up and he dipped her head toward the river.

"Say that again?" he said, dangling her over the water.

"Let me down, or—"

"Or *what*, you'll make me work for it like the other night? Go on then, Mariel, because I love the challenge."

Mariel squirmed, lifting her head just enough to see the river beneath her. Once, years ago, she'd found herself bound and upside down in a barn after a particularly spicy heist, and there'd been no one but herself to get her out of the precarious situation. When the others had asked her later how she'd done it, she'd said, *What kind of brigand would I be if I wasn't also an aerialist?*

With Erran, she was in no danger of anything except getting ravaged, which was exactly the danger she craved. So she swung herself as hard as she could, catching him off guard enough to secure her release. She'd planned for an elegant landing and a theatrical bow, but what she actually executed was a flat-bellied splash that stung from head to toe.

Erran was doubled over in laughter when she pulled herself to her feet. "You…You cannot have meant to do that."

"Shows how little you know me, princeling, because it was *exactly* what I intended." Mariel pushed her matted hair from her face, blowing to catch the wet strays. "Don't be jealous. If you're nice, I can teach you."

Erran moseyed over. He slid his hands down her arms and locked them around her back, snapping her close. "Oh, I know you well. And I have endless days and nights to learn everything you don't want me to."

Mariel lifted to kiss him. "Who says I don't want you to?"

She squeaked a startled gasp when he hoisted her into his arms. "I know you prefer to be a mystery." He locked his mouth to hers in a drawn kiss, and it sang through her veins. "My little mystery."

One reason Mariel hadn't seriously allowed herself to dream of love was because she refused to be a man's property. But every single time Erran used such claiming language—*my, mine*—her body, mind, and heart came into perfect unison. "Solve me then," she said in challenge and let him sweep her farther into the river, into the web of safety and imagination they'd spun together.

Erran had one hand wrapped in a root at the river's edge, the other looped around Mariel to keep her in place. Her head was nestled to the crook of his neck, and the feeling was so…so unexpectedly *right* that he was reluctant to leave the moment behind. He'd happily grow old and pruned there with her, watching the years pass with peace in his heart.

A fortnight ago, it seemed inconceivable that he could ever see the island as home, see Mariel as his partner. How it had all changed so fast was something he didn't question though. Doing so would let the darkness in and the light a chance to escape.

"Our clothing is likely dry by now," she said wistfully.

He smiled at the regret in her voice. But the day was waning, dusk soon to follow. They couldn't take the risk of being so exposed when darkness fell. "I ken it could use a few more minutes."

Mariel snuggled tighter against him and nodded.

Erran closed his eyes and let his breath flow smoothly in… out. His heart was as still as it had been since they'd washed up on Feck-All Island. But on occasion, one thought slipped in, a hint of the darkness awaiting them if they were ever rescued. "I need to say something."

Her breathing slowed. "All right."

"I know why you did what you did. I can't blame you. I even commend you." He let his words land, so she would better understand and accept the next ones. "But if my father ever found out, he would kill you."

Mariel snorted. "You'd like that, wouldn't you?"

The touch of her old animosity for him was a dagger to the heart. He fastened his mouth to her forehead and fought back the swell of sadness rising in him. "No, Mariel. I would be devastated."

She broke away and looked up, presumably trying to discern whether he was being truthful or mocking, whether to stay or run. "It's as I said before. Obsidian Sky is likely over."

"Likely isn't good enough." He gripped her face in his, deciding to hold back nothing. "I will give you all the gold you could ever want or need, to do whatever you want with it. More than you could ever steal. Whatever...whatever you want. Just please, *please* don't challenge him. He's a fair man about most matters, but he wouldn't be about this. The barons look to him to solve a problem that has affected them all, and he's been under so much pressure...If I have to beg you, I will."

"Erran..." Her face crumpled. "I'll stop, all right?"

"Promise." His voice was split with fear.

"I promise," she breathed. Her hand reached to cup his face. "I promise."

Erran kissed her in grateful relief, flipping her and pinning her against the bank with the temperate force she always went wild for. He couldn't let such a wonderful day end on a somber note. "Now, about this soap..."

"Guardians, are you trying to kill us both with infections?"

He traced his hands down her cheeks. "Would you not die happy?"

Mariel laughed, an utterly magical sound he wished he could summon whenever his heart was heavy. Her eyes had softened, glossing over. "I would." She pulled her expression into a mischievous scowl. "Unless the infection was painful and ghastly, in which case you better hope I die last because I would be one vengeful ghost."

"That is now the *second* time you've threatened to haunt me."

"How many times must I repeat the threat before you believe it?"

Erran tilted her chin and kissed her. "You're not worried *I'd* haunt *you*?"

"I don't ken you would be a worrisome specter." She frowned, her eyes fluttering upward in thought. "A little too nice, maybe, to scare anyone."

"If this is a ploy to challenge my masculinity so I'll despoil you to prove you're wrong..." He pressed his hard-on against her, relieved to have the words behind him, her response exactly what he'd been going for. "It's working."

Mariel cinched her arms tighter around him and dragged her lip through her teeth. "It better be, princeling."

Erran was in the middle square of Whitecliffe. The crowd was so thick, he couldn't see through it, but he knew it was the middle square, and not the east or west, by the scaffold in the center towering over all of them.

He couldn't remember getting there. The morning was lost to him, as were the preceding days, but the dread settling in his chest meant some part of him understood why he was standing and waiting to watch an execution.

Hamish came up beside him with a heavy, resolved gait. He hung his head, shaking it. "Ye donnae need to watch this, mate, aye? Some things are jus' more than a man can handle."

Erran started to ask Hamish why he was there, since his friend seemed to know more than he did, but the same trepidation stayed his words.

"We did all we could," Samuel said, appearing from thin air. "All we could, Erran. And we all tried, even Khallum. Even your mother stepped in."

"Let us take this from ye," Hamish said. "As yer best mates."

The sinking feeling intensified as the crowd's chattering lowered to a din. Someone called out an announcement for the king, and Erran was overcome with a relief that was just as confusing and elusive as the dread. If the king was visiting, then his father was probably making an example of some seditionist who had plotted against the crown, which had nothing to do with him.

A pulsing sound rippled through the air, but no one else seemed to take notice. Erran looked up at the sky, shot with green and gold, like it sometimes did when a cyclone was imminent, but the air was still.

The sound persisted, and he soon realized it was his pulse, so loud the entire world should have been able to hear it, but the other hundreds gathered were focused on the king's impending appearance.

He realized Mariel wasn't with him. He couldn't remember how he'd gotten there or the last time he'd spoken with her. There were other women there. His last fully fleshed memory was from the island, the day they'd washed their clothes in the river and she'd sworn to stop her brigandry. How relieved he'd been then, but it was all gone now, washed away in the creeping uncertainty of a moment that felt like a turning point, but he could not quite put his finger on why.

King Khain stepped onto the podium, and a full hush blanketed the crowd. "We are here because there are some laws that transcend Reach. Our system of lords and stewards is sacrosanct, and predates even the crown. I traveled here to set an example for all others who would be tempted to follow the example of the defunct Obsidian Sky. If you remove the head, the body will fall."

Mariel was dragged onto the platform, her entire body wrapped in chains.

"No!" Erran shouted, and everyone turned to look at him.

The king's eyes narrowed in annoyance.

"She promised to stop! Your Grace, she promised to stop. You can't—"

Hamish and Samuel each took an arm, but Erran wrenched away and shoved his way through the crowd. No one moved, and he couldn't move them. He felt like he was crashing into boulders.

"Have you any final words, brigand? Or shall we call you the Flame?"

"Call me whatever pleases you," Mariel cried. "For I am who I am and without regret!"

"Mariel!" Erran screamed, shoving and clawing to get to her, but with every step, he seemed to move farther away. "Mariel, tell them you—"

Hamish hooked an arm around his neck. "Do ye want them to kill ye too?"

"If they kill her, they've already killed me," Erran hissed and squirmed out of his grasp, only to look up and see the noose being placed over Mariel's neck. "Mariel, this is a mistake. Tell them what you promised me!"

But she couldn't hear him. The king had forgotten him. The crowd was chanting for her neck, their bloodlust becoming louder and louder.

Mariel lifted her head high, closed her eyes, and started to speak again, but the trapdoor was opened and she crashed through, squirming as the rope stole her life away. They hadn't even had the decency to hood her, and Erran could only watch, in utter horror, as the whites of her eyes filled with blood. Panic and regret splashed across her reddened face. Her legs kicked, swinging her aimlessly around. She would die the hard way because they'd left her rope too short on purpose. Of course it was on purpose. They wanted her to suffer, and she was.

The crowd suddenly opened up, all of them looking his way as they made a path for him. Erran's entire chest was on fire. Tears blinded his eyes. It seemed the day had robbed the air from his very lungs. But as he neared her, her struggling stopped. She met his gaze with what he could only describe as a soul-deep apology.

By the time he reached her, she was gone.

He used his sword to cut the rope, and she landed in his arms, limp and already turning blue. His hands were wracked with tremors, the pain—

Erran shuddered awake, drenched in sweat. He stared at his arms in a panic, remembering how she'd felt, her indelible warmth slowly draining into the ether.

But his arms were empty. And Mariel was fast asleep on the cot beside him.

He tilted his head back for air, filling himself with reality to shed the horrible dream. Except it had been so *real.* Most of his dreams were an amalgamation of experiences and observations, nonsensical vignettes, but not this one. This one had felt prophetic, like he was seeing exactly what would happen if he failed to protect her.

Erran breathed out and nestled back onto the cot, wrapping around her from behind. *Mariel.* The past two weeks had been dreamlike as well, but that dream he had no interest in waking from. It startled him to realize he no longer even *wanted* to be rescued. He could see himself perfectly content with the simple life they were making together.

He buried his face in her hair and inhaled, tethering himself to her scent, which reminded him of sandalwood. Of warm nights and comfort. *Real. This is what's real. She is what's real.*

Your nightmares can be just as real, a voice reminded him. *It won't be enough for you to protect her from the world.*

First, you'll have to protect her from herself.

FOURTEEN
A CHOICE IS A CHOICE

Samuel was not a man who forgot his facts or figures. Even with Hamish's fine navigating, he was sure they'd visited the same two islands seven times. Each time, Destin and Hamish squabbled over whether that was true, but Samuel knew. There were six islands. Two on the eastern side of the shelf; four on the other. He also knew which two they'd revisited, no matter how much Hamish insisted the trees were leafier each time, or Destin confidently countered that they were not, in fact, leafier but the very same leaves.

It had taken three days even to get clearance to sail and then another five of advancing and receding on their route, as storm after storm overtook the Gold Coast. There'd been no signs of Erran, Mariel, or her ship in the open sea—and no reports from the other ships recently ported of seeing them at all—and it had been Destin's suggestion they try the outer islands.

It was during their second week at sea when Samuel recalled a fact about the Eastern Shelf. The mysterious region threw navigators off course and was said to confuse their instruments, sending them in circles until they either surrendered or found themselves in trouble. Hamish then boldly declared that they would have to sail against the wind if they wanted to visit the western side of the shelf, which sounded like a surefire death sentence to Samuel, but he could conjure no better option, and he wasn't ready to give up on his friend. Erran was a mariner, a man of the sea. Mariel was tough and had learned how to survive through genuine trials, something Samuel had discovered from Destin, over one of their many cold meals aboard Hamish's monstrous ship, *Bella Yanna*. He'd learned a lot about the Ashdowns' upbringing. The more he listened to Destin recount the things they had to do to survive, to ensure the survival of others, the less sure he was that Obsidian Sky had been committing actual crimes.

He'd grown to like Destin, because though he was unpolished, he had a fresh-faced innocence that both explained him and made him an enigma all at once. He thought of him as *the kid,* even though he was older than all of them.

Unlike in the imaginative books his sister, Artesia, liked to read, where the heroes' struggles were milked for all the writer could give, they did not have to search every island before they finally spotted the wreckage of the *Mistwitch*. It was, in fact, the first island they found when they crossed into the western stretch of the Eastern Shelf.

They dropped anchor and rowed to shore.

"GONE INLAND. E+M," Hamish read slowly, his annunciation so slow and ridiculous, he lost his accent altogether. "Bloody hell. They were here." He clapped his hands and jumped in the sand. "Aye, they were here!"

Destin fell to his knees and sobbed.

Samuel gave his shoulder a squeeze as he passed him and joined Hamish near the exposed hull of the ship. "What do you reckon, mate?"

Hamish's eyes were full of unspilled tears. He could only shake his head.

"Well, I reckon they've been there, what, three weeks? Erran was trained for this. Mariel has lived off the land half her life. If they say they've gone inland, they have, and I expect they'll have found themselves a water source and a place to hunt, gather food. Shelter."

Hamish brought his knuckles to each eye and nodded.

"It also means they've had enough time to ready their shelter against predators. They'll have traps set, or other deterrents. Let's be on our toes."

Their trek inland was the easiest part of the entire voyage because someone had marked arrows on the trees. They followed them, finding first the river and the well and then, close by, a cabin.

A blanket hung on a makeshift line. There was a low fire burning in a rather large firepit. A spear, its tip coated in dried blood, was propped against the side of the structure. Beside it were a couple of crude traps meant for some kind of sea fishing, seaweed and other detritus tangled inside.

Destin brought both hands to his mouth.

"Do we knock?" Hamish whispered.

Samuel considered their options. A knock might be so unexpected as to be misconstrued for an animal that had wandered too close. Walking in without knocking might get the first one who entered speared or stabbed. "Let's call out to them. They'll hear our voices and know we're no predator. If they don't open the door, then we quietly and carefully enter. And step carefully, lads. Look for tripwire...branches that don't belong."

Hamish didn't wait for accord. He cupped his hands and shouted, "Oy, Erran! Mariel!"

Destin was next. "Mariel! Erran! It's Des!"

They waited a minute, then tried once more before deciding to cautiously enter the premises. Samuel was not prone to overanalyzing, but though the fire was fresh, he harbored a terrible fear they would walk in to find them both dead.

They're probably out foraging or hunting. Samuel went first, since it had been his idea, assessing the path for safety before inching slowly up the stairs. He glanced back at the other men before reaching for the handle, only to find there wasn't one. The door was cracked and had no visible latch.

Samuel gently pressed on the door, stepping in to find a surprisingly serviceable living area, and—

"Oh. Oh dear," he murmured, unsure *what* to do about the sight of Mariel's bare, sweaty back contorting as she rode Erran into next season. Erran's hands guided her hips, the two of them moaning and panting.

Well now we know why they couldn't hear us.

Samuel flung his arms out in a hapless attempt to keep Hamish and Destin from intruding, but intrusion had been their goal from the beginning, and the only conceivable way to keep the situation from getting worse was to announce themselves as swiftly as possible. "Erran! It's Samuel and Hamish and Destin!"

Mariel ceased her movements. They both froze. She slowly turned and then screamed, rolling off Erran, her hands crossed over her chest to cover herself.

"We'll…We'll just give you both…a moment…" Samuel stammered.

"Have we died and this is the afterlife? Nothing else explains what we just saw…right?" Destin whispered, as Samuel ushered them back down the stairs, wondering the same thing himself.

Samuel waited for Erran to stop pacing and sit on the log. Hamish and Destin were still inside with Mariel, and he hoped they'd stay in there for a spell, so he could have the conversation he needed to have with his friend.

"You must have quite the story to tell." He couldn't resist marveling at all Erran and Mariel had already assembled, the life they'd built in so few weeks. "One I'm interested to hear once we're safely aboard the *Bella Yanna*."

Erran massaged his temples, his attention pulled to the forest. "I can't believe...Samuel, I'm sorry. I'm having a hard time believing you're actually here. How did you find us?"

"I have a story to tell as well. Come, sit. We have more than enough work ahead of us."

Erran's abrupt laugh was dry and disaffected as he scratched down the beard growing along his jaw and lower cheeks. He picked the log across from Samuel, perching on the edge like he might flee at any moment. "This hardly feels real."

"Which part?"

"The part where you find us. The part where you show up right as..." He didn't finish.

Samuel had been calculating and tabulating the potential facts in front of him from the moment they'd reached shore, but the result had shifted considerably when they'd stumbled on the encampment. What he'd witnessed did not seem possible, but nor did very much about the situation. The only way to confirm was to ask. "Erran, may I make an observation? You can either affirm my thoughts or disavow them, or decline to answer at all."

Erran was bent over his knees, his hair a disheveled mess. "A Samuel observation. These are always interesting." His voice blended with the wind, and Samuel had to strain to hear him.

Samuel saved his smile, for Erran wouldn't see it anyway. "Setting aside the scene we walked in on for a moment, I cannot help but notice you seem...disappointed that we've come for you. Or at least not overly enthused."

The indignation came first, which Samuel had expected, but what he was not anticipating was how fast it collapsed into sorrow. Erran wore the dismal pall of a man who had just been told he had a month to live. "I don't ken what you want to hear, Sam."

"You know I prefer the truth, whatever the consequence. But it is yours to give, or not."

Erran snorted with a chuckle aimed at the sky. "Oy, you wouldn't understand."

"How can you know?"

His friend laced and unlaced his hands, sighing inwardly. He glanced in the cabin's direction, but the others were still inside. "Even I don't understand it, mate."

Samuel was grateful Hamish was with the others. For all his good intentions, his roughness would have shut Erran right down. "Try me."

"Only thing I know, Sam..." Erran raised his head and smiled wistfully. Laughed. "Is that these have been the most *bizarre* but also *wonderful* weeks of my life, and if I could...If I could...aye, I ken I'd live in this bliss forever. I really would."

The undeniable curiosity was almost more than Samuel could bear, but he had enough pieces to get a nominal understanding of the tableau of Erran and Mariel's island adventures. The wreck had pushed them into working together. Time had pushed them to make a home. And somewhere in the midst of it all, they'd come to understand each other. Develop affection for one another. "I can see the bond between you. It's palpable." He quickly clarified. "I'm not speaking of the sex, of course, you understand. I meant...after. What we observed after."

"Don't hurt yourself, mate," Erran quipped, humorless. "Aye, we bonded, but we bonded *here,* Sam. *Here.* Here, where we could be anyone—anything we wanted. Where none of the rest..." He shook his head, forming a tight line with his lips. His throat bobbed in a hard swallow. "But out there?" He glanced away when his voice choked.

Samuel decided it was as good of a time as any to tell him he was already apprised of the pieces Erran seemed unable to speak. "You should know, Erran, that Hamish and I are aware of Mariel's exploits."

Erran ripped his gaze to Samuel in a flash of panic.

"And will tell *no one*," he said quickly, before the veins in Erran's temples exploded. "We have already discussed it at length. No one has to know. Ever."

"Sam—"

"We'll swear a blood oath if it eases your mind."

Erran stared, dazed, at the fire. "Does Khallum know?"

"No. And he doesn't have to know."

"My…father?"

"I couldn't say, but I'd wager he's not familiar with her second life currently, or his search-and-rescue efforts would include bounty hunters."

"You mean assassins. He's been known to hire Riverhelm Revenants in the past."

Samuel wanted to reassure him that Steward Rutland would never murder his own daughter-in-law, no matter what she'd done, but he realized the statement wasn't entirely true. He couldn't know *what* Erran's father would do, because the situation was unprecedented. Obsidian Sky had plagued the Rutlands and their baronages for a decade. Their crimes would not be handwaved away. And it was reasonable to hypothesize that finding out they'd been hoodwinked by a woman would not sit well with the men either. "When Hamish and I told your father we planned to conduct our own search, I saw no evidence of this. He expressed nothing but concern for Mariel's safety."

"You told him about the *Mistwitch*?"

"No. We said nothing of where we were going, only that we would be gone for days, weeks if necessary. Our fathers received the same story. We were met with only slight discouragement, mostly reminders that they had authorities working day and night on the matter, but I suspect they found our offer commendable and decided not to hold us back. They don't know where we went. We will leave it to you to explain however you deem appropriate." Samuel smiled. "Just please let us know before we make port in Whitecliffe, so Hamish's, Destin's, and my stories can match."

Erran only nodded.

Samuel was oft considered the logical one of their group, good for practical advice but not as salient with matters of the heart. But it was with logic he formed the words he hoped would bring Erran comfort just the same. "You say you bonded here. That there's—and I'm taking liberties here—perhaps a certain magic about being stranded together and relying on one another, separate of the world proper, and it has allowed this relationship to blossom when it would not otherwise have come so far. But, Erran, there is nothing I see here but choice. You chose each other. Here. Out there. A choice is a choice. Only you and she can decide whether what you've built can sustain the return home, but please do not forget the power rests entirely between you, and nowhere else."

The others joined them. Mariel had a sling, with a few things inside, and a spear in her hand. Her expression matched Erran's: adrift and dazed. They both looked at each other, though not at the same time, and something about that made Samuel a little sad, like they'd missed an important moment.

"I ken we shouldnae waste what light is left," Hamish said.

The *Bella Yanna* was a much larger ship than the *Mistwitch*, far more capable of navigating the capricious Eastern Shelf. When Mariel told Destin about her own catastrophic voyage, he was stunned at how different their experiences had been.

They were below deck, in the galley. The others were on the upper deck, probably doing exactly what he and Mariel were doing, comparing stories.

He listened to Mariel tell many incredible tales about the wreck and surviving the island, but she tiptoed carefully around anything about Erran. Her eyes would light up as she'd talk about something they did, some problem they overcame together, but would then transition to a more practical recounting.

Destin realized she was doing this because she was afraid of his disapproval.

After everything she'd done, carving through the meat and bones of her own life to make space for his, it broke his heart.

"Mar, I want you to know…If you love him—"

"Desi." She rolled her eyes but without her usual energy or disagreement.

"I have eyes, you know."

"I ken you do, two of 'em. And you saw people doing what people do, and there's…" She rolled her lips inward and glanced out the port window. "We had to be a team. We had to rely on one another, or we wouldn't have made it very far."

"I only wanted to say…" Destin continued carefully. He'd never been amazing with words, not when they were children and they'd lost everything and not across the years watching Mariel spend herself on vengeance after vengeance. Her heart was too big, and so she'd sealed it off, because how else was she to protect it? "If you cared for him, you'd get no recrimination from me."

She scoffed. "How's that? When you betrothed me to him so we could take down his family?"

I was drunk, and I made a mistake. He gathered his thoughts before answering. "I never cared about all that the way…the way you and Remy did. I don't need it like you do."

"What?" She twitched her head.

"I said, I never cared about Obsidian Sky and the wrongs done to us and others the way you two did. It was always your show. Your effort. Your dream. I only stayed because you wanted me to, and you wanted me to because you didn't think I could manage my own self, and that's *my* fault. *My* failing."

Mariel studied him closely. "Destin, how long has it been since you had a drink?"

"Nineteen days." He could have recited the hours, the minutes, but those were for him. "I never had to think much before. I've had more time in my head these past weeks than I'll ever know what to do with."

She leaned forward and gathered his hands in hers. "I am *so* proud of you. So proud."

He angled his face away, embarrassed. "Aye. Thanks."

"And you did the right thing," Mariel said. Her voice lowered an octave, her expression solemn. "Telling Sam and Hamish. I know you're worried the others will think…but don't. They're loyal men, loyal to Erran, and Erran is…He won't let this secret leak out, and nor will they. So please don't berate yourself for making the only choice you could."

"I appreciate that, but I'm not sure the others will."

Mariel shrugged. "Then they don't have to know."

He flashed her a sad smile. "You don't ken they'll figure it out?"

"If they have anything to say about it, they can say it to me," she stated and gave him a fierce hug from the side.

"I feel the same about you and Erran. I can see it's more than you say it is, Mar. I can see it in his eyes. Yours."

Mariel folded her hands in her lap and buried her gaze there. "If I explained it, they'd never understand, especially Remy and Auggie."

"But what are you going to do when you get back? Return to hating him?"

"I don't know."

"I want you to be happy—"

"I said I don't know!" She sighed. "I was already beginning to think of the island as a permanent home. I wasn't prepared for...for this. And maybe, maybe we could get past my secret when it was only the two of us, but I don't ken...I don't see it being so simple when we're back in his world and he has to face his father. And I... I have to face the fact that the auction will now no doubt go ahead, and this time they'll win. They'll feckin' *win*."

"One moment at a time. Remember how you always told me that? To take life by the seconds, not think too far ahead?"

"Aye." She nodded, looking unconvinced. "Aye, I suppose."

He wasn't getting anything more out of her. She'd always shut down at the slightest hint a topic was veering too close to personal...dipping too close to peeling down the drawbridge of the keep she'd raised to protect herself.

But what Destin had seen in those few, precious moments was his sister had been *happy*.

And though he didn't have all the answers yet, he would make it his mission to protect that at all costs, like she'd always done for him.

Erran had been waiting for Mariel to return to the upper deck. His heart had been a mess the whole time, only half present in his retelling of events to his mates. They were restrained in their teasing, but it just made him more anxious, like they could read straight through to the uncertainty in his chest that felt an awful lot like grief.

Mariel had her arms wrapped around herself as she approached, like she wanted to make herself smaller. Guardians, how he wished he knew how to tell her he adored her for her larger-than-life self, that even a couple of hours without her had left his world unbalanced.

"Hi," he said when she looked up. His heart brightened at how she seemed to light up for him, but it fell again when she glanced around, as though worried about what others would think.

"Hi," she said and sidled in beside him. She talked, but then he did too, which led to an awkward dance of pointing and false starts until he finally held up his hands in surrender. "We need to all get our stories straight before we make port."

Erran knew he *should* have been thinking about preparations, but all he'd been able to focus on was figuring out how to reassure her nothing had to change, that they could still be whoever they wanted to be. "Aye, we still have some time."

"Samuel said no one has tied me to Banner, and Destin has offered to say the *Mistwitch* was his ship, so I don't have to explain how I came to have it." She chewed the inside of her lip, gazing stoically into the calm sea. "As for how we came to be *on* the ship, you and me, Destin had another good idea. We can say he wanted the ship moved from Sandycove to Whitecliffe and needed help, and you offered because he's family. When he was thrown in jail, we decided to take care of it so he'd have it waiting when he was released. We got caught in a storm, pulled into the Eastern Shelf, and the rest is...exactly as it was."

"That sounds reasonable," he said distantly. With every word she spoke, he felt the distance yawning between them, the unscalable chasm that had framed their marriage. It was happening so fast—too fast. "Mariel, I..." Erran abandoned the words, as they would have been inadequate, and drew her face to his. He brushed his lips to the tip of her nose, then the outer corners of her eyes before swooping down to reclaim her mouth with a fiery kiss that softened the edges of rigidity he knew was born of nothing more solid than fear.

"What if they're watching?" she whispered, her lips brushing his.

"Let them watch," he growled and claimed another kiss, which set his entire body on fire. "I'm not ashamed. Please tell me you're not."

Mariel rested her forehead against his chest. "Just...scared, Erran."

"About what?"

"Everything."

Erran gathered her hands in his and brought first one and then the other to his mouth. Behind her, the sun had just begun its gentle dip into the horizon, and the sky was a concerto of oranges and golds. A strange vision came to him, of the two of them standing upon the cliffs, repeating their vows with full hearts, but she was already scared, and he was determined to take the burden of her fears if it returned the smile to her face. "Listen to me. Mariel, look at me."

She blinked hard and did as he asked. Oh, how the tears there broke him. He would fix that too.

"I meant what I said on the island. I mean it still. Whatever comes, we'll face it together. We've weathered a shipwreck and boars and...There's nothing ahead of us we can't handle. Do you understand?"

Mariel swallowed as she nodded.

"I need to hear you say it."

She nibbled her lip again. A bead of blood surfaced on the soft flesh. "I understand."

"Trust me." Erran ran his thumb along the tiny wound and kissed her once more. "And I swear to you, we will weather this storm too."

LIGHTING A SPARK TO KILL THE FIRE

FIFTEEN
LIKE A DREAM

Three hours of interrogation, and Mariel was exhausted.

Four times she and Erran had recounted their story to Rylahn, Damian Law, and Argus Strong, the men hanging off their words like they expected them to change. Samuel had advised them to keep the core details the same but to add minor details to color out their stories on each retelling. He explained that was the way memory worked, revealing more and more layers as you explored deeper, and the stewards would know that as well.

They'll be hard on you, dears, but you will understand in the end, Hestia had warned them both, her red-rimmed eyes swimming with unspilled tears. She'd forsworn her colorful attire for a black gown that was borderline prophetic. *Trust it's necessary and do what is asked.*

"What's still unclear to me is why the two of you decided to address the matter of Destin's ship when he was jailed for suspicion of brigandry." Damian Law shifted a deep frown from Erran to Mariel. His eyes gradually pinched into slits. "Would it not have been a more suitable endeavor for once his name was cleared?"

"I knew—" Mariel said right as Erran blurted, "You see—"

Erran bowed his head in contrition and nodded for her to go.

"I knew my brother was guilty only of public indecency, a terrible result of his overfamiliarity with spirits. And while his disruptive behaviors were uncalled for, anyone who has spent five minutes with him would ken he's not half fit to care for himself, let alone…" She left the words to finish themselves.

"And you decided to spite me?" Rylahn asked, looking at his son. "When I told you to leave matters alone?"

"Father, with respect, you told me not to go to the jail, and I did not," Erran said carefully.

"Is it nay true you still intended to go there? And would have, had you not met trouble with the ship?"

"To the jail?"

Mariel cringed. Erran's attempt at naivete was painfully unimpressive.

"Aye, the jail. Your mother was nay convinced when you said you'd leave matters lie, and I had my own doubts."

Erran skated his gaze over the other men, his hands twisting in his lap. Sweat speckled his collarbone. Mariel hadn't realized what a terrible liar he was. He'd never needed to practice over the years, to perfect an ease in telling any story to any person to make it believable. Any remaining doubt he was fibbing about all the lasses in the keep disintegrated as she listened to him stumble through their story. "I would be lying if I said I hadn't considered it."

"And would ye have? Done it?" Argus Strong asked. It was startling to Mariel how much he and his son, Hamish, resembled one another, right down to the "intimidating" knit of brows. But he wasn't the problem, nor Steward Law. Rylahn needed the most convincing.

"I don't know," Erran answered. "I got little chance to think on it."

"Balingers require a crew. Five or more just to make her seaworthy, up to thirty for a proper sail." Rylahn hadn't shifted away from Erran. "You're usually more deliberate than this, Erran. Taking such risks isn't how I taught you."

"Aye, aye, but we were just trying to navigate the coastal waters, which I didn't expect would need an entire crew, Father. Nothing we haven't done before when shifting port."

"On smaller vessels," Rylahn replied, holding his intensity.

Mariel shook her head. "My brother has taken her out alone before. It was…It was *my* reckless suggestion the two of us could handle it."

"And my son was perfectly capable of refusing."

"Nay, because…" Mariel cut her sideways glance toward Erran, who stared at his hands as if they alone contained the answers to their conundrum. "He was trying to appease me, and I knew it, which was why I asked him."

"You manipulated him?"

Mariel sighed. Erran was still fixated on his lap. He looked ready to break. It was on her to finish this. "Aye, I suppose that's what I did. He'd been naught but accommodating, and I pushed it…pushed him."

"You're saying it's your fault?" Damian asked. "That you enticed him to this act?"

Mariel swallowed. "Aye."

"Nay." Erran whipped his head up with a drilling, solemn gaze around the table. "It's mine alone. I'm the sailor. She is not. If I hadn't believed we could manage the route, I would have procured a crew for the task. I miscalculated, and we both suffered for it."

Rylahn cocked his head. "Are you aware of the whispers coming out of Sandycove?"

Whatever had been on Mariel's face at the moment froze there. "Well, I—"

"I'm asking my son."

Erran shook his head tightly. Mariel noted his knuckles paling as he wrung his hands harder.

"Allow me to enlighten you on what I have been dealing with these past weeks." Rylahn cleared his throat. "It came to my attention that Samuel paid a man, Edwin Banner, a sum of gold to keep quiet about what he *thought* he saw. It involved a woman coming to his home, threatening him…"

Threaten him! I didn't even speak with him! Mariel ground her jaw to stop herself from correcting him.

"And ultimately fleeing for the Devon coast, his men in pursuit, whilst she cried out that she, and not some capable, cunning man, was the Flame. Seems there are whispers from some that this woman is none other than Mariel."

Everyone at the long table went silent. The only sound was leather shifting on seats.

Then Erran erupted into laughter. He threw his head back and slapped the table. "Mariel? My wife? An *outlaw*? The *Flame*?"

Chuckles passed through the other men as well, Damian lifting his brows at Argus as if to say, *I told you it was nonsense.*

Mariel silently stewed through the necessary but insulting dismantling of her accomplishments. *A little too convincing there, Errandil.*

"Aye, well, it had to be said, and now we can move on," Rylahn answered gruffly. "You hit the Eastern Shelf, which you've captained more than once before…"

"Aye, and were caught by a rogue wave. Actually, *I* was caught off guard, was thrown into the deck wall, and the rest is…"

"A blur," Mariel said. "Until I came to on the shore."

"If not for her, I wouldn't be alive."

"Well, we'd have *starved* if not for you. You had fish for us on the second day, and the boar, the one that almost killed me? Let's not forget my foolishness, getting my ankle twisted."

"You're the one who pushed us to find the well. The cabin."

"Which would have done us no good in the long run if you hadn't saved my arse from the boar."

"You saved mine first. And you kept me sane."

"Sane? I couldn't even identify a hallucinogenic mushroom properly—"

"All right!" Rylahn lifted his hands. He tapped the air. "We've been at this for hours. I think I've heard enough. Stewards?"

"Aye, I ken we have," Argus said, nodding.

"The two of you have been on quite the adventure," Damian said, "but an adventure is all it was. Erran, Mariel, we're so pleased you're both safe and back home, and would discourage you from any sea voyages in the near future, lest you tempt the Guardians further. Rylahn, we'll send you our full report within the week."

"Aye." Rylahn stood and shook their hands. "With gratitude, men."

"It was our honor, mate," Damian said. "Send for us if more is required."

"That will nay be necessary." Rylahn watched them leave. He flattened his hands to his vest and stepped away from the table, then came around to where Erran and Mariel were seated.

He knelt before both of them, bowed his head, and pressed a hand to each of their knees.

Mariel wanted to look to Erran for a read on what was happening but was too stunned to do more than gawk at her father-in-law, crouched in front of her in what almost seemed like submission.

"I promised the Guardians my entire kingdom for your return. If they ever come to collect, I will pay my debt with gladness." Rylahn pursed his lips and breathed in. "Welcome home, son. Daughter. I apologize for the interrogation, but may we now all put this unfortunate incident in our past, where it belongs."

"Thank you, Father." Erran leaned in and kissed the top of Rylahn's head.

It was over. Obsidian Sky was over. There were many moments she could assign to its ending, but Erran's father being confronted with her identity and dismissing it seemed the one most fitting.

And if it were so easily undone, had it ever truly mattered?

Rylahn used Erran's chair to push to his feet. He flexed his cheeks, clearing emotion to make room for business. "Get some rest, both of you, because we leave for Warwicktown at first light."

The revelation pulled Mariel from her gloom. "Warwicktown?"

"Lord and Lady Warwick have invited us to celebrate the birth of their second child, a daughter. Esmerelda. Lord Warwick has chosen Erran as Esmerelda's father-in-honor, so his presence is required." Rylahn stood but halted midway, his tight expression suggesting painful discomposure. "I should tell you, Yesenia and her husband will be there as well. They're visiting from the Easterlands for a few weeks, and she herself is coming as the bairn's mother-in-honor. I can assume this will nay be a problem?"

"Nay...of course not," Erran murmured. He scratched at the beard he hadn't yet shaved, shifting in his seat. "Not at all."

Mariel watched the way he tried to hide his uneasiness. That he had to hide it at all was troubling.

Inch by inch, the island felt more and more like a dream.

"I hoped you'd say as much. I've invited your brother as well, Mariel, in gratitude for his role in bringing you both home. Rest up, and I will see you both at dawn."

Erran couldn't take his eyes off his bedchamber door. Mariel was already inside, readying for a bath or already in one, and the only place he wanted to be was in it, with her. The longer he delayed, the longer it would be before he could assure her the Yesenia matter was nothing to be troubled by.

Instead, he was dancing around his sister's attempt to pull some admission or reaction from him that would feed her gossip mill.

"You know why they've invited us, don't you?" Sessaly was saying.

"Because all the great houses are coming," he muttered, sighing.

"Nay." She shook her head animatedly. "Nay, only us."

"What?" Erran cringed at how fast he'd reacted to her predictable ploy of presenting something ridiculous for reaction. "I need to bathe, Ses, unless that wasn't already pungently clear."

"I'm *serious,* Erran. The Laws, Strongs, Garricks, Leecasters…None of them are coming. And why should they? Wee little Esmerelda is only a lass. Hardly a cause to roll out the finery."

"It's custom to hold a fete when a lady is born. You, the princess of tradition, know that."

Sessaly flicked an affected glance at the door and leaned in, lowering her voice. "Father wants to put the whole messy Yesenia affair to bed. He's going to parade you and Mariel around like prize cattle to show everyone you've moved on."

Erran's hand went cold on the door's knob. "I *have* moved on. And he wouldn't…He's not one for games."

"You were made a fool in Warwicktown. Only there can you be unmade."

"Me? You're the one who just sat there while Yesenia had you about the neck, which you deserved, by the way, for goading her."

"All the more reason for Father to show everyone there's no more trouble." She lifted to peck him on the cheek, winked, and scampered off.

It was maddening that Sessaly's words had landed at all, how they'd crawled under his skin and burrowed deep. Adding to his misery was that what she'd said *did* make sense. Yesenia returning to the Southerlands was an opportunity to set the past to rights, at least in Rylahn's eyes. In his own…

He hadn't thought of Yesenia at all after he and Mariel had become intimate on the island. It was Mariel whose touch he needed to calm the tempest brewing in his soul—Mariel he already missed in the short time they'd been apart.

So why was he still standing in the hall?

Erran shoved inside. The sitting room was empty, but steam was rolling from under the privy room door.

He walked in and found her half-asleep in the water, her head rolled back and her arms draped over the sides. Her fingers brushed just above the stones.

Quietly, he shed his own clothing. Her eyes fluttered open, watching him undress. She said nothing, and there wasn't anything on her face he could read.

Erran peeled her away from the edge and gently nudged her forward before climbing in behind her. He settled his legs on either side of her and eased her onto his chest. Her head rolled sideways, her breath trickling into a sigh.

He reached for the crate with the soap and lathered some onto a sponge. Mariel closed her eyes as he ran the gritty, porous material along her neck and chest. He lifted first one arm and then the other from the water and washed them, pulling the sponge down and along each finger…around her nails. He dipped it again but left it under the water, reaching forward to clean her outer thighs, avoiding the old gash still healing. Mouth pressed to her shoulder, he washed her toes one by one. As he dragged the sponge along the inside of her leg, at last she shifted, murmuring a soft moan that was almost lost to the quiet.

Erran abandoned the sponge in the water and nudged her legs to the sides with his palms. "I want to make you come, Mariel."

She nestled her face tighter to his chest with a nod.

Erran choked down a lump of desire. Seeing her come undone under his hand, his mouth, his cock…there was nothing better. Nothing more beautiful, more erotic. He'd never said the words aloud because he didn't know *how*, but her openness to receive as much as he gave was a blissful contrast to his past experiences, which, with time, continued to be redefined.

He massaged her inner thighs as he worked his way inward, spreading her with both hands. She adjusted from the warm intrusion of bathwater. The heel of his palm settled into place, kneading ever so slightly.

Mariel twisted under the water. Her hands cupped under his thighs, her fingers digging deeper. Mere moments later, she whimpered, crashing.

When her shudders subsided, he lifted and turned her so she was sitting astride him. But it wasn't sex on his mind, despite the throbbing evidence to the contrary. He could only control his actions though, not his reactions.

He kissed her tears and eased her against his chest, wrapping both arms around her to convey what words could not.

"I should be glad we were rescued," Mariel said, her words warming against his heart. She climbed until she was settled over him and sank down, taking him in, but instead of riding, she curled back against him and said no more.

Erran kissed the top of her head over and over, his thoughts a heavy, twisted mess. He understood her perfectly. He should be glad they were home. He was…mostly. But he couldn't shake the terrible fear he'd left a part of himself on that island—the most critical piece. Mariel's sad distance only reinforced his dread, like she was, in her own way, saying good-bye to something they'd both only just opened their hearts to.

Mariel's heart was an ironclad fortress, built for self-protection. Her pulling away was not about a change in her own desire, but the fear *he* had changed, that he was incapable of feeling what he felt for her without the "magic" of the island. The only way for him to conquer it was to show her how wrong she was. About that. About Yesenia. Mariel had shut down at the exact moment Yesenia's name had been mentioned, and only he could fix it, by assuring her there was no place in his life, or heart, for the past.

First, he needed time with his own thoughts on the matter. Even before the island, he'd made his peace with the situation and had accepted the past was past. Hadn't he?

Erran knew what he wanted, but he had little time to clear his head of any remaining confusion.

If Mariel picked up on even a speck of it, the door they'd opened on the island would close, and he was not confident it could be reopened.

SIXTEEN
WARWICKTOWN

Erran spent the entire ride to Warwicktown searching for the right words to reassure Mariel, but every potential explanation introduced an additional complication instead.

She's married, I'm married could just as easily be *if neither of us were married, nothing would stand in our way.*

That was a long time ago was a copout, and anyway it was untrue. It wasn't so long ago. Sometimes that part of his life felt so recent he could reach out and touch it.

I'm with you now had a similar pathetic ring, as though she were the consolation prize in the whole sordid game of marriages. Somehow, *she never let me get so close, never opened herself up the way you have* sounded more like he wished the opposite had been true and Mariel was filling a mere gap instead of the whole hole she'd sealed.

The need for reassurance at all signified there was a problem, and that wasn't the feeling he wanted to leave her with when she was already going to feel out of her depth.

Even a simple *you have nothing to worry about* felt wrong, because what if he'd been misreading Mariel all along, and she actually *didn't* care about Yesenia?

Or about him?

His qualms about saying the wrong thing made it hard to say anything at all. He wanted to explain to her what to expect in Warwicktown, so she didn't feel like a fish out of water. He wanted to tell her the capital was a rougher, more merchant class town than Whitecliffe, dangerous and thrilling, but he had no idea if she'd been there. Asking felt like a way of revealing his impression she hadn't traveled much, which if wrong was insulting, if right might come across as condescending.

In the end, his overthinking kept him from saying much at all beyond remarking on the changing landscape as they traveled farther and farther west, into the more arid terrain of the Golden Coast.

"And what would *you* know about it?" Sessaly flipped open her fan and rolled her eyes, looking out the carriage window.

"About billiards? You're asking *me*, a man of ill repute, what I would know about gambling?" Destin sputtered, aghast. They'd been at each other for hours, and if Erran didn't know better, he'd suspect they were flirting.

"I don't even believe such places exist," Sessaly said flippantly.

"Speculation taverns? You're serious?" Destin snorted, turning toward Mariel. "Did you know there were people so sheltered as this?" He leaned closer when she didn't answer. "Mar?"

"Sorry. Aye, I ken you could say the same of us," she said, staring out the tiny window. "For what do we really know of the world of highborns?"

Erran, who hadn't been interested in the banter between their siblings until that point, broke his silence to fix the separation she'd chosen in her words. "You fit perfectly into our world," he said, giving her knee a squeeze.

Sessaly gagged. He shut her down with a look.

Mariel's smile was tepid…practiced. "No one fits perfectly into a world they aren't born into."

"I have to agree with our sister," Sessaly said. "The inanity of such an idea. But just because I agree with her, Destin, does nay mean I don't think you're putting us on."

"Then it's good I put no stock in what you think of my ethics."

"Ethics? Have you any?"

"How's your betrothed these days, Ses?" Erran asked. "Do you remember him? Aliksander, I believe his name was?"

Sessaly flushed. "I wouldn't know, seeing how busy the Laws were these past weeks helping Father locate your wayward self." She nodded in apology at Mariel. "I'm of course grateful *you* are home."

Mariel concealed a grin with a glance to the side, but the sight of amusement on her face cooled Erran's concerns some. "Of course."

"I had *hoped* to see him at Esmerelda's blessing, but…" Sessaly finished with a knowing look.

Erran shook his head tightly in warning, but Mariel had picked up on it. "But what?" she asked.

"Erran didn't tell you?" Sessaly laughed with her mouth wide. "Oh, my brother. He does like his secrets, always has."

"Ses." Erran scorched her with his eyes.

"Tell me what?" Mariel's suspiciousness was back.

"It was *supposed* to be a private event, for the family and the parents-in-honor, then Lady Warwick decided she wanted all the great houses. Even though Erran is the lass's father-in-honor, we had to politely decline, with the two of you playing happy families on some island, but then you came home, and suddenly the entire plan changed. Now us and Yesenia's new family are the only ones invited at all, the others completely off the guest list. So I asked Mother, and she told me the truth."

"That's enough," Erran said, knowing nothing could stop his sister on the verge of a revelation that would shift all the power her way. Even if he could convince her to ease off, Mariel wouldn't let it go, not with the distrust already settling into her tired expression.

"It seems Father views this trip as an opportunity to prove to all the Southerlands that his hopeless romantic of a son is no longer so hopelessly in love with Yesenia, our Lady Quinlanden, so all the rumors will stop swirling. I would expect to see them encouraged to interact as much as possible." Sessaly's mouth pursed in mischief. "So let us all hope his change of heart isn't just a ruse, for he's never been much of an actor."

"Ahh," Mariel said, paling as she shifted her focus back to the passing landscape.

"She's being dramatic, like always," Erran said, leaning close. He glared at his sister, who looked as satisfied as she should for the incendiary she'd dropped into his marriage, for no other reason than her own entertainment. He couldn't wait until she was Aliksander's problem. "Don't listen to her."

"It's not my business whether you are or are not still in love with her," Mariel murmured, shifting her legs away when he reached for one. "As I told you weeks ago."

Weeks ago. Before the wreck. Before the island. Before they'd bonded. Before, he'd seen his future with more clarity than ever before and with more desire than he'd ever known. How she could speak of it so glibly was either a sign of her easily shifting alliances or a cover for the pain Sessaly's words had inflicted, but he wouldn't solve it in front of the others.

"Ouch," Sessaly hissed, poking Destin with an elbow. "Did we touch a nerve?"

"We? Don't lump me in with your antics," Destin replied. "I'm with Erran. Don't listen to her, Mar. She's needling you for her own amusement."

"And what do you know of my amusement, Destin?" Sessaly said, blinking coquettishly.

"More than I'd like to but not nearly as much as I know about gambling, Sessaly."

"Sessaly," Erran said, firmer. Trying to silence his wayward sister had only ever made her more determined, but she'd inched too far, even by her standards. "That's *enough.* Unless you want me to punt you out of this wagon and leave you for the vultures."

"Father would murder you."

"A rather small price to pay for the relief it would bring."

"She can say whatever she likes," Mariel said. "Why should it bother me?"

"Even if it was true..." Erran said, but she was still faced away. She might have been listening, but so were the others, and there was nothing he wanted to say in front of them—especially his sister, who had a near-perfect memory and never missed an opportunity to unleash it.

"Oh. It is," Sessaly said confidently. "Whether Erran will prove him right or wrong is a matter for the Guardians."

"I'm not ruled by deities, nor should you be. I'm married now, so is Sen, and we're not children playing games, unlike you still seem to be."

"Sen." Sessaly snorted, her eyes flicking toward Destin. "So familiar. And I don't recall a silly little nuisance like 'marriage' stopping you before, aye?"

The carriage slowed. Erran craned to see the sea reappear below, the great bellows of the mine roaring with action. They had traveled down the steep slope into a city so packed and loud, he never quite felt at ease. It was the antithesis of Whitecliffe, a gentle enclave of coastal relaxation. Warwicktown was chaos personified, the capital of a Reach teeming with commerce, suffering, and grueling work. There were pockets so dangerous, even the Warwicks and their steel spines didn't venture there.

The keep itself was an enormous, utilitarian stronghold, with few defining features beyond the infamous Lord's Hall, where past and present Warwick lords held their council meetings. As boys, Erran and Khallum would play under the table with the serrated edges, wondering which council member would forget themselves next and lose another finger to their enthusiasm. They'd stand at the broad paneless window that overlooked the calmest stretch of coast in Warwicktown.

Erran had spent so much of his youth there, playing with Khallum and Yesenia and their little brother, Byrne. Like Khallum and Yesenia, Byrne, too, had been sold into a marriage chosen by the king and was wedded to the reputably formidable Lady Asherley of the Westerlands. Erran wondered if he'd be there for the blessing too.

Sam and Hamish and Lem had been there too, but back then, there'd been no one he'd spent more time with than Khallum—like their fathers, who had been inseparable friends in their own youth, a bond that had never dulled with time and responsibility.

But Khallum had become the lord himself, the one leading council meetings, on which Erran's own father sat—and where he would one day himself sit. How keenly he wished for his old friend's advice, which had always been a helpful balance to the wisdom of Sam and the crude affection of Hamish, but the moment Khoulter Warwick had died and left his son the heirdom had been the moment Khallum had shifted from mate to leader.

Shouts and whinnies filled the air. The carriage pulled to a stop and the door swung open, held by one of the Warwick attendants. The women exited first, Erran going last. Some of the others made gagging sounds, whispering about the stench of brine and shit that seemed to affect everyone but him. His second home.

His mother and father had ridden in the carriage ahead and were already headed toward the drawbridge, where a line of people were waiting to greet them. Erran craned to see, but the elevation was too low, the crowd of workers too thick as they scrambled to make the arrival perfect.

Mariel had drifted to the side, walking by herself. He moved toward her and slipped his hand through hers with what he'd wanted to be a reassuring smile, but he'd felt how weak it was and confirmed it in the droop of her gaze.

Khallum's gregarious laugh rang in his ears. He could hear his father and mother working their way down the greeting line, but he couldn't tell who all was there.

The crowd opened up, and Khallum rushed forward to crush Erran in a warm embrace. "Mate, fecking hell, next time ye crave adventure, just come with me to a Blackpool brothel." Khallum surprised him with a firm kiss on the temple. "Donnae ye scare me like that again, aye?"

Erran nodded through the unexpected clog of emotion. A shove from behind reminded him to keep moving. Sessaly. He glanced back and saw Mariel had somehow fallen back, behind Destin. He wanted to urge her to his side, but then Gwyn was kissing his cheeks, lifting her little dark-haired lassie for him to kiss as well.

"Welcome to the world, Esmerelda. I don't take the role of being your father-in-honor with lightness," he said, eyeing the sweet girl with the big, expressive eyes. Unlike Ransom, who took after his rough-featured father, Esmerelda would be a great beauty one day. "Thank the Guardians she resembles you, Gwyn."

"The Northerlands always comes through, one way or another," she quipped, and they both laughed. The king hadn't known it, or even cared, but he'd picked the perfect bride for Khallum. Women of the frozen north were tough and practical, like the women of the Southerlands, but had ice flowing through their veins. She knew good and well what her husband was up to, and she had more important worries to concern herself with.

Aunt Korah was next. Even Erran had always called her that, though sometimes, when being cheeky, Khallum referred to her as the Widow. She'd moved into the keep when Khoulter's wife had died, and she had helped raised all three Warwick children. Korah had also been the mastermind behind Erran's match with Mariel, springing into quick action to conspire with Rylahn when Erran had acted so foolishly.

"How fortunate you're already married, for with that lovely face, I'd have to rethink my policy of a man-less existence." She embraced him with a chuckle. "And how is wedded life, Erran? We chose for ye well?"

"Yes, well. Thank you," he said, instinctively searching for Mariel, but she was talking with Khallum.

"Do you remember my stepson, Evander?" She gestured toward a handsome redhead around the age of thirty.

Erran vaguely recalled that her late husband had produced a son out of wedlock, but he did not remember Korah being so gracious about it. "Aye. It's been…"

"Donnae trouble yourself. We've never actually met. She did-nae suffer me at all until recently." Evander raised both brows and chuckled.

Erran's eyes shifted back to Korah, but she was laughing too. "Aye, well, we are well met now."

"Aye indeed."

Next was young Ransom, hand held fast to his governess's. Erran knelt to greet him, amazed at how much the lad had grown since he'd seen him last.

Erran had only just stood again when he came face-to-face with Yesenia. Her tree-dweller husband hovered close, like he was ready to draw steel at the slightest infraction. *Not likely to do much with it though, is he?* he thought as he sized him up, remembering what a dove the man was.

"Yesenia." He leaned in to offer a hug but thought better of it, then withdrew his hand as well, wondering how stupid he must look to everyone watching. She was radiant, somehow even more than when he'd seen her last. She glowed with the confidence of a woman settled into her life as a wife and mother. Muted, but not gone, was the fire that had once compelled her every word and action.

"Erran." Yesenia's face split in a smile that brought him back to long mornings in the cove, mornings as exciting as they had been frustrating, for all the ways she pushed him to come no further to her than her pleasure. "You remember my husband?"

Erran cleared his throat with a hard grunt. "Corin." The man radiated with threatless warning as they exchanged handshakes, his hands surprisingly soft for a man's. "Good to see you both."

"Mhm," Corin said.

"We only got in this morning ourselves," she said, glancing between them with the tension of a woman readying to stop a fight. Erran wondered if he should prepare for one. "We left Torquil with Corin's mother. He's still a bit young for a long trip like this."

Yes, she was changed. Even her accent was softening.

"And Byrne? Is he coming?"

"Nay." Yesenia's face fell. "Asherley will be delivering any day now, and he didnae wish to leave her side. He seems happy, and that's all I ever wanted for him."

"Aye." Erran smiled, remembering how Yesenia had taken down bully after bully in her little brother's name. In the end, only the Garricks had had the balls and stupidity to go after the poor, sweet boy.

"And your wife? Mariel, is it?"

Erran's belly stung with shame at how quickly he'd forgotten Mariel. He looked over and caught her watching them. In her eyes was something he wished he could unsee. "Would you like to meet her?"

"Seems I will soon enough," Yesenia said pleasantly, nodding at Sessaly's impatience. "We'll catch up later?"

"Aye." His voice cracked. "Aye."

Erran stepped out of the greeting line and joined his parents in a daze. As he watched Mariel finish her own place in line, alone, he was confronted with another failure, and they hadn't even gone inside yet.

"You'll need to do better," Rylahn said, almost under his breath. "If not for the family name, consider your wife's feelings. She should not have to see her husband fawn over his childhood love, and so publicly."

"I didn't *fawn* over her. I was polite. I said hello to her and her husband, asked after her brother, and that was that."

"Defensiveness is a device of the weak. Learn from your errors, or you'll never be the man you should."

"Ah, give him a moment to find himself, love. Erran has moved on. Of course he has. You see how he adores Mariel. But sometimes we have to light a spark to kill the fire." Hestia kissed his cheek. "You both seemed so different when you returned, content with each other. Remember what's real, Erran, and what is not. Dreams don't warm our beds or our hearts. They only remind us how cold our lives are when we wake to find them only that."

Erran didn't need the lecture. He knew how it had looked. To others. To Mariel.

And he knew precisely what secret was burning a hole in his pocket and why.

He had no heart for his father's exploitative game, but he had no choice and would play it just the same.

This time, he would win.

Mariel greeted the Warwicks in a stupor. Her heart heated with anger, then shattered from pain. Over and over this happened until she was dizzy with confusion she was more than ready to be rid of.

The welcomers all blurred into one, a veritable mess of warmth and welcome. Only one stood out, a redheaded man who seemed unusually interested in her words and movements. She'd forgotten his name a second after he'd given it. His gaze followed her down the line.

The moment she stepped in front of Yesenia, she wished she hadn't. The woman was taller than some men, her dark hair plaited like a warrior's. She was dressed in the green and silver of her husband's land, but it was not a gown she wore. Her trousers and blouse reminded her of the way Mariel herself liked to dress, and something about the similarity made her ill. She glowed with a self-assurance that was alarmingly sensual.

It was no delight to see exactly how and why Erran loved her.

"Mariel, I cannae say how lovely it is to finally meet you," Yesenia said, snapping her in for a firm but warm embrace that seemed genuine enough. Maybe she was relieved to be done with Erran. Maybe she was putting on a show. Maybe Mariel's mind was working against her. Maybe, maybe, maybe.

"Likewise." Mariel forged a smile when she pulled back. She turned it on the man at Yesenia's side, a fair-faced blond with a gentleness that seemed radically out of place in the Southerlands.

A bit like Erran actually.

Mariel almost couldn't believe it. Yesenia and Erran had actually married each other, by proxy. They'd ended up with copies of themselves when they couldn't have one another.

"Mariel, a pleasure." The husband, Corin, kissed her hand. "You so remind me of Sen."

"I've heard this before," she said, trying to sound light and playful, the opposite of the darkness festering in her chest. "Now I see what a compliment such a suggestion is, however wrong."

Yesenia smiled. "Erran is a lucky man. I'm sure he knows it."

I thought he did. Mariel caught Erran watching. He stood with his parents and Sessaly, staring into the distance. "Ah, I'm sure we'll speak more later."

"I would like that," Yesenia said, annoyingly full of kindness.

Mariel shifted away from them in a daze of self-recrimination. Her hatred would have been justified if Yesenia had been the cold and unfeeling monster who had broken Erran's heart so callously, but the woman she'd met was perfect for him, a victim of the king's arrogance and who otherwise would have become the willing wife of her childhood love.

She joined her in-laws. When Erran couldn't even meet her eyes, she knew. She knew every one of her fears had been rational. What she didn't know was what to do about it.

"What does our itinerary look like, sir?" Destin asked the steward.

"You're free until the morning," Rylahn answered. "Settle in, catch a kip. Evening meal will be served in your quarters tonight." He turned toward his son. "Except Erran. We're due to meet with Lord Warwick for the next couple of hours."

Erran nodded, looking everywhere but Mariel's way.

"Mariel, would you like to see the coast with me?" Destin asked. The way he'd said it was so transparent, she was sure the others could see through it as well.

"Aye," she said, giving Erran one last opportunity to look up, to show her she was being emotional and paranoid.

But he only muttered a "will you see tonight" before shuffling off behind his father.

Erran's eyes glossed through the mostly transactional exchange between his father and Khallum. They sat across from each other at the table with the famously serrated edges, meant to remind any man there not to get too comfortable, spouting off about levying higher taxes for miners and building more ports in the empty stretch between Sandycove and Warwicktown.

He was so in thrall to his own malaise that he didn't even notice when his father left.

"Ye know you cannae fuck her ever again. Right?"

Erran whipped his head upward. "Come again?"

"You been here at all, Rutland, or dallying about in your own emotions as usual?"

"I was here," Erran replied. Khallum laughed at the lie, and he caved, joining in.

"I ken your father told ye why we uninvited the other families for Esme's blessing."

"Sessaly, actually."

Khallum snorted. "Aliksander will have his hands full with that one."

Erran grimaced. "Aye, well, right now she's gloating."

"Wasnae as bad as ye think," Khallum said. "Unless you're Mariel." He shoved back from the table without touching it and moved to the open window. The ledge was coated in a hundred years of bird waste, a faded tableau of chalky white and olive green. "What happened on that island?"

Erran blew out, whistling. "We crashed. We adapted. We survived. We..."

"Fucked? Finally? So we'll never have to hear about her scars or your freckles again?" Khallum chortled at Erran's polite silence. "Your father sent word you and Mariel had settled your differences. Had hoped to see signs of it myself, but I ken I'll be hoping until I'm dead and burning on the pyre, aye?"

"We *did*," Erran answered, unwilling to elaborate on what was a private matter. Somehow, it seemed wrong to tell anyone about all he and Mariel had shared, even his oldest friend. Sam had only been given the broad strokes, just enough to piece together a simple understanding. Hamish even less. "I don't know what came over me out there. I don't *want* your sister anymore, Khal, no matter how it looked. I'm happy for her. I've moved on."

"What's good for you is you'll have two days to correct that impression." Khallum traced his knuckles along the fossilized excrement. "I'm nay one to offer advice on the doings of the heart."

"That 'cos you don't have one?"

Khallum belched. "How's that?"

They both laughed. Erran relaxed.

"Gwyn is a good wife. That ratsbane king can gargle my sack into eternity, and he'll never hear a whisper of gratitude from me, but I'm grateful for her, every day. She isnae who I'd have chosen for myself, but she's right for me. Find the same true of Mariel, for you?"

Erran nodded.

"Ye told her so?"

"Not in so many words."

"Then do as I do. And show her what ye cannae say."

Show her. He'd tried the night before, in the bath, and had mucked up even that. But there was no point in asking Khallum *how* because he was the last person he'd take romantic advice from.

"How *are* you, Khal? With everything?"

"All this?" Khallum's boots scuffed the stone as he veered away from the window. "Wasnae how I saw it happening."

"I know."

"Well enough. Have my heir and a lassie to dote on. No doubt more on the way. My siblings are content in their own unions, so I donnae need to raise banners to free them. The Southerlands has its troubles, but I ken we're thriving as best we can, despite the ratsbane's increasingly criminal feckin' taxes."

It wasn't what Erran was asking, but Khallum already knew that. Khoulter Warwick had been a most unusual man, especially for a leader of Warwicktown. He could be equally cold and callous as warm and protective. Yesenia had adored him. Honestly, so had Erran. So many of his favorite boyhood memories involved the man, who had been as a second father to him. Hard but fair, and with a rare but incredible playfulness missing in most hardened leaders. "I miss him too."

Khallum tensed, facing away. "Aye. Every day."

"Shall we drink to his memory?"

"I'll send for the ale."

"Desi, I don't want to talk," Mariel said when their toes hit the sand. They had both removed their boots when they reached the tall grass lining the rugged shore. "So if that was your aim—"

"It was, and you knew it and followed me anyway," Destin said.

"Because I needed to get the feck out of there before I made an arse of myself!"

Nothing had prepared her for how awful it would be to see Erran so discomfited around his beautiful, perfect ex. Mariel longed for the days before the island, when she had no care of how he spent his time or how he spread his affection. At least then she'd known who *she* was still.

All she could think about was the two of *them* fucking in the cove, for hours and hours, like Sessaly had implied in the damned carriage.

"Do you not think he deserves some grace?"

Mariel spun on him. "Say that again?"

Destin pulled a patient breath through his nose. "Last time he saw her, he was still coming to terms with how he'd lost her. Does he not deserve a moment to put his thoughts together?"

"His thoughts?" Mariel shook her head. "You mean you couldn't read his thoughts, which were full of her?"

"Not in the way you think."

"And how would you know?"

"Because I know what remorse looks like on a man," Destin said quietly.

"Remorse he can't dilly her anymore," Mariel muttered, quickening her pace.

Destin stopped in the sand. "You're in love with him."

Mariel's breath stuttered as she turned, enraged. "How dare you suggest such a thing?"

"How dare *I*?" Destin laughed. "Is there some unspoken rule that one of us has to be a mess at all times?"

"Implying *I* am the mess?" Mariel asked in challenge.

"Implying precisely that."

"Oh, you...You're sober for a few weeks, and now you're the reasonable one?"

"I'll pretend you didn't mean to hurt me, because I can see you're hurting," Destin said evenly. "But I have to admit. It's unsettling to see you like this."

She blinked in indignation. "Like what?"

Destin blinked back. "Unhinged."

"You..." Mariel couldn't speak. She marched farther down the shore. "Why would I take advice on relationships from a man who has had dozens of one-night trysts and never returned to a single bed?"

"Because the fear that keeps you from recognizing what's in your own heart is the same fear that keeps me from wanting more for myself." Destin grabbed her arm and stopped her. "You're going to destroy your own happiness to mollify your pride, which is beneath you."

Mariel snorted and rolled her eyes toward the cloudy sky.

"You need to trust him."

"You saw—"

"You need to *trust* him, and give him time."

"Time for *what*? To decide who he wants to snog more?"

"You're being so crude."

"Not crude enough apparently, for I'm still no match for *her*." Mariel sank into the sand as the fight drained from her. She'd already wasted so much energy. "You think I want to feel this way? Like I am only good enough to live in her shadow?"

Destin laughed without humor. "Oh, I know damn well you do not." He sat next to her. "But closing down…lashing out… You've seen how it destroys others. You think I liked my spirits because I'm weak?"

Mariel softened. "I never thought you were weak, Des."

"Aye, well I am, in a way, because I see you doing what I've always done to myself. At even a glimmer of happiness, I shut down. I sabotage it before it can become anything real, for then I can wallow in a suffering that's safer than risking myself for the chance at joy."

"What do you suggest then, eh? I cannot watch…" Mariel's eyes stung with tears. "I hate feeling so…I won't be his second choice."

"Give him a chance to prove you're not."

"The proof is not mine to make!"

"Give him a *chance,* Mar."

"You saw—"

"A man whose behavior was being closely watched, by dozens of people waiting for him to fuck up. Do you count yourself among them?"

Mariel balked. "I wasn't *wanting* him to fuck up."

"Do you not think his own wife should be the one he can turn to, to talk about it?"

"To talk about his love for another woman?"

"You're doing it again." Destin shook his head. "If you really want to know where he stands, *ask* him, Mariel. Do you not owe him that much, at least? After everything you went through together? Would you not expect the same from him?"

"And if I don't like the answer?"

Destin smiled thinly. "At least you'll have one."

An attendant showed Mariel to her apartments. She'd expected to be alone and was surprised Erran was already there. He lifted from his chair the moment she came in, and he marched over and swept her into his arms with so much force, she forgot how to breathe.

He wrapped his hands under her ass and pulled her lower lip through his teeth. "I missed you," he purred.

"Did you—" Mariel's words dissolved when he backed her to a wall with a breath-stealing thud. Soon he was between her legs, yanking away her trousers, his fingers brushing the length of her and stealing her questions, which she needed to ask, and should ask, before she allowed even another second of intimacy.

It wasn't long at all before pleasure took the place of reserve. Then he was inside of her, her legs draped over his arms as he drove in so deep, she dug her nails into the wall to dull the sting of pain.

He watched himself take her, growing harder with every thrust. Her mouth watered with the thrill of such a fervent tryst, the realization she wished he would treat her like that more often, like she was the last drop of water in an endless desert. The thought pushed her over the edge, and she buried a scream in her sleeve as she climaxed.

Erran finally lifted his gaze to hers. His eyes narrowed in alarm. "Am I hurting you?"

"Nay," she lied, because even though she knew it wasn't her he was thinking of, she still craved the demand of his touch. She'd allowed herself to be weakened by him, but even that wasn't enough to push him away, as she should.

"Guardians, you…" Erran panted, his eyes rolling back as he came in a violent spasm. He gently lowered her and staggered back. "I'm sorry if that was…I just missed you."

It was the quickest sex they'd had yet, and she was ashamed to have enjoyed it so much. Ashamed to have been turned on by how electrified he'd been about his ex, as though Mariel drew power from the self-hatred his desire for Yesenia had caused.

"Think nothing of it," Mariel murmured, reaching for her trousers before he could see even more of her tears.

SEVENTEEN
OUR OLD SPOT

The morning delivered a lovely, balmy breeze wisping through the curtains, the only thing separating their room from the elements. Erran was still fast asleep after his bold showing the night before. Mariel wasn't ready to talk about what had happened, or think about her own role in their hungered rendezvous, which was even less clear to her in the dawn of day.

Mariel wandered down one identical hall after another until she happened upon the double kitchens. One side was full with staff readying for the day. She was more at home with the bustle of usefulness, but they wouldn't see it that way. They'd grow quiet at her presence, nervously waiting for her to make a request or leave. She was on the opposite end of the social hierarchy now. Nothing she said would change their feelings.

Mariel opted for the calm side, hoping to find at least a pot for boiling and a jar of tea leaves.

"Oh, Mariel." Yesenia turned from where she stood at the hearth, stirring something that smelled earthy and delicious. She smiled. "Seems we had the same idea this morning."

"Avoiding the awkward dance of trying to make unwanted small talk with the nervous kitchen staff?" Mariel asked before she could think better of it.

Yesenia laughed. "We were always cozy with our workers here, but it certainly isnae like that in the Easterlands."

"Never been."

"It's exactly the nightmare you're imagining."

Mariel laughed despite herself, despite imagining Yesenia with her legs clamped around Erran's head, writhing under his skilled tongue. "I didn't mean to intrude—"

"You're not." Yesenia unhooked two mugs and ladled tea into one. "Here."

Mariel tentatively stepped forward. "Gratitude."

"Donnae thank me just yet. The good tea is on the other side." She winked.

Mariel wanted to hate her. Oh, Guardians, how she wished she did. But there was a certain charm to the woman that made Mariel wish they'd met under different circumstances. They might have even been friends. "If I die, I'm holding you responsible."

"That's the spirit." Yesenia filled her own mug and nodded toward a small table, where the workers probably took their own meals. "Join me?"

Mariel suddenly froze. Small talk was one thing. Whatever Yesenia was offering seemed entirely another. "Oh, nay. I need to..." She gestured behind her.

Yesenia nodded. "Another time."

"Aye," Mariel said and rushed out, her heart a sprinting, dysfunctional mess. Embarrassed, she dipped into the first set of doors she saw and found herself in the midst of a modest library.

It wasn't like the indulgent cavern of learning Whitecliffe had. There were only a few shelves, half-full of books, and bins full of what looked like rolled maps. In the center was a desk far too large for the room, and she realized it wasn't a library at all, but an office.

The doors opened behind her. She turned and saw Khallum.

"Mariel." He latched the doors and smiled. "I'm glad ye came along this time."

She realized *this time* was a reference to the way she'd been excluded from Erran's last visit to Warwicktown, the one that had launched the entire messy affair and his campaign to rehabilitate his image. She'd fallen ill from something she'd eaten at the Spires, which she'd seen as a mercy. Only later did she learn just how much humiliation she'd been spared. "Esmerelda is a beauty."

"Aye." Khallum stepped farther in and leaned against his desk. "I ken I'll enjoy spoiling her."

"My father was like that. Always spoiled me, when he could."

"You two were close?"

Mariel nodded.

"Erran said you lost both your parents young."

"Aye."

"Condolences."

"It was a long time ago. I'm sorry about your own father, Lord Warwick. I always heard he was a fair and just lord."

Khallum nodded at the floor. He crossed his feet. "Aye, he was a good man. And call me Khallum. Your husband has seen me naked."

Mariel laughed awkwardly. "You're probably here to work, so I'll just—"

"I saw ye come in here and followed," he said candidly. "Thought we could talk."

What is it with all the cursed talking? "About?"

"This must be weird for ye, after all ye heard about Erran's last visit. But if I thought there was any *real* trouble to be had, I wouldnae have invited him or you."

"Oh, we don't…have to talk about this."

"Aye, but we do. May not be my business in other times or places, but it's mine here. Erran's an emotional lad. Not something

I understand leastways, but he doesnae understand me much either. He's always needed time with stuff, and I expect it's why his impulsiveness last time was such a disaster. If he'd had time to think on it, it would never have happened at all."

"Khallum." Mariel didn't know what to say. Leaving a conversation initiated by her host—who was also the lord of the entire Southerlands—would be rude. "I won't…You can expect no trouble from me while we're here."

"Or them," Khallum stated, a resoluteness underscoring the words. "Gwyn and Korah will be by your rooms around dusk to help ye get…all prettied up for the banquet tonight." He waved his hands as if discussing some rare magic he could never understand. "Not that ye need it."

She could tell he was being polite, rather than flirting, so she smiled. "I'll take all the help I can get."

"Aye, well you'll have more than you'll want." He chuckled. "One more thing, then I'll leave it be. Guardians know why Erran was infatuated with my sister for as long as he was. She wasnae as lovely as she seems now, trust me on that, nor was she exactly *nice* to the lad. Strung him about for years. It would be a shame for jealousy to ruin what seems far more durable than two bairns messing about ever was. Ye ken?"

Mariel nodded, wondering how often Khallum offered advice to others, and if so, if he was as clumsy with it as he was acting then. But she had no qualms with him or his intentions, which were steeped in loyalty for his best mate.

Khallum slapped his knees and stood. "As I said, good to have ye here, Mariel. Always welcome."

"Thank you, Khallum."

She waited for him to leave and then decided she was no longer interested in her tea.

Mariel set her mug on the nearest table and headed for the shore, where she could be alone with her thoughts and no men would deign to offer unasked-for advice about how she was supposed to feel about her husband still being in love with his enchanting ex.

Erran asked everyone he saw if they'd seen Mariel. A few said no, and a couple gave vague but incorrect suggestions, but the most useful piece of information was when someone said she was seen heading to the beach, alone. As soon as he heard it, it seemed the most likely answer, because he, too, felt a calling for the tide lapping over his feet. The sand between his toes. A reminder that who he'd been on Feck-All Island was who he could still be.

His failures only kept adding. The desperate sex he'd engaged her in had just confused her more. When she thought he was asleep, she'd slipped out to the balcony and quietly wept. Disgrace had kept him fixed to the bed, with the shame of knowing that if he had caused her sadness, he had no right to alleviate it.

He did know that if he didn't make it right soon, she would slip away from him altogether. If that happened, he wasn't confident anything he did would bring her back.

Erran had just stepped into the field of seagrass when a familiar voice called his name.

"Can we talk?"

Once, the sound had stopped time for him. The trill of her imaginative cursing had been a delightful gift, even when the cursing was aimed at him.

He turned, prepared to say no, but her grave expression stayed him. "Is something wrong?"

Yesenia nodded. "Aye, I ken there is, and I'd like us to clear the air. Put it behind us so we can all enjoy the celebration tonight."

Erran glanced down the shore. He didn't see Mariel, but he couldn't see much of anything through the dense brush and low fog. "Can we do this later? I need to find Mariel."

"It willnae take long."

He sighed through his teeth.

"Please?"

Erran nodded because he recognized the old determination in her. She rarely relented when she had her mind set. "I only have a minute."

"Our old spot?"

Their old spot. The cove. Where a key era in his life had started, thrived, and ended. "That seems unwise, given our history."

"And private."

"There's plenty of privacy inside the keep. Why not there?"

"Because I have a husband who may be feeling like your wife, and no one ever goes to the cove except us. I'd like to resolve this without more eyes on us, if possible. We had more than enough on us yesterday, and I'd ken your first night here was as cool as mine."

The cove was the very last place he wanted to be with Yesenia, but to say so would attach more meaning to it than it deserved. If he had moved on, the cove would mean nothing. It *did* mean nothing. "Let's be quick about it."

Yesenia led the way, Erran holding several intentional paces behind her as he checked to make sure no one was watching them slip away together. When she ducked into the grotto, he sighed and followed her in.

"Where's Corin?" Erran left his arms crossed, as though he couldn't trust them, which wasn't true. He could trust himself. But he needed Yesenia to see he wasn't going to suddenly launch himself at her like last time, even if she was the one who had invited him.

"He knows where I am and why," she answered, leaning against the rough cave wall. "I wanted to apologize. For how I left Warwicktown after I was married, without even a good-bye."

Erran shook his head quickly. "It would…" He almost didn't finish, but he needed to. For himself. For Mariel. "It wouldn't have lasted much longer, I ken."

She considered that for a few moments. "Maybe you're right. Doesnae matter anymore. When the king stole my life from me, I was so feckin' angry at the world, and I suppose at you too."

"At me?"

"'Cos I knew…I knew you'd move on. And ye should have. Of course ye should have. I donnae ken why it angered me so, especially when I'd fallen for Corin in spite of my monumental effort not to, but it did. And *then* I was angry at ye for still loving me, which is backward, I know. Ye couldnae have won is what I'm saying, because the rules of the game were never fair." Yesenia bowed her head. "We never got our closure. The king saw to it, but I sealed it with my stubbornness. If I'd have been kinder… clearer…what happened the last time we saw each other wouldnae have happened at all. It was out of character for you, which is how I know you'd reached the end of your wits. And I want ye to know, Erran, that I see my part in it now. And I'm sorry."

Yesenia's confession was as unexpected as it was informative. He hadn't thought of it from the view she presented, that she'd been angry at him for moving on after she'd done exactly the same thing. "There's no need to be. What's done is done," he said, replaying her words.

"I was also mad that you'd told me ye loved me, 'cos…" She seemed to gather her courage. "I loved ye too, but there wasnae a thing I could do about it. And it was a different definition of love than the one I know now."

Erran understood perfectly, but he didn't know how to voice to her what he hadn't even voiced to himself.

He had fallen in love with Mariel Ashdown, and the thrilling sensation utterly eclipsed anything he'd ever felt for Yesenia.

"I like her, Erran. I hope you two are happy together."

"Aye, I am happy," he answered, because he wasn't sure anymore if the same was true for Mariel. As much as he appreciated Yesenia's gesture, the longer they talked, the more uneasy he grew about being there with her. He regretted not pushing back harder. If anyone *had* seen, there'd be no end to the trouble. His reputation wouldn't recover this time, but worse than all of that, Mariel would believe nothing he said ever again.

"You should reassure her then."

Erran thought of the letter in his pocket that he'd written to give to Yesenia and decided it was no longer necessary. Maybe he'd written it more for himself anyway, the closure she had denied him before.

He patted his pocket and let his hand fall away. "I need to go find her."

Mariel watched Erran and Yesenia sneak off together. Her gaze traveled with them to the cove—the feckin' *cove*—and her body followed. She cursed herself for being such a jealous fool, for caring at all about a man whose caprices changed with the tides.

But the truth would relieve her burdens, as her mother used to say. There was no use pining for what wasn't. The sooner she recovered her heart, the sooner it could be hers again.

"I suspect she's intimidated by me," Yesenia was saying.

"Everyone is, which is how you've always liked it," Erran said. "I should head back before tongues start wagging. Maybe you should wait a moment after I leave."

"You were right. We should have done this somewhere else."

"Aye, but what's done is done."

An easy silence permeated the air. Mariel flattened herself against the rocks and told herself it was all right. It was better to know. Better to return to who she'd been before, impenetrable against such a vulnerable assault. Things had been good then, sometimes even great. Hard, yes, but she'd known what to expect and had known where everyone in her life had stood. Where she'd stood.

"You'll always be a part of me, Erran," Yesenia said softly. Her boots clicked on the rocks. "I'm sorry for never saying I loved ye back. I should have."

"Aye," he said with a laugh that sounded almost angry. "But ye always were willful."

Mariel didn't need to hear any more. She loathed herself for needing any of it, for thinking it would give her the strength to put these foolish, useless feelings back into one of the many tiny boxes where she placed all the inconveniences of her life. So what if they'd bonded on the island? Enjoyed each other? At least she'd learned she liked sex. She'd like it even better when her heart wasn't attached to the man underneath her.

She staggered back to the beach, her insufficient breaths a sharp contrast to the resolve in her mind. It was done. She was done. It was as simple as that.

But if she didn't want this anymore, why did it hurt so badly?

If she'd convinced herself to move on, why was the pain almost more than she could bear?

Mariel waited for a giant wave to crash onto the shore before screaming into the sea.

EIGHTEEN
HONOR

Mariel would have rather gouged her own eyes out than made herself "presentable" or attended the feckin' party. Fetes had never been her thing, but trying to pretend she was fine was just beyond her ability. Because of Erran's and Yesenia's duties to little Esmerelda, Mariel would have to watch them pretend they were over each other while everyone else studied her, hoping for a reaction.

In the hours since she'd discovered Erran sneaking around, she'd been plotting an escape from the marriage altogether, a union that was no longer practical or necessary, but there was one rather large problem she hadn't solved. Erran knew her secret, as did two of his closest friends, and she doubted he'd be as compelled to protect it if she was no longer his property.

Korah and Gwyn were unexpectedly delightful women, and Mariel liked them both, despite her temperament. Korah, the late Khoulter's sister, was a no-nonsense widow who seemed possessed of little warmth, but had a natural maternal air, something Mariel had noted in her almost-neurotic assiduity over the details of the elaborate gown the women had picked out for her.

Gwyn was just as matter-of-fact, but she fussed at Korah for pushing Mariel to wear something way beyond her comfort.

"This style is in season, Gwyn," Korah snipped. She tugged the short sleeves of Mariel's emerald gown down over her shoulders. "Perhaps you're worried because a shoulder-less gown would cause a woman to freeze to death where you're from, hm?"

"Or I simply believe a woman should wear what makes her feel lovely, and not succumb to the pressures of others." Gwyn had her vibrant red hair tied behind her. The one thing Mariel knew about her was she was the daughter of Lord Dereham of the Northerlands.

"It's fine," Mariel said, assuring them both with a grin that made her feel so damned foolish. This wasn't her—the formfitting gown, which revealed too much of her bosom, the painted cheeks and curled hair...The woman in the mirror was a stranger.

A beautiful one, she'd admit. Through some strange magic, they'd transformed her. But it wasn't real. Wasn't her.

It will make it easier to put on a brave face if it's some other woman who has to walk into the banquet and face her humiliation with a smile.

"See?" Korah lifted her brows in reprisal.

Gwyn gripped Mariel's shoulders and leaned in to whisper, "Don't let her intimidate you. You can wear whatever you want, however you want."

"Nay, I like this." *A mask. A facade. A means to an end.* "Besides, you're both wearing off-shoulder gowns."

Gwyn wore marigold, which made her hair even more fiery, and Korah a deep orange, less bold than matronly. They were both handsome women, for different reasons, and their gowns were suited for their complexions and personalities. Mariel supposed green did the same for her, as her dress was a near-perfect match to her eyes, but she knew nothing about fashion.

"Do you always hold banquets for the birth of a wee one?" Mariel asked.

"Nay," Korah answered quickly, like she was racing Gwyn to be the one to speak first. "Only our lassies, who have their honorary parents pledged to them at the banquet. The little lads are welcomed with a ceremonial hunt and their first blooding."

"Ransom had that?"

"Not yet." Korah flashed a disapproving look at Gwyn. "His mother has deemed him too young for the same tradition his father and grandfather and all before them took part in before they'd reached their sixth month. I ken he'll be betrothed before she relents."

"Korah," Gwyn said, sighing. "It's true I feel he's too young. I told Khallum we could do it at one year. That's my compromise. It's more than fair."

"Not everything requires compromise, dear," Korah muttered and put away the rouge and other oddities they'd used to turn Mariel into a changeling.

"Oh, you mean I could have just said no?" Gwyn sniped back, grinning at Mariel in the mirror. She adjusted some of Mariel's stray hairs, tucking them into the many pins she'd used to keep her updo in place. "You were beautiful before we dressed you up, Mariel. Beauty comes in many forms."

Mariel laughed. "You don't have to say that. I know I'm not much for…" She dabbed her hands on the gown. Her hair. "I like it that way, even if it isn't terribly exciting."

"You have a confidence about you that I've never had. Confidence is alluring. When you arrived yesterday, I watched every man on our staff look not at Yesenia or me or your mother-in-law, but *you*."

"My stepson among them," Korah groused. "Watch out for him, Mariel."

"I didn't peg you for a liar, Gwyn," Mariel said, narrowing her eyes. Other than the lingering looks from Korah's stepson, the only scrutiny she remembered was the embarrassment of being the third wheel in her own marriage. "I didn't feel the least bit confident yesterday."

"Isnae lying," Korah said from across the room. "You may not be traditionally beautiful, Mariel, but ye are beautiful just the same. And I ken, gown or no, you'll be fending off dances all night tonight. Your husband will have his hands full."

Mariel snorted. "I don't dance."

"Aye, but ye will, just the same," Korah replied. "Now, come. We're nearly late already."

When Erran returned to the keep, after failing to find Mariel at the beach, an attendant informed him his wife had returned but was being dressed and readied in their apartments, and men were not welcome. Then Khallum called him in on business, which they addressed while getting fitted for last-minute adjustments to their banquet garments, stealing any potential opportunity he might find to speak with Mariel before they were forced into a sea of people and expectations.

For a private event, there were many people in attendance—the merchant class, Khallum explained, the businessmen and women whose support was critical to the peace and prosperity of Warwicktown. Every one of them, Khallum said, were social climbers.

"You could have invited the other stewards if you were set on a big event," Erran said. He hadn't stopped searching for Mariel, but she hadn't arrived yet, and neither had Gwyn nor Korah, whom she'd been getting ready with.

Destin was across the room, talking with Sessaly and Hestia. It was good to see him at ease, like he belonged there. Keeping him grounded and happy—and sober—was the key to keeping Mariel's secret.

"Nay, because then these men wouldnae feel like they're on the top of the pile, would they?" Khallum grinned and toasted two such men as they walked by, beaming from the attention. "Besides, who really wants to be here? Not I."

"Nor I." Erran laughed. He spotted Yesenia dancing with Corin. It was an odd sight—the Yesenia he remembered wouldn't so much have lifted a foot in time with the music—but a good one. It would be better if they danced together all night, so Mariel could see the way of things.

"And there is my lovely wife," Khallum sang, opening his arms wide as Gwyn, looking fetching in a gold gown, stepped forward to accept his embrace. Korah was right behind, swishing by without a hello as she moved to a circle of women on the other side of the floor.

"Where's—" Erran choked on the word as Mariel entered, her shoulders pinched and unsure. Her dark hair was curled and pinned around her face, decorated with painted silver petals that sparkled under the candelabras. But it was the dress…How they'd found a gown so similar to her impassioned eyes was a trick of magic, surely. Her pale skin peeked above the low neckline, her breasts arced and perfect.

"Breathe," Khallum jested, leaning in with a laugh.

Erran's mouth was completely devoid of moisture. He cleared his throat and stepped forward, but Mariel breezed on by without even looking his way.

"Ouch," Sessaly said, skittering over with a scandalized expression. "Is there trouble between our little island lovers?"

"Sessaly, mind your business," Erran snapped. "For once."

"You are a menace," Khallum said to her. "I say that as your lord as much as your brother's friend."

Sessaly curtsied. "Thank you."

"Wasnae a compliment, lass. I'm not the steward, who'll endure your antics. You'll behave here, or you'll leave." Khallum swatted the air, and she backed away in stunned contrition.

"Excuse me," Erran said, breaking away to follow Mariel, but she was already dancing with her brother.

"She's catching the eyes of every man here," his mother said, slipping an arm through his. "Including yours. Why are you not with her?"

Erran didn't know why he told the truth. She wouldn't understand, and he was certain to regret it. "I think she's upset about Yesenia."

"Because you were so tongue-tied when you saw her yesterday?"

"I wasn't *tongue-tied*. I found my words fine, thank you."

"I was being kind. It was worse."

"Not because..." He checked to be sure Sessaly wasn't lurking, fishing for more fodder for her friends. "It wasn't for the reason you and everyone are thinking."

"Oh?" Hestia sipped her wine, waving and smiling at people as they passed.

"I'm committed to this marriage, Mother."

"How clinical that sounds," she replied. "Though *love* is rather distracting. Perhaps *committed* is for the best."

Erran groaned in exasperation. "Were you not the one who said there was no room for love in a marriage?"

"I said the two are typically exclusive of one another." She wiggled her gloved fingers at another woman. "Or can be."

"Do you have anything practical to offer, Mother?"

Hestia's smile faded when she turned toward him. "And when was the last time any of my lessons landed with you, aye? When you were five?"

"Say what you want to say." Erran watched, tense, as Mariel moved from Destin's arms to Khallum's. "I'm listening."

Hestia breathed deep. "I will not pretend I know all that's passed between the two of you. But I saw two very different people return from that island. And now they are, somehow, reverting to who they were before." She lifted her shoulders in a dainty shrug. "If you say you're over your dalliance with Yesenia, as your mother, I believe you. But I am not the one who needs convincing."

"I tried to find her earlier, so we could talk about it. But she—"

"Is avoiding you? Who could blame her? Her pride is hurt. Her heart...Well, who can say?"

Erran grimaced. "If she won't speak to me, then how can I make this right?"

"You try harder, son."

"Again?" Mariel asked when Destin traded places with Khallum. "When I said I didn't want to dance, I feckin' meant it."

Destin grinned and swept them into formation. "I should have said it earlier. You look beautiful tonight."

"Do I not usually?"

"I'm your brother, not a beau you can trap with words."

"When have I ever had a beau?"

Destin was quiet for a moment. "For a while, I thought you and Remy...might marry?"

Mariel laughed for lack of a better response. "That would never have happened."

"Mar, I *know* you were sweet on him."

"Aye, but I was sweet on Auggie more."

"Really?" Destin peeled back in surprise.

"You're shocked I like women as much as men?"

"Only that I didn't ken it sooner." He chuckled to himself. "Makes sense, I suppose. She's certainly always been in love with you."

"Has she? How do you know?"

"How do you *not* know?"

Mariel had always been unconscious of anything not directly connected to the survival of herself and others. One time, they'd all been out to a tavern for drinks and a man had joined them, talking mostly to Mariel all night. When he'd invited her home with him, hours later, she'd been so stunned that even he'd laughed about it. For days, the others had ribbed her about her obliviousness. "I suppose I never had time for distractions like that."

"Love isn't a distraction," Destin said.

"If not, then it's a weakness, and I refuse to be weak."

"Is that a confession?"

Mariel grimaced at the corner she'd unwittingly backed herself into. "Point to you."

"Erran has been staring at you all night. Were you aware?"

"I'm hardly aware of anything more than whether my feet are in the right place, Desi," she lied. She'd seen him watching. Trying to catch her eyes. Starting her way, only to retreat. It wasn't her job to coddle him or his reputation though.

"Why not dance with him? Huh? Seems harmless enough. There's only so much he can say when you're surrounded by dozens of others."

"I just—" She cut herself off when she noticed the redheaded man staring her way. He raised his glass. She frowned. "Do you remember Korah's stepson?" Destin spun, and she yanked him back. "Could you be more subtle?"

"Aye, what about him?" Destin's eyes narrowed over her shoulder.

"I ken he's quite rude."

"Rude? How?"

"*He* hasn't stopped staring at me since we arrived here yesterday."

Destin sputtered a laugh. "You really are oblivious."

"What do you mean?"

"I mean he's coming over here to take my place." Destin peeled back with a cheeky grin. "I should refresh my juice anyway."

"Destin, don't you dare—" Mariel plastered a polite smile when the tall man stepped in front of her. "Oh, ah, hello."

"I half expected to wait all night for a chance to dance with you," he said, brazenly taking her hand in his without asking.

Mariel was too taken aback to do anything but let it happen. She was still trying to figure out how she'd ended up dancing. "Evander, right?"

"I never much liked my name until I heard you say it." Evander grinned and spun them. When he snapped her close, she floundered her footing. "Say it again?"

"What? Your name? Why?"

Evander leaned in, and his lips brushed her ear. "Because nothing has ever sounded so lovely."

"He has some feckin' audacity," Erran muttered, slamming his mug onto a passing tray. Evander. Erran remembered why he'd never liked the scoundrel, even though he'd only known him by reputation. "And no decency. What kind of man holds another man's wife so close? In front of all to see?"

"Few men would make such a bold choice, and certainly no gentleman," Hestia agreed.

"*I* should be dancing with her."

"You should."

"But she's upset, and I'd only embarrass her."

"Equally embarrassing for others to see her husband hasn't even approached her, wouldn't you say?" Hestia leaned close. "But if you storm over like a jealous lover, you will only make it worse."

Mariel could pin a note to a tree with an arrow from a hundred yards, but she had no inkling of how to get rid of Evander. She caught Erran glaring, which was infuriating when he hadn't even asked her to dance. He didn't want her, but no one else could either? Was that it?

"Quiet for my sister!" Khallum boomed.

Mariel used the interruption to make a smooth escape from Evander.

The music died down. Everyone dancing dispersed. "I'm certain ye all remember Yesenia, and if you donnae, I ken ye at least remember her daggers. I know the Garricks certainly do."

Everyone laughed, a few whistling.

"Maybe *you* should give the speech," Yesenia said with a hard side-eye.

Khallum bowed and backed away, leaving her alone at the front of the room.

"All right, that didnae work," she said.

More laughter.

"So I ken I'm giving a speech."

"Speech!" someone cried and others joined in, including Destin.

Mariel gawped at him.

"It's tradition to feast when a Warwick lassie joins the family. I ken the last time ye all ate this good was when I was born, and my father was much more frugal than my brother." She paused for the chuckles, then turned behind her and grabbed something from someone. A candle. "I accept the noble charge bestowed upon me by my brother and Gwyn." She smiled down at the infant in the festooned cradle. "Esmerelda, as your mother-in-honor, I am sworn to love and protect you as your mother would, and will, if one day she cannot. Aye, where's Erran then?"

Mariel averted her eyes when Erran cut through the crowd and joined Yesenia.

Erran accepted a candle from someone with a tight smile. Yesenia narrowed her eyes from the side, something Mariel was also doing. "And what a feast it is!" he declared, his mouth pulling into the briefest wince. He shifted in place, squinted, looked around, and sucked his teeth.

He's nervous.

Yesenia gave him a prodding look.

"I, as well, accept the noble charge bestowed upon me by Lord and Lady Warwick." Both of his hands clutched the candle. His gaze traveled to the cradle with a lingering, thoughtful expression. "Esmerelda, as your father-in-honor, I am sworn to love and protect you as your father would, and will, if one day he cannot."

Khallum and Gwyn joined them, each carrying a lit candle, which they each tipped toward Erran's and Yesenia's unlit ones. All four raised their flames, then placed them into sconces on the wall behind Esmerelda's cradle.

Mariel exhaled through the applause. It was done. She could slip out without drawing too much scrutiny.

"Gratitude to you both," Khallum declared. "And now we feast!"

"Khallum, if I may…" Erran stepped forward with one hand on his vest.

"May what? Another speech?"

"Of a sort. I've something to say, and I'd like everyone here to hear it because I haven't the patience for fishwife gossip, and even less when it's wrong."

Khallum's brows fused in skepticism, but he stepped aside.

Mariel's body seized in one fluid clench. Evander, still hovering, made a *hmm* sound.

"Guardians," she whispered. "Someone needs to stop him…" Her head shook back and forth. Back and forth.

Everyone fixed their attention to a breathless Erran. His eyes were wide and wild.

"Some of you were here for my blunders." Erran scanned the crowd, and Mariel ducked behind the nearest person who wasn't Evander. "Aye, some for both. I suppose curiosity is normal enough, but lies are harmful, so I'll clear them up now."

"I can't listen to this," she said and turned to leave, but Evander grabbed her hand and snapped her back. She ripped it away again. Where was Destin?

"Yesterday, I saw someone I had once cared for and was pulled into the past for a moment, before I could remember myself. A past I have no need or desire for, not anymore." He licked his lips and gazed at his feet. "In being so unprepared, I hurt someone I care about very much, and I haven't known the words that can make it right again."

"The bastard," Mariel whispered, heartsick and disgusted. "He's trying to save face. So his father won't…" She couldn't speak.

"Mariel, come on, are you really so deluded?" Destin asked, finally stepping between her and the nuisance of a man who still hadn't left.

"The woman I married, she's so unlike me." Erran grinned to himself, casting his eyes to the side. "Oh, in absolutely every way. And how cross she makes me, how utterly fecking stubborn…" He grew serious again. When he glanced at Khallum in apology, Khallum nodded in encouragement. "But this is about me and how I behaved. And if she's still here tonight, I need her, and everyone here, to know how I feel about her. And that…"

Mariel refused to hear another word. He could rehabilitate his image without her.

She lifted the dress of her horrid gown and raced out of the banquet.

NINETEEN
THE LETTER

Mariel was a woman possessed, propelled by the aimless despair of the lost. As she traveled from the stones to the brush to the sand, she rode the rhythm of her beleaguered breaths.

Her world had started spinning the day she'd married Erran. Even her identity no longer belonged to her. The princeling had been a means to an end, and she hadn't once forgotten herself until the island. That cursed island, where everything had been the opposite of what it should, a world turned on its head and shaken until it was unrecognizable.

I need to be reminded of who I am and who I am not, she told herself as she slowed, nearing the jagged formation of rocks that had been the backdrop for the best moments of Erran's life. Someone had once told her a person always returned to the place of their greatest contentment, and he'd gone there *that very afternoon* with Yesenia, unable to resist the past for even a day.

Mariel couldn't compete. She didn't want to. Only in confronting her pain could she be rid of it altogether and return to the rightful path her life had been meant to take before she'd allowed her heart the pointless, painful detour.

She climbed carefully over the sharp boulders marking the entrance, almost disappointed when none cut her. Nothing signified life more than blood, the capacity to bleed. As a young lass, starving and watching her loved ones diminish by the day, she'd dig her nails to her thighs on her worst days, replacing one pain for another—a safer pain to mask the dark and terrible one from which there was no escape.

A pain caused by the Rutlands.

Her woes had come full circle, and it was a cruel twist of fate that her present agony was architected by her own weakness.

Mariel traced her hands along the walls. Was it there, she wondered, or there? Where had he pressed Yesenia to the rocks when he couldn't temper his lust another moment? Where had she lifted her skirt and invited him in?

Everywhere, her heart decided. The place radiated with the birth and death of Erran's happiness.

"Mar." Erran's boots screeched as he slid, wobbling for balance. "Mariel, stop. Stop and look at me."

So he'd followed her. Of course he had, for if he hadn't, then his obscene showing in the banquet would seem as disingenuous as it had been. The entire trip had been a rehabilitation campaign for him, and he'd won. He'd won them all over, and she shouldn't have cared. She shouldn't have cared a whit.

"Mariel, please. We really, really need to talk."

Her head shook because words were too hard.

"This distance forming between us…I *hate* it. I absolutely hate it, and I know…I haven't been myself here, and I know you see it."

Mariel keeled over a crag, unable to breathe more than stunted inhales, her exhales even more defiant. But if she said nothing, maybe he'd go away.

"What I said on the island was true. It ken it's the truest thing I've ever said."

"Then you *are* a professional liar, aye? You had me fooled for a while, but ah…" Mariel couldn't hold her tongue anymore. "Is it a Rutland trait, or is that one all your own?"

"I need you to hear me." Erran's boots squished on the wet rocks. "You owe me this much."

Mariel spun around, sputtering through a fit of false starts before finally saying, "Owe you? Owe *you*?"

"This isn't about my father, Mariel. It's about *us*, about two people who couldn't be more different, who found something in each other that they couldn't find alone." He looked like a sad little boy who'd had his favorite toy taken away, which seemed fitting, because that was all she'd been. His latest toy. "I don't believe it was only true out there."

"Why…" Mariel folded her arms around her, wishing it were enough to protect her from everything she shouldn't be feeling. "Do you want me to tell everyone what you said in there is true? Aye, I will. I'll lie for you if you'll just…just leave me alone."

"Lie…Mariel." His pursed smile was full of sadness. "Mariel. I know you don't believe that."

Mariel wiped her eyes and stormed over. "You don't have to play the fool with me, Errandil. I ken when it's just the two of us, you can be exactly who you feckin' are, and have been all along."

"*Stop* using my name as a weapon! It hurts me exactly as badly as you think it does." Erran surged forward, and she stepped back an equal distance. "I shouldn't have been so caught off guard seeing her yesterday, but there were all these eyes, this pressure of everyone expecting and maybe even hoping I'd make a fool of myself, and I froze. I'm not making excuses, only trying to help you see what might not have been obvious—and something I certainly didn't help by not talking to you about it before we even arrived. But *nothing* has changed for me."

"You're still going to pretend? Even now, you can't be honest with me. I *heard* you!"

Erran thrust his hands out to his sides with a bewildered gape. "Heard me what?"

"You and Yesenia. *Here.* Right feckin' here, where I'm standing." She slammed one boot onto the wet stone. Water splashed up around her ankle. "Likely other things as well, but I didn't stay around to find out."

"Me and Yesenia?" Erran took a deep breath. His hand traveled to his chin as he tilted his head upward. "If you heard us, then you'd know you're making all the wrong assumptions here."

"How she intimidates your craven little wife, aye? And you'll always be extra special to each other? Those assumptions?"

Erran's eyes closed. He went quiet, one hand traveling to his chest, sliding under his overcoat. He sighed. "I was looking for *you.* She found me first, said she wanted to talk. She apologized for how things ended, and aye…Aye, I ken she will always be special to me. I shouldn't have come here with her. I know that. But how could you…Why would you pick and choose my words to hurt yourself? Because I also told her I was *happy.* With *you.* And that even if she hadn't left as she did, it wouldn't have lasted, me and her. I believe that. Because there's lust and then there's…" His voice choked as he withdrew his hand from his jacket, pulling out a folded piece of vellum. "Read this."

"I'm not—" Mariel swallowed. "Nay."

He thrust it again. "Read it, Mariel. If anything we went through on the island meant…If it meant to you what it did to me, you'll read this and then decide how you think I feel."

Mariel leaned forward and snatched it from his hand, then spun back toward the sea before he could see through her tears… read more of her pain. She unfolded the paper, and the first words she read were *Dearest Yesenia.* "*Ah.* Nay, I will *not*—"

"It isn't what you think. Read it."

She snapped the paper in her hand, shooting him a final glare before shifting her eyes downward.

Dearest Yesenia,

This is all I never got to say. I didn't know myself then. I know myself better now.

Forgive me for my behavior the last time we saw each other. I was not myself then either.

I cared about you. Maybe even loved you. But those feelings were the last hurrah of childhood, which I'd been clinging to, harder than I should have. Losing you was the push I needed to be the man my father trained me to be.

I know this now, because I've given my heart away, and this time there'll be no getting it back. If someone or something takes my beloved wife from me, a piece of me will go with her. With hindsight, I see the two feelings are incomparable.

I don't want to hurt you with my words. I only tell you this so you no longer live in fear of me showing up one day to your ugly mansion in the trees to convince you to come home with me. You're exactly where you should be. I am too.

Your mate,
Erran

Mariel refolded the letter. Her hand shook as she tried to hand it back, but it slipped from her fingers and fluttered to the ground. Erran made no move for it.

"I planned to give it to her, but..." He shook his head. "I said what I needed, just with different words."

Her composure had deteriorated with every line she'd read, but she didn't realize she was hyperventilating until Erran rushed over and bundled her into his arms. He guided her to a boulder. "Breathe." He ran a hand down her back and kissed the top of her head. "Just breathe."

Mariel couldn't say for certain which word or line had done it, but something inside her had broken. It was everything at once, everything she'd believed in and everything she'd ever been. All she could do was bury her face in her hands and cry.

Erran lowered to a crouch and peeled her hands away, looking up at her with an expression so tender, she sobbed harder. "I *love* you, Mariel."

Mariel could hardly see him. Tears slid over her lips, landing in the washed-up sea. *I love you as well* was on the tip of her tongue, but what came out was "why?"

Erran laughed. "You're a hopeless romantic, aren't you?"

"Why, Erran?" She squeezed her eyes and wiped them on her bare arm. "Because I'm like her?"

Disappointment flickered in his gaze as he lifted her hands to his mouth. "You're not, actually. You're…just as maddening at times, I ken, but there's a warmth to you that makes me feel…" His throat bobbed. "Like I'm home. You've been putting others first for so long, you can't see how much you've been holding onto, how much love lives within you. But I see it, and I feel it. And since I'm in a confessing mood, here's another one for you." He gripped her hands tighter. "I wish we were still on the island. You'd be in my arms, and the world would feel right again."

Words of resistance formed in her chest, all the ways she could fight back, weaponize everything he was saying until it was nothing but another way of pushing her back down and into the sinking sand, where she was safe in the misery of her anger and sadness. Where all he'd done and was, every beautiful and maddening thing about him, belonged to her wounded parts and was no longer fresh and alive and taking up all the space of her delicate heart.

She pulled one of her hands from his and lifted it to his face. Tremors kept it from landing soundly, so he placed a hand over hers and locked it there with a short, sweet smile.

When her words failed her a second time, Mariel instead leaned down to kiss him. Her lips skirted his in the last of her uncertainty, the part of her still hanging onto the comfort of loss. But she knew—she *knew*. She knew, and that was the only reason it had hurt as badly as it had, because only love could break her so soundly and put her right back together, but in an order that finally made sense.

Everything, finally, made sense.

Mariel wrapped her arms tightly around his neck in her desperation to eradicate any distance left between them. It was hard to tell whose tongue was whose—who was more demanding—when they couldn't get close enough to satisfy the famishment burning through them.

"Not here," he said. He took her by the hand and led her out of the cove through the sea entrance. Their boots sank into the sucking sand, pulled by the ebbing tide, but he tugged her around the bend and up onto the dry part.

Mariel watched him lay his bespoke tailored jacket onto the sand and then he lowered her onto it. He peeled away his layers, the last of the sun's light coloring his tan skin with a peachy glow that brought her back to the most peaceful days of her life.

Erran helped her unlace her untenable gown. It took so long, they both laughed, but all amusement left his eyes when he climbed over her. He paused, his chest rising and falling, and just looked at her.

"Do you trust me, Mariel?" he asked. "What I said in my letter, do you believe it?"

Mariel nodded.

"Do you love me?"

More tears beaded. She bit her lip. Nodded.

Their bodies connected, sealing his questions. Her answer. As he moved in her, she saw the life she could have, the life she would have if she'd stop getting in her own way. Fate had brought her into a marriage with a man she was supposed to hate, but fate had nothing to do with how she loved him or how he loved her.

She wrapped herself around him, their flesh and souls becoming one, born anew of something far more terrifying and fulfilling than the armor she'd worn for so much of her life.

Mariel watched the sun set behind him and finally let go.

After, he held her until dusk became darkness.

When it was time to go back, he returned to the cove and came back with the letter. He tore it into pieces, glancing back at

Mariel before walking the remnants to the sea, where he scattered them.

"All you need to know is in here," he said, tapping his chest.

Mariel's words splintered. "All right."

"We can be whoever we want to be, Mariel. But being ourselves works just as well."

"If you ever..." Her mouth pursed.

"I won't. I swear to you." He took her hand in his and kissed it. "If *you* ever..."

"I won't." It was her turn to kiss his hand.

"We'll go in the back way." He grinned. "Quicker path to our bedchamber."

Hand in hand, they returned to the keep. With the night coming alive and the warm sand sifting between his toes, Erran had never known such peace. Such resolve. *Mariel and me. My wife.*

When she asked again why he hadn't given the letter to Yesenia, there was no accusation interspersing the question. She was simply curious.

"I ken I didn't write it for her at all," he said, after some thought. "I wrote it for you."

"Aye?"

He snapped her close to kiss her. Her contented titter lit up his entire soul. "Just didn't know it at the time."

"And the speech? Why would you do such a thing?"

"Are you having a go at my woeful public speaking?"

Mariel laughed. "You know what I'm asking."

Erran shrugged. "I didn't know how to talk to you, and it seemed like another way to try."

She drew her mouth into a scowl. "By saying all that in front of Guardians and all?"

"And why shouldn't they all hear about how a man loves his wife?" Erran pulsed his squeeze on her hand.

"So it had *nothing* to do with this campaign to make everyone forget what happened last time you were here?"

"I'd as soon forget it all myself," Erran said, half under his breath. He filled his lungs with comforting sea air. "I didn't think about it when I was doing it. Others can take my words however they wish. They were only meant for one person."

As they neared the tall reeds separating land from shore, Mariel slowed. "Erran, do you really think the two of us…knowing what you know about me, how I came to be your wife…Do you truly suppose there's a future for us? An honest one?"

"I could ask you the same," he replied. "After all that's been done to you and yours by me and mine."

"I still don't know what to do about that." Mariel pulled to a stop. She released his hand and gazed at the brush. "You're not your father. I know it. I don't see you like that. But he's my family now too. And how can I look my people in the eyes again, having joined myself to our subjugators without actually changing anything?"

Erran had been thinking about this very thing, ever since she'd told him the whole story. She might never see her father as he did, which was understandable. Rylahn was not an evil man. He was a businessman, sometimes ruthless and likely thoughtless. Yet if this were true, it should not trouble him to give back what shouldn't have been his to begin with. And Erran wasn't confident his father would do such a thing, even after hearing all Mariel and her people had been through.

"Do you trust me to figure it out?"

Mariel cast her eyes to the side in thought. After a sigh, she nodded. "I trust you to try."

Erran brushed a gentle kiss across her lips. "Give me some time with it."

She stretched a hand up to his face. "Don't expect an apology about today. But I'm glad I was wrong."

Erran chuckled. "Is that nay the same thing?"

"I assure you, it is not." Her face contorted to suppress a grin.

"Well, I *will* apologize, for not talking to you about how I was feeling about coming here again. Truth was I wasn't looking forward to dredging the past. I hadn't thought about her at all since you and I…" He sighed. "It brought a lot back for me, and not all good. I'm sorry for not just saying so. I should've told you how I felt before we came here."

She nodded. "We'll get better at this."

It hadn't escaped him that Mariel had yet to say the words herself. *I love you.* She'd nodded when he'd asked, but it wasn't the same. Still, it had to be harder for her. Even he could see that. For all she'd confessed to doing, her motivations for her transgressions had been selflessness. Justice. The Rutlands had fattened their coffers at the great expense of others, and were still doing so. Their battles were not the same.

All he could do was give her time.

Nay, it's not all you can do, but the rest will be much harder.

"Erran?"

He broke his daze. "Aye?"

"I don't know the way back to our apartments."

"Oh!" He laughed and linked their hands again. "That eager to jump me, are you?"

"Or to be out of this cursed gown," she muttered, lifting the sand-covered fabric with a disgusted look.

"Aww." Erran kissed her again. "You look beautiful tonight."

Mariel made a raspberry noise.

"Beautiful," he said again.

She made the sound again, louder.

"Feckin' *stunning*," he growled and swept her into his arms. Her euphoric giggle melted him. "Hope you're not too tired, outlaw."

Mariel was aching for the water steaming from the tub. Erran had called for it after she'd said they should consider not sleeping in sand, but it wasn't even about being clean. She needed the warm embrace after the emotional turmoil of the past days.

She stood naked in front of the long oval mirror rimmed with gold. Her reflection had always been a curious thing to her, for all her indifference to it. She'd come of age young and hadn't needed to worry about whether her hips were agreeable or whether suitors would be attracted or repelled. But her breasts were her singular insecurity. On an otherwise muscular frame, they were unnecessarily large and served no useful function in her endeavors. But until recently, her aversion had been mostly practical. Every piece of clothing Mariel had ever owned Augustine had had to tailor to make space for them. They perpetually got in the way, especially when she was using her bow. After a long day, her back hurt more than it should have, for her age. But like all burdens she'd borne for years, she'd learned to live with this one too.

She turned left…right, giving them more thought in the past five minutes than the past five years, and wondered whether such eyesores were pleasing to a man like Erran, or some unavoidable obstacle to work around as she'd always seen them. He'd given no sign one way or another. It was not a part of her he'd explored.

She lifted them in her palms, as she often did at the end of the day, relishing the immediate relief from taking the weight off her frame.

The door to the privy room opened. Mariel scrambled for her towel, but Erran lunged forward and steered her hand away. With his foot, he closed the door.

"Why would you hide yourself?" He resecured the towel on the hook and moved around to the back of her. "From me?"

Mariel shook her head at her reflection. She looked the proper fool standing naked, her hands crossed over her chest like a maiden caught unawares by a lake. His watching her worsened the bewildering shame.

One at a time, he peeled her hands away and laid them at her sides. She struggled through a breath, then held it as his hands replaced hers, cupping her breasts in his broad, strong palms. Hands that had touched her everywhere. Everywhere but there.

"My Mariel," he whispered before dipping down to kiss her neck. "Volemthe."

"I don't know that word." She fought every urge within her to look away. Nothing about her marriage had been easy, but his skill at finding his way past her defenses, of seeing her and knowing her, was as terrifying as it was intoxicating.

"It's a Vjestik word. It means *I love you.* I've picked up a few things in my travels." He brushed her hair to the side and kissed her crown. "I can say it in other languages, if you like."

Oh, yes, she thought, drawing her tongue along the back of her teeth. The foreign word, the accent…What a mystery he still was. In a world where she'd been most at ease when everything around her was known, she hadn't dreamed of how exciting it might be to live for the unexpected.

Erran's thumbs traced her nipples, sending her eyes rolling back. "Look at yourself, Mariel. Really look at yourself. See what I see, and you would never feel like you did when I walked in, ever again." He bent down and took a nipple in his mouth. Hot desire coursed through her. "Every time I look at you now, I feel this…this thought: *she's mine, she belongs to me*. But you belong to no one. It's I who belongs to you."

Mariel spun around and leaped into his arms. "You're half right, princeling."

"Mm." His fingers spread across her bare ass as he held her higher. "Which part?"

"Join me in this bath," she said between the safety of his kisses. "And maybe I'll tell you."

Mariel dreaded their pending departure. Not the leaving part, as she couldn't get out of Warwicktown faster. It was the good-bye itself, having to look everyone in the eye and pretend she felt no humiliation. She was adept at hiding her true self when she was the Flame, but that cool subtlety existed nowhere in Mariel herself.

It was a good morning to leave. They'd picked fair weather, and the soft-enough coastal breeze would keep them comfortable without waylaying them too far inland.

Mariel was the last to approach the farewell line, after Erran. Khallum leaned in to embrace her and whispered, "Don't ye dare break his heart." He kissed the side of her head. "Told him the same."

She smiled as she moved on to Gwyn and Korah, both women talking over each other through their insistence she was welcome anytime.

"Yesenia, it was lovely to see you again," Erran said, just ahead. He chastely kissed her cheek before moving on.

"It was…nice to finally make your acquaintance," Mariel said when it was her turn. She'd practiced the words, but they had the soreness of a still-healing wound.

Yesenia chortled. She looked as radiant as she had every day of the trip, her hair full and flowing, her masculine fashion giving her a dangerous sexuality even Mariel could concede was appealing. "Ye donnae mean it. And I ken I wouldnae either, were I you."

Mariel lowered her eyes with a laugh. "Aye. All right."

"It *was* good to meet you, Mariel, if only so I could see Erran will be fine, more than fine. He's where he was meant to be all along."

"He is. I won't let him forget it." Mariel left it at that, moving on.

Corin offered a sympathetic smile and a hug that seemed out of place, mumbling something about doing it again sometime, but she was glad for his understated good-bye. Glad her last memory of the place was the restrained comradery of someone who understood how something that could no longer hurt them could still be painful—maybe the only one who could.

Sessaly opted to ride with her parents on the return, likely on account of the whispers she'd been seen a bit too much with her brother-in-law.

"Are you going to tell us about..." Mariel nodded at the carriage ahead of them.

Destin groaned. "She's obnoxious." He nodded in apology at Erran. "Sorry. Since she's your sister and all."

Erran held up both hands. "Can't be angry with a man speaking the truth."

"She's betrothed to Aliksander Law, Des," Mariel said, though it vexed her to remind him. That she had knowledge or interest in the doings of the marriages of highborns was another slap in the face of her cause. Her deterioration.

"Why are you telling me, tell her!"

"Oh, I ken Mother is doing so herself right about now," Erran said.

"I'm nay interested in her...her whatever." Destin rolled his eyes and pointed his gaze out the window.

He is, Erran mouthed and Mariel laughed. Destin scowled at the passing hills.

She curled into Erran's welcome arms and nuzzled against his chest. His fingers brushed soft lines down her arm as he opened the book Khallum had given him, a fiction about two travelers stranded in a forest. One of his lawmen had confiscated it off a thug beating another man in an alleyway, and he'd saved it for his best mate, since he enjoyed reading so much, usually when he was at sea for a spell with long hours to kill. That was something new she'd learned about Erran. It made her like him even more. It made him even more real, a man of his own nature and creation.

Counting his heartbeats calmed hers. It was something she used to do when she was a little girl, when her nightmares had been so frequent and consuming. Her mother would come in and lie beside her until she fell asleep again, to the steady rhythm of her pulse.

"Any good?" she asked when he was an hour into his reading. Across the carriage, Destin snored into his sleeve.

"Hm? Oh, aye. It is." He kissed the top of her head. "It's about two people from different kingdoms who end up in the same place by some coincidence and then are chased by madmen into this enchanted forest. They escape, but then realize they're no longer in their own world at all. They have to work together to find their way home."

"Do they?"

He held up the book, his thumb marked about a third of the way in. "I'll let you know."

Mariel sighed and settled back in. He readjusted his arm to pull her closer. "Another world, eh? Sounds like the legends about the Hinterlands and the Medvedev lands."

"Legends are all they are." Erran chuckled. "If we could travel to other worlds, we'd know."

"Would we? Men are so secretive when they find something of value."

He took a moment with that. "True."

Mariel drew circles on his shirt with her finger. Once she said what she was about to say, it would be out there, and taking it back would be worse than having said it at all. But she'd been working the problem in the back of her thoughts for days, ever since their rescue. She had never halfway committed to anything, and her marriage could be no exception. She either wanted to be Erran's wife or she didn't. "When we get back, I'm going to tell my friends about us. And then, if they're willing, I'd like them to meet you."

Erran set the book down, marking his place with a scrap of leather. "I know it's no small thing for you to suggest it. And I'd love to meet the people you love. But you don't have to prove anything. If you say you care about me, that's enough."

"I do care about you, and this is why I want this. I can't be two people anymore."

"That I can understand. It's your choice, and I will respect whatever you decide." He paused. "I've been thinking a bit myself."

"While reading?"

"I sometimes do this thing…" He got quiet. "It's as though I can split my mind. Focusing on one thing lets me focus on another, and next thing I know, I've done both. I suppose it makes no sense to you."

"Nay, but it's interesting." She grinned up at him.

He grinned back. "If I asked you to show me your work, would you?"

"Show you…what?" Mariel sat up on the bench.

He scooted so he was facing her sideways. "You told me about decimated villages…the families. I'd like to see this with my own eyes. Not because I don't believe you, I do."

"And what will you do with this experience?" she asked warily. His heart was rooted by good intentions, but the people wouldn't appreciate being treated like curiosities.

Erran linked her hands in his. "It will give me time to wrap my own thoughts around the problem. I want to come to Father with a solution in my own words, with my own experience, in a way he'll listen."

Mariel almost didn't know what to say. The only thing better than robbing the stewards blind would be to influence a better world, a better way. But that had always been only a dream, an unpassable valley. "Will he?"

"I don't know," he said, quieter. "But he'll either listen or lose a son for his stubbornness. That should hurt more than any financial loss, but if I'm wrong, better to know, aye?"

TWENTY
BORDER TOWNS

As a boy, Erran would join his father on progress around their territory. Rylahn had instilled in him the importance of being seen by their people. The visits had stopped when he was still young, and until he'd asked Mariel to take him to the places she was trying to help, he hadn't equated the particulars of the timing.

Their visits had ended around the time Mariel's life—and the lives of the people she loved—had been taken from under her.

Whitecliffe was responsible for the lake district and the border towns of the Northeast. He recalled his father explaining that many of the villages were near enough to the Easterlands that they'd adopted their more gentile way of life. Their accents were near nonexistent, which was also true of many in Whitecliffe, they never uttered words like "salt and sand," and they preferred their seafood from ports north of the border, like Briarhaven, or from their freshwater lakes. But import costs were high, and they relied heavily on food from the land, land that, until roughly a decade ago, they'd owned and farmed.

Mariel had explained they'd only have time for two villages: Everspring and Mistgrave. Erran at first had questioned whether Mistgrave was the best use of their time, since they'd recently visited Loch Ethereal, but the dark look she gave him, paired with the words *you saw what you were supposed to see,* reminded him he was there to listen.

She had little to say on their ride northeast, and he left the silence for her to command.

Everspring was beautiful on the approach. It had the same lush forests as at Loch Ethereal, which reminded him of his boyhood visits, when he'd pretend they'd stepped out of the Southerlands altogether, into a whole new world. He never told his father about it. Rylahn had never outwardly discouraged Erran's imaginative side, but he hadn't seen value in cultivating it either.

They rode under a trellis of broken metal. "E ring," it read, the letters spaced so far apart, it made no sense. It took him embarrassingly longer than it should have to realize it had once been the town's name, the entrance to what should be as picturesque as the past half tick of riding, but he already knew would not be.

He swallowed his dread and followed Mariel underneath.

The road more closely resembled a path, used enough to be rutted but not enough to be clear and clean. Weeds grew over the sides, some in the middle. Cratered holes were full with the remnants of a recent rain. There were so many, they had to navigate around them.

Erran's first question weighed on his tongue—*why have the roads not been tended with tax funds?*—but he already had the answer. The first of many there'd be no point in asking.

"There used to be training guilds along this row." Mariel's first words in over an hour. "Whitechurch will never let the guildhalls go elsewhere, but many apprenticeships start here. *Started* here."

Erran followed where she pointed and saw a line of attached, pitched buildings. All of them were missing windows. Most had also been mined for boards and other parts. They seemed to belong to a time before. He remembered the fact about the training guilds, and his last visit to Everspring returned in startling relief—the vivacious town center, as full of people as Whitecliffe. A mordant stench of decay had replaced the absolute assault of so many great foods cooking at once. Citizens had eaten right there in the town, around a fountain, which he could now see was not only overgrown with weeds like everything else but had crumbled away in parts. The basin was missing an entire side, and rainwater ran down it like a sieve.

"Where do people..." He shook his head at his folly.

"Live?" Mariel veered south, down another inconspicuous path. "Not here. Not anymore. A few families stayed because they had nowhere else to go. I don't know how they've fared. I don't have the heart to find out. We'll go to Mistgrave now. There's more to see here, but...I don't have the heart for that either."

Erran hadn't realized how pitched his pulse had become until they were clear of the main village and back in the woods. He adjusted in his saddle, working up his courage for whatever was next.

"You can ask questions if you want, Erran. I know you're being respectful, but it's better you know."

He cleared his throat, wondering where to begin. "You said this resulted from land seizures and taxes?"

"The land seizures came last. It all started with taxes on the food we grow. We'd always paid fifteen percent, but it was after... Well, it was after a visit your father made here years ago when we received the news taxes had been doubled to thirty percent. The number increased exponentially with profits. Wealthy farmers either moved away or were thrust into poverty almost overnight. I ken he saw all the plenty and couldn't allow an opportunity to pass. Mind, this was in *addition* to the sixty percent land tax, which is the highest in the entire Reach. Then and now."

Erran invited the acerbity of her sting. He would neither look away nor shy away from the truth she was offering, which was a gift, no matter how deep the ache in his chest.

"And then," she said, the gentle forest passing them by. "It was raised once more, to forty percent. The wealthy, as I said, most just moved to another region, under another steward. They could do that. But the rest, the everyday families, were already living harvest to harvest. They had to ration. Children were prioritized, getting most of the greens and fruits because they needed them to grow. Gradually, the lack of nutrients started affecting the men, who could no longer tend their lands like they once had and couldn't afford to hire help. And when they could not pay their taxes, because there were no longer any profits, they were given no clemency. No time to make it right. If taxes were due and unpaid on a Tuesday, the repossession agents would arrive on Thursday."

"That's so unjust," Erran whispered. "Mariel, I swear to you, I'm not defending him, but it's so hard to imagine my father doing this. I feel like I hardly know him anymore."

"Honestly, Erran, I ken your father didn't know the extent of it. Most men like him prefer not to, so they can sleep at nights. They delegate the tasks to barons and guards and give them full discretion over the management of things. The last time we saw him around these parts was right before the famine started."

"Nay, he knew. Some part of him did. It's why we never came back," Erran mused aloud. He constructed a clearer image in his mind. "He couldn't face it." He swallowed. "Because he's a coward."

"Most men are, when they have the privilege to be." Mariel rewrapped the reins in her hands. "Few men have that luxury though."

Erran didn't ask what had happened to the displaced working-class families. Mariel had already given him a grim view when she'd told him about her parents. Her sister. How many other thousands of mothers and fathers and siblings and bairns had their own stories? How many generations had ended so rich men could grow richer, beyond anything they could ever truly need?

I love you, he wanted to say. *So much so that I want nothing more than to reverse time and fix all of it, even if it means we never would have met.*

She went silent again until Mistgrave. They entered from a different road than the one he remembered from their idyllmoon, which was, as Mariel had shared earlier, the point. Like Everspring, there were remnants of an old sign, but none of the lettering remained. It was merely an arch.

"Remy and Augustine lived just north of the border, in the Easterlands, but they didn't escape any of this. When the blight came, after the land wasn't turned over properly each season, it spread to their family's land as well." Mariel sighed. "And the steward of their land, I ken, saw how well the efforts had gone for your father and instituted the same ones there. It happened to them in the same order. Crops died. Adults were next. Then the land was taken. Almost seems like there's a formula to it, doesn't it?"

Erran nodded through his overwhelm. It was a grief weighted heavier by guilt, compounded by the shame of daring to feel sadness for something he was indirectly complicit in. Had directly benefited from.

"Our homestead on Loch Ethereal was transformed into a retreat for the rich, like many other lake properties, but most of the land..." She turned down another path, which winded downhill, and they emerged onto a cliff overlooking a massive valley. Within it were various shades of death brown and, between those sparse patches, what remained of homes. Some had been burned out, others stripped for parts like the main row of Everspring.

"This is all I have in me today, Erran." Tears raced down her face, spilling off her chin. "I just cannot...cannot relive it all."

He stretched a hand between their horses. When she took it, her fingers almost limp in his, his composure crumpled with all he wished he could say. But none of it would have made a bit of difference. Words were as useless as the hollowed-out hovels that had once housed vibrant, loving families.

"I will..." Erran forced back the despair that was not his to claim. "I will..."

"I ken you'll try." She squeezed his hand and released it. "I don't want to lie to you anymore, so you should know I'll be visiting my friends tonight. I'm going to tell them it's over. Obsidian Sky is done. Don't follow me. Don't...ask me where I'll be. Just trust me to know what I'm doing and let me do it."

He nodded. The valley blurred through his tears. "Aye, Mariel. Whatever you need."

Destin might have been many things, but a liar was not among them. He'd humiliated himself and others, had failed to live up to his responsibilities, and had been a liability, but he did not lie to the people he loved.

He truly struggled with his decision not to tell Mariel the Obsidian Sky meeting had been moved an hour earlier, so he could have some time with the others himself before she arrived. There were things he needed to say—and they need to hear—and she was already burdened with enough pressure. He could take this one from her.

Alessia nestled near Magnur on the far log. From the haze in her eyes, she'd already been drinking before she'd arrived, but Magnur was stone sober. Even when he drank, it had little effect on him.

Remy and Augustine hovered on different sides of the second log, each staring in opposite directions.

Destin settled on the third and took a moment to warm his hands on the fire they'd built before he'd arrived.

"Aye, so what's this about then, Des? And why the secrecy?" Alessia blurted. When she leaned forward, Magnur put a hand on her back. A recent development. Or an old one Destin had failed to notice in his thrall to the drink.

"Did something happen to Mariel?" Remy asked. "She *did* come back, right?"

"She's fine." Destin's throat was as dry as sand. He wished he'd had the forethought to bring something without spirits to drink. He'd left his waterskin at the Spires. "A little worse for wear. Nothing the steward's healers couldn't resolve."

"The steward's healers." Alessia snorted and looked toward the sky. "That acclimated is she?"

"Auggie said the whisper in the Spires is they were on an *island?* Just the two of them?" Remy seemed like a man trying *not* to put a story together, like he was hoping Destin was there to disavow him of whatever his imagination had stitched into a tapestry of despair.

Destin nodded, bent over his knees. Mariel might have been unhappy with everything he was about to say, but it wouldn't matter for long. "If they hadn't been together, neither would have survived as long as they did."

"But how...I donnae ken how they got there." Alessia looked incredulous.

"After she split from Remy and Auggie in Sandycove, she rode for Devon, where the *Mistwitch* was anchored. The guards pursued her all the way there and she...jumped from the cliffs and swam to her ship. She didn't know Erran had followed her."

Remy shook his head, frazzled. "And he jumped in after her?"

"Aye."

"And we're expected to believe that the...the silk-stocking *princeling* would risk his own neck for her?"

"I ken the truth doesnae require belief," Magnur muttered. He stared at the fire, expressionless.

Remy tapped his hand in the air, glancing to the side with a distrustful wince. "Did they *mean* to end up on the island? Why did Mariel think...Nay, this isn't adding up."

"She wasn't expecting to run, and she followed her instinct," Destin said carefully. He took a moment to read his friends, see where they were at with things. Magnur was simply listening, unruffled as always. Alessia was enraged, though there had to have been more to it than Mariel and Erran. Remy was in denial, and

Augustine was unusually quiet. "But they got pushed off course in the Eastern Shelf and crashed. They're both lucky to be alive."

"I'll never celebrate the survival of a subjugator," Alessia quipped. "But aye, happy about Mariel."

"And they were there for *weeks*? The whole time, just the two of them?" Remy was still catching up. His inability to do so was a matter of will.

"We really thought she was dead," Augustine said softly. She wiped her eyes. "We…"

"Aye, weeks. Erran's mates were the ones who put it together. They—" Destin abruptly cut himself off. They had every right to know, but they'd inevitably put it back on him. They'd never believe Sam and Hamish had known just enough to prompt Destin's memory.

It didn't matter. Or wouldn't, after the night was ended.

"They what?" Alessia's tone verged on hostile. She'd never liked him.

"They knew Mariel was the Flame." Destin wished again for something to wet his throat. "They knew she was there to stop the auction. And they said—"

"Whoa, whoa, whoa!" Alessia leaped from the log. "You cannae just drop that on us! What do ye mean they *knew*? How, Des? How, 'cos ye told 'em? Ye did, aye?"

Magnur tugged her back down.

Destin lowered his eyes. "Mariel told Banner's men, and Erran and his mate heard."

"Well, I donnae believe ye. Why the feck would she do such a thing?"

"Auggie and I were there," Remy said faintly. "She was trying to…to pull the guards off of us."

"And why are we only just now hearing about it?"

"There seemed no point." Remy buried his face in his hands.

"It was more than what she said that tipped them off," Destin said. "No one else knew about Banner, just the steward and Erran.

And…Mariel. There was no other reason for her to be there that morning."

Alessia turned her ire on Augustine. "Remy, aye, he's too far up Mariel's cunt to ever say a word crossways, but *you*? Never said a feckin' word about her saying what she said."

"Mariel's reasons are her own," Augustine said into the forest. "Nothing came of it anyway."

"Ye donnae ken this affects us all?"

"She'd never name any of us," Remy stated. "Never."

"'Cept, they know Auggie, aye? She *works* for the silver spoons. And it wouldnae be hard to tie you to her." She pinched her finger, squinting. "Just a *wee* bit of digging."

"Then that's our problem, Alessia." Remy met her wild stare. "You were more concerned with saving your own ass. Remember?"

"And why has this nay reached everyone's ears by now? Wouldnae the attempted capture of the Flame be news far and wide?" Alessia demanded.

Remy shook his head at the sky. "Maybe you should go back to your blacksmithing."

"Aye, you'd like that! So I willnae keep showing ye all the holes in your story!"

Destin cleared his throat so Remy would ease off. "Listen, listen. These mates of his, they're no more keen on the public, or the stewards, learning the truth than any of us are."

Alessia burst into maniacal laughter.

"I *mean* it. They love Erran. And Erran…" Destin clenched from head to toe, like a man expecting to be hit. "Loves Mariel."

"Guardians on feckin' high, you are nay serious!" Alessia flung her arms out, her mouth hanging wide. Magnur had given up trying to subdue her and just shook his head at the forest floor. "Nay, nay, nay, you're telling tales, Des, because the Mariel *we* know—"

"Loves him back." Destin's tension eased. The words were out. The truth was out. But the airless silence was almost worse than Alessia's unhinged ranting. "Being stranded on an island you never expect to leave will do that, I ken."

"Ye *ken?*" Alessia was seething. Her nostrils flared as she whipped her gaze around at the others. "Are none of ye gonna say anything about it? Remy? Aug?"

Remy and Augustine wore identical looks. Dazed. Wounded. Heartbroken. Even with all the hours and days and years he'd lost to the drink, Destin hadn't missed how *both* Perevil siblings had been in love with Mariel. Mariel acted like maybe she was in love with them too, but Destin understood something about survivors that she perhaps did not.

It wasn't surviving if the injuries were self-inflicted, over and over.

If a better way was never found.

A way out.

"Is *this* why you asked us here early? Too much of a coward to tell us herself?" Alessia asked.

"She doesn't know I'm telling you, and she'll be plenty angry for it, I'm sure." Destin scratched his head. He needed to hurry. Mariel would arrive soon, and he had somewhere to be before she got there. "She wanted to tell you herself, but I did it instead, because I knew how you'd react, and she doesn't deserve that."

"*Deserve*? She's betrayed us! Betrayed herself!" Alessia elbowed Magnur, aghast. "Say something!"

"You want me to say something?" Magnur ran a hand along his beard. "I joined Obsidian Sky for the freedom ye all offered. If we're free to come or go, free to be involved or nay, then either Mariel is free to love as she chooses or I ken you all have been lying to yourselves all along." He grunted as he stood, towering over the group. "I'll be retiring now. Give Mariel my love. I'm grateful she's home."

Alessia gaped at Destin for several intense seconds before leaping from her log and racing after Magnur. "Wait! Mag, wait!"

Destin slowly exhaled, taking his time. "I can't tell if that went better or worse than I expected."

"She's…She's pretending, right?" Remy was still lost to his fantasies. "An exceptionally long con?"

"I've seen them, Remy." Augustine's voice cracked and shattered. "At the Spires. Seen them myself."

"What?"

"Before, she could hardly make herself be civil. A bairn could've seen through her act."

"What are you saying?"

"There's an ease about her. When she's with him...she has to pretend *not* to love him. I'd hoped and prayed I was wrong, but—" Augustine slammed her mouth shut. Tears flowed down her cheeks. "You know, if I know Mariel, she's embarrassed. She'll believe she's lost the part of herself we love and respect, and I..." She wiped one eye, then the other. "I'll nay contribute to that."

"But she *can't* love him, Auggie. It's impossible." Remy's eyes flared wide in his desperation.

"Why, because *we* love her?" Augustine shook her head. "Remy, I told you before. Erran is well loved by his people. For his kindness...his uncommon empathy. Maybe she sees in him what others do, or maybe she sees that, through love, she can do more than she's ever done with us."

"She'll never persuade a monster to stop terrorizing."

Augustine shrugged. "Maybe. Maybe not. But she'll do all she can. You know that."

"When Mariel gets here," Destin said, "she's going to call for an end to Obsidian Sky. Not for *him.* For you. Your names are known because you were there, but Erran, his mates...No one wants to take this further. It dies here. In this forest. And we let it die."

"You make it sound so simple," Augustine said. "Like there aren't now three highborns who know two-thirds of the names of the outlaws who terrorized them."

"Nothing about our lives has ever been simple, Augustine." Destin searched for her gaze and locked it. He felt the full weight of his question as it left his tongue. "Aren't you tired?"

More tears spilled. "Of course I'm tired, Des. But if *we* tire, where does it leave the people suffering?"

"There will always be suffering, but adding to misery with our own doesn't ease theirs. Sometimes enough is enough. We've done enough."

Destin had decided to leave before Mariel arrived. He'd delivered her message for her, for better or worse, and the two she owed the most to were still there.

He knew in his bones they'd never see Alessia or Magnur again.

Destin stood. "She'll be here soon. I can't tell you how to feel. And yet, try to remember all she's done for us. It's not for us to decide where and how she finds her happiness. But we can try to be glad she's finally found it."

"Where are you going?" Remy asked.

"To do what's necessary," Destin said. "Before I no longer can."

Remy and Augustine were the only ones there when Mariel arrived. Augustine recounted everything Destin had said, while Remy offered only sighs.

Mariel felt herself paling with every revelation. She'd planned to tell her friends herself about Erran, in her own words, but her brother had *taken* that from her. In doing so, he'd driven off both Alessia and Magnur, and she might never get a chance to explain things. And then he hadn't even stuck around for the aftermath.

"I see," she said when it was all out. "Was he on the drink again?"

Remy shook his head with a short laugh. "He was as lucid as I can remember him."

"Why then? Why would he say all that?"

Augustine slid in beside her on the log. "He wanted to help you. And we love you, Mar. We always have." Augustine's face had been hidden by the evening shadows, so Mariel hadn't seen her tears before. "It defies all logic, but if you love Erran, who are we to tell you it's wrong?"

"It is wrong." Mariel wrung her hands over the warm fire. Everything she'd planned to say had to be scrapped. The team already knew Obsidian Sky was over. They'd learned the truth about her darkest secret but also her greatest joy. "Nay. Nay, it isn't wrong. What he and I went through would bond anyone, but..." *But it was more than that. I see him, who he's meant to be. And he sees me as I am and loves me all the more for it. He sees what made me, and he would do anything to keep that hurt from others.*

"But you love him, and that's that." Remy stood, dusting his hands down his pants with a hard breath out. "A quite unexpected twist, but you never did anything halfway."

Mariel looked at his sister. Her first love, in a way. She and Remy had both filled that need, and she'd fulfilled theirs. But she saw now there were phases to a life, and she was no longer in the one that had held them so cosmically close. "Auggie?"

"Oh, ah, I ken we'll manage," she said, squinting tears away. "It was time."

"Time?"

"There can be no momentum from a slow horse," Remy answered for her. "We'd been slowing for some time now. All of us. The heist before the auction wasn't our best work. We left tracks. We...doesn't matter. All things have a season, and this season has been over for longer than we chose to admit. Now that they know our names, it's over regardless."

She sensed more unsaid. "But?"

Remy sighed. "But now we have to figure out what to do with ourselves, aye?"

"There's something...else, Mar. I have a confession," Augustine said quietly. "When I told you about Erran bedding all those women, it wasn't true."

Mariel smiled gently. "I know."

"I didn't mean to lie to you, but once it was out, I couldn't take it back. I ken I was fearful you'd see he was different, and would fall for him, just as you did, in the end. I'm sorry."

Mariel had suspected as much. "There's no need for apologies, Auggie. I understand."

Remarkably, neither seemed mad. There was sadness trailing between them, mostly unsaid, but they'd exhausted enough of it before she'd arrived, and she'd come upon the precipice of their acceptance. She supposed that had been Destin's intention, to spare her the worst of it, but she would have liked the opportunity to have decided for herself.

"Erran has already promised to send gold where it's needed. He's committed to this cause too, just…legally," she said, but at the mention of his name, they both went sour, exchanging disgusted looks. They weren't there yet. Maybe they'd never be. It was enough for one night. She could only take one step at a time.

Above the rest, they were still her family. With their vigilantism behind them, perhaps they could even act like one.

"Where did my brother go? He didn't say?"

Remy shook his head. "Only that he had to do what was necessary. You know Des. He rarely makes sense."

What was necessary. The words were simple enough, but why did they settle in her belly like an undigested pit?

"You should go," Augustine said, lifting for a chaste cheek kiss before turning and wrapping herself in her shawl.

Remy kissed her next, brushing awfully close to her mouth. He made a soft sound against her flesh before withdrawing. "This is one end, but it's not *the* end."

Mariel was crying too. "What I wish for the most is for it to be the beginning of something too, something we've waited a long, long time for, all of us."

"Time will tell." Remy blew her an air kiss and darted off after his sister.

TWENTY-ONE
THE FLAME

Mariel rode back to Goldsea Spires in a haze of wistfulness and melancholy. Her parting with Remy and Augustine had gone as well as it could have, but it was as Remy had said: time would tell. A part of her had died with the dissolution of Obsidian Sky. Whether it was a part she would miss remained to be seen.

The ocher sunset glowed behind the hills and cliffs of the coast. She took it in. There was so much beauty in the world that she'd taken for granted, or had simply overlooked in her single-minded purpose. It had robbed her of more than a normal life. It had taken sunsets and sunrises. The comforting smells of baking bread or fresh rain. Life's great beauties had been no more than practical measurements, tellers of time or indicators of potential impediments. No small joys for her.

Guilt had settled over her long before she breathed in the start of dusk. Enjoying anything when others still suffered was a luxury, one she'd railed against for so long, the words and sentiments were habit. And now she would benefit from these luxuries, even though they had nothing to do with her choice to stay with Erran. Her children would never miss a meal or know the true meaning of need. And a part of her was so glad for it, so relieved to not pass her trauma to another generation, that it only deepened her shame.

No matter what, she'd always be the Flame. It wasn't a name; it was *her*. Not even retirement could take that from her. Erran had promised to help her people, and she believed him. She'd never surrender her principles, not even for him.

She'd just commenced her final approach up the cliff to the Spires when a rider raced up in a plume of dust. Before it had cleared, she could see it was Erran.

"Mariel." He panted, skidding to a stop inches from where she was waiting. "Destin was arrested tonight. Again."

Mariel pulled her hood back, unsure if she'd heard him right. "*What*?"

"Destin…" He put a hand to his chest and breathed deep, trying again. "Destin was arrested."

"But why?" *Said he had to do what was necessary.* "Erran, tell me he didn't…"

Erran's woeful air was the only answer she needed, but he told her anyway. "He claimed to be the Flame again, but this time…" The trepidation woven through his words and expression had her terrified of him continuing. "He gave details. Lots of details. About many of your heists. He knew far too much, the guard told my father. Far, far too much for it to be incidental." He massaged his mouth. "And, ah, this time he was sober. He said…"

Erran's words trailed, muted, into the background. The sunset burned her eyes, obscuring her path, as she rode toward the keep, loosely aware of nothing but the horrible nightmare she'd had so many times over the years. Destin saying the wrong thing to the wrong person. Destin swinging from a scaffold. Destin gone, gone, gone when she'd spent the past decade building and fortifying protections from the cold cruelty of life and reality.

She heard her name in the distance. Erran was calling for her, and his voice was close enough that he couldn't be too far behind. Did he know what she intended? Did she?

Oddments of the meeting she'd missed felt like memories. She *saw* Destin telling the others about her and Erran, about why it all had to end. She was right there with him, listening to his intentions and standing witness to them, but her own voice was locked. There was nothing to add, no words that would connect past to future.

Mariel leaped from her horse before she'd reached the long staircase. She narrowly prevented injury by landing in a crouch, her palms springing off the ground as she leaped back into motion. There wasn't time to think, but her unending thoughts spun anyway, filtering through disorienting memories and premonitions. She was aware of every inch of her own flesh, tingling from the inside as she raced through the doors, her instinct overriding her courage. Her ears rang, forming a barrier from the anxious questions being hurled her way.

All the while, Erran screamed her name.

She ignored the guards who tried to stop her outside of Rylahn's office and stormed in, flinging the doors wide. An irritated frown was etched his face, deepening into worry as he took in the state of his daughter-in-law.

"Mariel. I know you're—"

She stormed in, Erran hot on her heels, and slammed her hands onto his father's desk. "You cannot hold him. You cannot, because it's *me* you really want, Rylahn. Me. *I* am the Flame, and I can prove it."

"What's this about?" Rylahn demanded.

"She's mad with grief, Father. Let me take her to our apartments," Erran exclaimed. "Mariel, come on. Please, we can talk about this somewhere quiet."

"Nay, we'll talk about this here." She pulled herself erect and met her father-in-law's disordered gaze. "What my brother knows, he learned from me. He learned it all from me, but he has nothing to do with it. I kept him safe because he wasn't built for a life like mine, and I'll tell you…" Pausing to catch her breath, she glimpsed the horror in Erran's expression, and she nearly regretted what she was about to say. "I'll tell you something I did not even tell him. About Banner. So you know I'm not just trying to save him."

Rylahn blinked at her. He turned his attention on Erran. "What's this? Huh? What is this, Erran, a jest? This isn't the time."

"Your son has nothing to do with this!" Mariel boomed.

Rylahn recoiled in his seat.

"I married him to get close to *you* so I could take back every last feckin' thing you've stolen from me and mine and every other last feckin' person in your fiefdom! I lied and pretended and schemed and all the while loathed every last one of you. Every…" Her restless gaze landed on a horrified, pale Erran, and for a moment, everything around her slowed to a crawl. Her heart caved deeper into her chest, knowing she'd already said so much—and would say more. *I'm sorry.*

"Mariel, I'm trying to be reasonable here, but what you're saying is utter *madness.*" Rylahn stood. "Erran is right. You're upset. You've had a great shock, and—"

"Destin didn't know about Banner because he was in jail. He knows only what I told him. Ask him what Banner's wife looks like. Portly, with a hairy mole just at the corner of her chin. What she was wearing. A violet gown laced with yellow daisies. Ask him! See if his answers match!"

With each word, bits of her happiness flaked away. The contentment of Erran's scent after he'd exerted himself to provide for them. The pride in his eyes as she became adept with his makeshift spears. The way he grinned every time she'd said something they both knew was ridiculous. How beautiful he'd made her feel, when she hadn't known how wonderful it could be.

"Mariel." Erran sank onto a chair and buried his face in his hands.

But Rylahn just stood there. Staring. Calculating. "Is there anything you wish to recant?"

Mariel pinched her shoulders back and shook her head. "Not a word."

Rylahn flashed an inscrutable look at his son and marched around the desk, passing them both. He muttered something to his guards.

"Why?" Erran looked as lost as she felt. His elbows were on his knees, his hands open in surrender. "Mariel, I asked you to trust me."

"I do trust you, Erran," she said, but her eyes were focused on the door, on whatever future awaited her now that she'd outed herself to save Destin. "But my brother will never hang for my crimes."

"You'll both hang," Rylahn said. Boots thundered in the halls. "Consider it a kindness, for it's far more merciful than either of you deserve."

"Rylahn, he has nothing to do with this!"

"Guards," he said, so calmly she half expected attendants to appear through the door and not the twelve burly men who did.

"Father, you do *not* have to do this. Let me talk to her. We'll explain—"

"Erran, if you knew about this, I will never look at you the same."

"Just *wait*! You cannot take her away!"

"I can," Rylahn said calmly. "And I will."

"She's my *wife*!"

"Would she say the same? Did you hear a word she said, or were you listening with your cock once again?" Rylahn snapped once, and the guards swarmed around her in a storm of thunder, blocking her from Erran.

Mariel stepped forward and held out her hands to be tied. Instead, she was thrust forward into motion, dragged on both sides so her feet lifted off the stones. She'd been preparing for the moment for most of her life. Had imagined it, including how she'd comport herself. The words she might say.

How bold she'd been in her fantasies.

How stupid she'd been, thinking she was ready to die.

Perhaps that had been true, before she had known love.

Several of the guards broke away to subdue Erran, whose desperate protestations followed her out the door.

Mariel was dragged from the room and into the hall, realizing she had no idea where they would take her. Did the Spires have cells or a dungeon? Would she be thrown in with the violent criminals in the village jail? Taken straight to hang, to avoid a scene?

Erran screamed after them. It brought her back to the island, to the howls of the dying boar holding onto the last vestige of life.

A door slammed.

Erran's screams progressively disappeared into the ether of the past. Of a life that was beautiful for what little she'd lived it, a taste of what happiness was for others. It was always going to end this way, she finally understood, the toes of her boots skimming halls she'd walked freely. There was no justice for the powerful, only those who dared stand tall against them.

Life as the Flame was only possible without regrets.

But she had one.

Mariel wished with all her heart she'd told Erran she loved him.

THE HEART IS
INCAPABLE OF LIES

TWENTY-TWO

THE TWO PILES OF FRUIT

Mariel had given up on tracking time about twenty days into her house arrest. One of the staff had told her yesterday it had been two months. She couldn't imagine what Rylahn was waiting for. His indecision wasn't a good look, for a leader who had the rare and precious opportunity to make an example of the biggest thorn in the side of the powerful.

She supposed he was embarrassed he'd let a criminal into his own house…let her marry his heir. Perhaps if he could uncover the names of the others, Mariel's involvement might blend into the background and lessen the scandal. But the longer he held her, the more judgment would come down on him for his hesitation.

But *something* about her scared Rylahn. She'd yet to solve what it was. House arrest in his own keep, no public declaration of her capture, no singing his victory far and wide…Those were not the actions of a man who should be on top of the world, parading his prize in a triumph for all.

Even if he was cautious about how it would look for Mariel to be the face of it all, he could have made an example of Destin, but he hadn't. Yet.

She'd been treated surprisingly well. Fed the same meals she would have eaten if she were free. Attendants were sent to assist her, and her clothing was taken to laundry. They'd even unbolted one of the windows, so she could enjoy fresh air. That had been a recent change, Hestia's doing. Mariel hadn't asked for it, but she was grateful to breathe in something other than the same air she'd been stuck with for weeks.

The apartment was on the topmost floor of the keep, isolated from the bustle she had been used to, in a quiet corner overlooking the sea. She spent many of her hours sitting upon the bench she'd pulled to the window, reliving the day Erran had leaped into the sea after her. The day *everything* had changed.

She hadn't seen or heard from him since the evening she'd been locked away. Whether it was Rylahn's doing or Erran's, she couldn't know. It hurt the same.

The door opened behind her. She didn't bother looking. It was noontide, the hour of her first daily interrogation. That meant it was Rylahn, come to whittle her down. Hestia would be by just after supper for her own round, with her softer touch to balance the approach.

"Are you still treated well?" He always opened with the same question.

"Aye." She always responded with the same answer.

"Do you need for anything?"

"Nay."

"Very well." His chair scraped the stones as he dragged it to the window.

"How is my brother?"

"Still on house arrest, like you. Never misses a meal." His answer never changed, but that was why she asked every time, because as long as Destin was still in the keep, he was safe. She was still grateful every day that Rylahn had moved him from the jail, even if his reasons hadn't been altruistic.

The subsequent silence was for the question she never asked—couldn't ask. *And Erran?*

"Mariel." Rylahn straddled his chair across from her. "Sixty-one days you've been in here."

She nodded at the window. Sixty-one days then. "And sixty-one days you've asked me the same questions over and over, because that's how men are taught interrogations work. You wear the person down with repetition until they give you what you're after."

"I have never interrogated you. I have been kinder than most of my peers would be." He watched her. What did he see? A woman beaten? Hanging onto…what, she didn't even know. Not her freedom, which would never be hers again. Not even Destin, whom she had no power to save. "But this has gone on long enough. This morning, right now, will be your final chance to give me the names of your cohorts. Just give me *two.* I know there were more, but I'll settle for two."

"And when I don't?"

"I have another way of getting what I need. But the only thing that can help *you* and your brother is your cooperation right now. If I get what I need without having to resort to extraordinary measures, I'll free you both."

"And what happens to my friends?" Mariel asked in challenge. She needed to hear him say it.

"They will hang," he responded calmly. "As they should. As you should. But I find myself unable to make the order against a woman my son, for reasons I will never comprehend, loved."

Loved. Not loves. Mariel's pulse raced from the sudden jolt of pain. "What does free us mean? Release us so some other man can claim the catch? Run from one prison into another?"

He chortled, passing a hand around the room. "A prison? Mariel, have you ever experienced prison? True prison? Your food would be moldy and rotten, if you were fed at all. You'd pray for the gallows, for at least you'd be free of the rats who don't wait for you to die, only to sleep, before they feast upon you. And the cold…Have you ever been cold in the Southerlands? Ask a man in prison. He won't even have an answer, for all it will bring back."

"And that's what awaits me, isn't it? If you 'let me go,' as you say." She wasn't sure why she was antagonizing him, because she had no intention on day sixty-one of giving up the names he'd asked for since day one. Even if he was good on his word to release her, she'd never give up her friends.

One thing heartening her was knowing Erran couldn't possibly have outed Remy and Augustine, or his father would have their heads. However else her husband felt about her, he'd been good on his word. Samuel and Hamish too.

"I couldn't ken what awaits a creature like you." His green eyes briefly narrowed. Sometimes, it was Erran looking back at her. She hadn't realized how closely the men resembled each other until she'd been forced to stare at the steward for so many days on end. "If it does, it will not be me or my doing which puts you there."

She had no reason to believe him, though she did, but her belief in his word had no part in her refusal to speak. There was no freedom for her if it came at the cost of her friends, who had followed *her* vision, *her* passion. Destin would feel the same. If not, he wouldn't still be under house arrest, dealing with the same daily interrogations.

"Mariel." Rylahn leaned in, offering his "be reasonable" sigh, which she'd become familiar with even before he'd locked her away. It was Erran's sigh. It had the same light exasperation he often tried to temper when she was being wittingly unreasonable. Except when Erran did it, he was never cross for long. Tenderness wasn't far behind. "Help me help you and Destin. Your mates will be discovered before long either way. You were never going to be able to run forever. All you're doing is deferring the inevitable."

"If that were true, you would not have wasted sixty-one days with me," Mariel replied. "You're no further along than you were two months ago. And I will nay contribute to getting you closer. Aye, no matter the cost."

Rylahn rolled his tongue along the inside of his mouth. He glanced out the window, nodding. "I've been coming for sixty-one days because, despite what you've done, Erran was fond of you. He's well rid of you now, and gladly, but it would still hurt him to see you swing. I've been trying to spare him that pain, but..." He stood abruptly and checked his pocket timekeeper. "You have until I leave this room to change your mind. First, let me tell you why you should. When I leave here, I'll be publicly announcing the go-ahead of the private auction your actions delayed. The location, the properties, all of it will be tacked upon tavern walls, banks, anywhere anyone with eyes can see. Everyone who wants to know will know. Can you think of anyone *you* know who might want this information? Who might show their faces on the day?"

Mariel's blood cooled. It was a shrewd move for Rylahn, baiting Obsidian Sky, and two months ago, it might not have worked. But Augustine would have learned by now where Mariel and Destin were. Remy would have pulled Alessia and Magnur back in to solicit their help. They were smart enough to bide their time, but then again, a refresh of the auction might be exactly the dangling promise to smoke them out of hiding. There was an equal chance of them seeing the trap as walking into it.

"I see you understand." Rylahn checked his timekeeper. "Your answer."

Mariel locked his gaze and spat at his feet.

Rylahn pursed his mouth and whistled. "Aye, well at least I can look my son in the eyes and say I tried." He spun and marched out. The air whooshed with the soft slam of the doors. Mariel flinched.

When her composure returned, Mariel rose and went to the desk to withdraw the vellum and ink that had been left for her to write her confession. Instead, she composed a letter to Erran.

There was almost no chance of it making it to him. The attendants had no reason to betray their steward to aid her.

And if it made it to him, there was even less of a chance that he would do as she asked.

More than likely, her words would hasten her demise.

Tell OS to be vigilant and trust no temptation. If you ever loved me truly, then do this one last thing for me. I release you of your obligation to me. No matter what lies your father puts in your ear, I did and do love you. The heart is incapable of lies.

Mariel folded the letter and waited for her attendant.

Erran's eyes glossed in his mindless study of the portrait hanging above his father's desk. The man, bedecked in the boldest, gilt admiral's uniform he'd ever seen, was their ancestor, Drummond Rutland, who had built Goldsea Spires many years past. His statue graced their cliffside—if "graced" was even an accurate description. It was the tallest statue in the kingdom, by no small margin. Some of the mariners had dubbed it Drummond's Cock, a shining, phallic beacon of protection that kept them from veering too close to shore.

"I will tell you what I tell you every day, son," Rylahn said as he stormed in. His gait was heavier, more pronounced than it had been on any of the prior days Erran had sat waiting for him in his office. "She's a criminal. Criminals have but one code of honor, and that is protecting other criminals." He ripped his chair out from the desk but didn't sit. His eyes closed through his slow breathing exercise.

"Today was different," Erran noted aloud. He gripped the arms of his chair and leaned forward. "Wasn't it?"

"Different in that we near the end." Rylahn tapped his chest and sank onto the hard wood. "I offered her one last chance, and she threw it in my face. Two months I've put up with her, for you. So now we do it my way."

Erran's hands tightened on the chair as the room wavered. He'd had almost a season to practice the calm his father required for such conversations, but the turmoil within had no outlet.

Every night before bed, he screamed into the sea, but it couldn't come close to repairing the peace he'd felt with Mariel wrapped in his arms, safe against his heart. There was no relief from the absence of it, or the fear he would never again possess the power to save her.

To do so would start a war. Son against father.

One that, after two months of his wife being locked away, he was ready to fight. To bleed for.

To die for.

"Did you hear me?"

"Aye," Erran murmured. He cleared his throat and said it again louder, knowing his father loathed mumbling. "I heard you."

"You're nay going to ask me?"

Erran suppressed everything he should have said, for it had all already been tried and had failed. "I have no questions unless the answer involves my *wife* returned to me, safe and unharmed."

Rylahn groaned with an exasperated look at the ceiling. "Have you not learned from the Yesenia fiasco? Can you not see how a woman might use what the Guardians gave her to confuse you?"

"You look down upon me for loving someone who deceived us, and I understand why you might." Erran released the chair and brought his aching hands to his lap. "But I have tried these weeks to tell you why, and you have refused to hear."

"That your wife was a vigilante who married into our family to take from us? Aye, I heard you."

"Nay," Erran said slowly, breathing steadily out. Whatever had happened between his father and Mariel had been a turning point. The restraint Erran had been channeling all those weeks no longer served any need. Either his father released her or Erran would call upon every person Mariel had ever aided to help him do it himself. "That she was righting wrongs done upon her people. That her heart is bigger than the White Sea, and her intentions pure. Her actions should spark reflection, but instead they draw threats and retribution. You ask me if I can learn from my mistakes, but respectfully, Father, can you?"

Rylahn's face distorted in irritation. "Is this your mother's doing? Has she coddled you too much, made you soft?"

"Did you hear anything I said? Mariel only sought to return to her people what rightfully belonged to them! Do you ken she asked for a life as an outlaw? Always on the run? Always looking over her shoulder? Can you not see how we bear responsibility for creating her?"

"Oh, aye, and how she's indoctrinated you!"

"Nay, Father. What she's done is open my eyes!" Erran sprang to his feet and dropped over his father's desk. "With *love*. You can turn your nose when I say it, but Mariel loved me, and I love her still."

"Erran, a woman like her is incapable of love."

"A woman like her is afraid of love, for how can she know that, too, will not be taken from her?" Erran sucked through his teeth, suppressing the fervor raging so hot within him, his face was a blazing mess. But he'd already gone too far to stop. "What would you know of love, Father?"

"Think with your *head*, son. Not the one between your legs. She *used* you. And because of your lack of cunning, she nearly won."

"If you believe that..." Erran pushed angry breaths through his nose. "Why have you not killed her? Or her brother? It's not like you to spare someone who has wronged you."

"Do I have to make it so clear?" Rylahn thrust a hand toward the door. "Your harlot bride and her ne'er-do-well brother were the only ones who could reveal the others. Unless you already know their names?"

"Have you given her *any* of my letters? Even one?"

Rylahn laughed. "You know I haven't."

"There, *right* there." Erran slammed his palm onto a stack of paper. "If you didn't believe she loved me, you wouldn't isolate her so! You would allow her to see me. But you know she would not turn me away. You *know* she wants me there, and this scares you! It scares you that she's right, and that you've caused all the harm and suffering. I've never seen you so scared. Because if your own son would…"

Rylahn's jaw clenched. "Would what, Errandil?"

"You know, Father, even Sessaly believes this has gone too far." Erran wiped the fresh sweat from his face. "She sits outside of Mariel's room and knits, hoping her presence might bring Mariel *some* comfort. Doesn't say a word. No one knows she's there. Does that sound like our Ses?" Erran laughed bitterly. "Nay, I ken this is a revelation to you as well, for if you thought she was in any danger of helping Mariel, you'd have barred her from the wing just as you have me."

Rylahn's unsettling calm didn't make it to his eyes, two dilated balls of rage. "You have a fortnight to make peace with her end. By then I will have what I need, and I will watch, knowing I was *more* than fair, as she and her mates swing from the scaffold I will have built with my own hands. Now leave me!"

"If you harm her, even a hair on her beautiful head, you will never see me again," Erran warned. The dark, boiling pressure had risen into his neck. Spots troubled his eyes. "I will raise an army—"

Rylahn threw his head back and cackled. "And who would follow you, son? What man would go against their steward to save a *thief*?"

"The same men who lost everything because of you," Erran said and shoved away from the desk.

Rylahn's pause was icy. "How long have you known?"

Erran shook his head with a cold sneer.

"How long?"

"Long enough."

"You would forsake everything you have trained for? All you were born for? For a woman who loathed you, tricked you, and seduced you into believing her lies?" Rylahn's anger had become disgust. "A man so easily swayed by the wiles of a lass is nay fit to lead a household, let alone an admiralty."

Erran wasn't sure who he was anymore, who he should be. He knew only that either love was enough to save Mariel or it would be what damned them both. "Then give it to someone else, and I will take her in its place."

Rylahn's revolted grin peeled back over his teeth. "In the end, Erran, you will walk away with neither."

Erran turned his hand to a fist and rapped the doorframe with his knuckles. "We'll see."

Mariel twitched and nearly fell out of her chair. Her legs slipped from the cushion to the floor as she wiped the drool from her mouth, but the sight of Hestia *kneeling* in front of her was so disarming, she couldn't even remember what she'd been doing.

"Good to see you resting," Hestia said, as though she meant it.

Even in her bitterness toward all Rutlands not named Erran, Mariel had recognized the way Hestia had been slowly introducing small luxuries to her routine. The window. A soft robe for after her baths. Even the water was hotter now, and she had two attendants minding her across the hours, despite that she required none. Sour wine had been replaced with a light, refreshing cider, and there was always, always fresh fruit awaiting her in the morning.

"I didn't mean to," Mariel mumbled. She buried her face in the shawl still wrapped around her and sloughed off the dried remnants of sleep.

"Aye, well you need to, pet. Rest all you can." Hestia removed Mariel's stockings and dragged a basin from nearby. She settled Mariel's feet into the cold water.

"Ah! What are you doing?" Mariel recoiled with a gasp, but Hestia gave her a chiding tap and she relented.

"It will help with the swelling," Hestia explained.

"What swelling?" Mariel squinted at her feet in the water.

"How are you feeling otherwise?"

"Same as I've felt since the day you threw me in here."

"Really?"

No, not really, but Mariel wouldn't let any of them have the satisfaction of knowing the stress was making her ill. Some mornings she couldn't eat at all. And the exhaustion was befuddling, with how little room she had to roam.

"Perhaps you are one of the fortunate ones." She stood, casting a frown over the center table. "I'll call for more fruit."

Mariel glanced at the bowl to be certain, but there were still plenty of oranges…starfruit. She hadn't touched the cherries either. "I have enough."

"You should eat more."

"Hestia, why do you care what I eat? Whether I have air?" Mariel asked, sighing. "Why does any of this matter when I'll be sent to the gallows soon?"

Hestia went to the fruit and separated it into two piles. "Because you will not be going to the gallows, Mariel."

"How so?" Mariel turned, but Hestia clucked her tongue, and she stayed put. Her obedience was maddening, but the long nights and rough mornings had taken most of the fight out of her.

"My husband has sent word of the auction, which is to be held in a few days. His announcement includes double the land initially offered."

Mariel curled her toes in the chill water. "He's taking *more* land from *more* people who don't deserve it?"

"He has to stir their anger somehow. Anger leads to mistakes, and mistakes will end this unfortunate matter." She dusted her hands and put half of the fruit back in the bowl, turning her nose at the discarded pile, even though it had been brought just that morning. "One can hope anyway. We are all ready for this to end. You as well, I imagine."

She was, but she and Hestia seemed to have different ideas of what the end looked like. "Then how can you say I won't hang? He'll get what he wants and have no use of me."

Hestia crossed her arms with a heavy exhale. "Oh, pet. He was never going to execute you. It was your brother he was trying to spare, and now you've given him no reason to."

"What do you mean he was never going to execute me? Why has it been two months, then? And why..." She stopped. She needed answers to those questions before asking others.

"He had to be sure you weren't carrying our heir," Hestia said coolly.

Mariel snorted into a laugh. "So what's stopping him now?"

Hestia walked slowly over. She reached behind Mariel to gather the shawl and wrapped it around her. "Poor dear, you've been without a mother so long, of course you couldn't know." She pressed her lips to Mariel's forehead. "You *are* with child, Mariel. And we do not execute mothers. A child needs their mother, but how involved you get to be in their life depends wholly on what you say and do next."

Mariel watched the hearth wither and shrink and then passed out.

TWENTY-THREE

A LIT TORCH INTO A GASEOUS MINE

Erran had slept only in small stints since the day of Mariel's imprisonment, but he'd been fast asleep when the screams rang out.

He bolted upright in his bed, still fully dressed on top of the blankets, and launched into a coughing fit. His eyes stung and burned. Breath was trapped in his lungs.

Smoke.

Fire.

Erran staggered from the bed, shielding his eyes on his way to the door. The metal handle seared his hand, and he withdrew it with a sharp hiss. Flouting the pain, he reached for the nearest cloth he could find, his coat, wrapped it around the burned flesh, and tried again.

The hall was a disarray of panic. There, the smoke was thicker, choking the air. Attendants hurried each direction, slamming into each other, ignoring orders to help get everyone out.

Mariel was still in the upper hall, tucked into a corner. If the workers were running for their own lives, no one would be running for hers.

Erran brought his wrapped hand to his mouth and stumbled sideways down the hall, squinting to protect his eyes. He couldn't hear anything over the exodus. The smoke was so disorienting, he didn't realize, at first, that he'd passed Sessaly's door already, but when he saw no one else there, he reached for the handle. One girl running by screamed, "She's nay there, sir. I already checked!"

He wasn't taking anyone's word for it, so he opened her apartment and charged inside. Fire engulfed Sessaly's entire bed. Some windows behind it had shattered, flames licking through the glass. A beam had crashed down through the tester, allowing the fire to work upward through the wood.

He checked her privy and closet, but she wasn't there either.

Erran coughed and backed into the hall. He was knocked sideways by someone barreling toward him, but he kept on, sightlessly stumbling toward the nearest staircase.

He started up a stair and was shoved into the wall again. A faint apology followed the offender, but Erran didn't care or blame them.

Upward he ran, passing a dozen more fleeing staff on their way down. Some paid him no mind. Others gave him a wide-eyed stare that read, *You're going the wrong way*, but no one said anything, for they were all doing as he was, with clothing pressed to their mouths to preserve their health for as long as they could.

He was equally hindered by the smoke as he was the stinging tears pouring down his face. The fire seemed contained to the lower floor, but the fumes had risen, and the hall was clogged with them. One last person flew by on his way down the hall, and he hoped it meant the others had already gotten out. He wished he'd asked someone for help, for he had no idea how he was going to get Mariel out of a locked room without a key.

But when he reached Mariel's apartments, the door was open. He entered just in time to see his father scoop Mariel into his arms and hoist her high against his chest.

"Erran, *run*!" Rylahn screamed, coughing through the second word.

"You go first!" Erran cried, pumping his arms to encourage his father to go, go.

His father briefly seemed like he might argue. He shook his head, tucked it against Mariel's, and sprinted past, Erran directly behind.

The fire was in the hall when they reached the residential level. The shortest path to the outside was through the flames, but Rylahn charged in the opposite direction, practically leaping onto the staircase as he hustled downward with Mariel, skipping steps.

Both doors to the entrance were open wide, and Erran could see beyond that there were already hundreds on the front terrace, huddled in horror. His mother and Sessaly had to be out there. Destin too. He couldn't believe otherwise.

When they passed through the doors, Erran turned toward his father and held out his arms. Rylahn passed her over, careful to leave the pillowcase over her mouth.

Erran ran with Mariel to the edge of the outside steps and set her down underneath a tree.

"Mar. Mariel." He shook her, but still she didn't wake. "Mariel!" He murmured an apology and gave her cheek a slap.

"The most terrible dream," she muttered. Her eyes slowly opened and widened. "*Erran*?"

"There's a fire in the keep," he replied, forcing himself through hacking coughs. Over her head, he watched a long, blurry line of men racing back into the keep with water buckets, his father among them. "Can you walk?"

Mariel tried to sit. He helped her to her feet, but she was too unsteady, so he slipped an arm around her waist and half carried her across the veranda. He heard his name called out, and he followed it and found his mother and Destin standing with several of their closest attendants.

"Oh, my son, thank the Guardians!" she cried and flung her arms around him, sobbing into his shoulder. "Please tell me Sessaly followed you."

Erran's stomach plummeted. "I thought she was with you. She wasn't in her room."

"Oh, Guardians!" Hestia howled and charged back to the entrance, but it was Mariel who stopped her.

"If she's in there, they'll find her," Mariel said. She stumbled a step, her eyes fighting closure.

Erran tightened his hold around her waist.

"I saw your husband go in with the others, with buckets. He'll find her, Hestia."

Destin was crouched, breathing through his threaded hands. He abruptly sprang back up. "I'm going to help."

"Desi!" Mariel cried, reaching for him, but her protestation did nothing. He ran off to join the others, and only Erran's quick reflexes kept Mariel from darting after him.

Erran smoothed some hair from Mariel's eyes and kissed between her brows. To see her in the flesh, after so many weeks apart, sent him reeling with how powerfully he loved her, even more with absence. He had a devastating urge to use the chaos to run as far away with her as their legs could take them. But he couldn't leave with Sessaly and others still missing. "Are you hurt?"

She shook her head, speechless and teary.

"I don't just mean from today, Mariel."

"Nay," she whispered, hoarse.

He whispered his gratitude to the sky and kissed her on the mouth. "If something had happened to you…"

Mariel swayed, and Hestia charged forward to help catch her. Erran suspiciously noted his mother's concern for someone they'd kept locked up for months.

But she was his mother first, and if he needed her to protect his wife so he could help others, he knew he could trust that.

"You'll look after her?" he asked her, following the line of men rushing in and out of the burning keep.

"Will I look after her? Of course, dear. But, Erran—"

"Don't tell me not to help, Mother." He cradled Mariel's face in his hands and crushed a fierce kiss to her mouth. "I *love* you, Mariel Rutland. Whatever happens, never believe in any other truth but that one. Never listen to anyone who says otherwise. I never gave up on you, and I never will."

He tried to smile through his fear, but his mouth would not obey. Reluctantly, he released her, but one of his father's pages came rushing over, waving something in his hand.

Erran snatched the folded paper, right as Hestia and Mariel appeared over his shoulders.

"You took everything from us," he read aloud, "and now we take everything from you. The land returns to the people in two days, or your daughter will be lost to the sea. Yours in vengeance, every man, woman, and child you've aggrieved."

Hestia gasped, smashing her hands to her mouth. She screeched her daughter's name into her fingers.

Erran closed his eyes and pocketed the letter. "Is this…" he asked Mariel, quiet only enough for the two of them.

"Nay. We don't operate this way. They would never do this," she said. "But they might…They might be able to find out who it really was."

There was something distant and worrisome in Mariel's eyes, and he sensed it wasn't about the fire or Sessaly or anything immediately clear. He would ask later. What *later* looked like was a matter for the fates, but the one thing he knew for certain was she would never be anyone's prisoner again.

"Wait with my mother." Erran spotted where the men were getting the buckets and pointed himself that way. "And tell her what you just told me, Mariel. We must do everything in our power to get her back."

Mariel nodded. Her eyes were squeezed closed. She paced from one foot to the other. "Wait—"

He looked again at the line to keep from losing it, then let his eyes travel back toward her.

"I love you, Erran." She pressed a hand to her mouth. "Please be safe."

The night started in flames and ended in embers.

Mariel waited with the others in the carriage house in solemn silence. Destin and Erran arrived first, and she launched herself at them both, hooking one arm around each. They were covered in soot and stank of wood smoke but were unharmed.

Rylahn came later. He entered quietly and sat in the tall chair they'd left empty for him. It took some time before he had anything to say.

"Everyone escaped. Most of the damage was in Sessaly's apartments, where it's believed the fire originated. Who started it, how they got in…" He leveled a drained, accusatory glance Mariel's way.

Hestia opened her mouth to speak, but he stayed her. "There's no need to apprise me on the letter, love. I already know."

"Rylahn, we *must* do what they say." Hestia's crestfallen expression became more wilted with every word. "That's our lass. Our Ses."

"We do not negotiate with radicals," he grumbled and drilled his gaze at the stone wall.

"You don't mean to let them hurt her." Erran looked dumbfounded. He peeled away from Mariel and approached his father. "Father?"

"Did I say that, Erran?" Rylahn pushed the words through a hard clench. His stony gaze persisted. "Look to your wife. She knows where your sister is."

"If I did, I would go for her myself," Mariel said, rising. "This isn't the work of Obsidian Sky, Rylahn. We have *never* harmed anyone."

"Haven't you?" Glaring, he scratched his fingernails down his neck. "Aye, you know more than you're saying."

"I know it wasn't us!"

"Do you expect anyone to believe that?"

Erran stepped between them. "The auction announcement threw a lit torch into a gaseous mine. How many people saw that? How many people are slated to lose everything? Mariel's right. Obsidian Sky would have sabotaged the auction, but they wouldn't have set fire to our keep. They wouldn't have taken Ses. They wouldn't have risked Mariel's or Destin's lives." He glanced at Mariel briefly. "And they look to Mariel for direction. They wouldn't undertake such a violent act without her nod."

"You opened the window for her," Rylahn said to his wife.

"Darling, you're tired. Who was going to see any message all the way from the sea?"

"I sent no message. I—" Mariel rushed off when a bout of nausea gripped her. She made it as far as the handwashing basin before she lost her belly.

Erran pulled her hair out of the way and traced a hand down her back. "I'll send for a healer."

"Nay, it's…" Mariel rested the back of her hand against her mouth, but then more came up. "I'm not unwell."

"Inhaling smoke can be deadly. I'd feel so much better—"

"Erran, I'm with child." Until she said the words aloud, the revelation hadn't felt like a truth belonging to her at all. It still didn't, though her surprise was embarrassingly unearned. They'd lain together dozens of times and had taken no precautions. Maybe it was as Hestia had said, and she'd suffered from the lack of mothering into her adolescence, but it wasn't that she hadn't known better. She understood good and well how bairns were made.

"You're…" Erran took several steps back. One hand scraped his face. The other hovered just over his mouth. "You are?"

"Mar, is this true?" Destin asked. She heard his chair creak from the shifting weight.

"Hestia said" was all she could get out before she vomited again.

"All the signs are there," Hestia said. "And she has not *bled* the entire time she's been in convalescence."

"Is that what you call being imprisoned, Mother? Convalescence?" Erran snapped. He placed his body between Mariel and the others, lifting her chin to catch her eyes. He breathed in and held it, his mouth inflating through the release. "You're not spending another day locked away. Not fecking one." His head moved only slightly over his shoulder. "Do you understand me? I will take her tonight, and you will never see us again."

"We'll speak on it later," Rylahn replied, weary.

"We'll speak on it now." Erran laced a hand in Mariel's, and together they returned to the sitting area. "She stays with me. That wasn't a question, nor is one coming."

"Of course she stays with you, love," Hestia said swiftly. "We'll work out the other troubling details another time, when we're not…" She sighed.

Mariel wanted to speak up in her own defense, but even opening her mouth made her queasy. Erran doing it for her was startlingly satisfying.

"By other details, you mean her brother, who will also not again be locked away?" Erran asked in challenge. His hold on Mariel tightened. "We need to find Sessaly, but you also need to understand the way of things. She's my wife. He's our family."

Rylahn shot to his feet with a forceful grunt. "She's not your *wife*, Erran. She's a *thug*! I did not raise you to be so willfully blind!"

Erran swallowed hard and spun to face Mariel. "I'm offering you an annulment. Right here, right now. You can leave with as much gold as you want, and you never have to see me again. This is your way out, Mariel. I won't stop you."

Tears spilled over her lids. She shook her head. "Never."

"And if instead all I could offer you was obscurity? A quiet life without any of what you've had here?"

It was horrifying, baring her heart in front of those who thought so little of it, but Erran needed her to say it, and he needed his parents to hear it. "I only need you, Erran." She trapped another wave of bile to add what *he* needed to hear. "And our child."

"And should their crimes be swept away, merely because your heart has softened?" Rylahn asked. One shaking hand gripped the mantle.

"Yours were." Erran stood tall, challenging his father in a silent standoff. "For who had the power to hold you to account?"

Rylahn shook his head as though shedding the conversation entirely. He sucked in a sharp breath. "It's late. It's been a long night. We'll reconvene at first light about our Sessaly." His hand lifted at Mariel. "She stays with you but under guard. She will not leave the grounds until I say so. Her brother as well."

Erran nodded once in understanding.

"Where are you going?" Hestia asked when Rylahn slipped his vest back on and headed for the entrance. "Are you not going to catch some rest?"

"To call my banners. Until we know the size and shape of our foes, we must assume we are at war."

He slammed the door.

Erran undressed and bathed his wife not because she needed it, but because he did. The weeks apart had demoralized him in a way he'd never experienced, and he'd accepted it could only have happened because he'd never been so teeming with purpose.

She was his purpose.

He no longer cared how she'd come into his life, only that it was her choice to stay when it would have been so much simpler for her to go. Only if *she* wanted to leave would he allow it. He'd stand aside for no one else.

It wasn't just about the two of them anymore though. Erran pictured the life growing within her as he slid the soapy sponge along her belly, still smooth enough he wouldn't have known if she hadn't said something. He didn't know how to ask her if she was happy about being a mother, or to tell her how thrilled he was at the prospect of fatherhood. Neither seemed appropriate with so much unsettled.

He was bursting with things to say. Maybe she was too. Maybe the long, lingering moments when her eyes commanded his were the message.

But nothing that came to his tongue was enough.

So he didn't say anything.

Nor did she.

Erran cleared his mind of the worries of tomorrow and carried his wife to a foreign bed in a building he hadn't been inside of until that night.

She curled against him.

He folded himself around her, his thighs cradling her and his arms crossing over her, forming a shell.

His eyes closed.

They were on their island again, just the two of them.

The island could be anywhere.

Anywhere they were.

It was true before, and it was true still, and in the midst of so many lies and deceptions, it was the only truth that mattered.

TWENTY-FOUR

THE REMNANTS OF HIS TYRANNY

Neither Erran nor Mariel had slept overnight. She'd finally crashed at dawn, and though she'd made him promise not to let her sleep for long, it was clear she needed it, so he was going to have to break that promise.

The first things he'd noticed, when the chaos of the terrible evening disintegrated into a thoughtful quiet, were the sunken dark crescents under her eyes. Her languid movements lacked precision. Even her words were heavy and cloying, like she had no access to the right ones and stumbled instead through whatever her mind allowed. She slurred through her thoughts, only half finishing sentences.

She'd said enough for him to know what mattered. Where they stood. Their reunion was muted by their worry for Sessaly, but that was where his crazy idea had taken root. When he'd suggested it to Mariel, she'd nodded like it was obvious, like it wasn't merely the right answer but the only one.

The problem was there was no way to get her out of the carriage house to see it through. His father's guards circled its small perimeter, forming a tight, armed wall. He wondered how many knew *why* they were guarding Mariel and Destin—and if they'd even care.

Mariel wouldn't approve of his choice to go without her, but there wasn't another way around the problem of her restrictions. Obsidian Sky wouldn't hurt Sessaly, but they weren't the ones behind her kidnapping. Not all bandits had the same objectives or ethical limitations. There was nothing about the situation to be taken for granted.

Erran kissed Mariel on both temples. He tucked the coverlet around her shoulders, careful not to wake her. He wondered if he should leave a note, but decided not to. His absence would speak for him. His results would speak louder.

He found his father in the kitchen, hovering his spoon above a half-crusted bowl of porridge, which smelled much better than it looked.

"I'll be out for a bit," Erran said from the door. "I'm asking the guards to stand down and let me pass."

Rylahn didn't react.

Erran scoffed and turned to leave.

"Where?" His father dropped the spoon and looked up. "Going where?"

"To do what I can to fix this."

"Leave that to me."

"Do you have a plan?"

Rylahn pushed the bowl away. "My men are ready when I give the order."

Erran couldn't help laughing. "Ready for *what*? For whom? We don't even know who is behind this."

"Don't we?"

"You're the wisest man I know, Father, but you are being deliberately and unlawfully thickheaded about this because you're embarrassed." Erran stood tall in the face of his impertinence. He hadn't spoken so out of turn with anyone in authority before, and definitely not to his own father, whom he feared and respected in equal measure.

But Rylahn just shook his head with a tired look at the hanging candelabra. "Your judgment is a mirror, son. You slept beside this woman for months. You were intimate with her. You say you…you *love* her. From that, a man can draw but two conclusions: either you are blind and lacking the faculties to discern danger, or you were in on it with her. I've spent hours trying to decide which would be worse, and it might surprise you to learn I'd rather my son be a criminal than an imbecile."

Erran would have made himself small at such admonishment before, but the accusation landed with only the softest thud. "Then it may surprise you further to learn I am neither. I'm not blind to what Mariel has done; I suspected something was off from the start and had just about confirmed it, just before the Banner mess. Then the island happened, and there was nothing to be done but listen to what she had to say about it all and try to make sense of it. The more she talked…" He shrugged. "Aye, the more I saw myself as she must have. If you truly believe you've done nothing wrong, then you'll see no reason not to listen yourself."

Rylahn's mouth formed the faintest sneer. "To a criminal? Who lies?"

"To my *wife*."

"Not for much longer." Rylahn inched back from the bench. "I've asked my solicitor to file for an annulment."

Erran snorted. Months of reflection had hardened him. "Then I'll marry her again. I may do it anyway, for the first time was cheapened by your hastiness."

Rylahn gaped at him. "What *happened* to my son?" An animated hand followed his words through the air. "What has she *done* to you?"

"Opened my eyes." Erran's sadness returned. What could be worse than a man who had ordered or allowed the atrocities done in his father's name? A man who stood by every one. "Just give the land back, Father! What does it really mean to you and the barons? How does it compare to what it means to the families who are now homeless? Whose children will starve and die? The lineages that will end just so you and your friends can be only slightly richer?"

"This isn't about gold. You know it isn't, even as you stand there and indict me. Laws are laws, Erran. When men cannot pay taxes, there must be consequence, or all men will see there is none, and there will be mayhem."

"Laws you created! Laws that benefit only you and your cronies. Is it not your duty to protect all citizens, not just the ones who share a table with you?" Erran snapped. His blood was on the rise, and he should have stopped, before he went too far. But everything had already gone too far. "This greed and ignorance will get Sessaly killed, and I..." He ran a hand over his mouth and glanced down the hall, toward the entrance. "I will not let it happen. Forgive me or don't. My eyes are already too far open to ever close again."

They'd gone rounds for weeks about the Mariel-and-Destin dilemma.

Though Obsidian Sky was ostensibly defunct, Remy, as second in command, had called an emergency meeting the night Augustine had returned with the news the Ashdowns had been made prisoners at the Spires.

Remy hadn't wanted his sister returning to her duties at all. There was far too much risk anymore. The steward might not know their names, but his son did, and unlike Mariel, Remy had no trust for the princeling. The man would fold when the right threat was dangled before him. If not him, then he had two other friends who knew just as much, and who had even less incentive to protect their secret.

But Augustine couldn't have been swayed. Mariel needed an ally inside, and there was nothing else he could say. Any influence he'd had over his sister had inevitably faded, and if it had been him with a coveted job at the Spires, he would have continued going back as well.

None of the group could agree on a way forward. Magnur wanted to assemble a line of trebuchets and fling a slew of boulders at the walls until they released her. Alessia suggested hiring assassins to sneak in under the cover of night, which was more feasible in the short term, but murder would raise the bounty on their heads to amounts no man could resist—and Remy wasn't sure he wanted that on his conscience. Augustine's plan was simply to listen and wait for the right piece of information or opportunity. With patience, it would reveal itself, she insisted.

Remy, the Tactician, had no better suggestion. So wait they did.

For two long months, they waited.

Until the princeling himself showed up at his door.

Magnur answered, greeting the craven bastard with a sword to the neck. Alessia flung the door wider, brandishing her own steel with a flick of her wrist. Remy could have stopped them, but he wanted to see how it played out first.

Erran hoisted both of his hands in cool submission. He didn't look the slightest bit afraid. Remy wondered if that might change, if he learned just how much the two wanted him dead—and that Remy himself was probably the only thing standing between Erran and his final meeting with the Guardians.

"Please hear me out. I'm here on Mariel's behalf," the man said. He craned his neck back for relief, but Magnur's sword tip followed him. The princeling flinched when blood ran down his neck and into the opening of his shirt, but he didn't try again to withdraw.

"Or your daddy's," Alessia retorted. "Donnae ken I'd like to take the chance of being right. How about you, Mag?"

"Nay, best to be safe."

"Mhm, *Mariel* taught us that."

"Aye, we'd be a fool to forsake her wisdom now."

"'Specially not for this squint who got her and her brother locked up."

"Listen. *Please.*" Erran's arms flagged. His elbows lowered to his sides. "Remy. Could you call them off?"

"Me?" Remy chortled. In truth, he hadn't decided what to do about the princeling's sudden arrival. He hadn't calculated it into the possibilities, because the man was a true wild card. Mariel loved him—trusted him—but the rest of them had no reason to. For all they knew, the Rutland guards could be lying in wait in the alleyways for an ambush.

But in his years as an apprentice to one of the greatest tacticians in Oldcastle, he'd absorbed the importance of not overlooking a variable for risk alone. The safest way forward seldom led to the most desirable outcomes. "Mag, check the street. Alessia, watch the door."

"Not taking my eye off this one for a moment," Alessia grumbled. Her eyes narrowed to slits, like a feral cat's. "He's wily. Kens he's too smart for his own good."

"Whatever I am, I'm also a man who loves his wife and respects..." Erran scrunched his face as he brazenly reached upward to shove the sword aside. He grunted and massaged his neck, daring to look maddened by the whole thing. "The work you were all forced to do because of men like my father."

"And you, squint." Alessia spat on his boot. "Ye benefit just as much as the others."

"Aye." Erran didn't break her wild gaze. "I have. I do. And it needs to change."

"Is he armed?" Remy asked.

Alessia slapped her hands all over Erran's body. Remy could almost respect how the man was taking the small assaults in stride. "Nay. Which makes him a fool as well."

"Go on, both of you," Remy said, shooing them with his hand. "I'll hear what he has to say."

Magnur and Alessia circled Erran on their way out. Alessia charged at him, but all he did was regard her behavior with indifference.

The man is exhausted, Remy realized. Augustine had been at the Spires when the fire had broken out, and she had come home just long enough to tell the others what had happened. She'd returned to the keep, not for the Rutlands but for the women she'd come to see as her friends, other workers still dealing with the shock of the night's horrors.

"Sit," Remy ordered. "I'd offer you a drink, but I'm rationing."

"I'm not looking for hospitality." Erran slipped warily onto the rickety chair across from Remy. He glanced back at the door, probably expecting the other two to launch a surprise attack. It wasn't out of the realm of possibilities, no matter what he'd asked them to do. "The fire last night. Was it you?"

Remy laughed. "I thought you were here about Mariel."

"I am."

"My sister said she wasn't hurt. Nor Des."

"They weren't," Erran said, "but whoever was responsible has also taken my sister as ransom. Mariel says it wasn't you, and if you say the same, I'll believe you. But my father will not. He's convinced it was Obsidian Sky, and if I can't find who was actually responsible, you'll all be hunted to the end of your days."

"Worried for us, are you?" Remy smirked.

Erran bowed his head into his tented hands. He kept himself like that, letting the time pass. "If I have to run away with my wife to protect her, it's what I'll do. But do you ken she'd even go, if the rest of you were in my father's crosshairs? She'd put herself on the gallows first. Tighten the noose with her own hands. You know she would. There's no end to this until it all ends. I need a name, Remy. I need to know who has my sister, and Mariel believes you can find that out. I need my *father* to see it was *you* who gave it to me. I'll guarantee your immunity if this happens. In writing."

Remy couldn't decide where he landed on the man's sincerity. He hadn't wanted to believe Mariel had actually fallen for her mark, but he found it even harder to believe the man could love her back after learning her secrets. A woman who had married into his family to rob them blind? Nay, his "love" didn't add up.

Yet he could see nothing but distress in the highborn sitting across from him. Whether his words were true, *he* seemed to believe them. "You mean your father will grant us immunity, aye? He's the only one with the authority."

"Aye. That's what I mean."

"And how do you ken you'll pull it off? He'll agree?"

"He will when I tell him it's the only way to get Sessaly back."

"A man like him cannot even conceive of the value of what he's stolen. Why should I believe he sees the value of his own blood?"

"Because he loves his daughter. And he'll get nothing until he signs." Erran spread his hands over the table. "You've already disbanded. Your work is over either way. Tell me your price. If immunity isn't enough, tell me what will be."

"I almost feel bad telling you this, but you're severely overestimating your father." Remy crossed his arms and leaned back. "This started with his ill-considered public announcement about the auction."

"Aye." Erran nodded wearily. "He wanted to get your attention. Instead, he got someone else's. I need to know who."

"He did get our attention. We saw right through the trap." Remy chewed the inside of his lip, thinking. He no more believed in Erran's lofty hopes than he did the steward's magnanimity, and he didn't particularly care *what* happened to the spoiled debutante daughter of a tyrant, but he loved Mariel and Destin. Whatever else was true in the web of deceptions and offers, as long as Rylahn Rutland believed his daughter-in-law was involved in his downfall, he would never relent in his mission to destroy her. Even if Erran got her to run, they'd never find peace. Never stop looking over their shoulders. The same fate awaited the rest of them too. "Where are Mariel and Des now?"

"Safe."

Remy scoffed. "How specific. You want me to put trust in you, yet offer none in return."

"Nay, for if you send those two rabid lapdogs after her, they'll both be killed. And it would break my wife's heart. She's suffered enough."

"How do you know your sister didn't perish in the fire?"

"We were given a note."

"What did they ask for?"

Erran held out his hands. "The return of all lands taken."

Remy laughed. "Your answer, then, seems simple enough to me."

"I've said the same to my father, but he's..." Erran pursed his mouth tight. "A man possessed. He's been humiliated. He believes this requires answer."

"Then how does giving him a name help anyone but him?"

Erran flopped back in exasperation. "Remy, he *will* find Sessaly. He's called his banners. Do you ken what that means?"

"You think me stupid?"

"He will find those responsible, root them out, and make examples of them. Then he'll continue until he finds you...your sister...those foul creatures who answered your door. Mariel will live because she's carrying his grandchild, but Destin? He'll have no use for him."

"What did you say about Mariel?" Remy sat back.

"She's with child." Erran glanced away. "Are you a father?"

Remy shook his head, as much in response to the simple question as to make sense of the far less simple emotion Erran's words had prompted. He hadn't even accepted Mariel's fondness for the princeling, and she was already having his child?

"My mate, Hamish, he told me all the colors of the world change when you become a parent. Nothing has been the same in my head since Mariel told me last night. Nothing. Not a single feckin' thing. Before, I loved her enough to come here and risk my neck, but now I come to you as a man hoping not only to protect his wife but also his child." Erran leaned in, stretching across the table. "You and me, we can end this. Tell me your price, Remy, and I'll see it done."

The man in Remy wanted to send the princeling soaring through his window and into the road. The tactician in him appreciated the opportunity the offer presented. A way out. A way to save them all. A way to help others beyond anything they could accomplish as vigilantes.

He *could* track down whoever was responsible for the attack on the Spires. Secrets were rarely so for long, and for the right price, they didn't exist at all.

"My price…" Remy rubbed his chin. "You already named one. The ransom letter named the other."

"The land returned. Immunity." Erran nodded. "Anything else?"

Remy would have laughed at how simple Erran's words made the whole thing sound if there'd been any humor left in his heart. "Aye, there's one more."

Erran nodded for him to continue.

"It's not enough for him to reverse what he's done. He needs to *see* it. With his own eyes. Not send his men, so he can hide behind ignorance. He needs to *face* what he's done. I want Rylahn Rutland himself to ride through the remnants of his tyranny, and if he refuses, then you're on your own."

TWENTY-FIVE

A NEVER-ENDING CONUNDRUM

Erran laid out the terms to his father, speeding through the parts he sensed wouldn't be received well, which was, to be fair, most of them. He'd expected a fight, but all he got was a turgid silence and a stare so rigorous, he wondered if his father had even been listening.

"You went to Obsidian Sky," Rylahn said at last. He drew each word out with exaggerated emphasis. "So you *do* know. You *do* have names. *You've known all along*." He wedged his tongue between his teeth and clamped down. "Your wife's imprisonment is on you. *You*. You had the power to free her, and you didn't."

"She wouldn't have wanted me to free her if it meant you executing her friends." Erran's defense of his choice wasn't as strong as it sounded. He'd made the same argument to himself, every single day of Mariel's confinement. Those weeks had been unbearable, but he could not have faced her if he'd given into the urge. "I'm still not telling you. I'm sorry, Father."

"Are you?" One of his father's eyes twitched.

"Mariel wasn't the woman I wanted to marry. Yet when you told me to, I did, out of loyalty to you. And now she's my wife, and I love her, and my loyalty belongs first to her. As it should. As yours is to Mother. As you *raised* me to act."

Rylahn's eyes rolled. "Do not hurl my teachings in my face as twisted lies. Your loyalty to her should have ended the *moment* she told you who she was."

"Aye, perhaps," Erran said, nodding. "Instead I listened. It wasn't easy to hear. Was even harder to see. But that isn't the man I want to be, blind to the results of my own accounting, my own choices. When we were on the island, everything she told me was so hard to accept because the man she spoke of was not the man I know. My father is an honorable steward, I told her, a man who loves his people. Loves his wife, his children. It just doesn't reconcile with my own experiences, and yet…" He cast his eyes aside, finding his words through the twisting discomfort of a life slowly crumbling. "I believed her. I opened my eyes to what she was telling me, and I am not…" His mouth tightened with a surge of sadness, an awful gut-punching of grief that held just as much guilt as anything else. He'd never needed to rely on his words for anything so crucial, and he had no confidence in his capability, only his sincere desire to help. "I cannot return to the person I was before she showed me the man I want to be. If you're honest with yourself, you'll find I'm becoming the man you raised me to be as well."

Rylahn shook his head at his desk.

"I need you to hear me this time when I tell you what she means to me. *Father.*" Erran waited for his father to look up. "This isn't lust. She's nay Yesenia. She is the realest thing I've ever felt, held, touched. She's the most incredible woman I have ever known. Without her, there is no sunset, no sunrise. No color in this world. Not for me. And I *believe* in her. If you make me choose, I will choose her." He tapped his chest. "But I'm asking you not to, because it doesn't have to be this way. You're not like Yesenia's in-laws, those feckin' bootlicking tree-dwellers who conspire with the crown against their own people, but that's where this has all led us. Starvation. Homelessness. Death. You're better than this. The Southerlands is better than this. So many times I've told Mariel and the others that you're a good man, and this is your chance to make me an honest man."

"I don't even know what to say to you anymore, Erran," Rylahn said. His eyes were so red and heavy, Erran doubted he'd slept at all. No matter how tough he was acting, he was terrified. He loved Sessaly. He was the singular reason she'd become a spoiled brat, because he'd overindulged her, given her everything she'd ever asked for. When he'd been tough on Erran, because he felt he had to be, for his daughter, he only had tender kindness. There were times it made Erran jealous, but his mother reminded him that Sessaly would become a woman and be offered in marriage to the most strategic match their father could find, and it wouldn't matter if she loved him or even liked him. Her life would become the property of her husband, and her choices as well. Until then, Rylahn would give her the world to make up for it.

"I propose," Erran said cautiously, "you start with one of Obsidian Sky's asks. Just one. It will cost you nothing except your time."

Rylahn threaded his hands and waited.

"Ride with me through the lake district."

"Erran—"

"You're the steward, and you should do this anyway. It's part of the job. And if you find that what you see is the image of the province you intended to build, then there's nothing more I can say."

"You want me to ride through lands I've ridden through a thousand times?"

"I remember when the visits stopped, the same time the taxes went up and the land seizures began." Erran shook his head. "Set aside for a moment that others want you to do this. Don't *you*?"

Rylahn rubbed his temple with his fingers. His heavy breathing sliced through the quiet. "Go check on your mother, please. She's not handling this well."

Erran's heart sank. "Will you not even consider what I'm saying?"

"Please," Rylahn said. He stood with an old man's energy, slow and creaky. "I have somewhere I need to be."

"Mariel," Destin pleaded, "I know how you feel about him, but it's not *safe* for us here. Either of us. There's naught he can do about it, and you know it."

Mariel wasn't sure how to tell him he was wrong, because she didn't actually believe he was.

They were sitting on a bench in the center of the maze that had been sculpted upon one of the lower cliffs on the Rutland estate. It sat at the outer barrier of where they were allowed to wander during their lockdown, house arrest with more legroom. But at least now she could see Erran…draw strength from him, which was not an easy thing for Mariel to admit, but her marriage had been a series of self-challenges that had made her stronger than she'd been since her parents had left her and Destin to fend for themselves.

But it didn't mean she was strong enough to fight the Rutlands.

"You're going to have a baby," Destin said. He pulled her hands into his with the urgency of a child.

"That's what keeps me safe," Mariel replied. She withdrew her hands, folding them into her dress. "But *you're* not safe. When Erran returns, we'll talk to him about getting you out of here. He'll know a way to sneak you past the guards."

"You're only safe until you deliver!" Destin spun on her in frustration that said, *You're not getting it,* but she was. She was an incubator, at least to Rylahn. Maybe to Hestia as well. Certainly to the men and women whose salaries they paid. But she was, at most, a couple of months along. There was time to figure out what to do about her predicament. Destin's required a more immediate answer. "Mariel!"

"I won't leave without my husband," she said stoically, stubbornly. Erran had been gone when she'd woken that morning, and while he hadn't left a note, she suspected where he'd went. He should have been back already, and the fact that he wasn't left a dark crevasse of fear and uncertainty in her belly. Remy and Augustine wouldn't hurt someone Mariel loved, but Magnur and Alessia were less predictable. Their short fuses were rarely lit with reason. They'd lose no sleep over taking a life if they deemed it necessary. "And he would never let them hurt me, Des. I know you think he's weak—"

"I think he would die to protect you, and if you stay, he might get the chance." Destin groaned softly under his breath. "Is that what you want? To force a conflict?"

"Force a…" Mariel scoffed and gestured around. "We are already in conflict, Des. *Someone* tried to burn the keep down. They kidnapped Sessaly. Don't forget we weren't on the side with the torches. We were the ones being torched."

"The steward is convinced it was our people behind it. You won't sway him otherwise."

"Maybe I won't have to."

"How so?"

"I ken Erran went to see Remy today."

Destin did a double take. "Pardon me, *what*?"

Mariel sighed. "I didn't ask him to, but he knows they can help. They might be the only ones who can help."

"What would help is if the steward gave the feckin' lands back to their rightful owners. It's not an unreasonable ransom demand, Mar, and he won't. Not even for his own daughter…"

Rylahn was beyond reason. One day, Erran would be the steward, and he would right the wrongs done, but how many years would it take? How many more would die before then?

She couldn't say the words aloud because they truly frightened her, but for the first time in her life, Mariel didn't have a plan, nor did she have any power. The one card she'd thought to play was beyond her ability because she wouldn't get ten steps beyond the perimeter before the guards dragged her back. Erran had played it for her, but he was even less likely to win with it than she would have been. Even if Remy agreed to hear him out, it wasn't the same as listening.

And as much as she wanted to continue helping her people, she wouldn't do anything that risked the safety of her child.

How could she tell Destin she'd given up though? Even in his pleading, he was looking to her to say what came next. To give *some* sort of direction. But the only fight she had left in her was the one needed to protect her own.

"You won't leave without him?" Destin crossed his arms. "And I won't leave without you. Seems we have a conundrum."

Mariel laughed. "When have we not had a conundrum, Desi, eh? Our whole lives have been one never-ending conundrum."

Crunching steps in the maze had them exchanging wary looks. None of the guards had followed them in. She'd heard one of them whispering about how easy it was to get lost inside.

But it was Rylahn who emerged from the path. Alone.

"Mariel, might we speak? Just us?"

Destin stood, making himself big with his stance. "So you can interrogate her more? Nay. You've something to speak about? Speak to me."

Rylahn swept his eyes over Destin. A flicker of...*something* was there, but it left before she could understand. "You and I have matters as well. I'll find you later."

"You misunderstand me. I won't leave her to be harassed by you."

"It's you who misunderstands, Destin. Now leave us."

Mariel nodded to show him it was all right.

"Mariel," Destin hissed.

"It's all right," she said. "He can't hurt me."

"I'll be *just* at the outside of the maze. I'll hear if you yell." He backed away with his dark gaze fixed on Rylahn.

The moment he was gone, she regretted it. Vulnerability crawled through her marrow. She was alone and undefended, with a man whose life would be drastically simpler without her in it. Even if she screamed, no one would come. Not for her.

"Where's Erran?" she asked, hoarse.

"Helping his mother. At ease, Mariel. I'm not here to hurt you." Rylahn gestured at the bench. "May I?"

Mariel inched farther to the left.

Rylahn sank onto the bench with the stiff awkwardness of one who had forgotten how to sit. He slapped his hands atop his knees and said, "There's something I need to tell you, and there's no point in wasting breath getting there. I knew your mother. Ofaelia. When she was still a Braeloch."

"My mother?" Mariel retreated into her shock. More questioning she'd been prepared for. Harassment. Threats even. He'd shown her an entire arsenal of tactics over the past weeks. But not once had he ever mentioned her family. "How?"

"My father's grocer purchased our cabbages and carrots exclusively from the Braelochs."

"All right. And?"

"He liked them so much, he eventually went into business on the side with her father, Cohle." He shook his head and blew a pursed breath. "Your grandfather's vegetables were the best in the region. The land around the lake is fertile and generous, which you know. His peers said he should raise the taxes to pocket from Cohle's success, but my father didn't want the man to suffer. *We can both eat more*, he used to say, so instead, he invested by doubling the Braeloch lands. In turn, Cohle tended that land for free, and all profits for the extended acreage belonged to the Rutlands. It seemed overly generous, even for my father, but I was just a boy—fifteen, perhaps, the last time I went with him. I didn't yet understand the ways of men.

"Your mother was a few years older than me. Ah, Ofaelia was a force. A sharp wind when a breeze would suffice. Southerland women often are, but she was different. Cohle used to say she could command the skies themselves. I always knew the moment she'd stepped into the field because the birds would fly to this large tree at the north end of the property and wait for her to finish her business before returning."

No one had ever described Mariel's mother to her that way. By the time she was old enough for memories, her mother had been whittled down by the demands of a hard life. The image of Ofaelia storming through a field, sending the birds aflutter, seemed a fiction too great for a man of Rylahn's voided imagination, but there was nothing in his face suggesting he was being anything but earnest in his remembrance. "She never mentioned you."

"Aye, she wouldn't have. I was a mirror to her shame." Rylahn squinted at the midday sun. "But we were friends, I think. Father's deal meant more visits to Mistgrave and the lake. I liked talking to her. For all she unsettled me, there was an ease to the way she moved through the world that was foreign to me. It was as though she never needed to question where she stepped, for she was confident the world would adjust to her stride." He looked upward with a sigh that was almost wistful. "What I didn't know then, inexperienced in the ways of men as I was, was that my father had more than gold on his mind when he made the deal with Cohle. I wasn't the only one who looked forward to visiting the Braelochs."

Mariel turned so she could look at him better. She held her patience to let him finish his own way. Whatever else his words intended, they were a confession, and there was a reason he'd chosen her, his greatest antagonist, to hear it.

"Ofaelia tells me one day she's with child. For the first time in our acquaintance, she seemed unable to find her words, but she finally gets out that it was my father who put her in that state. She assured me there was nothing untoward, that they were *in love*." Rylahn scoffed. "Aye, and in the next breath said my father wanted nothing to do with any of it. The whole time, right under my nose. While I'd be learning the harvest with the men, she and he were rutting like barn animals in the stables. It was the only time I ever saw her cry, and I did nothing. I didn't understand why her confession had turned me inside out. She was five, six years older than me and never looked at me with anything but the regard of an older sister. But first love can be a dangerously powerful thing. Erran knows. I could do little but watch him tear himself in two for someone…" He trailed off. "He had to learn the hard way. As I did. But in my woundedness, I chose not to believe her. I called her a liar who was trying to destroy my father and our family, and I promised she'd come to regret her lie. That the next time she saw me, I'd be there to collect on my promise."

Mariel's hands formed a knot in her lap. It was too much, all of it, but he hadn't spoken so openly about anything to her before. He might never again. And what he was saying, it made some sense, more sense than a man who comported himself as a decent conscientious steward caring for naught but gold. She could deconstruct his words later, but she might never hear them again if she stopped him now. "Are you actually suggesting Destin is your father's *son*? That's he's your…*brother*?"

Rylahn made an ambiguous shrug. "It was because I believed her I was so full of rage. Not long after, she was married off to Astin Ashdown, another local farmer, and several months later was a mother. My father sold the land to Cohle for a fair price, and our visits stopped. We found another farmer to supply our cabbage and carrots, and the name Braeloch was never again mentioned. Even on progress, we gave the lake a wide berth." He paused briefly. "Two years later, my father was dead—heart stopped when he was out riding. No physician could tell us why, when he was otherwise in perfect health, but I knew it was her. And in her absence, it was all too easy to let the blame fester, to replace the grief. Anger is always easier, is it not? I ken you know better than most."

His story was so utterly preposterous, but Mariel could neither move nor speak. She stared at her lap with a dread still forming.

"I didn't return until I was steward myself. She wasn't the same woman at all. A wisp of who she'd been…a mother twice over, another on the way. I dealt with her husband only, but I would catch her watching me from the window. Hiding. Not once did she come down. And I looked at the land, the prosperity, and contrary to my vow, she'd not suffered at all. She was thriving. And I was still grieving my father—my youth. It was blinding, how furious it made me. I knew nothing else. I couldn't make myself see her again, so I delegated stewardship to my most ruthless officers, gave them some…ideas on how they should govern, and walked away from it. You know better than I what happened next."

"Aye, because you were a craven bastard who couldn't even face the wreckage of his own tantrum! And you made *everyone* suffer for the actions of one, actions that had naught to do with you at all!" Mariel's breathing pitched and crashed. The dull roar of the surf beyond the maze reminded her she was alone and isolated with a man who loathed her—and apparently her mother—enough to destroy an entire region in the wake of a broken heart that he should have had the better sense to subdue.

Rylahn didn't even seem to hear her. "Years later, when Korah Warwick came to me with a list of ten potential brides for Erran, I nearly fell out of my chair when I saw the name Ashdown. Number eight on a list ordered by importance of birth. No one expected any serious consideration to be offered beyond the third name on the list, but ah, I chose you. Korah, Hestia, even the late Lord Warwick asked me to reconsider. The Rutland name is second only to the Warwicks, they said, as if I didn't know. Any marriage made must reflect that." Rylahn flexed his hands over his thighs. "I told them a highborn wedding would require planning, dowries…contracts upon contracts. The Ashdowns weren't even barons anymore. They'd been stripped of lands. Titles. They'd fallen so far, I didn't even need your signature, Mariel. I could have wed you to Erran either way. Even after all my explaining, they still didn't understand why I would let my son, my heir, marry someone so far beneath him. Even I couldn't quite see the edges of the grudge I'd held for so many years." He bowed his head, pulling his hands across the back of his neck. "When I look at Destin, I see my father. When I look at you, I see her. Ofaelia."

Mariel wanted to avail herself of the dagger in her boot so she could press it to his throat and carve the truth away, but his words had unlocked the final box of her childhood confusion. How and why it had all changed so *fast*. Why she, a pauper, had been chosen for a prince. The disproportionate disgust Rylahn held for Destin, despite his string of excuses for the reasons he couldn't send him to the gallows. The only disconnected piece of the puzzle was that Rylahn had told her any of it.

And then she knew.

"This is some final confession, but you're not dying," she drawled. Her hands wrapped around the bench. Her legs readied to spring. The sea was just ahead and beyond. Rylahn's leg was so bad, she wouldn't even have to run fast, just fast enough for him to lose her trail. A quick climb over a bush and she'd be free. The rest she could sort later. "Tell me, will you wait until I've delivered to dispose of me, or do you wish for my child to die too?"

"If only either would proffer the peace that has eluded me for so long." Rylahn sank deeper against his thighs. His head faced the ground. "But peace and I are unacquainted." He abruptly sat tall. "I won't hurt you, Mariel. My son loves you, and I love him too much to break his spirit when he's only just discovered he has one. But as I've just given you my testament, I'm asking for yours in return. For your full honesty. Will you, for once, give me that?"

Mariel cautiously settled back down, crushed so far to her end of the bench, she was half climbing it. "Don't ask me for names. Those I will never give."

"Do you actually love my son, or is it just another one of your lies?"

"Aye, I do." Mariel felt lighter suddenly, not in the confession but in answering the question from the one person whose belief in her was absent. "It would be far, far easier for me were it all a lie."

"Then tell me how that is possible, after all your hatred for us? After *ten years* of vengeance, why *him*, the son of the man you most hate? For if this is not retribution, it is one hell of a happenstance."

Mariel already had her answer, for the many hours she'd spent contemplating it. She only had to decide how much was for others and how much was for herself. "I saw his heart, and I knew it was good. And when I gave him mine, he treated it with the utmost care. I knew he would never do to me what his father had." He didn't deserve the rest, the most vulnerable and raw parts that were hers alone, but she said it anyway. "He was the first safe place I've known since I lost my parents and sister. Anger *is* easier. There were years it was all I could consume. Love, forgiveness...They take so much more from us. They give us everything to live for and everything to lose. Nothing about loving Erran has been easy, but that's not his doing. My armor was so thick and calloused, I've forgotten how to remove it. Still is. Yet somehow, he's discovered a way, and bit by bit, I've let him."

Rylahn frowned, considering her words. He stood. "I'm going to ride through the lake district with Erran."

"You have?" Mariel rose with him, stunned. Her pulse hastened again, as though the fragile trust they'd built was crumbling. "Why?"

"He asked me to." Rylahn stretched a tentative hand toward her. It landed awkwardly on her shoulder with a quick squeeze. "You'll obviously do as you please, but I hope you will leave speaking with Destin to me."

Mariel nodded remotely. The late afternoon haze only added to the surrealness of a moment she still didn't understand. "Why... Why did you tell me all of this?"

But Rylahn didn't answer. He cast another squinting look toward the sky and limped back to the maze path.

Erran wanted Mariel there. It was her story to tell, and he had no right telling it for her. But his father would only go if they went alone.

On the ride to Mistgrave, he told him why.

About Mariel's mother.

About Destin.

The aftermath of his fateful choice.

And then he stunned Erran again when he revealed he'd told all of it to Mariel first.

"The truth is I've been here plenty in recent years. I come alone." Rylahn led them down an unfamiliar path, which took them deeper into the woods. "To a place Mariel might want to see. You could take her sometime."

Erran was still fuddled by everything his father had said, and so casually. He didn't care about some place in the woods; he had questions, too fucking many of them. But his father refused to answer any.

Rylahn pointed as they entered a small clearing. There wasn't much beyond the brush and fallen leaves, but in the center was a cairn. Stones of similar size were piled and stacked. "I made this for Ofaelia." He nodded sideways. "Eh, maybe for Astin too. And their young lass. Never learned her name."

"Whoa. Whoa, whoa." Erran shuffled in front of his father. "You cared enough to build a memorial but not to *fix* everything you upended when your feelings were hurt? If you wanted to honor Mariel's mother, *that's* how you do it. Oh, and her name was Angelika."

Rylahn's knuckles went bone white as he twisted his reins. "There are things I didn't tell you about the auction. There's a reason it was necessary."

"What does the auction have to do with *anything* I just said?"

"The contract I signed with the barons who took over the lake," Rylahn said, "gave them fifteen years of prosperity. At the expiration, all authority was to revert to me, their services no longer required. The decrees they'd instituted and upheld would be undone, though they'd keep anything they'd earned in that time. But they wanted to renew the arrangement that made them very wealthy men. Why wouldn't they? A taste wasn't enough. It never is."

The entire ride, memories from Erran's childhood had become wisps of remembrances in his thoughts, only to be reframed with everything he'd learned about his father. Celebrations he'd held with other men had obviously been about the land confiscations. The barons who would approach Rylahn in the villages about his "beneficence," sealing their proclamations with knowing looks, made far more sense. And, however illogical, Erran at last had an actual answer why carrots and cabbage had always been forbidden in their kitchens.

But it all added up to one thing: the man he'd known as Father was not the man others had called friend.

Still, he was there. Observing. Confessing.

"I should hope you wouldn't want to renew such a foul arrangement," Erran replied when it seemed his father was waiting for one.

"I never intended for it to exceed the fifteen years. That was more than enough time to make a point, and a year in, I already had deep regrets. I never foresaw how...bad it could get if I wasn't there to oversee their choices. But if I reneged on a contract I signed as the steward of this land, then it would undermine all contracts, all laws. I cannot be above judgment. No man is." Rylahn dismounted and crept toward the cairn. He crossed his arms as his shadow spread over the rocks. "The barons threatened a coup if I didn't sign for another fifteen years."

"And? Do not all the soldiers of our region answer to you alone?"

"Power is a curious thing, Erran. It may be absolute, but it is never absolutely yours." Rylahn dug into his pocket and withdrew a round, smooth stone. He set it atop the pile. "Review our histories some time. You'll see the way power in the Southerlands has transferred hands, often brutally. Read closer and you'll see why."

Erran glanced at the darkening sky. They hadn't even started their ride through the villages, yet he craved home. Mariel. He missed his sister. His father's conscience was a burden too big for Erran to carry. Rylahn would either honor the ransom or he would not, and the persuasion for such a choice had lived nowhere but within the man himself. "Dusk is fading, and we still have more to see. You can tell me whatever else you have to say at the inn."

"We're not staying the night. Everything you need to show me, I've already seen." Rylahn mounted and turned toward the road. "The auction was my compromise to the barons for ending the contract. It was an immediate wound inflicted on the people to avoid greater injury. They agreed, on the condition I put an end to Obsidian Sky and make an example of its leaders. No one wanted that more than I, so of course I agreed. Heartily. I had no inkling two of them belonged to our family."

A terrible thought came to Erran. "It wasn't brigands at all who took Sessaly, was it? You know who has her?"

Rylahn stiffened. "I have my suspicions."

"Why would they demand you return the land then? Land *they* wanted."

"They're testing me to see where my loyalties lie, if I have a weak spot. There's at least two of them who still have their eyes set on my seat and welcome any excuse to make a play for it." He spurred forward and back onto the road.

Erran caught his father's pace. "Ah. And with this more recent agreement, you thought you could appease them with the names of two Obsidian Sky outlaws. You didn't care who, as long as it wasn't your daughter-in-law or…or brother."

Rylahn didn't answer.

"And the auction?"

"What about it?"

"Do you still intend to take all that land and give it to the men who watched entire families wither and die for their own sick benefit?"

"How else do you propose I bring your little sister home?"

Erran thought for a moment. There was something about the whole retelling that didn't sit right, and it went well beyond the words themselves. "Those barons, did they commit any crimes in the act of…service?"

"Aye. You know they did." Rylahn snorted. "Many."

"Crimes they could be punished for?"

"If someone had the mind to, I ken."

"These same men who held others to account could be held to account?"

"If you're suggesting—"

"I am." Erran stopped riding and waited for his father to do the same. "Look, if the men who benefited from the land confiscated from criminals are they themselves criminals, then you have legal basis to confiscate those same properties. They'd be yours to allocate as you please."

Rylahn shook his head. "I've already thought of that, but there are dozens of them, Erran. You're not seeing the scope of the matter. We arrest one, the others know before we blacken their doorstep."

"Don't you see? All this happened for a reason. *Mariel* coming into our lives happened for a reason!"

His father sounded exhausted when he slowly said, "Son, I'm not following."

Erran's glee was concealed by the darkness. Mariel would have dozens of better solutions, undoubtedly, but he liked to think she'd be proud that he'd added to his cunning through her education. "You have an auction happening *soon.* Where all these criminals will be gathered to purchase more confiscated lands."

Rylahn watched him, drained but attentive.

"Grandfather used to say any man could be a prolific fisherman if he stocked his own pond." Erran couldn't be certain the idea was a good one, but it *could* work. "The auction is a stocked pond, Father. Your pond. I ken if you really mean to undo the hurt and make things right, it's time to go fishing."

TWENTY-SIX
ONE MILLION WAYS

Thirty-seven. The number of barons arrested.

Three hundred sixty-eight. The properties confiscated from said barons.

One hundred ninety. The properties returned to their rightful owners.

Twenty-two. The days it took to oversee the successful transfers.

Ten. The years it had taken to prove Mariel's life's work had not been for nothing.

One million. The number of ways she had come to love her husband.

It hadn't been as smooth as the facts and figures suggested. The barons wouldn't give up their wealth and status without a fight, and there'd been a half dozen small uprisings from loyal serfs hoping to gain favor if their baron emerged the victor.

One skirmish ended with a guard killed. After the perpetrator was ceremoniously hanged in the Whitecliffe village square, the uprisings stopped.

Not every property had been neatly returned. Some were deemed appropriate forfeitures. For those currently imprisoned, they could plead their case once they paid their debt to the law. For those egregiously behind on taxes, they could reapply for their titles when they produced twenty-five percent of what was owed.

Rylahn had held the barons in the jail for two of the past four days, long enough to search their lands for Sessaly. But it was Remy and Alessia who'd found her eating breakfast with the wife of Baron Hundson, who was happy for the whole ordeal to be over—less so to discover she had sixty days to vacate her land.

Mariel sat across from her father-in-law in his office, in a seat typically occupied by men of importance. Erran was beside her but had nudged himself slightly to the side. His occasional smile showed his contentment in her taking lead on the ceremonious end of years of strife. She saw pride in his gaze, but it was she who was proud of *him*, for contriving a conduit to peace that avoided war. For convincing his father it was the best way forward.

"Everything we talked about is there." Rylahn nodded at the long sheet of vellum she'd unrolled. He nudged the inkpot and quill her way. "Land has been returned to those eligible through a re-review of crimes and unpaid taxes. Those who were ineligible have a path for reclamation. Taxes have been lowered to a standard twenty-five percent but will scale for farms who reach specific profit levels, as defined here." He leaned over his desk and tapped the page in the middle. "The third section details what we agreed to about the democratic elections for elected law officials. This should ensure repossessions are fair and in accordance to laws that are not unbalanced."

Mariel could hardly read through her tears. All those years she'd turned their aggressors into one-dimensional monsters who would respond to nothing but threats. Rylahn had a long way to go to redeem the harm he had caused, but if she'd have known there was more to the man, they might have settled matters so much sooner.

"Will it not be legally dubious if a woman signs?" Mariel asked as she reached for the quill.

"Your brother, Baron Ashdown, will also sign. And right there, you see where Erran will sign, promising to uphold the fairness standards when he takes the mantle of stewardship as his own." He returned to his seat. "*You're* signing, Mariel, as a symbol of your commitment to quietly put an end to your own activities. No one will ever know it was you who brought all this to a head, because that knowledge comes with the risk of your bigger secret being discovered. And it can never, for if the public finds out, your fate will be beyond my authority."

Mariel dipped the quill in the pot but hesitated before leading it to the page. The past rushed forward to remind her to never trust anyone but herself. Anything that seemed too fortuitous was either a trap or a missed opportunity for one.

"What is it?" Erran whispered.

"Doesn't seem real." Ink dropped onto the table. "I keep thinking about the way Yesenia and her husband trapped his brother into signing something like this, but there was no true accord. It won't be long before Aidan Quinlanden finds a way to undo all of it."

"My father isn't Aidan." He gripped her knee. "He's a fallible man who did a terrible thing and knows it. Whether you can forgive that is a matter I cannot advise you on. But if I didn't believe his heart was true, Mariel, we wouldn't be sitting here. We'd already be halfway to the Northerlands in search of a new life."

"Is there a reason you're whispering?" Rylahn asked.

Erran seemed ready to make something up, but she'd come to the table in good faith and expecting the same. "Steward, I want to believe you're in full support of everything on this page."

"You'd be a fool to." Rylahn scoffed. "You didn't come this far trusting anyone's intentions."

"Not an especially comforting response," she replied.

"It's not me you should trust. It's him." He nodded at his son. "I have, at best, a year or so left before retirement comes calling.

My leg has reached the end of its travails, and I no longer have the belly for politics. The two of you will be leading this region soon. Managing the barons will become your burden. If the Guardian of the Unpromised Future is less capricious than they say, the son will do better than the father ever could."

Nothing could undo death. Starvation. Grief and tears and injury and suffering. Not even the treaty collecting ink splatters beneath her quill. It was a thought that had kept her up many nights. The best she could ever accomplish as the Flame was trauma avoidance. Not even the Guardians could turn back time.

But Rylahn was linked to her twice over. He was both her father-in-law and Destin's half brother. Erran was right; he wasn't Aidan Quinlanden, who still stood by every terrible thing the Quinlandens had ever done. Rylahn was a man capable of change and evolution, and if she couldn't accept that such change was possible, then there'd never been much point to her work anyway.

She drew a deep breath and traced her signature on the line, adding one last rogue inky dot at the end. She passed it to Erran, and he leaned in to do the same. "What happens now?"

Rylahn pulled the page to his side of the desk and signed. "Pamphlets will be made and distributed across the region. Elections won't happen until springtide, but I've put a temporary stay on any seizures until they've taken place."

"And Obsidian Sky?" Erran asked. "Will there not be discontent when you make no arrests?"

Rylahn had held true to his word on immunity. But putting their names on any document, even if the document assured their freedom, was not something they could take back. It would have exposed them forever. In the end, Remy and Augustine accepted the offer, but Alessia and Magnur chose to protect their anonymity.

"When the thieving stops, they'll eventually be forgotten," Rylahn said. "If not, there are plenty of men set to die for other crimes. Pick two, get them to sign a confession in exchange for a handsome sum to their families when they're gone."

Mariel leaped up. She suddenly needed air, to breathe in the brine of the sea and drink in the roar of the endless surf. What she would miss most about life as the Flame were the nights in the forest, sleeping under the stars. Sometimes she'd stay at Remy's or the hovel Destin had won gambling, but she always returned to her bundle of tattered blankets, Augustine beside her, smiling. They'd never needed words, and anyway, neither were very skilled with them. The culmination of so many years and so many tragedies spoke for them, allowing brief pockets of joy that words would have sullied.

Erran watched her strange behavior but said nothing. He'd come to respect her long silences…her sudden remembrances. He'd held her through her nightmares, and rarely asked about them, but was a most attentive listener when she chose to share. He gave her space to be whatever she needed to be, but he left room for her to return, and she always did. She always would.

"Walk with me?" she asked him.

"Walk with *me,*" he said, flicking a brief, conspiratorial glance at his father. "I have something to show you. Something I've been waiting…" He breathed out hard, laughing. "A long time to show you."

Mariel narrowed her eyes, glancing back at Rylahn. "You know I don't like surprises."

Rylahn nodded at them both, giving the ink one final blow before rolling the vellum. "Be back before supper. It will be the last one before Sessaly is wed to the Law boy, and your mother will be cross if you miss it."

Erran was prepared for Mariel's suspicion, but he could take it. It was better than ruining the surprise.

Until a few days ago, he hadn't even been sure there would *be* a surprise, with how last minute everything had come together. He had Hamish and Samuel to thank for making it happen so fast. His father to thank for the final touch.

"Erran, just tell me. You know how I feel about things like this," Mariel pleaded as he led her down the hill toward the wharf.

"I've spent months on this, and I *will* get my reaction," he teased, tugging on her hand. She groaned and stumbled after him.

"Maybe I'll deny you it for your insolence."

"Maybe you won't be able to, for all your awe and wonder."

"You overestimate yourself, princeling."

"And you underestimate me, outlaw."

Mariel creased a sulking grin he wanted to kiss right off her face, but if he didn't make the big reveal soon, she'd lose her good humor. He'd taken her the long way to the wharf to keep her from seeing the gift before he was ready, but her restlessness was palpable through her playfulness.

They emerged at the base of a cliff, which concealed anything to the east of them. He tried not to chuckle at Mariel's attempts to figure out what she was supposed to be so in awe of, pleased with the knowledge she would neither discover it nor guess it until he was ready.

He gently pulled her onto a long pier. The tide was high and water lapped the pilings and splashed up through the boards, soaking their boots.

"I just don't—" She staggered to a stop with a gasp. Both hands flew to her mouth to trap a whimper. "*Erran*."

He'd been down to the pier early that morning to survey the final work, but now that she was with him, the real present was seeing the rebuilt *Mistwitch*, anchored and bobbing at sea, through *her* eyes.

Mariel's hand stayed fixed to her mouth. Small sobs escaped through her fingers. Her head shook and shook, her eyes traveling back and forth between him and her rebuilt ship.

It had taken six trips to haul the wreckage from Feck-All Island to Port Worthing, where Samuel had overseen the work himself. They'd had to source some new wood and other parts, but Erran had been clear: it was not to be a replica, but the vessel herself. The same one Mariel had proudly earned besting men at their own games. As much as could be preserved, must be.

"How?" she squeaked.

"I'll walk you through every detail later," he said with promise. He pulled her against him and planted a kiss atop her head. "Shall we?"

Mariel eyed the rowboat tethered to a pylon. "Now?"

Erran turned toward the mainland. "Or we could go back…"

"Nay, nay," she said quickly. A delightful smile split her reddened cheeks. "I want to see her."

He helped her in and rowed her to the ship. When she tried to reach the ladder, he offered her a remembrance of the last time they'd boarded the ship and pinned her to his side instead, then took them both up.

"I have a confession to make," she said. "Sometimes I think about you carting me up this ladder, and it's all I can do to breathe."

"Oh, aye? How about that day? Were you struggling to breathe in my presence then?" He hoisted her over the side and onto her feet.

"I was struggling not to kick you back into the sea."

"How shortsighted would that have been for your fantasies?" He joined her on the deck, straightening his vest.

"There were no fantasies until later, I assure you." Mariel tilted her head, looking up and around. Her smile grew with her slow inspection. "She looks the same but somehow different."

"About two-thirds of her parts are original." Erran guided her down the steps of the sterncastle and onto the main deck. "The sails were only torn. Augustine stitched those, with some direction from a shipwright. The rigging had to be completely replaced, and there were two massive holes in the hull. The wood must have been lost at sea, along with the rear mast, which I had rebuilt. Samuel oversaw most of the work, so it's him you'll want to dress down if anything is—"

Mariel silenced him with a bawling kiss as she jumped into his arms. "Thank you. Thank you, thank you, thank you." She purred against his ear. "*Thank you.*"

"Aye, it was nothing, Mar," he said, but there were tears in his eyes too. Every tear he had ever shed, for better or ill, had been for her.

"You must have started this right after I was imprisoned." Her legs slid down his sides until she was standing again. She wiped her eyes and glanced around with another wondrous sweep.

"Not long after."

"How did you keep this from your father?"

"Samuel had the work completed in Port Worthing."

"But Rylahn clearly knows *now*."

"Aye, and while he's still not sold on a woman skipper, he agreed to give the *Mistwitch* a permanent spot at port." Erran nodded at the rigging. "Shall we take her out? The skies are calm. Sea is fair."

Mariel's grin brightened her entire face. "Will you show me how you…" She gesticulated her arms like she was playing a harp.

"Trim the sails?" He pulled a grin to the side of his mouth.

She nodded eagerly. "Aye. That."

Erran laughed. "I'll teach you anything you want to learn. She's your ship. I'm just here for the ride."

Mariel leaned against him. His arm circled her.

"Mariel, before we go…" Erran looked down at her. "We've rarely spoken about the child coming."

"Oh. We haven't, have we?"

"Are you happy about it?"

Mariel's forehead scrunched. She aimed toward the sea. "Are you asking because you're not?"

"Nay." He reached for her face and took it into his palm. "I've always wanted a family. But I don't know what your wants are."

"I always wanted one too. I just didn't ken one would ever be mine to have." Her smile was at first sad but then, gradually, brightened her eyes as well. "I *am* happy. Or I will be, once she's here, and I can stop worrying every little thing I do is hurting her."

"It's not. Mother would tell you, believe me." Erran fused his brows. "She?"

"Oh, I don't know." Mariel shrugged. "Don't look at me like that, Errandil. It's just a feeling. I've no magic in me. My mother had some. They say it sometimes runs in families, but neither I nor Destin inherited any."

"If our children ever do manifest magic," Erran said solemnly, thinking of his own gift of intuition, "we'll send them to the Sepulchre for proper training. The king is coming down hard on families who try to hide their magic."

"I haven't even met our child, and it breaks my heart to think of sending them away for so long."

"Then don't think of it until we must." Erran wound his arms around her back and swept a kiss from her forehead down to her mouth. "I'm ready to instruct."

Mariel backed away, affecting a sloppy salute. "I'm ready to learn." An impertinent grin spread across her face. "But, ah, I ken we should stay in calm waters this time?"

"You certain? I know of this island..."

Mariel scowled. "Maybe we should leave the danger and excitement for others, now that we're starting a family."

"Danger, yes." Erran snapped her close. "Excitement, never."

"If you're trying to seduce me, all you have to do is, ah...trim those sails."

"Is that all, lass?" Erran traced his hands up and down her back. "Trim your sails?"

"Are we speaking of the same thing?" Mariel cooed, swaying in his embrace.

Erran grinned. "Let's find out."

EPILOGUE

Destin couldn't stop smiling as he watched Augustine and Hestia compare thoughts on the guest placards.

He didn't realize how glum he must usually look until several asked after his unusually cheerful disposition. Caught off guard, he told them he was just happy for his sister, who was celebrating five years of "choiceful wedded bliss," as she'd called it. She and Erran had remarried just after Agnes was born, and they considered that their true anniversary feast day. Now Agnes was five, and little Esther was two and a half, and their little family was complete.

But he had another reason for his joy, and it was the child he and Augustine were expecting. It was yet early to be announcing anything, though they'd told Mariel, Erran, and Remy, of course. They'd been married two years and trying for a child since. He wanted a huge family, with as many bairns as Augustine was willing to deliver—like Sessaly and Aliksander, who, hardly five years into their own union, already had as many children.

"Respectfully, Stewardess, how often do people *sit* at one of your celebrations?" Augustine asked, her tone good-natured but her face splotched with pink frustration. She'd become one of Hestia's most trusted attendants, no longer her seamstress. Instead, Augustine oversaw a team of them. One of Destin's favorite things to do was secretly watch her inspect their work, moving from gown to gown with criticisms that would seem nitpicky to others but was what set her apart from others in skill. Every detail mattered. Details were what others would notice, speak about, and marvel over. If even one was amiss, it was a reflection of the stewardess herself.

"But when they *do*, Augustine, we must ensure their experience is a pleasant one."

"Are we hoping to avoid fisticuffs or fishwife gossip?"

Hestia narrowed her eyes but laughed. "Both, I ken."

"You need say nothing else." Augustine gathered the cards at the table they stood by and flounced off to rearrange them.

Destin nodded at his sister-in-law, and Hestia returned the greeting. He was always fully aware that he served as a reminder that the Rutlands, however distinguished, were not above scandal. She'd been kind, if cool, since the truth had come out about Rylahn's father and Erran's late mother. Rylahn had been warmer, attempting in small ways to forge a bond with his much younger half brother, but Destin would never forget, or fully forgive, how the choices the steward had made had harmed so many lives. Rylahn's monthly visits to the lake district were evidence of his remorse and desire to do better, but the dead were just as dead.

"Can I help?" Destin asked his wife, right as Agnes and Esther went tearing by in their matching lavender gowns. Agnes was screeching the notes *lalalala*, and Esther was taunting her, twice as loud, with *woowoowoo.*

Augustine caught Esther before she tripped over her taffeta, quickly righted the girl, and sent her back into action. She laughed as she watched them play. "They're both such spirited, beautiful lasses."

Destin sighed wistfully as his gaze followed his nieces. Some whispered about Agnes and the twist in her spine, which no healer had resolved. Physicians had no cure for it either. It might get worse. It might improve. No one could say. None at the Spires tolerated unkindness about it. Rylahn had once escorted a man from his halls at sword's point for making a drunken jest about how there were plenty of men who were aroused by mutants.

"Oh, you asked if you could help! Aye, aye. Where do you ken Yesenia is best sat?"

"With her family seems prudent." Destin leaned in to read the cards. The options were Damian Law, Esta Garrick, and Sessaly, with each table seating two. "Hm. Perhaps not."

"Hestia prefers unlikely pairings that encourage fresh conversation," Augustine said.

"Then Esta is out." Destin plucked the card from the stack. "Unless you *want* both of Erran's past bedmates at the same table?"

Augustine's eyes shot wide. "Oh. Aye. Right."

"And Sessaly is out." Destin pulled her name as well.

Augustine looked confused.

"Never heard the story about how Yesenia put hands on her neck?"

Augustine laughed. "Steward Law it is!" She neatly folded the name and placed it across from Yesenia's. "Esta and Sessaly together then?"

"Esta has enough piss in her to keep Ses in line."

Augustine finished placing the cards. She crossed her arms, examining the dozens of tables she'd helped to arrange over the past couple of hours. "Well, it will have to do. Guests are already arriving."

Destin lifted her hand and kissed it. "As you said, no one will be sitting, and even if they do, they'll sit wherever they please."

"Hmm." Augustine leaned against him. She smelled of cinnamon and linens. In their Obsidian Sky days, it had been wood smoke and pine. What a difference five years made, though there was a persistent part of him that missed those nights...the adrenaline surging through them as they'd passed ales around, recounting the close calls from whatever heist they'd pulled off. The excitement of children playing adult games, he sometimes branded it when he was feeling morose, but it *had* meant something. No matter what he'd said to Mariel, those years were just as important to him. So many had looked to them for hope, and they'd offered as much as they were able. It was a touch bittersweet that they'd been able to do far more as Rutlands. "I will miss it here when we go back to Mistgrave."

Destin had been delaying their move for years. He spent about a third of his time at his estate on the lake, the rest in Whitecliffe with his wife, but there were responsibilities a baron couldn't neglect. It was harder to work from afar. His sailor's apprenticeship under Aliksander was only a seasonal obligation. "Are you not surprised to hear yourself say that? About a place like the Spires?"

"Home for me is wherever you and Mariel and Remy are. The girls. I don't care about all...this. I'll just miss them is all."

Remy had been dividing his time between Oldcastle, where he taught business law, and Whitecliffe, where he helped influence it. "Mistgrave is closer to the universities. Maybe you'll see him more often."

"Or less. He's been coy about it, but I ken he's met someone there."

"A woman? Really?"

"Aye, surprises me as well, but the way he's been acting, I expect an announcement soon."

When they were younger, Destin assumed Mariel and Remy would wed, and he would wed Augustine, and they'd continue on as a family. Both the Perevils had danced their way in and out of Mariel's heart, but proximity was not passion. What Mariel had with Erran was. What Destin had earned with Augustine was. "When he learns he's to be an uncle, he won't stay away for long."

"He must have known we were talking about him." Augustine nodded at the middle arch in a row of thirteen, where Remy was propped, eating an apple. "Ugh. He's already pillaging the feast tables. I'll find you later?"

Destin kissed her. "Aye. Go on."

He was still laughing when two children crashed into him. He looked down and found his nieces, each wrapped around a leg. "You both have deviance in your eyes. What are you up to?"

"Uncle Des! Agnes said..." Esther screwed her face in thought. Her dark curls framed her soft, round face. "You have pie."

"I have pie? What kind of pie?" Destin frowned suspiciously at Agnes. "Have you been telling tales to your sister again?"

Agnes shrugged, her green eyes glinting with mischief. She flashed a quick tongue at her sister, winking from behind a band of reddish hair. "I might have said it."

"Now, you both know there'll be no pie until after you've eaten proper," Destin said, gathering an arm around each of them. They groaned in unison. He lowered his voice to a whisper. "But I ken I might know where we could steal a *bite.*" When they squealed, he flashed them a look of caution, flicking his gaze toward the arches, where their parents were helping with final preparations. "And *don't* tell your cousins, or Aunt Ses will have my head."

They scampered off, waiting for him to follow. In the distance, between the arches, he caught Mariel watching and smiled. She touched a hand to her mouth in return.

With his heart full to bursting, Destin went off to spoil his nieces.

It was almost everyone. Hamish and his brood. The Laws. Augustine and Remy. Khallum and Gwyn had made it with their children. Even Yesenia had traveled down with her son, Torquil, which was a surprise because Erran hadn't invited her.

"It was me," Mariel said as they watched their guests mingling around the open terrace. "She's a Warwick, and the Warwicks are like kin to you. I saw no reason to not at least extend the invitation. Torquil is a handsome boy, aye?"

Erran squeezed her hand. "You didn't have to, but it was a lovely gesture."

She smiled. "I wanted to."

It was a gorgeous evening for a party. Candles flickered but held strong against the gentle breeze. A band of musicians played lively ditties on the pipes. The spits of meat roasting just beyond the veranda had him salivating, but he was too excited and nervous to be hungry.

For all he knew his wife, there were still times he couldn't guess her reaction. His big idea had been taking form for over a year, and he'd somehow kept it a complete secret from her. He knew how much it weighed on her heart that she could bear no more children. Neither Agnes's nor Esther's births had been easy, and they'd nearly lost both mother and child. He couldn't fix what the Guardians had taken, but he could offer her something else. Both Remy and Augustine had endorsed it, Destin as well, so Erran knew it couldn't have been a *terrible* idea, but still his nerves were balancing on a razor's edge.

"Did you see what Alessia and Magnur sent? For the girls?"

Erran chuckled. He'd seen, all right. The mysterious bandits had politely refused their invitation, but Alessia had sent two child-size swords, crafted herself. *Start them early or regret it later*, her note said. *Kisses, Auntie A and Uncle M.* "I ken we might give them a couple more years before we introduce them to the armorer?"

"Aye, maybe more than a couple." Mariel laughed, shaking her head. She turned to him, stifling a yawn. They'd been chatting and laughing and fielding well wishes for hours, and she'd been fading for half of them. "You seem a touch off tonight."

"Me? Oh…" He hugged her from the side. "Thinking about Father, I ken." It was half-true. He'd watched Rylahn become an old man almost overnight. His dark hair was mostly gray. The cane he used for his leg was no longer elective. A year past, he'd ceded leadership to Erran, though had stayed on as adviser to his son. Erran had taken a step back from the admiralty, promoting

Aliksander to commodore. The stated reason was so he could be home more with Mariel and the girls, which was certainly a big part of it, but it was also the sense his father had few good years ahead.

"He looks happy tonight." Mariel nodded at the dance floor, where Rylahn was shuffling in embarrassing gyrations with Agnes, Esther, and Charles, Sessaly's oldest son.

"He loves being a grandfather. Don't ken I ever saw him half as happy as a steward." Tears suddenly clouded his vision. He sighed.

"Are you *sure* you're all right?" Mariel asked, worry written in her eyes.

Erran turned toward her, offering his full attention as he pulled her hands into his and brought them to his mouth. "Mariel, I have *never* been happier."

"Then you're up to something." Her eyes narrowed to suspicious slits. "You are, aren't you?"

He lifted his shoulders. Grinned. Her easy read of him lightened the trepidation some.

"You miscreant." She jabbed him with her shoulder. "Are you going to make me look bad when my gift to you is underwhelming?"

"Depends. What's your gift?"

"No point in waiting anymore, I ken." Mariel's gaze traveled to the raised dais on the other end of the veranda. She winked, handing Erran her glass of wine, and broke away in that direction.

Khallum, chatting with Samuel and his father nearby, excused himself from his own conversation and started off after her.

"Everyone, hush!" Hamish's booming command echoed from one end of the veranda to the other. "Your lord has sum' to say!"

Khallum smirked at him and stepped onto the dais. "I see all the glossed eyes out there, so I'll keep this short. A little over five years ago, most of ye came here and witnessed a most enchanting takedown of our beloved Errandil, by the tongue of his beautiful lass right here. She told us *all* about his prolific freckles. His dubious and inconsistent salt-and-sand brogue."

Everyone laughed.

Khallum opened one arm and Mariel stepped into it, blushing. "I ken she's changed her mind a bit, as she's asked to start over and tell us what she *really* loves about a man she couldnae have possibly wed by accident, for she's done it twice now. Mariel?"

Erran had no idea whether his lovely wife was about to offer an even more impressive assessment of his weaknesses or something entirely different, but he was strangely excited to find out.

"You look green, mate. You shouldn't." Samuel chuckled, stepping in beside him.

"Aye? And what do you know about this?"

Samuel nodded for him to listen.

"Thank you, Khallum. I…" Mariel breathed in through a small gap in her mouth. She glanced nervously to the side. "Well, I ken I should start by telling you all how little I thought of my husband the last time I stood here." She chuckled nervously, and the guests followed suit. "Perhaps an unnecessary clarification, if you were here. Made a bit of an arse of myself actually."

"Tell us about his freckles again!" Augustine hollered.

"He has more than his share of those," Mariel said. "I'm nay good at this, so I'll just say what I came to say and then everyone can return to enjoying their ale and boar." She shuffled in place, her gaze on her feet. "Years ago, I was *supposed* to tell you all one thing I loved about Erran. Seeing as I did not love a single thing about him at the time…" More laughter brought a touch of a smile to her pale, anxious face. "I could not. But now…" She looked up, her lips parting. Her mossy eyes glistened. "I find the question is still impossible, for there's nothing I don't love about my husband. I could tell you all about his kindness. His gentle patience with our very strong-willed girls. His eagerness to teach others of the many valuable things he knows. A work ethic that exceeds what's expected of him. The way he knows when to speak and when to listen. His full and giving heart that never runs out of capacity." Mariel wiped her eyes with a brief chuckle. "Aye, but you all just want to hear about his freckles, right?"

Cheers and stomps rippled across the stones.

Blood rushed to Erran's face. He glanced at Samuel, who had a handkerchief to his own eyes, but there was nothing to say.

"Too bad." Mariel grinned. "For they're all mine." She found Erran and held his gaze with a soft, sleepy smile. "Every last one."

He couldn't wait to take her to bed. To press his flesh to hers until two were one, to feel her heart beat against his, their own flutter of harmony.

But there was something else he had to do first.

"I love you, Erran. You already know this, but I ken it was time everyone else hear it too. Just this once anyway." She nodded at Khallum and marched away with her head down so the others wouldn't see what Erran had, that she was overwhelmed and crying.

Khallum moved back to the dais. "Erran, any amendments to make to your own statement from the past? Ken to tell us what ye love about this lass?"

Erran couldn't take his eyes off his wife. "There's nothing to say!" he shouted, his urgency for her swelling with her every step. "For I love feckin' *everything* about this woman."

Mariel folded into his embrace, set to a chorus of *ahhs*. "I had so much more I wanted to say," she said, lamenting into his chest. "But I got nervous."

"Oh, love." Erran smashed a kiss atop her head and crushed her close. The girls joined them in the hug, and he tucked them neatly in. He was often asked if he was disappointed he didn't have a male heir, but his answer was always the same. *I have everything I could ever need. I will never want for more.* "My girls. My lasses."

"Daddy, did you show her?" Agnes asked. She tugged on his arm.

"Even the girls know?" Mariel peeled back with a suspicious look.

"They wanted to help." Erran ruffled both of his daughters' heads. Agnes frowned and smoothed her mussed hair down.

"Remy and Auggie helped as well. Des. Mother. Father. Sam. Hamish."

Mariel retreated in mock offense. "Who *doesn't* know?"

Erran kissed her nose. "You. Ready to find out?"

Mariel distrusted surprises because they had previously been preambles to the darkest moments of her life. Obsidian Sky had been as much about control as correction. In a world that had slipped from her fingers at every turn, she'd found solace in creating something no one else could shape or define.

But Erran loved to surprise her. He seemed to live for her annoyance-turned-delight, and over time, she'd come to trust there *wasn't* some tragedy lurking behind every lovely gesture. Just a man who loved his wife, and delighted in showing her.

As with all his surprises, she couldn't guess where he was taking her. They were headed to the north end of the property, through the thick brush separating the Spires from the main road into the village. She'd never been up there because the entire section was cordoned off and abandoned. The path was barely traversable, hardly discernible in spots. But Erran wouldn't take their daughters anywhere dangerous, so Mariel put her faith in him and followed with blind trust.

Erran walked ahead, Agnes's hand in his. Mariel held Esther, who, despite her enthusiasm only minutes earlier, had crashed on her shoulder and was softly snoring away. They were both such different girls, her daughters. Agnes—named for Angelika, who had often been called Agnes—was feisty and unpredictable; Esther, thoughtful and introspective. It was too early to say for sure, but it seemed her youngest was manifesting some magic as well, which meant they'd have to send her to the Consortium of the Sepulchre in the Skies for a formal education when she turned seven. To do otherwise would mean a life of secrecy or exile. But Mariel couldn't even think about being parted from her little butterfly, so she tried not to borrow against the future's worries.

So much about the past five years had been like a dream. The family she hadn't believed was possible exceeded even her biggest dreams, but it was the gift of helping others that caused her heart to continue growing even beyond motherhood. Beyond the gold and the returned land and the other corrections she'd persuaded Rylahn to agree to, she still wanted to do more. She took the girls into the village twice a week to serve food for those who struggled to afford it, and every month, she traveled even farther with them. Teaching them the service that had shaped her life was the greatest gift she could ever give them, and they had come up with their own creative ideas for how to provide aid, which was a gift without measure.

The path veered west and abruptly opened into a small, overgrown courtyard. A fountain, cracked but still trickling water from two of the six spouts, sat at the center, covered in snaky vines and old moss. She almost didn't notice the smallish lodge beyond, because there was a tower that stretched so high, she was stunned not to have seen it from afar.

Esther stirred as they slowed. She yawned and slid from her mother's arms, then landed squarely in the dirt before scampering to her father. "Did you tell her? Did I miss it?"

"Just in time, butterfly," he said. She had an inclination to shrink around her rambunctious sister, due to some early challenges with self-confidence. *A butterfly is always beautiful, even before others can see it,* Erran had said to her once, and she'd liked it, so it had stuck. "Agnes, do you want to tell your mother about this place?"

Agnes nodded and spun proudly toward Mariel. "A hundred years ago, us Rutlands lived here."

Mariel frowned, dubious. "This modest keep? You think I don't know Rutlands love their pomp?"

"That's what Daddy said you'd say!" Agnes seemed eager to continue, so Mariel gestured for her to do so. "They did live here, Mama. But it was too small."

"Ye ken?" Mariel laughed, passing a smile between all three eager faces.

"Then Daddy's great-great…" Agnes's brows fused as she tried to recall what she'd been told. "Daddy's *ancestor* built Goldsea Spires instead." She looked to Erran for validation.

"Very good, lass. Ancestor is the right word."

"Well, I had no idea," Mariel said. "Lived here almost six years, and I just learned something new. Didn't even know this place was here. Thank you for the lesson, Agnes."

Agnes bowed and backed theatrically to the side.

"I know it still needs work." Erran squinted as he surveyed the area. It was truly hard to imagine the Rutlands living so humbly, but there was a charm to it that the Spires lacked. The thatched roof on the main building was cozy and welcoming. The tower, intriguing. She wondered what it had been like to pass a meal inside…how children had played in the surrounding land before it had been lost to time. "We did as much as we could before the rainy season, but we'll finish up when it passes."

"We're moving here?" Mariel asked, watching Erran try to read her. The idea of austere living was appealing, but it was hardly a place for a steward to do business and entertain guests. "Is that the surprise?"

"Nay, love." Erran's hard swallow betrayed his nerves. Whatever he was about to say, he'd had time to work up to it and was still uncertain. "It's for you."

Mariel was confused. "Me? You want *me* to live here?"

"No, silly Mama." Agnes's laugh rang through the night. "Daddy said you miss work, and your work was helping people. He said you could help people here as much as you want. They can come here."

Esther tugged at her hand. "Mama?"

"Yes, butterfly?" Mariel murmured, her thoughts drifting. *For you. For your work.*

"Do you love it?"

"Aye, lass," she answered, though she was looking at her husband, trying to understand. She was already spending much of her time in the village, even if it did sometimes feel like they were only putting ointment on a wound.

"I specifically recall you talking about how people…" Erran's voice caught. "Died simply because they could not afford care when their injuries or illnesses were easily cured. Now, I don't ken to know how to fix that, but I suspect *you* have some ideas. Perhaps what you need is a place to see them come to life."

Mariel pressed a hand to her mouth so the girls wouldn't hear the blubbering building in her throat. "Erran…" She shook her head, unable to continue, recalling what he hadn't said. The conversation that had given him the idea hadn't been about Obsidian Sky at all. Right after Esther's birth, when the physician had told her there'd be no more children, she'd experienced a breakdown that had lasted months. Motherhood filled the need within her to nurture and protect the vulnerable, even more than before, but she'd envisioned their family as being bigger, somehow. Having it taken from her hadn't dulled the joyfulness she took from mothering two beautiful, perfect little girls, but how she felt about the whole thing was actually much more difficult to define than words could provide.

But Erran had understood. He'd read her just fine. He'd known precisely what she meant, what she needed. The purpose she'd been unknowingly seeking for over two years.

She rocked into him and gave in to the tears. Agnes and Esther rushed over to join.

Erran tilted her head back, inspecting her. "Will it suffice?"

"Will it…" Mariel laughed through her sniffles. "Your heart, Erran. It's too big."

"Too big? Or just big enough for my three beautiful lassies?"

"Mama, I wanna help!" Agnes cried. "I wanna help those men too, like we help in the village."

"And women, Ag," Erran said, one hand on the back of her head as he grinned at her. "Mayhap children too."

"Can I help?" Esther was so quiet, they barely heard her, but Mariel was always listening for her daughter's sweet voice.

"Of course." Mariel choked up as she crushed her children against her. Erran had been busier of late, but she'd assumed it had to do with his duties as steward. Never in her wildest imaginings would she have foreseen what he had really been up to. "You both can, just as you always have."

Erran snaked a hand behind her neck and drew her in for a lingering kiss. *More. Again. Always. Forever.*

The girls made gagging sounds, but Erran *tsk-tsked* and said, "Nay, nay, girls. I want you both to see what it looks like when a man loves his wife, so you'll never accept less for yourselves. There's no shame in a man who wears his feelings."

"Revolting," Agnes muttered with an eyeroll to her sister.

Mariel met her husband's eyes over the heads of their perfect children. She could read his heart as well as he'd always read hers. He knew her better than she knew herself sometimes, and he had been showing her, in ways small and large, for over five years.

She couldn't predict how many years awaited them or what they might bring. Tomorrow was not promised. Nothing in life was ever certain. She knew it better than most.

But in the moment, in that perfect slice of time under the moonlight, wrapped in the love of her husband and children, she had everything she could ever want or need.

My heart, he mouthed over Agnes's head.

Through her tears, she whispered, "My heart."

"Shall we get the girls to bed?"

"It is *way* past their rest time, Daddy."

Both of them soundly objected, their parents grinning through their unspoken conspiracy. Erran took Esther; Mariel, Agnes.

Mariel let him deliver the best part. He'd more than earned it.

Erran winked at her and shifted Esther higher in his arms. "I ken it wouldn't hurt to eat some pie first."

The Book of All Things continues with a new story in *The Virtue and the Vixen.*

ALSO BY SARAH M. CRADIT

KINGDOM OF THE WHITE SEA

KINGDOM OF THE WHITE SEA TRILOGY

The Kingless Crown

The Broken Realm

The Hidden Kingdom

THE BOOK OF ALL THINGS

Blackwood Cycle

The Raven and the Rush

The Poison and the Paladin

Southerlands Cycle

The Sylvan and the Sand

The Flame and the Forsaken

Guardians Cycle

The Altruist and the Assassin

The Belle and the Blackbird

The Virtue and the Vixen

Darkwood Cycle

The Melody and the Master

The Hand and the Heart

The Wolf and the Witchling

Sceptre Cycle

The Claw and the Crowned

The Duke and the Disciple

The Tempest and the Tides

THE SAGA OF CRIMSON & CLOVER

THE HOUSE OF CRIMSON AND CLOVER SERIES

The Storm and the Darkness
Shattered
The Illusions of Eventide
Bound
Midnight Dynasty
Asunder
Empire of Shadows
Myths of Midwinter
The Hinterland Veil
The Secrets Amongst the Cypress
Within the Garden of Twilight
House of Dusk, House of Dawn

MIDNIGHT DYNASTY SERIES

A Tempest of Discovery
A Storm of Revelations
A Torrent of Deceit
A Squall of Sedition
A Chaos of Awakening

THE SEVEN SERIES

Nineteen Seventy
Nineteen Seventy-Two
Nineteen Seventy-Three
Nineteen Seventy-Four
Nineteen Seventy-Five
Nineteen Seventy-Six
Nineteen Eighty

VAMPIRES OF THE MEROVINGI SERIES

The Island

and more

THE DUSK TRILOGY

St. Charles at Dusk: The Story of Oz and Adrienne

Flourish: The Story of Anne Fontaine

Banshee: The Story of Giselle Deschanel

CRIMSON & CLOVER STORIES

Available as a single collection, The Shorts

Surrender: The Story of Oz and Ana

Shame: The Story of Jonathan St. Andrews

Fire & Ice: The Story of Remy & Fleur

Dark Blessing: The Landry Triplets

Pandora's Box: The Story of Jasper & Pandora

The Menagerie: Oriana's Den of Iniquities

A Band of Heather: The Story of Colleen and Noah

The Ephemeral: The Story of Autumn & Gabriel

Bayou's Edge: The Landry Triplets

AS RIVER CHASTAIN (CO-WRITE WITH ELIZABETH BURGESS)

THE COMPLICATED ROMANTIC LIFE OF ROMY DELACROIX

Silvan

Bastian

Dane

For more information, and exciting bonus material, visit www.sarahmcradit.com

Sarah is the USA Today and International Bestselling Author of over fifty contemporary and epic fantasy stories, and the creator of the Kingdom of the White Sea and Saga of Crimson & Clover universes.

Born a geek, Sarah spends her time crafting rich and multilayered worlds, obsessing over history, playing her retribution paladin (and sometimes destruction warlock), and settling provocative Tolkien debates, such as why the Great Eagles are not Gandalf's personal taxi service. Passionate about travel, she's been to over thirty countries collecting sparks of inspiration, and is always planning her next adventure.

Sarah and her husband live in a beautiful corner of SE Pennsylvania with their four tiny benevolent pug dictators.

www.sarahmcradit.com

www.ingramcontent.com/pod-product-compliance
Lightning Source LLC
Chambersburg PA
CBHW020245030826
48979CB00030B/2629/J

* 9 7 8 1 9 5 8 7 4 4 4 6 8 *